Encounter

When Religions

Become Classmates —

From Oregon to India & Back

Kathy Beckwith

2 WONDERS

For inquiries about author visits
or other books by Kathy Beckwith, please contact Kathy at
www.kathybeckwith.com.

Published by 2 Wonders, LLC
www.2wonders.com

Cover Art by Lea Lyon | www.lealyon.com
Cover & Interior Design by Masha Shubin | Anno Domini Creative

ISBN: 978-1-7374777-0-9
EPUB ISBN: 978-1-7374777-1-6

1 3 5 7 9 10 8 6 4 2

A warning to the reader:

THINGS CAN GO wrong in common events, and things do go wrong in this story. But there are events included here that you might overlook as ordinary-sounding, and miss the reality that they are of special risk. Be alert to this extremely serious warning about rock climbing:

Climbing can be a dangerous sport, where a fall, equipment failure, rockfall, weather, or human error may result in injury or death, even falls from short distances.

In other words, please do not attempt any climbing, including bouldering, because of this story. Climbing should never be attempted without proper, thorough, and qualified training.

Dedicated to
the spirit of
wondering
that is within each of us.

With gratitude

for the kind help of
Kip Beckwith
Malini Devanandan
Navneet Kaur
Sharon Michaud
Penny Milton
Gretchen Olson
Asha Sathyaraj
Vijendran Sathyaraj
Steve Scholl
Jyotsna Sreenivasan
Paul Wiebe
and the critiquing readers –
Alanna, Bill, Joyce, Kelley, Lee, Maj, Nissi,
Ranjit, Russell, Sara, Tanja, and Wayne –
for SCBWI, including Kacen's caution
and the calm eyes that echoed "You will,"
for Sisterhood,
for Lea Lyon and her caring,

and for the Animators in my life,
both here, and there.

Table of Contents

PART I

Taking Flight

Annie stepped out of the plane into the warm Mumbai night. She had expected to go directly into an airport transit room, unable to see India until they reached Hyderabad. But here she was at the top of a stairway, looking out over the tarmac at the Mumbai terminal.

"What was I thinking?" she whispered.

The family she had joined up with in LA, friends of friends, moved down the steps in front of her. The woman looked back up at Annie, and told her, for the fourth time, just to follow the transit crowd. "They'll soon have you off for Hyderabad, just an hour's flight onward," she said.

"I'll be fine," Annie said, trying to sound convincing. "Thank you so much for letting me travel with you." She paused on the bottom step and watched the LA family join those going in another direction, leaving her alone in the crowd, on the other side of the world. That was the plan, of course. They would go on by train to visit family in Pune. Annie would catch a connecting flight to Hyderabad. But as she touched her foot to the ground, the feeling washed over her again – that her parents' first reaction might be right, that she should have just watched some movies about India for now, and then come when she was in college, that this was a mistake. She could have been completely happy finishing her junior year right there in Ridgeway, with friends she had known since kindergarten.

The transit crowd quickly moved ahead, and Annie rushed to catch up. As she walked toward the Mumbai terminal, the thought crossed her mind that even after all she'd done to get here, she'd rather be leaving India for Oregon, with this semester somehow already over. She forced the thought away with "I wonder ... I wonder ..." It was a good time to try out her pledge – to be open and curious and wonder instead of being afraid, or instantly judging what seemed too different. Suddenly the words were there to finish the sentence. "I wonder why that lady is kneeling, touching her hands to the ground and then to her forehead." Annie watched and saw tears in the woman's eyes as she stood up. "Maybe she's coming home," Annie thought.

IT ACTUALLY WAS a mistake of sorts, Annie's being there. She had never intended to come, just like she had never intended to be one of the winners of a national scholarship essay contest. It was just an assignment Mr. Snyder made their class do. Her mom and dad had no idea Annie had entered any contest. When they found out she'd won, they were dumbfounded. "What was Mr. Snyder thinking?" they asked Annie. Her mom didn't wait for an answer but went straight to the phone and called the school. Mr. Snyder had left for the weekend, so she talked to the secretary, Elaine, and asked her to leave a message for Mr. Thompson and Mr. Snyder, to let them know first thing Monday morning that Annie would not be accepting any scholarship to go to India.

Annie spent most of that Saturday searching the Internet and found that one of the two schools participating in the India scholarship program was an international, multi-cultural Christian school. She decided that was the one she would try for, thinking it might sway her parents to be more receptive to the idea. They finally did agree to look at the school's website and "think it over," though Annie was sure it was just to prove to her they were listening, and that they hadn't already decided she couldn't go.

Annie was ready for change. She loved Ridgeway High, but there were so many times that she just couldn't push away the screaming ache inside. Her mom and dad had both told her that time would help, but it was the opposite. Annie was angry and more confused than ever. Any little thing could have stopped that accident. If God had any power at all, it wouldn't have happened. If only Annie had not insisted on a party in a corn maze... life would be so different.

She had just stopped talking about it and had let them think they were right, that time was helping, but it hovered like a black cloud over everything she did, everywhere she went, everything she thought about.

It didn't help that things were messed up with her and Param and Danny. Annie had been walking a tightrope the past few months, afraid if she leaned too far one way or the other, she'd fall and lose them both. Danny stayed in his just-friends mode, but still was mad that Annie wanted to hang out with Param so much. As much as she loved Danny, she wasn't going to let anybody say who she could and couldn't be around. The truth was, even though she couldn't figure him out, she liked Param. A lot. But now he seemed to be back-tracking, treating her like any other girl, not someone he could ever really love, as if he were suddenly more concerned about his parents' expectations than about Annie. Which her mom and dad would have been thrilled over.

Her whole being fought against the idea that Param was forbidden to her because he didn't know the right God, according to her parents, and she to him because India wasn't in her bones, according to his. Not that they had said it outright exactly like that, against him or her, but Annie knew the bottom line. She should marry a good Christian. Period. Param should wait for a good Indian girl. Period.

So how do you get India in your bones, she wondered. Would five months of living there do it? And who is this Right God, anyway? If Param doesn't want to work for her, does any of that even matter?

His parents were just as controlling as hers. Her mom and dad asked her one night not to date Param, just let him be a classmate. God's plan for her life, they said, surely did not include the struggle and heartbreak that would come from being with someone who did not walk with the Lord. For sixteen years Annie had accepted things like this. But that night she couldn't do it.

"Who is the Lord, Mom?" she cried. "And where is he when you need him? Can't you just leave me alone?"

They had not tried to stop her tears or her dash to her room, and no one mentioned that night again. Annie settled for keeping her feelings for Param hidden from them. And from Danny, the one she could never hide anything from. It didn't work. He knew. And he didn't like it. But he never did anything to change it. It didn't matter that she loved him too. He didn't seem to get that, and expected something different, something more, to happen automatically. Or maybe she just imagined it all.

Sometimes she didn't even know what she wanted, except for things to be easy, like they're supposed to be when you fall in love. At least if she were in India, she couldn't do anything about anything for a whole semester.

Param's mom called the Kartens that weekend when they were "thinking it over." She'd heard the news about the scholarship, but evidently not that Annie's parents weren't letting her go. She assumed that their biggest worry would be the flight over, and she had the solution. Friends of theirs from LA were planning a trip to India on January 4th. The timing was perfect. If Annie could get to LA, she could go the rest of the way with this good family.

Annie overheard her parents talking that night. "Maybe God put this opportunity in Annie's life for a reason," her dad said. "We certainly didn't plan it, nor did she, really. She's had a rough time, Meg, and it doesn't seem like it's over yet. Annie's reaching out for something."

"But India?" her mom countered. "It's too far, and too unknown. Besides, this isn't the time to let her leave. We need to support her now more than ever. She still blames God. I'm not sure she would even reach out to Him for strength for such a trip, and she needs to be able to do that."

Annie was tempted to run into the living room and announce that she would take care of herself, that she wanted to go, but she hovered around the corner in the kitchen and listened.

"She would be in a good environment," her mom conceded, "and the non-Christian elements she runs into may just serve to strengthen her faith. At least it would take her mind off all that's happened these past three months. But India? Do you think she'd be okay?"

"I've always wanted to go to India," her dad said at last.

"What? You've never told me that."

"Well, ever since college, at least, but I never saw it happening," he replied. "Annie could do it, Meg, and she needs something. It's a unique opportunity. She's changing, and it scares me."

Annie wanted to yell out that she wasn't changing at all, that she was just waking up. Instead she slipped into the room. "Were you talking about India?" she asked. They sat up past midnight talking, looking at the school's website, talking some more. The next day her dad asked their pastor if it was crazy to think of sending Annie off to a boarding school – Megha Malai International School in Tamil Nadu, South India. The pastor said it sounded familiar and called them back that afternoon with a glowing report from a seminary roommate who had gone there for high school when his parents worked in India. He recommended the school highly and gave the pastor contact information for the school's alumni group in Portland.

Param's family also made a call and confirmed that Annie could travel with their LA friends. From LA on there would be just one short flight on her own before she'd meet up with the other scholarship winners and the chaperone in Hyderabad. They would visit that area for most of a week and then head off for the new semester at the school.

So against all odds, after several more days and evenings of discussion, Annie's parents shifted their talk to details of her trip, and she ended up with an airline ticket and an invitation from the Admissions Office at MMIS.

ANNIE WAS STILL at home for Christmas. It was a good time, a healing time, and she let the anger that she had unleashed on her parents over the last two months melt away through all the traditions they loved about Christmas. Right then, it seemed that she didn't need to struggle against them or God or confusion. She would soon be away from it all.

The last Sunday at home included a farewell for Annie at church. The pastor's sermon was about two Greek words for time – *chronos*, regular clock-ticking, calendar-turning time, and *kairos*, an "ah hah" critical moment of insight, when things fall into place, the time you first realize something that suddenly makes sense. That was what he wished for them in the New Year – *kairos* moments. She was ready for a New Year in which things made sense.

ANNIE CRIED ON and off half way through the flight from Portland to LA, until she realized the man next to her was watching, and she forced herself to stop. She wanted to go, to mix with these kids from all over the world who found their way to a boarding school in South India. But when the time came, it was hard to leave home for somewhere she'd never even imagined, with no one she knew. It was a relief to meet up with Param's friends at the LA airport.

During the LA to Hong Kong flight, Annie had noticed that her blond hair was definitely in the minority, but now, en route from Mumbai to Hyderabad, she began to notice that she was also in the minority with English, except when people talked directly to her. She wondered why no one thought she spoke Swedish or German, which she didn't, and she wondered what language, or languages, they were using with each other.

"Char budgee," Annie wrote in her journal, because the flight attendant had repeated it twice clearly, and then the man in a long white skirt-thing sitting next to her had said it too, and checked his watch. Annie had tried talking with him earlier, but it didn't work. "No English," he said kindly, and turned back to his *Namaste* in-flight magazine.

Annie realized she must have been staring at the flight attendant, for she explained, *"Chaar baje* – four o'clock. We'll be arriving at four, Hyderabad time," she said in easy English. It was early morning, though it hardly mattered to Annie. With missed flight connections in Singapore, Annie had been traveling for almost forty-four hours. She glanced at her watch, still on Oregon time – 2:20 in the afternoon, yesterday. She was almost half a day late coming in, and she only hoped the scholarship group – Lori, Ketsa, and Jen, and Ms. Dunlop, the chaperone – had gotten the email she sent from the Singapore airport.

The man in the white skirt finished his boxed apple juice and cucumber sandwich and dumped the containers onto the floor of the plane with a swish of his arm across the fold-down tray. Annie automatically reached to pick them up for him, and then, glancing at him as he folded his tray away, realized he had meant to do it. "What the heck!" she wrote in her open journal, then crossed it out and wrote, "I wonder why the man sitting next to me just dumped his garbage on the floor of the plane."

As they approached Hyderabad, he looked at her and smiled. "*Chaar baje*," he said, as the plane hit the runway. He turned his watch toward Annie. It was 4 o'clock to the minute. "*Chaar baje*," Annie responded as she reset the hands on her watch. She smiled at him, but in her heart, she knew the smile was also for the Indian day that would soon dawn.

Annie Karten, Oregon's girl, said to herself, "Okay, India, I'm here. Let's hope I survive."

~ Ten Months Earlier ~

PART II

Skunk Naps
(Oregon)

Don't judge me. I did enough judging for everybody. But unless you grew up in Ridgeway, in my family, at my school, you don't know what you would have done. Besides, we never had anyone in our class die. So we thought it couldn't happen, or wouldn't happen. Or we just didn't think about it. If we had, I know that hats or turbans wouldn't have seemed so important to any of us. And we would have stayed out of the corn.

But you can't go back. It's bad enough remembering. Especially when you know you were the person who caused it. I hate that thought. I hate it.

Annie

CHAPTER 1

"**W**ait up, Annie," my friend Katelyn called. "Look what's headed up the hall behind us!"

In ten seconds of watching the new girl, I could tell she was going to have a very hard time at our school. I doubt that I was the only one who thought that. Everybody stared as she walked into our Civics class. Which is normal when somebody new comes, especially if they come in March, which no one does. But if you were trying to fit in, you'd wear jeans and a nice shirt your first day. Not her. She had bright red, spiky hair, poking out from under her black velvet hat, and she wore a long gray skirt. It went to the floor, with stuff written on it in marker. Instead of smiling or just coming in and sitting down, she stared back. Locked her eyes on us. That's weird.

"Welcome, Ms. Paulmann," Mr. Snyder said. "We have a place reserved for you there by the window. I only ask that you remove your hat in class."

It's a thing with Snyder. But it doesn't bug us anymore, because he's a great teacher.

"I wear it all the time," she said. Like that was an answer. We really stared then.

"Not in my class."

"Okay," she said. She turned and walked out the door. Just like that.

"Oh, my gosh!" Katelyn said.

WE SAW HER in the office lobby between Civics and English, her black velvet hat still on. But she was not the biggest news in the office that morning. Her marked-up skirt and black hat were nothing compared to a new boy and his dad, I assume, talking to our principal, Mr. Thompson.

The boy was really nice-looking. The other thing somebody would notice instantly was their turbans. Of course, I've seen people wearing turbans, on TV and in movies, but never in person. Ridgeway, Oregon, is definitely not turban country. Cowboy hats, yes. Ducks and Beavers caps, totally. Almost everybody in Oregon is for one team or the other. Bob Marley crocheted colors, yes; that would be Danny. But turbans, no.

My first thought was, how are they going to fit in? I sort of hoped Ridgeway would be nice to them. Actually, I hoped my own parents would be nice to them. Religion is fairly big in my family. To be honest, it's huge.

And what I've been realizing recently is that our church in Ridgeway is not super inclusive. We hear how certain adults talk, criticizing other religions, but for most of the kids my age, our reality is different, even if we don't say much. I'd guess that 25% of the kids at our school are Mormon, plus some Catholics, so we live with diversity, and it definitely doesn't keep us from being friends. Still, I had a hunch people at church, and maybe even some kids from school, would consider turbans a whole different category of diversity. I said a little prayer for the new people.

I also noticed the new boy looked like the sports type and instantly hoped he'd go out for our track team. Which, by the way, I'm on, and which has a history of setting records at both district and state. I run distance. Although I love school most of the time, running keeps me sane. So track is logical. Not just the meets, but all the running I do to be ready for them, or just to run.

"Looks like Ridgeway is becoming international," Katelyn

said. She didn't sound excited, like I was feeling, but we had to get to English.

As we walked in the door, I saw Danny already at a computer on the Internet. "Did you see those people in the office?" he asked. "Look at this. They're Sikhs. I thought so. New material for you Christians wanting to throw the rest of us to the lions."

He wasn't talking to anyone in particular, so nobody answered him. Danny gets a little carried away sometimes. But he's a really good friend. I've known him since we were babies. He teases me about my religion, but not to be mean. I think he wants to make sure I don't go overboard, so he has to act like he doesn't buy into it. If there weren't certain things Christians have to believe and do, and it all just depended on your heart, Danny would be in. He went with our youth group to build houses in Mexico during spring break of our freshman year, and on the last day, he was the one chosen to give the key to the new family. He cried, because he knew how happy they were. That's his heart.

Danny's super good at anything to do with computers, but sometimes he speed-reads the Internet, and doesn't get everything right. I decided I'd look up Sikhs myself to see if they were possibly some brand of Christian, like Greek Orthodox, which Danny told me about once. That would make things easier.

Class was starting. I scooted into my seat, and opened my copy of *Hamlet*. A thought came to me: If Snyder makes that girl take off her black velvet hat, will the Sikh boy have to take off his black turban?

Evidently Tani, that's the new girl's name – taw-nee – also thought it was a good question. Emily was Office Aid that period, and told us that when Paramdeep said he was in Civics, Tani blurted out, "You're gonna have to unwind that fancy hat, friend." Exact words. Emily reported it all at lunch. Danny said Paramdeep will get by because his is religious tradition, not just something you wear for fun, but Tani will be squashed. Mr. Snyder does not budge. She doesn't know that yet.

Two volunteers from our PEERS group were assigned to eat lunch with the new kids, so Tani and Paramdeep ate together, in their hats, with two juniors. You have to be a junior or senior to be selected for PEERS. I didn't think it was especially fair to pair somebody up with someone they wouldn't want to hang out with, simply because they were new on the same day. I'm a pretty good judge of people, and I could tell right off she wasn't his type. I also thought they should have introduced Paramdeep around to the rest of our class, but they didn't. They could have at least asked a sophomore to eat with him. I would have volunteered, with Katelyn.

Jackson Evans, this kid I haven't been able to stand ever since he came to Ridgeway in fourth grade, went up to Tani in the cafeteria and told her hi and welcome to this f'in' school, I suppose to let her know that if she's the dirty mouth type, then he's her man. I just shook my head when I overheard that. Jackson is hopeless.

It took nerve, but I caught up with Paramdeep as he left the cafeteria. "Hi, I'm Annie," I said. "Welcome to Ridgeway." He smiled and said thanks. And he goes by Param, not Paramdeep. I told him there was an informational meeting after school for everybody who wanted to go out for track. And then I said the dumbest thing I have ever said in my life: "You look like you'd be really good." Which was bad enough, but what came out was, "You look really good."

I could have died.

But this Param is like no other guy I have ever met. He just smiled again. "Thanks, Annie." Like my name was important. Like he hadn't noticed the missing words. Then he added, "I didn't know about the track meeting, and we've still got some moving in to do this afternoon, but it sounds like fun. Maybe I could talk with you tomorrow about the meeting."

Yes!

CHAPTER 2

We're not a class that thrives on drama, but we are human, and we were not about to be late to second period the next day. We had to see what Mr. Snyder would do about Tani. Danny actually took dollar bets from people: if she'd walk out again, never show at all, or for 100:1 odds, Snyder would give in. We'd never bet on the last one. That's just not Snyder. Nobody ever paid up on bets anyway, but that didn't seem to faze Danny. He was constantly lining up bets on everything. So although we have electives all over the school first period, the entire class, and some kids who are not even in our Civics class, ran to be there at the door by the time Mr. Snyder arrived.

"Good morning, ladies and gentlemen," he said as he walked past us into the room. As if he expected a regular day.

"Pay up, Danny," Jason Harding said. "She didn't show." But just as the bell rang, in came Tani, black and purple skirt this time. And black velvet hat – on her head where she knew Snyder would not want it – with her short red hair sticking out from under it like yesterday. She sat down in the desk he had pointed out when the trouble started.

Mr. Snyder takes roll by just glancing up at us. We were totally watching him when his eyes lit on Tani's hat.

"Please remove your hat, Ms. Paulmann," he said, and went on checking the roll. He didn't look at her as he said, "It is my understanding that you were given a copy of the student handbook, and were told that I have a no hats policy in this class. Period."

I suddenly remembered Param was supposed to be in our Civics class, and wondered if "Period" meant turbans too or what Snyder would think about it.

I didn't have to wait long. Right then, Param came running up to the door.

Mr. Snyder looked up. "Welcome, Mr. Singh. Paramdeep, is it?" he asked. He didn't even comment about the tardy, or the turban.

"I go by Param, Mr. Snyder. And I'm sorry for late arrival. I got lost coming from Photography."

"Having learned my name balances out the tardy. I'm glad you're here."

I never thought about anybody getting lost in Ridgeway High School. It's not that big. Besides two years of classes here, most of us have been coming to high school games and programs since we were in junior high or even grade school. Param took the empty seat in the back.

"All right, class, we're going to hear a bit of Scott Joplin's ragtime music to set the tone as we look into some specific governmental changes in the 1900s. Then we'll talk about where you might have heard this kind of music before and how it came to be... Ms. Paulmann, the hat," he added. Like that was all he had to say.

She got up and walked to the door. Like she didn't care about ragtime music or Snyder or school!

"You owe me a dollar, Danny," Katelyn whispered. "She's walking out."

But Tani stopped at the door. "I am going to get a drink, Mr. Snyder," (which we don't do during class) "and then I am coming back and sitting at my damn desk" (as if swearing will impress him) "to listen to Scott Joplin. My mom plays *Maple Leaf Rag* better than anybody I know, Mr. Snyder Sir. And we danced to Joplin music. My little sister, my dad, and me. For an hour."

There was something fierce in the way she said it with her teeth clenched. "It's more than music, Mr. Snyder. I have a right to be here, and I will." She whirled around the doorway into the hall.

"Was she crying?" Katelyn whispered.

I shrugged instead of answering. We looked straight ahead at Snyder, but with our eyes a bit sideways so we could watch the door, too. Then he walked over and pulled the door closed, I suppose to keep her out, but maybe to keep the music in. "Mr. Snyder Sir" is probably our coolest teacher, and I guess we're sort of protective of him.

Tani was standing at the door before the first song finished. Mr. Snyder should have locked it. She walked in and went straight to her desk. Put her hatted head down on her desk with her arms crossed over it like somebody was going to beat her up.

Mr. Snyder didn't say or do anything.

"100:1!!" Katelyn scrawled on a note for Danny. "I could have been rich!"

"Nobody bet that he'd cave," Danny said quietly.

CHAPTER 3

It bothered us that Snyder would bend his rules just to accommodate Miss Tani A.B. Paulmann. Emily saw on her papers in the office that she had two middle initials, and we decided that they probably stood for "Above and Beyond" the rules.

Danny eventually asked Snyder why he backed down, and if he was discontinuing his hat rule or what. It was a waste of time. All he found out was some quote Snyder told him that didn't make sense: Ponder passion, pursue doubt. And that he appreciated us removing our hats in class, as always.

"Then why not her?" Danny had asked.

"That would seem reasonable, wouldn't it?" Snyder said.

Why Danny let it go at that, I'll never figure out. He should have said, "If that would seem reasonable, and if it's a rule, then why are you letting her break your discipline system?" But sometimes even nice teachers can be intense, so I guess I can't blame Danny for not pressing it. I do know Snyder would talk about real things, though, because he told us all about his rodeo accident when he was in high school. How he actually had to learn the word for *pen*, because he had a head injury that wrecked his verbal. And what it was like for him when other kids called him deformed because of his scars. Somehow, he managed through all that and ended up an awesome teacher.

The irritation of Tani wearing her hat eventually subsided into something like a weed seed stuck in your sock but you're in too much of a hurry to stop and take off your shoe to check it out, so you just keep walking. She kept wearing her hat, and Snyder kept ignoring the fact that she did. It didn't help Tani's acceptance with the class. If she was going to be Miss Above and Beyond, so be it. We left her alone. She pretty much kept to herself, except for lunch.

You know how cows turn into their own stanchions when they come into the barn, every single time, the very same one? Like they own it or something, and no other cow messes with their territory? Well, it was like that with Param and Tani in the cafeteria. Because they ate at that table with the PEERS their very first day, they evidently took it to be their place, and they both went back every lunch. Miss A.B. talked to him too. Who wouldn't? Every time I looked over, they were deep in conversation. It bugged me to see Param get stuck with her, but he must have thought we had assigned places, because he kept doing it even though we invited him to eat at our table.

"I'll catch you after lunch," he'd say, and he would, but after he'd wasted most of the lunch period with her. Maybe she was his community service project. She sure didn't seem like his type. He was obviously psyched on life and she was the total opposite. He's cool. It wasn't his nice clothes. Or even his looks, but he did have this perfect skin color, like the best tan, and a sleek metal bracelet he wore every day. He also had a runner's build. But what I really liked was, he was nice.

I was in the gym shooting hoops after lunch one day, and he came in and watched us. He complimented kids he didn't even know for the shots they made. And I noticed that he didn't laugh when people made fun of other kids. That's not your usual. He must do it sometimes. I mean, everybody does even if they don't want to, but since he'd come to Ridgeway, I hadn't heard him bad mouth anybody. Not even when some of us were railing on a teacher we frankly can't stand, for good reason. He just walked over to his desk and sat down and let us keep talking until the teacher walked in and we shut up.

But when I found myself really staring at Param was at track practice the first time I saw him pole vault. He was good. Like a hawk soaring to the top of a Ponderosa pine and then diving to the creek on the other side. I saw that happen once. Param made it to 12 feet that day, so I got to watch him repeat that soar and dive several times.

"They must have had pole vaulting in India," I said to him after our first meet, in which he placed second. India was where he was born and probably lived before coming here, Emily told us.

"I played cricket, mostly," he said, "but switched to track when we moved to the States. I like pole vaulting." Then he added, "You ran a great 1500, Annie. I'm beat after 400. How do you manage the speed on that last half lap?"

I didn't tell him it was my fastest time ever, and that I killed my lungs because I heard his voice over all the others yelling, "Go, Annie! Go!"

MISS A.B. FINALLY took her hat off. Not the way we expected.

We were already well into our early 1900s era Civics projects when she and Param came to Ridgeway, and when nobody invited her to join a pre-existing group, she signed up for the only project nobody had taken – a report on Charlie Chaplin. When Snyder announced she'd be presenting the next week, Katelyn whispered, "Bet she plays sick." Tani hadn't volunteered one word in class since her ragtime music outburst. Even when Mr. Snyder called directly on her, she hardly talked.

But now, three weeks later, not only did she not play sick, but when Snyder called her name, she stood up and walked her long skirt to the front of the class. She was wearing a shawl too. Then right in front of all of us, she unzipped her skirt and let it and the shawl drop to the floor. It happened so fast that we couldn't even be shocked, and there she had on underneath it, black pants, a white shirt, and a black jacket. Out of her pocket she pulled a bow tie that she clipped to her shirt collar, then a fake mustache she pushed up under her nose. She reached into a bag and pulled out a rounded hat. In one fast swoosh of her hand she had replaced black velvet with this Charlie Chaplin hat.

Katelyn coughed. "What was that?" she mouthed.

"What?" I whispered.

"Birthmark? Grossity? Watch when she takes the hat off."

Tani nodded at Snyder, and he started the music. Joplin music again. Most of us knew Charlie Chaplin from the silent movies they played during a Roaring 20s dance our freshman year. He was funny, and we watched him as much as we danced. I doubt that anybody in our class thought Tani could be Charlie Chaplin. I sure didn't.

We were wrong.

She walked up to this imaginary door and turned the knob. It was locked. She fished around for a key, in three or four pockets, but didn't find one, so she crawled up on an empty desk that she or Snyder had set up, and pretended to open a window and crawl in. Hard work, I guess, because once she was inside, she reached back into her pocket for a hanky, a real one, to wipe the sweat off her forehead. An imaginary key fell out.

We could tell exactly what was happening. She picked up the key and with a very serious look on her face, like this was the only logical thing to do, she crawled back out the window, unlocked the door, turned the knob, and walked in.

She took a step forward and bowed.

Talk about shock! How could anyone with such a bad attitude do that? Somebody in the back started clapping. I turned around and saw it was Param. Two or three other kids joined in, and the rest of us just looked at her to see if she was under some spell or something, and what she was going to do when she sat down.

"Excellently done, Ms. Paulmann!" Mr. Snyder said. "I sincerely appreciate your allowing the spirit of Charlie Chaplin to shine through you to us today! Class, let's show Ms. Paulmann our appreciation." So we all clapped. Tani actually smiled. The first time since she came.

But the magic of Charlie Chaplin disappeared the instant she took off the hat. I saw what Katelyn was talking about. A huge birthmark on the side of her head. Purple and pink, and yellowish mixed in, bubbly and rough at the same time, and no hair on it. Can't they do plastic surgery on heads? She obviously thought no one would see, the way she slid one hat off and the other on, but I saw, and so did Katelyn.

That was when it dawned on me that Snyder must have found out about the birthmark and agreed to let her wear the hat. That makes more sense. What a big mess over nothing. You would think she would have tried plastic surgery. But maybe they can't implant red hair into a birthmark for some reason. Danny said that he knows for a fact that birthmarks look different than a head that's been through a motorcycle wreck like his dad's, and he'd bet 50:1 that Tani was in a major wreck not more than a month back. But then, Danny loses a lot of bets.

I thought about telling Tani that I really liked Charlie Chaplin.

CHAPTER 4

My mom freaked when she came to our next track meet and saw the boy I had been talking about.

"Annie, who is he?" she asked with a nod behind her to where Param was standing. I had a hunch the turban might throw her, since I found out for sure that Sikhs are not Christians, and I hadn't mentioned anything about his religion to Mom.

"Param Singh."

"Singh? That's the new boy?"

"Yes, Mom."

"You didn't say anything about him being a... Where is he from, Annie?"

But before she could interrogate more, Param bounded up.

"Hi, Annie. Is this your mom?"

When I introduced them, Param held out his hand for Mom and smiled. "So does Annie come from a family of runners?" he asked. I could tell that Mom was pleased with that, because running is her thing to keep in shape, and we do run together sometimes. Dad's thing is basketball with men from the church, but Mom and I run, and since we're two-thirds of the family, Param was basically right. When Mom smiled, the thought flashed through my mind that she might just make an exception and let me date a non-Christian if she got to know Param.

I liked our family rule when Mom and Dad first made it. I think I was thirteen at the time and some gross guy from high school had just asked me out. I was relieved to tell him I couldn't date till I was sixteen. I didn't bother to add, "and then only Christians." In the meantime, I can do things with groups of kids.

Danny is the only exception because he's grown up around us, and our moms are friends, and my mom also knows I love him, but not in-love kind of love. Besides we don't really "date." We just do things together. We ride our bikes or go for walks down to the river or make pies, stuff like that. And talk about everything. And my parents think he's really smart because he can fix anything that goes wrong with their computers. He was already a computer geek in junior high, or maybe even grade school, but he took it as a compliment. Then during our freshman year, he discovered this group from Athens, Greece, called Computer Greeks, and he's been doing computer stuff with them ever since.

But recently I had caught myself thinking that May 29th, which is my 16th birthday, was only two months away, and I started imagining what it might be like to be alone with Param, totally alone.

I had a hunch that Mom would not relax her policy for someone in a turban. It seemed too drastic. Unless he became a Christian. That little thought got me in big trouble. With Danny, of all people. I asked Danny if he thought Param would ever become a Christian. Big mess. Danny assumed I wanted to go out with Param, and even though I did, I realized a little too late that it was not the best for Danny to know. He is the last person I expected to freak. It made him mad, even though he was jumping to conclusions.

"He's not right for you, Annie," he said.

"What are you talking about?"

"You've told me why you won't go out with somebody who's not a Christian. He's way more than 'not a Christian.' He's something else on purpose. Something he wants to be."

"Danny, what? I just asked you a simple question – if you thought Param would ever be a Christian. And I'm not going out with anybody."

It was quiet for a minute. I knew Danny was just being protective, but it felt different than that.

"What, Danny?" I said again.

"Annie," he started, then broke off and walked away from me. He turned back and said, "Well, before you do anything, ask him about the fancy bracelet you think is so cool, and the knife he carries…"

"What are you talking about? Danny, get back here!"

Very unlike Danny, he didn't say another word, just turned and walked away.

"What knife?" I yelled after him.

But Danny was gone.

CHAPTER 5

I should have just ignored that comment. But it's like noticing the door wasn't locked when you come home and you wonder if somebody forgot to lock it or if there's a robber inside waiting to kill you. So I asked.

"Danny, what were you talking about yesterday? What knife does Param carry?"

"It's a Sikh thing," he said. "Ask him."

"Danny, come on. What's with you?"

"Annie, you don't get anything, do you?"

And I stopped. Because I wondered if Danny's eyes were watering.

I GUESS THAT'S where it all started. The rumor, or the truth, that Param had a dagger he kept in his backpack. I'm not saying Danny spread it, because he says he didn't, that he was just trying to get me to think about what I was doing, and possibly some kid overheard him. Next thing we knew some parents had called in asking if the school was aware that a boy from India had a weapon at school. Emily got the scoop from the office. She overheard the principal tell Elaine that people were so ready to stir up trouble. They asked if the principal had interviewed this family to make sure they all had "appropriate papers" to be in our school district. And had he gone over the rules with this boy – in English?

I have to give it to Danny, that he instantly came out of whatever was bugging him when Emily told us that. He walked right over to Param's desk, even though Spanish class had started, and told him that if he had a knife of any kind, he'd better dump it quick before the office gets to him. Param looked confused, and didn't do anything, and thirty seconds later, here comes Mr. Thompson, the principal, saying he needed to see Param.

Things happen fast around Ridgeway, but they don't finish fast. Param never came back to Spanish. And he wasn't at track practice. So we knew something bad had gone on at the office. Kids said they saw Param's mom in with the principal, really upset.

My mom heard more about it than I did by afternoon, and when she picked me up from track practice, she asked me if Param had been suspended, and was it true that he was threatening some kids with a knife.

Whoa. That was hard to believe. But it still gave me a bad feeling in my stomach. I wanted to defend Param, but to be honest, there was something else. Should I be thinking of dating somebody who I hardly knew who might have a whole other layer of them because of how they grew up? At least I knew Danny through and through.

We were shocked to see Param walk into Civics class the next day. Everybody knows it's an automatic minimum two-day suspension for weapons at school, and that's just for the guys who forget and leave their pocket knives in their pants' pockets. If it were a dagger or something real, then it's expulsion plus some psychological examination and a bunch of other stuff, and here Param was back in class. But he wasn't his usual self. No smiles. Straight to his seat in the back.

Tani took it upon herself to walk over to his desk, and without saying a word, reach her arms around his shoulders from the side in a hug. Rather dramatic.

Snyder was onto something. He started some orchestra music. "We're taking a break from the 1900s," he said. "There is something more pressing that bids us take a look. Mr. Thompson suggested this might be a good time to do it. Mr. Singh, your knife please..." And he held out his hand toward Param, who seemed to know what Snyder was up to.

The whole class turned to watch, though we knew Thompson would have already taken it away. Param reached for his neck and removed the chain he was wearing. He held it out for Mr. Snyder.

"I carry a symbolic knife, Mr. Snyder, which I wear on this chain. It would not be appropriate to carry a kirpan to school."

"A kirpan?" Snyder asked.

"A big version of this," Param said, placing the chain and the tiny, tiny dagger hanging on it in Snyder's hand. It reminded me of my old charm bracelet, only a little bigger.

"You mean all the hubbub of yesterday was because of this?"

"I suppose so, Mr. Snyder."

"Mr. Singh, have you ever threatened anyone with a knife?"

"Never, Mr. Snyder."

Param suddenly smiled.

"Mr. Singh ...?"

"Well, once when I was four or five, a monkey stole a tiny cup of *ghee* right off my plate of rice. She spilled it on the floor and then sat in the window sill licking the inside of the cup. I love *ghee*, but I was afraid of monkeys, so I made a paper knife – actually about ten of them – and waved one at the monkeys the next time they bounded into the courtyard. They never took my *ghee* after that, so yes, Mr. Snyder, I suppose I did use a knife as a threat once."

"What in the world is gee?" Katelyn whispered. I think Katelyn sometimes misses the point. But I didn't know either.

Then Mr. Snyder did a cool Snyder-thing. He motioned for Param to come sit in the Royal Chair.

"All right, ladies and gentlemen," Snyder began, "Mr. Singh and I have discussed things, and he has agreed to talk with you this morning. I would invite us all to begin with questions about his faith, his cultural traditions, his family, his ties with India and the Punjab, and the circumstances of prejudice and/or acceptance that he has encountered since moving to the US at the age of twelve. Who would like to start?"

Katelyn didn't even raise her hand. "What's gee," she called out, "and did you really have monkeys running around inside your house?"

CHAPTER 6

W hen we got done, fifty-five minutes later, I knew I loved Param. I loved Mr. Snyder. I loved our whole class. And I wished Snyder would dump the 1900s and do that to every single person in the room.

Sikhs are okay. Actually, better than okay. They care about their families. They started equal rights and women's rights from the very beginning of their religion, way in the Middle Ages or sometime. And that wasn't easy when people were stuck in castes, and women belonged to men, and there was fighting between Hindus and Muslims. They also believe there is only one God. That's good, because that means they aren't the ones who believe in praying to a bunch of stone or metal statues, which I know for a fact makes some Christians lose it. I get that.

Danny apologized right out in front of the whole class for the mess about the knife. He said he'd read something on the Internet about Five Ks being important to Sikhs, one being that they carry a knife. Since Param seemed to be a real Sikh, Danny assumed he'd follow the rules. He said he shouldn't have assumed.

Param actually turned it into a compliment to Danny and thanked him for wanting to learn about his faith. That was probably the beginning of their friendship. I wondered if maybe Danny wouldn't be jealous any more. Or whatever it was that made him suddenly act so weird around me.

Param said Danny was right about the five Ks, more or

less. His symbolic dagger was one of them, a pledge that he as a Sikh will always fight against evil and injustice. Actually, his cool steel bracelet was another K – a kara. And the fact that his turban covers his hair, which starts with a K, which he hasn't ever cut and holds a special comb called a kangha. The fifth K is something to help them keep their priorities straight. He didn't say what exactly, but I'll ask him later.

Then we switched to Param telling us about his home in India, and the monkeys that jump over the compound walls, and the international school he attended. He told about coming to the US, and then somebody asked if anybody ever thought he was weird because he wore a turban.

"Probably a lot of people," Param said, "but they wouldn't have, if they had been at my *dastaar bandhi*." He smiled as he described the ceremony they held for the first tying of his turban. I wish I would have known Param then and he would have let me come. It sounded like something good that you remember for a long time.

Before his *dastaar bandhi*, Param said, he wore a cloth, a *patka*, over his knot of hair. "Once some kids cornered me and ripped my hair down out of its knot."

We were pretty quiet when he said one boy took the cloth that covered his hair and blew his nose on it, then threw it to the ground. I thought that people in the US were really mean. The kind of thing Jackson Evans would think of. But then Param said that was when he still lived in India.

"I wasn't really sorry it happened," he said. "Afterwards, that is. At the time it was bad. But later my mom and dad and two uncles sat with me and my sister and we talked a long time about why people hurt each other. They'd had their share of trouble, and for some reason that made it easier." Param paused, and I could see his eyes watering.

"This brings back memories," he said softly, "and makes me hope that Ridgeway won't be a hard place to live."

That's when our class did it. We stood up. All of us. And clapped. A long time. It mattered to Param. He sat in the Royal Chair with tears running down his cheeks. Mine too. He was more beautiful than ever because I knew his niceness was way deep in his heart, and he was real and not ashamed to be hurt or to be loved.

For some reason I turned and looked at Tani. She was standing there, looking up at the ceiling. Her mouth was open, and I realized that she was crying too, silently. Her black velvet hat was in her hands. I wanted to go over and hug her before Katelyn saw. I wanted to put my hand over her birthmark, in case it hurt. I had a hunch her tears weren't for Param, but for herself. But I didn't move. Even though I knew something was wrong. I usually don't just go up to somebody I don't especially know. Besides, the bell rang and everyone gathered around Param.

CHAPTER 7

That emotional thing about Tani faded pretty fast. You can't get too worried about somebody who's cold and gloomy. But one thought didn't go away like I wished it would: What would she say if Snyder had her sit in the Royal Chair? What's the deal with her so mad at everybody when she doesn't even know us?

The Royal Chair is an important piece of furniture in Snyder's room. He mostly uses it to honor somebody for their good work. They can do that – sit in the Royal Chair – or pet his hedgehog. It's a cool little critter he keeps in the bottom drawer of his desk, a toy. He's way crazy, we know. Probably no other teacher in the world does stuff like that, but like I said, Snyder is cool, so weird things turn into a class all their own – fun. I got to pet the hedgehog once when I sang a solo in the school talent show. It didn't have anything to do with Civics, but Mr. Snyder said I did a great job, and did I want to stop by and pet the hedgehog? And bring witnesses. That's a part of it. Four other kids came with me to watch and cheer. I was so proud!

Anyway, it kept bothering me that Tani could be a perfect Charlie Chaplin one day and dance while her mom played the piano for an hour, and the rest of the time it was like she was dead, or a shadow of somebody that was reflected into our room, just sitting there, except this once when she was standing up crying. It didn't make sense. I wondered if she had a story like Param's.

Danny said everybody has a story, even though it might not be as interesting. Even Jackson Evans probably had a story, and Danny would bet a dollar that I'd find out three cool things about Jackson if I pretended I was a newspaper reporter and called him up for an interview. Danny can give you a guilty conscience at times. I said I wasn't that desperate for a dollar, but it did get me to wondering if Tani was ever in school plays someplace before Ridgeway. And where she used to live. And if she really could dance. And if she'd try to ask Param to the girl-asks-boy spring dance that our class was sponsoring in two weeks.

I decided to ask him myself.

Not as a date, because I couldn't do that to my parents before my birthday. And for some reason it seemed like I owed it to Danny too. So I asked Param like it was a general announcement that our class was sponsoring the dance and it would be great if he could come. He said it sounded like fun, and he'd try to be there, but afterwards I felt blah.

The worst happened. Danny told me about it, just to bug me, I think. Tani asked Param to the dance. I don't know how Danny got all the details, but evidently Param said his parents probably wouldn't want him to date, but he was hoping he'd get to go to the dance and he'd like to dance with her. "So you can cross him off your list," Danny said. "He can't even date!"

I just looked at him. "So?" I hate it when people say "So?" but in this case there was nothing else I could say.

"So, I found out more, too," he said. "On the Internet. Unless his family is pretty radical, they'll not only restrict his dating, but they'll plan on him marrying a Sikh."

"Danny, why are you telling me all this?" I asked, mad. It was like he wanted to get my reaction to Param dancing with somebody else, and not dating, and not dating me, and not ever being able to marry me, all with one hit. Danny can be so exasperating! Did he think I'd ask him since Param was already taken? No way. I decided not to go to the dance. I'd stay home with my mom and dad and play *Clue*. And cry. But in the end, I decided to go. By myself, which was fine with me. Because some of us girls do that. And we have a lot of fun.

I had almost two weeks until the dance to stay mad at Danny, but I couldn't. I never can. Danny is not purposefully mean. Besides, he has all this good credit built up with me because of everything we've done together, so when he grinned at me at lunch the next day, and offered me his fried chicken, which we hardly ever have at school, I grinned back. That was that.

But what happened at the actual dance was the shocker. Our school has this great new tradition of beginning every dance with dance lessons. We griped when last year's seniors started it, but it was so much fun, we won't have a dance without doing it now. It gets everybody into it, even shy guys who don't like to dance but come because there's nothing else to do in Ridgeway. They teach three kinds of dance every time, to start things off. Swing is one of them, then some kind of folk dance, and then something random. This time the something random was country line. And what happened was that one of the PEERS who Tani ate with that first day announced that she and Tani were going to teach us a line dance. No way! Her in that long gray skirt with permanent marker stuff all over it. And her black velvet hat.

Talk about a worm turning into something else. I would almost say butterfly. She was standing up on the stage. She bent down and rolled up the edge of her skirt to where some ribbons hung, and she tied them up so that it looped up to her knees. The music started and she smiled. She clicked her heels together and then kicked and turned and stepped and crossed over and all the while called the instructions of what she was doing into a hand-held mic while we watched. Like she was a real line dance teacher. This was the same person as in our Civics class?

Right then I decided I was going to find out why she wore long skirts and didn't fix her head and how she learned to dance when she couldn't talk to us, and while I was at it, I'd ask her to keep her mitts off Param. Not really. But I did pray right then that God would help me know for sure what I should do. I also asked God if it really mattered to Him if I dated a non-Christian if the person believed in God as much as I do. And I prayed that I would love everyone, even Tani. But especially that God would help me know what my heart was doing with Param.

And then I wondered if Param and Tani would meet up somewhere after they left the dance.

CHAPTER 8

Sometimes I pray and don't carry through with my hunch because I'm not sure if it is God or me talking. But this time I thought maybe God was answering my prayer with a feeling that I couldn't just push away, that I should invite Tani to The Night Thing at church. It's the biggest, funnest party ever, for our youth group and kids from other churches, plus kids from school who don't go to any church, so they'll be familiar with us and maybe come back later for other activities. I asked Danny, of course, who comes every year but never seems to make it to church, and I asked Param. I didn't know if it would be against his religion's rules to go to a church, so I told him it was just a fun party that happened to be at our church, with a devotion at the end.

Then not because I wanted to, but because of the feeling that I should, I invited Tani A.B. Paulmann. She said right off, "Yes, I'd like to come. Thanks." Just like that, which surprised me, and then asked me which church I went to.

"I'll see if my dad can drive me in," she said and then turned and walked away.

"We can probably pick you up if you need a ride," I called after her.

I had to talk to her a couple more times about The Night Thing, because we do this activity with photos, and each person has to bring one from home. And to make sure she had a ride.

"If my dad is sober," she said.

I knew immediately that was a puzzle piece. I just hate it when I find out that parents are drunks. It's so unfair. I suspected that had something to do with Tani's attitude. It also made me realize How much I love my dad for not being a boozer.

I was sort of glad when she called before the party and asked for a ride. I like to see somebody's house. You find out if they're rich or not, or sloppy or neat, and what their family looks like. I didn't know where Kinsey Lane was, where she lived, but my dad did. Only she had walked out to the end of this long driveway to meet us, so I couldn't really tell much except that they lived in an old, but okay, farmhouse. I didn't see her mom or her sister anywhere, and I supposed her dad was drunk, so I didn't say anything about that. I did wonder why her mom didn't drive, but figured I could find out later.

Not knowing what else to say, I asked Tani if she remembered her picture, which she had. And then we were quiet. I looked out the window at the corn fields around her house.

Dad is a talker. "You folks raising that corn, Tani?"

"No, we just have the house. The people down the road do the fields."

"So do they grow corn where you come from?" he asked.

"Maybe somewhere, but not in my neighborhood. I lived in Seattle all my life before Ridgeway. I don't remember seeing corn fields."

"Great place, Seattle. Annie's mom and I lived there for a year right out of college. Do they still let sailboats on Green Lake?"

I wondered how he could just make up things to say to a total stranger.

"Yeah. I watched them sail all the time when I ran the lake path."

I never thought of Tani as a runner. Like she'd trip over her long skirts.

"Annie, I think we better get our garden in," Dad said. "That corn's a foot high." And then to Tani, "Ever run in a corn maze?" Like she's one of my friends he's known forever.

"What's a corn maze?"

I was the one to answer, because Dad's never done a maze himself. "It's really fun," I said. "They chop the corn stalks into a tall maze at the end of the season, and you can go through the trails every which way trying to find your way out. Sometimes we do it at night with flashlights. That's the best!" And then for some reason I added, "We'll do it this fall."

"Okay, Annie," she said. First time she's ever said my name, and I instantly regretted it. I didn't know if I wanted her really knowing me. This was just an invitation to a party, not to be best friends and step in where Katelyn and Danny and my other friends were. What I should have regretted was talking about the corn maze.

THE NIGHT THING was as good as ever. We had a hay ride around town, and came back for hotdogs and s'mores behind the church. Then we went inside to play games in the dark with glow sticks. Danny and I started a round of Sardines by hiding in the baptistery. I hoped that wasn't sacrilegious, but Danny said God was not some old grouch and would think it was fine, and even the youth pastor thought it was funny when we got twenty kids in that little tiny room and started laughing so the rest of them found us by the noise instead of the glow from the light sticks.

At midnight, we started the serious time. We sat in groups of four and talked about our pictures. I asked Param and Katelyn to be in Danny's and my group. I noticed that some other kids had let Tani join them. The youth pastor did a devotional with a Scripture, and then he lit candles and started beautiful music. He had us hold hands in a long line and led the line first into a circle. Then breaking away and doubling back, he wound us past each person so we'd be able to look them in the eyes and silently ask God's blessing on them.

I wondered if Param would be nervous, and if he was asking the real God for blessings. But he fit right in. When we came to each other in the serpentine, he reached out for my hand, which you don't have to do. He looked right at me, and I know my eyes answered "yes." Yes to what, I wasn't sure. But before he moved on, he whispered, "God be with you, Annie." Like he knew what the words meant and wanted that for me. All I could do was whisper back, "Thanks." I wanted to slip out of the serpentine so that nothing could erase the warmth of his hand and the thought of being wrapped inside his blessing, but we went on in opposite directions. I suppose the others couldn't hear my heart pound.

Tani didn't do the blessing walk. She went to the bathroom, I guess, and never came back until the whole thing was over. She missed out on something good.

To kill time while we waited for my dad to pick us up, I asked Tani if I could see her picture. It was not what I expected.

I had this weird feeling that she looked like me, except for the red hair. A Mickey Mouse sweatshirt and jeans, just like what I wear, standing next to a really normal looking family. Her dad seemed nice, not like a drunkard, and her mom was beautiful. Red hair, just like Tani's, but her little sister had dark brown hair like her dad's. And then I noticed that the side of her head with the birth defect was toward us. And it was beautiful red hair. Nothing wrong. Nothing there except a regular head.

"When was this taken?" I asked.

"Right before Christmas," she answered.

"It's beautiful," I said, but I was wondering if she'd been in a motorcycle wreck right after that, like Danny guessed.

Dad pulled up right then and we walked toward the car.

I just rode along while Dad asked us all about the party, mostly talking to Tani. I didn't mind. It gave me time to think about Param.

CHAPTER 9

It was by accident that I got to know Tani.

Track practice was canceled because the coaches had some big meeting, but I remembered only after the buses left. So I decided to hang out until the usual time Mom picked me up. I could have run on the track on my own, but nobody else stayed, so I headed into the computer lab, just as Tani A.B. was heading out. We crashed.

She dropped two textbooks and we both bent down to get them. That's when I noticed something on her skirt. The one she wore her first day at Ridgeway. With the permanent marker writing.

"I'm sorry, sweet Tani," it said. My mouth read it out softly, but she heard me.

"Oh, that's okay. I think I bumped into you," she answered.

I looked up at her. "Oh, yeah, I am sorry, but that's also what your skirt says, right here." She was still kneeling down, gathering her things, and I pointed to the words.

She nodded her head, but gave no explanation. Then I really looked at her skirt: "Don't go. Stay and dance with me. I love you, Red." It was signed "Jek."

"Who's 'Red'?" I asked.

"Me," Tani laughed, pointing to her hair.

"Who's Jek?"

"A kid from my church in Seattle."

"Your church? You went to church in Seattle?" I asked.

"Yeah. That's not so radical, is it?"

I didn't answer. It didn't seem likely, but I guess I had to believe her. I really wanted to know why she wore such a weird skirt to school. And a bunch of other things. Nobody else was around, so I sat down on the floor beside her and said, "Where'd you get this skirt?"

"They gave it to me. My youth group. When we left."

"You have a youth group?" I asked.

"Had. In Seattle. We moved, and left all that behind."

"Why?"

"Because my sister was killed." She wasn't looking at me, but was rubbing her hand across the messages on her skirt. "In a car wreck with my dad."

"Oh, no," I said. "The sister with brown hair in the picture?"

She nodded her head. "Jenny."

I waited, because what do you say when you've just heard something like that? For some reason, I scooted up next to Tani and put my arms around her. She started shaking. She gathered her knees up to her chest, but she didn't push me away, and she cried.

What is there about feeling bad that you can't let others see? Right then, in the middle of this, Miss Holland walked out of the computer lab and locked the door behind her. She saw us on the floor.

"Are you okay, Annie?" she asked me. "We're fine," I answered. "Just waiting for my mom to come pick me up." I say dumb things sometimes, and this was dumb, but I didn't know Miss Holland all that well. She walked on down the hall toward the office. I smoothed Tani's skirt and found the words, "I'm sorry, sweet Tani." I put both our hands on those words and waited for her to look up at me. And then we both cried, even though I didn't know pretty, brown-haired Jenny.

"You want to walk the track?" I asked Tani. She kind of rolled her head and I decided that must be a yes. I took her hand and we dumped our things at the side of the steps. I was glad the track was empty. We walked half a lap before she said anything more.

"It was my fault, Annie."

Darn. "Were you driving?" I asked.

"No. Dad was." We walked some more. "But I made it happen. The wreck. All in like ten seconds. My mind. My words. And my dress. Now everything is done, forever. And it can't ever change."

She cried like she had in Civics class, face looking up but tears streaming down her cheeks.

"What happened?" I whispered.

"We were on our way home from Tacoma, where my grandparents live, and where I had just bought a dress for the Winter Formal. I was holding it on my lap, in the back, and I looked up and there's this skunk ahead on the road. Just that fast, I remember thinking, we can't hit it. The smell would wreck my dress for the dance. That's what I thought, Annie. Nothing else. Just that my dress would be ruined and I couldn't wear it. And I yelled, "Dad, don't hit that skunk!" He swerved. I didn't know what happened when you swerve fast, that the car could go out of control like that ...."

She started crying hard, and I steered us toward the bench beside the track so we could sit down.

"It was all mixed up then. Like an explosion. Screaming. I saw Dad's hand reach out for Jenny, who was riding up front with him, and we were all tumbling over and over and then sirens came and people came, and they covered Jenny up. And they took Dad away in the ambulance. And they took Jenny away, and then I realized they were taking me away, too, but I wasn't hurt. I wanted to be hurt, Annie." And she sobbed, "I wanted to be hurt so bad. And make them uncover Jenny."

We didn't say anything for a long time. I thought maybe that's all she wanted to tell me. But then she added, "I only said one thing on the way to the hospital. I remember. I asked a man what happened to the skunk. 'The skunk?' he asked, like maybe I was crazy. And then I went to sleep.

"Dad wasn't awake for Jenny's funeral. We were worried he might die too, because he was in a coma for almost three weeks. But then he just woke up and saw Mom first and asked her where the girls were. She was so relieved she just burst out crying, and he knew then that we had died, but Mom grabbed me beside her so Dad could see me and I could tell by his face that he thought we were alive, and he said, 'Oh, thank God, I haven't killed my girls.' That's what he said. That he hadn't killed us, but I ran out of the room then, because I knew he'd have to hear that Jenny was dead. And I knew it wasn't Dad who had killed her, but me. And I had wrecked things for Dad forever."

This is bad to say, but in the middle of Tani telling about such a horrible thing, I could see this skunk walking across the road as if nothing had happened. I wondered if some other car hit it. I wished it did. I'm so sorry my brain thought about the skunk then. I tried to make it quit, because it was so stupid, and then Tani was talking again. But I guess she was thinking about the skunk, too.

"If God is good, if God is in charge, then why didn't he have that skunk take a nap?" she asked me or the track or nobody. "For ten seconds. Just a ten second skunk nap. And let us pass before it came out on the highway?

"There is no such thing as God, Annie, or else he's warped. A skunk nap could have changed the whole world. That's not a very big miracle. My mom is always sad. My dad is always drunk. And all that happened to me is an ugly scar on the side of my head that the doctors say will mostly go away. And I am so far away from anybody who loves me or could ever forgive me for what I did." She started sobbing.

Then, for no reason, I said, "I forgive you, Tani." Like I'm

God. And I hugged her and held her, and I cried too. After a while we got up and walked and then ran two laps, even with Tani in her skirt, until we collapsed on the steps where we had dumped our books.

CHAPTER 10

I would have argued with anybody else who said God is warped. Criticizing God is not a good idea, especially not name-calling. But it came to me that Tani deserved to call God warped, Big Time Warped, if she wanted to. He'd forgive her for that when she was ready.

I kept thinking about skunk naps on and off that evening. Or why God let Tani look up and yell at her dad in the first place. She could have looked at her new dress the whole time and he could have hit the skunk head on. If the dress was stinky, she and Jenny would have gone and picked out another one. They would have grown up and been in each other's weddings, not one of them gone to heaven, missing the whole rest of life on earth, and the other one being sad forever. It didn't make sense.

That night I dreamed I was walking inside a long building with little cubby holes on the walls, like we had in grade school. Each one was stuffed with raccoons, sound asleep. But then I looked closer and saw they were skunks. I tried to leave the room quietly so they wouldn't wake up and spray me, but I was wearing a long skirt and I tripped on it and crashed into Mr. Snyder's globe stand. The noise woke all the skunks up at the same time, and they started falling out of the cubbies.

I think I woke up then and knew I was dreaming, but I tried to get back into the dream to see if I could get out of the building, or maybe that was a part of my dream too, because then I realized they were really raccoons after all, with skunk tails. God had messed up and made them all wrong, and nobody had told me.

I know dreams are crazy, and of course I knew where this one came from, except for the building, which I've never seen, and the cubby holes, which I haven't seen since third grade. But the bad thing about that dream was, I couldn't forget it or the feeling that I'd been tricked and nobody told me that God messes up sometimes. Somebody should have told me that. Maybe not used the word "warped," but at least hinted that God wasn't all He was made out to be.

It crossed my mind that maybe it was a good thing Danny was waiting to become a Christian, because at least he'd have time to figure out what God was really like before he believed in Him. Which I never did. Figure out, I mean. Because they wrapped God up in a box with shiny paper and curly ribbons and handed Him to me when I was a baby, or at least really little, and I just took the box and got what they gave me, and knew it was what they said it was. I guess I never really looked in the box before.

Until Tani.

AT TRACK PRACTICE I asked Param, out of the blue, "So who is God, anyway?" I wanted to hear who was in the box they gave him when he was little.

"What?" he asked. I didn't blame him. It wasn't a fair question on the spur of the moment. So I changed it a little bit as we started running laps. "Who do Sikhs say God is? Where is He?" I really wanted to ask right out if he thought God let people die when He could have prevented it, but I didn't.

Param stopped running, so I did too. He looked at me like I was joking, but then I guess he saw the look on my face, and he answered seriously. "Where is a little easier than Who, I guess. God's everywhere. He's in you and in me." We started running again. "It's like that song we sang at the party at your church, about the light. We have something like that too."

He quoted me a saying: "You are the light manifest." I remember that much, and then something about God being in me.

"I like that scripture, Annie. *You are the light manifest.* I learned it when I was little. I didn't really think about it then, but I do sometimes now. I think about being God's lamp."

"So what do you think God is really like?" I asked. We both stopped running. Track wasn't the important thing right then.

"I wanted to draw a picture of God once," Param said, "but I didn't know how to make the lines, so I asked my mom how tall God was and what kind of a head I should make. I still remember what she said – that I shouldn't try to draw God because God is more than I could ever think of. She said that I must remember that God is bigger than everything and closer than anywhere, even right here within Paramdeep. I believed her." He paused. "Why are you asking me this all of a sudden?"

"I don't know. I guess I just wondered if we had the same God, and if you really believed in Him, and if you did, how you handled some of the bad stuff that He lets happen."

"Like?"

The track coach saw us standing there talking and called out something that neither of us heard, but we both knew meant he wanted us to get moving.

"Later," I said.

CHAPTER 11

The next week in Civics we got school time to start figuring out some God stuff. Only I didn't realize that was what we were doing, and actually Snyder probably didn't either.

He is so funny. We walked into class and there was Snyder in a gorilla suit.

"Today we begin our study of another indicator of the life and times of the pre-Depression era, ladies and gentlemen. In this very room, in just one week's time, you will be transported to Dayton, Tennessee, 1925, where you will take part in the Scopes Trial."

I had never heard of the Scopes Trial.

The next moment Snyder had leaped up onto his desk and was scratching like a monkey. "So is man a lineal descent of an ape-like being, or did God, in the beginning, create heaven and earth, and Adam and Eve?" Pause. "Or both?" Pause, scratch. "And perhaps more importantly, do we have a right to explore these things in a classroom in Dayton, Tennessee, in 1925 or at Ridgeway High today, for that matter?"

He dropped to a crouch and pulled a banana off the bunch he had sitting on his desk.

"Was John Scopes a criminal, a guinea pig, a rebel, a pioneer, a blasphemer, or a devotee? And what about Doc Robinson, the owner of the ice cream store where the textbooks containing this evolution 'heresy' (pause for banana) or this 'scientific theory' were sold?

"But enough of my chatter. The names of the cast are listed on the board. Each of them is described in the handout I will give you. Please read through it to see what character you would like to portray."

"What if we don't want to be in a play?" Trevor asked.

"I can't conceive of that notion, Mr. Brown. I'm sure you will make an excellent witness in this case."

"Can I be the gorilla?" Danny asked. Snyder took off the gorilla head, smiled, and put it in the bottom drawer with his hedgehog.

As I read the handout, I knew right away what part I should play. It actually sounded like something that could happen today in Ridgeway, only we don't have a courthouse. I knew I should be a witness for creation. There's plenty of evidence they didn't have back in the old days that shows how God really did create the earth in seven days the way the Bible says and it just looks like it took a long time. I knew I could get some DVDs from the church. But then I remembered I couldn't show them at the trial for evidence, since they didn't have DVDs in 1925.

Then I noticed the description of Clarence Darrow, attorney for Mr. Scopes, who was the teacher who let the kids read about evolution. Darrow was a big wig from Chicago who evidently took the case to prove a point – that freedom of speech and freedom to study different viewpoints has to be allowed. He wanted the trial to hit the whole country to draw a lot of attention to what he thought were bogus laws. This teacher, Scopes, was up for a fine – $100 to $500 – which was probably a lot of money back then, for teaching something besides the Bible.

Snyder had sample speeches too. I read some of Mr. Darrow's and Mr. Bryant's. Bryant was another big wig attorney who said Scopes was guilty. It reminded me of a debate I watched once, when I found out later the speakers didn't necessarily believe the position they were defending. They just learned how to present that viewpoint. I wondered if I could do that – pretend. I walked up to the board and wrote my name on the blank space next to Clarence Darrow.

Mistake. I should learn not to do things the minute I think of them. Clarence Darrow has a huge part. As if I didn't have enough to do without learning a lot of questions and speeches. I could have just been a witness, on and off in a few minutes. What is worse, though, is that Danny and Katelyn decided to be on Mr. Bryant's side. And Param and Tani had decided to work together. Darn! I was so involved in reading the stuff that I didn't even realize people were grouping up and having fun.

So I told Snyder the next day that I wanted to change, and he said I couldn't. Well, he talked more, but that was basically what he said. So I was stuck being Clarence Darrow, who thinks people like me who know Creation is true are basically dumb and hiding their heads in the sand. I didn't really like it, pretend debate or not, but I just decided if I was stuck, I might as well try to have fun and be a really cool attorney for Mr. Scopes. Who was Scopes? I turned and looked at the board to see who had signed up for that part. Gross!

Jackson Evans.

Me, defending Jackson Evans? No way. Jackson wouldn't volunteer for anything. Somebody must have signed him up for John Scopes. I definitely was not defending Jackson Evans.

I never would have talked to Jackson Evans on my own. I can't stand his filth. Mouth, that is. He has this attitude that nothing is worth anything. And shocking people by being mean is a game. I had no desire to defend him on anything. Let him go to jail for teaching that the Bible is bogus. He deserved it. I told Snyder I didn't want to interview him.

That didn't work out well. It sort of hurt when Snyder just looked at me and said, "Annie?" With a question mark. As if he were saying, "Is this you? Are you going to be this petty?"

Major guilt trip. He didn't say anything more, so unhappy though I was, I walked up to Jackson Evans and said, "Let's talk."

"Why?"

"Because I'm your attorney, Jackson!"

"Why?"

"You're Scopes, and I'm Clarence Darrow, if you didn't notice!"

"And you want the glory of defending me?"

For Pete's sake! That is exactly the kind of thing Jackson Evans would do. I went straight to the board and erased my name, regardless of Snyder.

"Oh, is the Clarence Darrow part available?" a quiet girl named Sondra asked. I couldn't think why she'd volunteer for the part. She's smart, but not outgoing enough to be a lawyer.

My mouth answered, not me. "No, I'm just rewriting my name better." I turned and walked back to Jackson's seat.

"Jackson, the answer is No. Annie does not want the glory of defending you. You are not exactly the nicest person to defend, if you want to know the truth. But Snyder said I can't change roles. So we're stuck with each other." I know that was not a very Christian thing to say, but I was not exactly feeling my best right then.

"And I hope you'll act like a decent teacher," I added, "because this whole thing will stink if you don't." Maybe Jackson hadn't seen my eyes get watery before, or maybe he does have some feelings, because he surprised me.

"Annie, I'm not going to say 'f-you' on the witness stand." Soft. He said it softly, like he wanted me to believe him.

"Okay, Jackson. And no pushing my head in the toilet." I had been mad at Jackson Evans for six straight years because I heard he did that to some kid in our grade school when he first came to Ridgeway.

"What are you talking about, you bitch!"

"That! That's exactly what I'm talking about. I'm not working with you."

I guess we were louder than I realized. When I turned to go back to my desk, the whole class was staring at us. And Snyder looked at me like I was some big disappointment. Like I felt when I cheated in Algebra in 9th grade.

"I'm not Clarence Darrow, Mr. Snyder."

"I'll do it." Sondra called out.

"All right, Ms. Crandall," Snyder said to Sondra. Just like that. He wouldn't even fight for my rights. I took the bathroom pass off the wall and went into one of the stalls and cried till the bell rang.

I THOUGHT ABOUT skipping track practice that afternoon. Too many crappy things all at once, I guess. Maybe coach would think I was absent. I could just run home instead of around and around the track, which would be more exercise anyway, and I wouldn't have to fake being happy. But coach saw me before I could decide, so there I was. Once I got going, it felt good to run. The frustration over Jackson Evans and Snyder, and the God mess with Tani, went straight to my legs. It felt like I was running a PR. I didn't care if my lungs burst open. I didn't care if I fell and got hurt. I ran and when I finished the last lap, I collapsed. I rolled over on the ground and bawled.

"Got a cramp? Come on, I'll walk with you." It was Param. He reached down to pull me to my feet, then put my arm up around his shoulder and his arm around my waist. We walked, and I cried, and he didn't say a word, which I was glad for. We ended up at the side of the pole vault pit where I first saw him sail like a hawk, and I slid down to the ground. He knelt, then sat beside me, and in the same movement guided my back gently to lean against his chest. I still cried.

"Hey, Annie, what hurts?" he whispered.

He probably knew by then it wasn't a charley-horse.

"Right here," I cried, crossing my arms over my heart. "I don't know. Bad day, I guess." I should have felt stupid to cry in front of him, but I didn't care.

He crossed his arms over mine and held me tight. And then I knew. It wasn't just Jackson Evans and Snyder's look of disappointment. It wasn't just god-boxes and Tani's hurt. A restless something deep inside me was coming out and knocking against my skin. Against the very arms that were holding me. And I knew the words it was going to say: Why can't I love this other God's boy in the turban? Why isn't my God big enough for him too? Why can't I just roll over and put my arms around him and hold him back? We could decide together who God is.

Another thing about Param is that he doesn't always have to talk. He doesn't have to interrupt you to say something more important. He doesn't even have to know everything. He just sat with me and waited.

"So will you get in trouble for doing this?" I asked him at last. "For holding me?" He put his chin down on the top of my head and held me even tighter.

"Not if nobody knows," he said.

MOM WAS LATE. I was the last one at the track.

"Hi, Sweetie. Sorry," she said as I got into the car.

"That's okay, Mom."

I guess we were thinking about our own things, because the car was silent most of the way home. Maybe she felt she wasn't being mom-ish enough, because right as we pulled into the driveway she asked, "How was your day?"

"Super," I had to say, because I couldn't stand the idea of God and teachers and my mom all being against me on the same day. She would probably try to fix everything and tell me that Tani would be okay, and that hard things happen, but God is still in charge, and she'd tell me Snyder wasn't mad at me and I could apologize to Jackson Evans. She'd probably even want to get me reinstated as Clarence Darrow. Right then I just needed her to leave me alone.

CHAPTER 12

W e got extra points for dressing up like our trial characters. It could have gone either way – like somebody would make fun of the idea and then nobody would think it was cool to dress up. But Snyder was pretty smart. He brought in this huge old trunk, his Peace Corps trunk he said, so treat it with honor and he'll tell us its story sometime. The trunk was full of suit jackets and vests, hats, baggy dresses that could fit even fat girls, a couple of shawls, and a graduation gown and gavel for the Judge Raulston. Even some shoes and umbrellas. It swayed things to the "let's be crazy" side, and we all grabbed clothes out of his trunk like it was a privilege to wear this old stuff.

People got into their roles. We usually work harder for Snyder than any other teacher, but this was even more than usual. It felt good.

My first job was to find another part, so I'd know if I needed a jacket and vest or one of the old dresses. I grabbed all three out of the trunk and was hoarding them till I decided. I found out there was this other guy, Dudley Field Malone, a helper to Sondra, or rather to Clarence Darrow. It still sort of bugged me that she took my part, but I knew I had to get over that, and the outline said Malone gave a major speech for the defense and that I would get to examine some of the witnesses. It sounded okay to me, so I put the dress back in the trunk. I'd be Dudley Field Malone. Nice name.

Snyder said he had a movie about the trial, but he didn't

want us to see it until later. So we read a few paragraphs about our roles, and used a script that outlined the basic order of things. The funny thing was, we got involved for real. People starting talking about the Bible and what it said, whether it was really true or truly real, as Sondra put it. She said people in her church don't get hung up about whether or not an actual whale swallowed Jonah and barfed him up after three days, but they think about what else the story could mean. I never once in my whole entire life, ever since pre-school Sunday School class when I first heard the story of "Jonah and the Whale," ever imagined someone would think it didn't really happen.

"This whole thing about what we should or shouldn't be taught in school isn't so far-fetched, you know," Danny said. "It's just like the argument going on right now about whether they can teach birth control, or do they adopt a district policy on abstinence as the only way. Like they're afraid we'll all go sex wild if we hear the options. As if we didn't know."

"Or make smart choices to not go sex wild," Katelyn added. "I wonder if the school could ever back the wait-till-marriage theory. Or talk about chastity as a reasonable option anyway."

Right then something weird happened. I still don't know what it was. Danny turned and looked right at me. I don't think he meant to. It was like he was thinking, not looking at me. But then his face changed, and I could tell he knew what he was doing. He smiled, then shrugged, as if to explain it away. But it was too late. His smile gave me a funny feeling, and made me catch my breath. It reminded me of the time we had sat in the porch swing at his house and talked about my chastity ring and my pledge to keep myself for my husband.

"I like that idea, Annie," he had said. It gave me a funny feeling back then, and I pushed it away. But this time I didn't feel like pushing it away. The feeling that Danny was deep down mine. And really cute when he smiled like that. That maybe I underestimated Danny sometimes. That maybe I shouldn't take him for granted so much.

"There's always such a big disconnect between what they say at church and what we study at school," Katelyn was saying.

"Some people like it that way. It protects us from what people can't figure out but say they know," Trevor added. "And it adds to the circus effect of life."

The circus was one of the great things about the Scopes trial project. Snyder didn't make us keep to just research and speeches before the judge and jury. He told us about the hotdog and lemonade stands that sprang up in the town, and about the booths selling books on evolution and religion. He told us about the ape parade through town, with real apes dressed up like people in ties and hats! We spent two whole days making "extras" to help set the scene. Some kids brought toy monkeys, and Snyder let us hang his gorilla suit on the door to let the whole school know what we were doing.

In the end we moved the trial out to the courtyard, which was what really happened in Tennessee when it got too hot without AC inside their courthouse. Snyder took a big chance and asked the principal for assembly time for the whole high school to come watch us. Two assemblies, as it turned out. Talk about pressure. Knowing we'd have almost three hundred kids, divided into two batches, standing around watching and listening to us provided even more incentive to learn our roles. But that just made it seem more real. In fact, we made three hundred paper fans to give to the good people of Dayton, like they did in 1925, so they'd get the idea of how hot it was supposed to be.

We were hooked up with portable microphones. It was almost like a play, but without all the parts written down. The funny thing was, Trevor, who asked if he had to be in it at all, ended up being Reverend Cartwright, the local preacher who opened and closed the sessions with prayer. He went a little overboard blessing the judge and the holy truth of the Blessed Bible and the prosecution – Danny and Katelyn – but I guess that's what Trevor thought happened, and maybe it was. It made me curious about what Trevor thought about God. And if he ever prayed for real.

But the funnest of all was Param and Tani. I wanted to be jealous. Actually, I was. Snyder said they could share the job of the announcer for WGN radio station. But in the end, they were so good, I let it go. They learned all kinds of things about the 1920's and what things would be advertised on the radio. The judge purposely called some extra recesses in the proceedings just to let them do their thing. It was every bit as good as Charlie Chaplin, only this time, I did tell Tani, and Param, how good they were. And I made a vow to work with Param the next time we had a school project.

Our class and most of Ridgeway High School knew we had done something awesome by the time the jury gave their verdict: Guilty. Guilty of teaching the theory of evolution in a Tennessee school. Sondra was a great Clarence Darrow. She walked up to the jury and told them they basically had no choice but to find her client guilty as charged. The jury looked puzzled. They were supposed to. They pretended not to realize this was bigger than just Dayton, Tennessee. Now people all over the country would pay attention. Sondra grinned and cried out, "Yes!" which I'm not sure was a typical saying in the 20s or even typical for Sondra. Then somebody in the jury cheered and Snyder had us line up and take a bow. We hadn't planned that ahead of time, but we had no trouble. Everybody felt proud, in the good sense of the word, and we got a long applause.

CHAPTER 13

I won't say that one good teacher, or one great class project, can change the rest of the school year, but something was different after the Scopes trial. I tried to be a little nicer to Jackson Evans. And Tani began to fit in. Nobody ever referred to her as Miss Above and Beyond again. We pretty much got back to being a class which had known everybody since kindergarten, but we opened up a little more and added others in, whether or not they totally fit. I guess we felt a part of each other because of familiarity if nothing else. Like if we met up across the country in New York City someday we'd treat each other like long lost friends from Ridgeway, Oregon, because we all went through the Monkey Trial together.

Not everything changed. I mean, we still ate lunch in the same groups around the same tables, according to who we were, but occasionally if everybody but one person was gone at a table where they usually sat, people would notice and tell them to come join their table. At least the rest of the year was a little more – inclusive, I guess you'd say. And more fun, because you saw things about people that you hadn't noticed before. Like Sondra. She got chosen as our class's May Day princess. I think her being Clarence Darrow somehow changed people's opinions that she was just a 4.0 anti-social, and we saw her as somebody who can use her smarts and is bold enough to dress up in Snyder's old suits and hats and be a lawyer.

She actually cried when it was announced she was a princess. May Day is a big deal for our school and the town of

Ridgeway too. If you look at the walls by the office, you'll see old, old pictures of May Day celebrations – dances and the queen and court in City Park. They go back more than seventy years. At last, it was our class's turn to wind the May Poles. I think everybody should know how to wind the ribbons on a May Pole. Like you have to do math and read at a certain level and give a speech to graduate. Why not dance the May Pole as a requirement? It's beautiful, and you weave this awesome pattern down the pole, all together. It makes you a part of Ridgeway's history, and you remember that when you graduate, maybe more than math.

We chose our own music for the May Pole Dance, and the PE teacher taught the whole sophomore class how to do it. Both boys and girls. The school has a bunch of poles stored under the stage, so there are enough that everyone in the class can take part. We decorate the May Poles with huge bouquets of flowers on top and whatever colors of streamers we want, and we close the ceremonies with our dance. It'll be another tradition to talk about in New York City if we meet up in seventy years. Maybe better than the Monkey Trial. So when it was all over, I asked Dad if he could make a May Pole for our meadow. He thought I was kidding. "Maybe for your wedding day," he laughed. Actually, I'd love that. I want to get married in our meadow, or at least have the reception there, and May would be a beautiful time of year.

After May Week the school year began winding down. The days turned mostly sunny and warm. Even though there were projects and papers due, we knew we could survive it, so we lightened up.

Our track team placed second in districts overall, with three people plus our boys' relay team qualifying for State; the baseball team "had an enjoyable season," their coach reported in assembly, meaning they didn't do so well; and the softball team was district champ, headed for State in June. There would be just eight days of school left after Memorial Day weekend, which was also my sixteenth birthday. At last.

CHAPTER 14

May 29th. The day I could go out with someone alone. In junior high I told my mom she could change it from my 16th birthday to my 21st, because there was no one I wanted to date. She just laughed. But I was serious. That was not the case now with the thought that Param could be my very first real date. I didn't know that somebody else already had a plan for me. It was my best bud Danny, but I didn't learn that until the day was almost over.

We celebrated my birthday a day early – on Sunday. Mom and Dad took me out for breakfast – fresh strawberry waffles with whipped cream, which is a birthday tradition we have, and then after church, Gram and Gramps came over for dinner. We had lasagna, my favorite, and salad and chocolate cake with dark chocolate frosting, chocolate ice cream, and sixteen candles.

We did it Sunday because they had agreed to let me go to the coast on my real birthday. With a friend. It was good that I started this all three weeks early, convincing them that it was reasonable and the only birthday present I really wanted. The driving part alone took three or four days of persuading that we'd be okay. They brought up a gazillion arguments – there'd be lots of cars on the road, more traffic than normal, people irritable trying to get home after the long weekend, sharp curves along the Salmon River, cars known to go off the road, a whole different thing than driving on county roads, a hard thing for any teenager to manage, even if they are a good driver. Which I knew. I also knew they were assuming it was Katelyn who was going with me and they thought she'd be driving us. She's the oldest kid in our class and has had her license for over a year, whereas I've only had my permit for six months because I had to wait for driver's training. And Katelyn is my friend, so they're used to having her drive me places. They have confidence in her judgment.

When the idea had settled for a few days I admitted that Param was the person driving. They had a minor freak-out. Actually, major.

"We don't even know him, Annie. We don't know how he drives. Does he even have his license? Besides ..."

I didn't let them go there. "Yes, he's a good driver." Besides the driving factor, which they didn't like, I had to convince them that even though this was the Big 16, it wasn't a date, because of the Christian vs. non-Christian thing. And because Param can't date even if I can. I'm not sure either Mom or Dad was buying into this, but they seemed to soften a little.

"We'll think about it," Dad said.

I think Mom was secretly happy to learn that Param's parents restricted his dating. I also think the only reason they even considered my plan was because it was my birthday, not because they were happy about any part of it. I will admit that at that point, I wasn't above applying "It's-my-16th-birthday" pressure, if that's what it took. Besides, they would have felt differently about me going with Param if they had let themselves get to know him.

So I was getting ready to ask Param if he thought he could go, but instead I was talking to Katelyn and said, "I really want to go to the beach on my birthday, and ..." She didn't let me finish the Param part.

"Yes!" she said. "Awesome idea, Annie! Your folks will let us?"

I must have nodded yes, because she didn't miss a beat. "Fantastic. I'll drive our van. That way seven of us can go. Who do you want? Me and you, of course," she laughed, "and Danny, Param, and Trevor," who she had started liking, "and … should we ask Tani? That's five. Two more … Emily, for one? Maybe we should save the other place just in case my mom makes me take my brother." She paused, then started counting on her fingers. Actually, I think that's already seven, so I'll tell Mom my brother can't come.

"Let's eat at Mo's for clam chowder since it's your birthday. Maybe they'll give you a free clam!" she said. "Maybe we'll even find one of the glass floats they hide on the beach. You've always wanted one, right? It's going to be the greatest birthday, Annie. I should have thought of this plan for my birthday!"

Actually, I love Mo's clam chowder, and she was right about me hoping for years I could find a glass float, so I couldn't be too mad at Katelyn for destroying my very first date with Param. Even though I was officially going to call it an outing, not a real date. I decided that Mom and Dad would probably like this idea better anyway, which made me feel a little less guilty about the pressure. They finally agreed, after talking in person with Katelyn about the roads.

WE GOT TO the beach about 10:30. We decided to go on down to Wild Iris Bay State Park and then come back to Mo's for lunch. It was a beautiful day – sunny and a little windy, but that just meant there were all kinds of kites to watch. On the pathway to the sand right where you start onto the beach, Danny stopped us all and read the hazard sign out loud: Never turn your back on the ocean. Watch for sneaker waves and rolling logs et cetera et cetera. I didn't make fun of him. I don't take the ocean for granted. It is probably the most beautiful place in the world, but it's also way powerful. I learned that when I was a little kid.

We were jumping the waves with my cousins from California

when I got knocked down. Salt water filling your mouth and lungs, upside down in some tumbling water cage with sand scraping all over you is no fun. Mom said I cried like crazy, but they were right there to dip me out, and in a couple of minutes I was back in playing. So I didn't mind that Danny read the warning. I didn't want anything bad to happen on my birthday.

There's this rock at Wild Iris Bay, usually surrounded by water, but the tide was still pretty low so we walked out to it. We could see starfish on the sides of the rock, and sea anemones in the tide pools.

"You might not believe this, Annie," Param said, "but this is my first time touching the Pacific Ocean. Our family has been going to drive over ever since we moved here, but we haven't done it. One thing I know now is that the water's a lot colder than the Atlantic. And a lot, lot colder than Kerala or Goa."

"Where's that?" I asked.

"Two of our favorite places in India. The beaches are warm and you can play in the water forever. But I haven't seen those," he said pointing to the sea anemones.

"Touch them," I said. "Really gently."

"They don't hurt you?"

"Little tiny critters, maybe, but not us. Their tentacles just feel a little sticky." He hesitated, but crouched down, and I took his hand and brushed it over the waving green tentacles. As the animal closed up, I looked up at Param. Gosh, he was beautiful.

"Wow! And there are so many of them," Param said. "I wouldn't have even known they were here. Pink too, besides all the green. And look at that sea star!"

I loved his reaction. He knew how amazing this all was. Which is cool, because it is amazing. We waded around the base of the rock, checking out barnacles and mussels and pools where little fish darted every which way. I told myself right then that we'd come back again to this very place. Param and I.

"Come on!" somebody called. "Let's go check out that

cove." We could just barely see around another outcropping of rock at the north edge of the beach where the cliff came down to the sand, enough to tell there was a little place isolated from the rest of the beach. "If we go between waves, we can get around the edge without even getting wet," Danny yelled back over his shoulder at the rest of us. We ran for the spot and timed the waves perfectly, making a dash around the rock between two big waves, one smashing up against the outcropping just before we made a run for it, and the other doing the same once we were safely past.

No one was there but us. It was perfect. We played in the water, then buried each other's legs in the warm sand, which meant we had to wash off in the water again. Tani got everybody to build me a big multi-layered sand cake, with fancy seaweed decorations on the sides. All I had to do was gather sixteen sticks for the candles, which I did, and they sang to me. I made a wish and pretended to blow them out. I didn't tell what my wish was. You're not supposed to tell, but I couldn't have anyway. Danny said I had to do it again because he hadn't lit the candles, so he took out a lighter and got a few of them going, and then before I could blow them out, he gathered them up in a little bunch and started a tiny fire. We gathered some driftwood and built it up to campfire size and just sat around it and talked. I was completely happy.

Then I got an unexpected birthday surprise. I knew that whales swim off the Oregon coast on their run from Alaska to Baja, where they have their babies, and sometimes we've been lucky enough to see them spout. But I've never seen one up close or rise up out of the water like they do in the movies. And then suddenly there it was, straight out from the cove, swimming along maybe half a football field from the shore. It didn't rise up, but we could still see it. It just stayed near the surface, and sometimes disappeared in the waves and then would show itself again. It was huge. We all watched for a while and then Danny pulled a Frisbee out of his backpack, and we played Ultimate. The last couple of tosses, the waves seemed bigger than usual, or the water was coming in, and we realized we had gradually been working our way toward the back of the cove to stay out of the water. It was Param who cut our fun short.

"Are we trapped in here?" he asked.

CHAPTER 15

We stopped playing and looked at the water and the rocks and saw how much the tide had come up in two hours.

"How are we supposed to get back to the normal beach?" Param asked.

"Oh, my gosh," Katelyn said. "The tide's in big time."

The spot of sand where we had run to get around the corner of the rocks into the cove was nothing but ocean spraying against steep rocks. I looked up the beach. The other end of the cove was worse, nothing at all except the cliff meeting water. The land behind us was beautiful but way too steep to climb, even overhanging in places, and offered no way out. I had an awful feeling that we had made a huge mistake not watching the tide, turning our backs to the ocean while we played and while it changed. From where we were, we couldn't see anyone on the main beach, and I wondered if everybody had headed for home, or, if anyone was still there, if they'd be able to hear us yell over the roar of the ocean. What would they do even if they could hear us?

It had suddenly become a horrible day, even with a sand cake and a whale. I prayed that God would get us out of this mess. For a while we stood and talked about what options we didn't have. Then we all watched four or five waves hit the rocks to see if there was a low water time. There was once that I wondered if we might have been able to dash fast and wade through it. But the next one was way too high. We would have been covered with ocean, which can pull you off the rocks and out into deep water in just seconds. There was no way we could make it. Dang! I felt like crying. I wished we had never come. I even blamed Katelyn in my mind for getting all of us in this situation, because she was the one who took my idea and turned it into this whole beach day with everybody invited. But down deep I knew we had all gone along with the idea to make a dash for the cove.

"The tide's coming in," Danny said. "And by the looks of the beach here, we won't have all that much longer before the cove is underwater too. We don't know what's north, even if we could get out that way, which looks pretty impossible, so we're going back the way we came in, and we better do it now." He pointed out a way we could climb just above where the waves were mostly hitting, and even though it was steep and rough, it looked to us like we could make it. I have to hand it to Danny. He's crazy a lot of times, but this time he was totally serious and determined.

"Once we start, keep moving fast," he said, "and keep scrambling over the rocks, okay? Go high and use your hands and feet to keep your hold. If the water hits, hold on to anything there is to grab." He had us line up in some kind of order, that I'm not sure made any sense, but Danny thought it did, so we did what he said, Param leading the way, and Danny coming at the end. I was somewhere in the middle, after Emily and Katelyn, and I was scared to death. Danny told us to go, and we all moved fast up onto the rock, but my feet were underwater, then my shins and when a wave hit, it splashed over my knees onto my thighs. I think I was crying, but I know I yelled for people to hurry. Emily slipped and a wave came over most of her, but she held onto the rock and Katelyn reached over and pulled her back up, and the two of them bounded on ahead.

I moved as fast as I could, and knew that Trevor was

coming right behind me and Tani and Danny behind him. Another wave. It washed up almost to my waist, but I grabbed the same rock hold Katelyn had used and I didn't fall. There was a lull then, between waves, and we kept scrambling, leaping from one rock to another, sometimes letting our hands lead the way, sometimes our feet.

At last I bounded down onto the sand on the other side of the cove, into about a foot of water and instantly ran up onto dry sand, away from the ocean. Following, just a breath behind me, was another wave carrying something huge and dark, and I realized then that the whale had moved into the shore, or was dead and being washed ashore, and was almost on us. Trevor bounded past me, and I glanced back to make sure Tani and Danny had cleared the rock, when it happened.

A log, bigger than anything I've ever seen on the beach slammed into the rocks, exploding in our ears and spraying water everywhere. Tani and Danny leapt down onto the sand, soaked in the spray. The log hit and swayed as if it might try to break its way into a resting place on the rocks; then as the water receded, it rolled off and crashed back down into the foam. I stared at it as the surf again rose and picked it up, the end of the log disappearing around the corner into the cove where we had played. I looked back at the rocks we just crossed. The log hit exactly where, just a few seconds before, Tani, Danny, Trevor and I had scrambled.

Another wave hit. We were out of the water, but I instinctively ran, and so did the others, and then I fell down in the sand and cried. We were huddled together. Tani was crying too.

"Sheesh, that was bad!" Danny said. "Did you see where that log hit?"

Nobody else said a thing. We were soaking wet and we were quiet. A man walking a dog down the sand turned back toward us and yelled, "Everybody okay over there?"

Danny yelled back that we were. I could hear another

voice, closer, saying, "Fool kids. Think they're indestructible."
But I didn't look up. How could he think we'd do something
like that on purpose? We walked back to the restrooms by the
parking lot without saying a word. We had enough sweatshirts
and jackets and a couple pair of extra shorts between us that
those soaked the worst could get semi dry. Katelyn put some
beach towels out on the seats of the van, and told us not to get
it too wet, or she'd get in trouble. There wasn't much choice.
We loaded in.

We didn't stop at Mo's. Nobody said anything as we went
by. It was a quiet ride. Katelyn put a CD on, but even that
didn't change the mood. I realized I hadn't even thought to
look for a glass float.

"Dang," Danny said at last. "I wanted to go out with you
on your sixteenth birthday, Annie, not drown everybody
in the ocean. Or get you killed by some giant redwood log
crushing you against the rocks."

I stared at him, not sure that I heard right.

"You didn't get us killed," Tani said. "We all decided to
cross back over."

"It wasn't your fault any more than anybody else's," Trevor
added. "Besides, we probably would have drowned if we stayed
there. It was getting worse, not better."

Quiet again.

"So was that whale we saw really the log?" Emily asked.

I couldn't help it. I laughed. At the craziness of it. It was a
log all along, not a birthday whale. Funny how you see things
as good surprises when you're happy. Maybe it was one of those
nervous laughs people do when they can't think of something
normal to say. But it was crazy enough to make Danny laugh
too, and that broke the gloom and doom.

"Hey, isn't anybody hungry?" Danny asked.

"I am," Param said.

"Me too," Emily added.

Katelyn slowed and pulled off onto a wide spot on the shoulder of the highway. A quick glance at traffic, and she pulled back onto the road headed west. "I for one am starved, and I love Mo's clam chowder. Let's go to the beach, you guys!" We cheered. Katelyn popped in a Dixie Chicks CD and turned up the volume full blast. She and Tani and I sang along, and finally Emily asked for the words from the CD case so she could sing too. Danny yanked it away from her and joined our noise. We pulled into Mo's, still wet around the edges, but ready for lunch. It was 3 o'clock, and there was no line.

"Perfect timing," Danny said. As the waiter seated us, he added, "This is a birthday party for my friend, Annie." I think he said it so they would let us come in regardless of being wet. He pointed to me. "So maybe you could sing to her." The waiters did. We had a great lunch.

"Give me two minutes," Danny said as we headed outside after lunch. We assumed he had to run back in to the bathroom, so we waited in the van. He returned and said we had to go to the beach – just a block behind Mo's, and it'd only take a minute.

"Look for it, Annie," he said once we got to the sand.

"For what?"

"Guess."

"I don't know. What?"

"What did you want to find?"

"I never told you," I said.

"I know. But it's here. Hiding in plain sight."

So we all looked, and finally Danny started calling "hot" and "cold" as I moved between the driftwood piles.

"Boiling!" he said. I looked down, and right at my feet, lightly covered in sand and beach grass was a swirling green and blue glass float. I knelt and brushed the sand away. The glass sparkled as the sun hit it.

"Danny, you are sooooo good! It's beautiful. I've always wanted one."

"I know," he said, and his grin sparkled like the glass. "You're my bud. And you're sixteen today."

They sang "Happy Birthday, Dear Annie" as we walked to the van. Katelyn pulled a big sack with tissue paper puffing out the top from the back of the van.

"We all went together on this," she said.

I peeked in, then reached my hand in and pulled out the cutest little stuffed kitten, holding a mouse in its paws. But the kitten wasn't going to eat it, you could tell. The look on its face was super innocent, like, "What do I do with this little guy now that he's here?"

"It reminded us of you," Tani said. "Nice." She reached out and gave me a hug.

"Me too," Danny said, and then they were all instantly in a mass hug, me in the middle with a precious glass float in one hand, and a kitten with a mouse in the other.

"I love you guys!" I said, because I did, totally. "Thank you for doing my birthday with me."

ON THE WAY home Emily rode up front with Katelyn, and I knew she'd make sure Katelyn stayed awake. I rolled an extra jacket in a wad and put it against the window so I could lean my head against it. I thought about Mo's and about the hugs and then kittens and kites and sea anemones and Param's hand. Group dates aren't such a bad idea. But what did Danny say about going out with me? Did he mean a date? I looked at him in the seat behind me. He was watching me. I know my face turned pink. I could feel the warmth. I smiled and held up my glass float. He nodded and smiled back. I wondered when he got it. I loved that he hid it for me instead of just wrapping it up and handing it to me. That was Danny. I couldn't remember telling him I wanted one, but I must have.

Then I thought about how Danny had stayed calm and made a plan, and got us back over the rocks. It all made me wonder if I'd been treating him like the ocean – forgetting and turning my back on it, taking it for granted as if I could play Ultimate and it would always be there just the same and I could come and go as I pleased. I know now that's not really true. The tide shifts, and logs appear and change everything.

The log. Would I ever tell Mom and Dad what could have happened on my sixteenth birthday? I'm sure they prayed that we'd all be safe. I had even prayed that God would get us out of the cove, but I didn't even think to ask God to keep a log from crushing us to death. I guess He did that on His own. Or was it all just crazy chance? What's the difference between a skunk nap and a whale log? Nothing. Absolutely nothing. Except we were on our way home, and Jenny was dead. I slid my hand over Tani's on the seat next to me and was glad she couldn't read my mind.

CHAPTER 16

S nyder offered twenty-five extra credit points if we went to graduation and listened to the speeches. Most of us went, but more because we had such a great senior class that year than because of last minute extra credit. And then our sophomore year was over. We were half way through high school. I wasn't sure I wanted it to go that fast, but at the end of the year, everybody – no matter how much you love or hate school – is ready for it to be over. Me included.

Especially this year, because I had lined up my first real summer job rather than working for my parents or Gram, or babysitting. And more especially, because no matter what, I was going to make sure it was the summer I went out with Param.

Or so I thought. A week after school was out, Param's mom took him and his sister to Woolgoolga, Australia. To visit relatives, which I could hardly imagine – relatives in a place called Woolgoolga, Australia! And they were going to be gone for the whole summer. Sheesh! The best plans sometimes get messed up by things out of your control. It was going to be a very long summer.

The day after Param left, Danny called. "I have an idea," he said. "I think we should ride our bikes out to Grand Island and do Loop Road."

"How many miles is that?" I asked.

"Ten out there, then six around the loop, and ten back."

"I can't ride twenty-six miles without working up to it," I said. "I did that before, and my bum and my legs were so sore I couldn't walk for three days."

"Okay, then I'll get my dad's pickup and we'll take the bikes out to the Island and just do the loop."

"When?" I asked.

"Saturday."

"Who all's coming?" I asked.

Danny was quiet. Then he said, "Me and you. It's a date, Annie."

"What! Danny, what?" I laughed. "We don't have to go on dates. We can just do bike rides."

"Please, will you go on a bike ride date with me on Saturday?"

I waited for him to say something more. The phone was quiet. "Of course I will," I said. And then I wondered what I had gotten myself into. What was Danny thinking? I guess I'd find out on Saturday. The thought made me grin.

IT WAS A good summer to have a job. Katelyn got hired as a camp counselor-in-training. They wouldn't even let her use email, so she could have been in Woolgoolga too, for all the good it did us. Other than a few Saturdays and Sundays, Danny was going to be working way long hours for his dad and his uncle on their farms. So, with Param gone, I basically had no major circle of friends left. I began to look forward to Saturday's bike ride.

That day changed things for me, and Param wasn't even here to know. Or maybe it didn't change things. But it made me know more about myself. What I might do when I wasn't putting on the brakes, afraid of losing something that I love. Someone I love.

Danny was first my little-kid friend and then he was my growing-up-together friend, and finally my forever-friend, but we never kissed. Or were romantic. It just didn't fit, and besides, when once or twice I thought about it, and thought I might like to, I remembered some stories from girls who had boyfriends they had broken up with. They all had promised to stay friends, but it mostly didn't work that way. Somebody's feelings were always hurt, and they started not liking the other person. I think that's why I decided in junior high that it wasn't going to happen to Danny and me. He was too great to risk not liking. Or having him not like me. My heart would break.

So I crossed him off my possible love list, which actually had no one on it. I guess Danny would have been my entire list if I hadn't decided that having a boyfriend was a bad idea. I just stuck with that and eventually believed it more and more until it was true. At least until Param came.

But Danny did something that Saturday to put a crack in my plan. We were half-way around Loop Road when he stopped his bike and pointed out a dirt road going through some trees, toward the river. He said it led down to a farmer's irrigation pump, but that it was a great place for our picnic. We both had brought things to eat in our backpacks. But Danny, unknown to me until he pulled it out, had also brought an orange tablecloth and fancy red and pink paper plates, cups, and napkins. And fried chicken, which I love. And potato chips which I also love. And tuna sandwiches, which was his assignment. I added carrots and celery and dill pickles, and chocolate chip cookies. So it was a great lunch. As we finished, a big blue heron landed on the river right in front of where we sat.

"A sign," Danny said.

"A sign?"

"The right time. A sign that the universe is lining up right for us – no rain, fried chicken, dill pickles, and our first date."

"Danny, we've gone on lots of bike rides before."

"I know."

"Then?" I asked. I wasn't teasing him. I was suddenly curious to know what he'd say. I was sitting there with Danny next to this orange tablecloth with chicken bones on fancy paper plates, and I thought maybe there was something else, something that I'd pushed away for a long time that I might want to let back in. And I wondered if Danny might have wanted it too. We just looked at each other, and I could feel myself wishing him toward me.

Danny looked at me. Then he let his eyes fall. I guess he didn't feel the wish. He looked down at the tablecloth and began to gather things up and put them back in our backpacks.

He started up the hill for where we left our bikes, then turned back and offered me a hand. We walked hand in hand to the top of the hill and then he let me go.

He shouldn't have.

Right then Danny should have realized that if he had tugged me toward him, I would have come. And we could have held each other and I would have let myself kiss him, and everything would have been different. We couldn't have just gone back to pretending. We both would have known that I've loved him all this time, even though I didn't let myself think it. That would have been the new truth. And he would have felt it too, and we would have kissed again. We would have spent the summer becoming each other's, knowing anybody could come back from anywhere but it wouldn't matter to us. I would finally be done being afraid of loving Danny.

Instead we got on our bikes and finished the Loop. And because it never happened, just that fast we became best buddies again, like always.

As we rode back toward the pickup, I began to think it was probably the way it should be. That the heron meant we were friends forever. And I should be glad not to risk that. Besides, Param would be back in August.

CHAPTER 17

I never questioned what Tani was doing for the summer, though I know Dad stopped by their house to see Mr. Paulmann a couple of times, and told me I should give Tani a call. Dad didn't understand that the school year had been so hectic, that it was healthy for me to just be a hermit for a while. It seemed like a good time to get started on my new job and the pile of books I wanted to read over the summer. I didn't especially need Tani right then. Parents don't realize how perfectly good it is to be alone and not worry about being nice or doing something good for somebody else.

Of course on Sundays, which I had off, I did things – church and my grandparents and hikes with Mom and Dad back over on the Coast and in the Gorge – but mostly I was happy to stay home or call Danny and go walking on the road by his house. Especially now that I had my license and could drive myself over there.

My new job was at Abbey Road Produce Stand, selling to both locals and the Portland-to-Coast traffic that came through Ridgeway. I loved finally earning some good money, but it was more than the money. There were things I never knew happened at a job.

I had heard of the Abbey three miles outside Ridgeway, and knew that the monks made books or fruitcakes or choco-late. I couldn't remember which, because there's another abbey not too far away which makes the things this one doesn't. Our family wasn't really up on the Abbey. We had gone there once when I was little because friends invited us to walk in the Abbey's woods, which the monks welcome. But evidently Pam and Eva, owners of Abbey Road Produce Stand, not only knew the Abbey, but believed the monks were totally smart. So, they incorporated monk stuff into their business.

The day I went in for my job interview, I knew Pam and Eva were like Snyder – the kind of people you just go along with and try new things for, because they're so awesome. You know you'll end up loving what they do, and loving them. Which I did.

We started work at 8 a.m. but the doors didn't open until 9:00. We had setup and sorting to do that took some of that time, but even that waited for twenty minutes while we started with a devotional first thing every morning, compulsory, or at least everybody came. Usually it was out in the back where the fountain was set up, with music, and with flowers all around.

I never imagined getting paid to go to church. But that's the other thing. It wasn't really like church or at least not our church. I'd never done silent meditation before, so I just called it silent prayer so my mom wouldn't freak if I accidentally mentioned it. And yoga! Some days we all did yoga, which I didn't mention at home in case it's another religion entirely. I think maybe it's Buddhist. We listened to beautiful music and poetry and sayings. One was a prayer to the spirit of the wild earth. I thought about it all day long, but I definitely didn't mention that at home. If I get a job that doesn't start with devotional time, I may actually do it at home before I go to work. Maybe that's why Dad says he likes his prayer time in the morning.

They have a little corner with spirit-lifting books, Eva calls them, and candles and pictures and cards. There's a basket of tiny rolled cloth blessings printed out, tied in ribbons. And all of this is next to the jars of jam and honey and pickles, next to the stands and boxes of fruit and veggies. "Balance," Pam said. "I've learned from the monks that it's all about balance." And she struck a funny, tippy pose and caught herself before she fell off balance. "Balance and homemade bread." Which we also sell.

Pam and Eva also encouraged volunteer work. So we each got two hours a week off with pay to go somewhere and volunteer. We just had to make a little display of what we did on the produce stand's bulletin board.

I didn't even know what to do. That's how bad I am at volunteering. We supposedly had service projects at school, but they usually ended up being litter clean up around the school or in the bleachers after football games. Sometimes we picked up litter in the park or along the nature trail. All that did was make me mad at people who throw stuff down on the ground. And spit. Gross.

Pam heard me singing a camp song back at the loading dock and asked me if I'd ever thought about helping out at a care center for stroke victims. I wondered how she thought of an idea like that. She went into a storage room and came back with a guitar. She handed me a chord book, two song books, and two CDs to go with them. I tried to tell her I didn't know how to play guitar, let alone help people who had a stroke, but she didn't listen. She said I could learn, and people like Eva's mom, Myrtle, and her friend Lydia would love somebody like me. So that's what I ended up doing.

I learned six guitar chords in one week. I trimmed the fingernails of my left hand short for doing chords and kept the right hand nails long for strumming, and all ten fingers got really sore. But I learned how to play.

What was harder was learning the old-time songs. Luckily, Mom and Dad had heard them all, so we put on the CD and sang them every night after supper. They're actually fun songs. Funny and love-y and silly and some sad, from the 1940s and 50s. I guess that was my volunteer homework, but it ended up being a great thing to do with Mom and Dad. Dad even made up some bass harmony parts that sounded really good. I didn't realize he was such a good singer. I didn't have to practice the words on the second CD she gave me. They were all hymns and old choruses from church that I knew by heart.

The next Wednesday afternoon I met with the Maplewood Care Center therapist, Stacey, who told me what to expect, and then introduced me to Myrtle and Lydia, who shared a room. The women were both in wheelchairs when we came in. They looked like sisters. Something was different about their faces, but I wasn't sure what. They looked from Stacey to me, and Myrtle waved a hand around in the air in greeting. I waved back. Stacey introduced me, but when I said "Hi," they didn't answer, either one of them. Just nodded their heads.

Stacey prompted them. "Can you say 'Hi' to Annie, Myrtle? She works with Eva at the fruit stand." Then she repeated "Hi, Annie" three or four times, and finally both Myrtle and Lydia said it with her, though the Annie part didn't sound right. Eva had told me that her mom's speech was mostly taken by the stroke, and I assumed it was the same for Lydia.

Then I sang along with Stacey, and played guitar chords on "My Old Kentucky Home." After Stacey and I sang it through once, she invited Myrtle and Lydia to sing, and I couldn't believe it. They sang the words. Song after song. Not perfect, but they sang along. And then Stacey let me play "Jesus Loves Me" all by myself, and they sang every word with me. I actually stopped singing and had to let them finish the last "...the Bible tells me so" by themselves because I started crying. I don't think volunteers are supposed to do that, but I suddenly felt how sad it was that these two ladies had songs in their hearts, and probably a lot of words too, and yet they were all trapped up inside of themselves.

I was sorry that I cried, because I didn't want to hurt them or make them think there was anything wrong with them, but I couldn't help it. Especially when Lydia held out one arm to me in a hug. Then I cried all over both of them, but I promised I'd come back, and I think they were okay with that.

I didn't wait until my next volunteer day. I went after work on Friday. Stacey wasn't there, but the ladies seemed glad to see me. I brought a book this time, instead of my guitar. It was a book of sayings that Eva had loaned me. She told me to read the first part of the saying and let Myrtle and Lydia finish the ending. To help keep their vocal cords in practice, Eva said, and just for fun. "But they can't really talk," I protested. "They try, but they can't make the words come."

"You just wait and see," Eva said.

I opened the book and read, "A stitch in time saves ____."

"Nine," Lydia said.

"Twinkle, twinkle, little ____,"

"Star," Myrtle finished.

"A penny saved is a penny ____."

"Earned." Clear as a bell, Lydia finished the saying.

"She was born with a silver spoon in her ____"

"Neck," Myrtle said. And then she looked at Lydia and raised her eyebrow, as if surprised herself by what she just said, and they both grinned. I couldn't help but laugh, even though I didn't actually know that saying.

One of the aides walking by the door just then said, "Mouth. She was born with a silver spoon in her mouth." But Myrtle and Lydia and I looked at each other, and I think we decided it was funnier the way we had it.

We did a whole page of sayings, and then we sang two hymns, "The Old Rugged Cross" and "Wonderful Words of Life." Before I left, we sang "Jesus Loves Me" again. And I cried again, but this time because I loved singing with them and because I was glad I wasn't out picking up litter and getting mad about spit on the school steps. This was the exact opposite and I was witnessing courage instead of stupidity.

I asked Dad if I could take his digital camera to the care center the next Wednesday to take pictures for my bulletin board display, but then I changed my mind. I asked Eva if I could borrow some pictures of her mom before the stroke, and if she had any of Lydia, who was Myrtle's friend, not her sister. She did, of them riding horses together when they were fourteen, and one of Myrtle when she was sixteen. My age. They looked so different. There was another photo of both of them with their grandkids. I put Eva's pictures in sheet protectors and pinned them on the bulletin board, along with one of us singing together that Stacey took my first day. I didn't tell anybody, but I also put a little stack of print-outs up by the cash register that I downloaded from the Internet on five signs of a stroke that you should never ignore. I never asked Eva how her mom's and her friend's strokes happened or when. I wasn't sure I wanted to know. It was enough for now, just to sing. And then I got a crazy idea.

CHAPTER 18

Can people dance in a wheelchair? At least maybe you could move around a little, or move part of you even if another part didn't move. It dawned on me that I should call Tani after all, and ask if she'd come with me to Maplewood to teach line dancing. I didn't mean standing up or anything, but I knew that Tani had a great music collection, and I suspected she could make dancing even sitting down fun, because she loved it so much.

So I called. I think she was surprised, because she didn't say much at first and let me just talk about how I ended up at the care center and why I thought it would help Myrtle and Lydia if she could come. I finally heard a little laugh, and she said, "Sure, even though it sounds a little radical."

The next Wednesday afternoon, she got her mom to drive her into Ridgeway and they picked me up at the fruit stand and we all went together to Maplewood. Tani brought her CD player and country music, and I introduced her and Mrs. Paulmann – Robin, she said we should call her – to the ladies. I'm not sure what they thought, but they listened and they watched Tani as she pranced and kicked and stomped in front of them. They smiled their half smiles. When she told them it was their turn to dance, Myrtle raised her eyebrow, like she was asking a question.

"No, you really can," Tani said. "Do like this." She grabbed my hand and swayed to the music. "Okay, your turn," Tani said to the women. Myrtle reached her hand out and held onto

Lydia's and they began to rock their shoulders back and forth a little bit. I was so excited that I hugged Tani when the music stopped, and then Myrtle and Lydia. I begged Tani to come back with me the rest of the summer.

We expanded our repertoire. We did more wheelchair pushing than dancing, and took our ladies and other residents outside too. The staff at Maplewood got to know us and trust us and seemed glad we could do special things like that. We never told them about Tani daring me to race Mr. Davis against Mr. Taylor who she was pushing. We had to move their wheelchairs into the street, because the sidewalk was too narrow for them side by side, but it was a dead-end street with no cars or any bumps, and the men laughed and told us not to tip them over. Which, of course, we wouldn't do. But later we decided in case they told on us, maybe we shouldn't call it a race, just fast walking.

We also stopped by the Ridgeway Library and got our favorite picture books to read each time we visited. I was so glad our librarian at junior high insisted we keep reading picture books, or that idea might not have come to us, and Myrtle and Lydia would have missed *Mr. Nogginbody Gets a Hammer*; *Maggie and the goodbye gift*; *Happy Birthday, Moon*; and *One Thousand Tracings*. I never learned exactly if they had or hadn't read those books, but it didn't really matter. They liked them, and all the other ones we read.

Tani also sang with me. I loaned her my CD from Eva and she memorized all the songs. We both decided there should be a comeback of 1940s songs, or we should get Mr. Kelly, our choir director, to do an old-time concert and invite the senior citizens of Ridgeway, maybe even some from Maplewood, plus people like Mom and Dad who also know the songs. Or we could take the choir to Maplewood and sing there if the kids would do it.

When I told Tani I would miss the next Wednesday and

Friday because we were going to San Francisco, she said not to worry, that she'd go by herself. I looked at her right then and realized how much she had changed since she came to Ridgeway last March. Or maybe it was me who changed. Either way, I knew I loved her. She was so much more beautiful than when she walked into Snyder's class with her black velvet hat. And I don't mean that her head was healed and her hair mostly grown back over the spot, which it was.

I almost missed her life. If she had moved back to Seattle before the Scopes Trial, or before my birthday on the beach or before Maplewood, I would have forever told the story of this sassy sour girl in a long marked up skirt, with an ugly birthmark, who came to our school for a few weeks to try to bring Snyder down and take a new boy away from me, though I wouldn't have said the Param part out loud. But here she was, singing quartet with Myrtle and Lydia and me and heading up wheelchair races, and helping people dance when they couldn't move.

God found a way to let Tani and me share our love. And I was so glad.

CHAPTER 19

We saved our family vacation until the end of summer. Mom and Dad and I went to San Francisco, where we combined a church conference with doing Ghirardelli's Chocolate Factory and Alcatraz Island, cable cars and fire-roasted eggplant sandwiches. Which you don't get in Ridgeway. It was so fun. I came home feeling it had been a perfect summer, ready for the one last thing to do – the big corn field maze party.

Katelyn was back from camp, so I called her and Tani and had them come over to help plan. We made the mistake of designing an invitation and emailing it before I checked out the basics with Mom. I had volunteered our house after the Olson's Corn Maze. Mom didn't care. She loves to have people over. But when I called the Olson's, just to make sure the cost was the same as last year, they said the cool weather had delayed the corn a bit and they wouldn't open till the second weekend in September. They asked if I wanted to schedule our party for opening night. By then school would be on, and football and volleyball, so there was no point in having it as an "end of summer" party.

I called Danny right after I hung up with Mrs. Olson, not knowing what else to do, and good old Danny said he'd pull through for me and find another corn patch.

"Where?" I asked. "Olson's always open first. Nobody else will be ready either."

"I'll find something. Don't worry."

"In one day?"

"Believe in me, Annie!"

"I'll love you forever, Danny!" I said.

"Just hold that thought," he said laughing, "and save me a hug." Which I needed about then. It made me smile that he'd say that.

"I'll find someplace they're about ready to harvest," he said. "They'll never notice a little maze in the middle for a couple of days."

"Danny! You can't do that!"

"Don't worry. You want your party, don't you?"

"Yeah, but I don't want us to get in trouble."

"We won't. They'll think it came down with the rain."

"What rain?" I asked, but Danny just laughed.

I must not have felt totally okay about it, because when Mom asked what I was planning to do, I told her Danny was checking out other mazes. I didn't say, "other corn fields." She was already stressed enough with me. She said I should have planned better, and done my calling first, and of course I would have. It wasn't like I tried on purpose to wreck things. We just got back from San Francisco and I couldn't do everything at once. Olson's always opened the end of August. I couldn't help it if they messed up my plans.

Danny called back that evening. "Want to go with us to check out a corn field?"

"Who's us" I asked.

"Me and Param."

"He's back! Of course I want to go!"

Wrong thing to say. Or wrong amount of excitement in my voice.

"Come on, Annie," Danny said. "Let's not do this."

"Do what?" I meant it.

"We walk together and talk together and you make me feel

like I'm important to you, and then Param comes back and you go crazy."

"That's not being crazy. That's being excited to see a friend who's been gone all summer. And you are important, Danny, forever. You know that."

"Okay," he said. "But I'm mad at you. And next summer we all go to Australia so we don't miss anybody most."

"Deal," I said. I knew Danny wouldn't stay mad. That's another thing I love about him. But sometimes, inside me, I wish he'd get mad. I wish he wouldn't just joke it away, and that if he really wanted me, he would do something about it. Like he could have, but didn't, on the bike ride on Loop Road in June. And on all the walks between then and now. I wish he'd just out and tell me. Or do something. But that's not Danny, I know. I wonder why sometimes.

"So I'll call Katelyn and Tani," I said. "Where are we going?"

Mom overhead that. "Going? When?"

"Mom ..."

"Annie, I'm not staying up all night to make all the food for your party while you go out running around. You need to commit to this. You can just drop the maze and play volleyball here."

I think that was her point all along. Mom and I usually get along okay, but she wasn't being reasonable right then.

But I turned Danny down, told him to call Katelyn and Tani, and stayed home to cut veggies and make sandwiches and cookies, and I was mad at Mom the whole time.

About 9 p.m., when we were finally done, I called Danny's. His mom said they weren't home yet but should be back soon. I asked Mom if I could use the car to go over to Danny's. She seemed a little more reasonable once the work was done.

Danny lives out in the country on the other side of town from us. There's a road that you can see from the dip near his house that he and I walked on a lot, ever since we were in grade school and our moms knew each other from Friends of the Library. It goes around some bottom land, another farmer's corn mostly, near his house, and you can see the river along the back side. It's beautiful.

We always went around the edge of the field or down the open strips where the irrigation machine goes. Except the one time we went inside the corn. It was awesome. We walked down the rows under a high corn roof. Danny in one row, me in the next. And it was so far away from the world that we lay down in our rows on the cool dark ground and looked up at little snatches of blue sky, and we talked. First about all the aphids on the leaves and then about everything.

We'd gotten in trouble though. For not walking around on the road. They said we could wreck the corn. But I still think it was because we were out of sight and they didn't know what we did in the corn patch. We didn't do anything, but we could have. I think of that sometimes. When we walked back out of the field, I remember thinking that if you can do the awesomest thing in the world twice, Danny & I will lie down in corn rows again sometime.

But the field wasn't empty that night. There were lights. And from the sound, I guessed there were a couple of those big corn cutters starting on the field. There was another sound too. The fire siren in town went off right then. We can hear it even out in the country. I said a little prayer for whoever needed help. It's kind of a tradition with our family to do that. And like always happens, the coyotes hidden in the woods started howling along with the siren. Weird, I know, but I guess they think it's their big cousin coyote somewhere calling them. But I forgot about sirens and coyotes the minute I spotted Danny's blue Honda Civic parked on the side of the road just ahead of me. I pulled over behind it.

So this was where Danny was going to have our maze. In his neighbor's bottom land corn field. They always cut that field for silage, down to the ground, but I know for a fact that the farmer is a little grouchy, especially when people ride their horses through the corn to the trail along the river. I doubted that he'd want us to knock the corn down to make a maze. And if Danny talked the cutter driver into doing it for us, we'd have major highways, not trails. The cutters are huge, way too big for the paths we need for a fun maze.

I decided to leave the car parked and walk over to where I could get a better look at the field below. Suddenly I was hit with flashing lights in the distance. A cop car. And then I could see a fire truck or emergency vehicle following it. I hopped back in my car just to be out of the way as they passed by. I wondered where the fire was. I hadn't noticed any smoke on my way out.

But they turned right before they got to me. Down the roadway into the field.

I had a bad feeling. Ever since our kindergarten field trip to Martinelli's farm, I've had to push thoughts out of my mind about those corn choppers. Everything I ever pushed away came rushing back, and suddenly I knew it was mixed up with Danny being in that field. I prayed to God that he was safe, but the feelings didn't go away. I swung the car back onto the road and headed for the corn field. A pickup came from the opposite direction and caught the rescue truck, following on its tail lights. I bumped down the road behind the pickup, stopped the car down on the level and started running toward the lights.

The guys from the fire department were on the run too. Big flashlights were leading their way into the corn toward the sound of a horn honking. Another group carried a stretcher. Running. Talking into their radios. I couldn't hear, but I knew I needed to hurry. I picked a row and ran and ran until I could see the lights, and the cutter, and a bunch of people. The first person I recognized was Jackson Evans, standing in the headlights of the corn cutter. Waving his arms, waving the rescue crew toward the back of the machine.

"Hurry, man!" he was saying to no one in particular. "Hurry. They need help back there. Hurry, man!"

I thought Jackson looked stupid, waving his arms and jumping around. Somebody needed to calm him down. But they were hurrying, so I guess he thought he was doing what was needed. When the last bunch rounded the cutter, Jackson crumpled down on the ground on his knees and started bawling. Right in front of me, though he had no way of knowing I was standing there in the corn a few feet away from him.

"What's wrong, Jackson?" I asked. But I didn't wait for an answer. I had to find Danny.

Why does your heart tell you something, something you just can't shake off, and then it's all wrong? The first person I saw, talking to an EMT, holding onto his arm, was Danny. I started crying. I guess because he was okay. And then I saw Katelyn off to the side and headed toward her. There was somebody in the middle of all the people. On the ground, but I couldn't see who.

Katelyn saw me coming, and turned and grabbed me. "Annie. Annie... "

"What! What's happened?"

"Annie, it's so bad. It's so bad."

I held her shoulders to make her look at me. When I saw her eyes, I knew how scared she was. "Katelyn, where are Param and Tani? Did they come?"

She nodded her head, tears streaming down her cheeks, as she pointed to the group huddled in front of us. And then Jackson Evans was there with us too. I hadn't waited to hear Jackson say what happened. I should have. Jackson was the one who really knew, it turned out. I should have asked him and remembered because what you realize is that the next day it gets blurry in your head, who was where and who said what.

As best I remember, they were just making Param lie flat on the ground until they could check him and ask him some questions, and then somebody helped him up. He was okay, just something about his arm. The EMTs who had been with Param headed for the group that was between the corn chopper and the wagon.

"Automatic trauma entry. Unconscious patient," somebody was saying into the radio.

"Activate Life Flight. We're going to need an engine company to set up an LZ."

"Abdominal ... treat for shock ... respiratory rate ... airway ... tube her ..."

It was a jumble of words I couldn't even understand, except for Life Flight. I knew that means somebody's hurt bad.

"It's Tani," Katelyn finally said. "Annie she's hurt. Bad. She couldn't talk to us. She was just lying there, not moving, and they hooked her up to some IV bag. I don't know if she's even ..."

"Katelyn, What? What are you saying? She's alive. They're calling Life Flight. She'll be okay. Just stop talking. Stop it." But I was going crazy too.

And then I heard Jackson, crying, saying "She'll be okay. She'll be okay. She'll be okay." Like he was begging somebody to hear him and make sure he was right or crying himself into believing it.

I guess we were loud. Danny and Param saw us and came over, and this is what I'm not sure about. Something changed. Somebody heard them say to cancel it. What? "Cancel what?" I think I yelled, because an EMT came over and put his arm around me. I think it was our wrestling coach at school, but it might have been Brett from the market in Ridgeway.

"She's dead," he said, and then as if we couldn't hear that, he continued, "I'm so sorry. The medics did everything they could."

"NOOOOOOOOOOOOOOOO!" Jackson screamed, his arms straight in the air, then pulsing down with fists clenched. "Stop the chopper! Stop the chopper! Don't let it get her!"

He was wild, and Danny grabbed him. "The chopper's off, Jackson. It's off!"

Jackson ripped away from Danny and started to run toward the cutter or Tani or the EMTs, and then he stopped. They had covered her.

"Oh, God, what's happening?" Katelyn cried. We slid to the ground, and there in the opening in the corn, I prayed that God would undo this. That it wouldn't be true. That Tani was okay. Because right then I thought of Tani's Jenny-sister and her dad, and I knew God had to keep Tani alive for him. They should pull the cover back off, and help her up like they did Param. Oh, please, God. Please!

I GUESS JACKSON understood better than I did that Tani was really dead. He lay right down on the ground on his belly and rocked his forehead back and forth against the dirt, and he sobbed. Param grabbed Danny's arm and told him to get down beside Jackson, and there they knelt, one on each side of Jackson, bending over him, patting his back, stroking his hair, talking to him. But it didn't help. So Param lay down close against Jackson's side and put his arm tight around him, his cheek against Jackson's, under Jackson's long hair, and held him that way. For a long time. And finally Jackson quieted and was as still as Tani. One of the EMTs tapped Danny on the shoulder, and Danny stepped away from us. Another EMT got down on the ground with Param and Jackson. I don't know if that's what they're supposed to do, but it was good.

After a while Danny brought the guy he was with over to

where we sat. Jackson was sitting up now. They needed to ask us some questions.

"She wanted to ride on the cutter," Danny said. "Jackson shook his head no from inside the cab, but she said she'd never get another chance."

"I didn't think she was coming on," Jackson choked out. "I would have stopped. Oh god, I would have stopped, or yelled at her to get away, or something. I don't know what. I thought she was just playing, and too close at that, so I turned the cutter. Shit! I turned the cutter away from them, but she was already on the steps and she fell. The next thing I knew I was hitting the brakes. And flying off the cutter. But she was down. Bad. The wagon had come around and was on her. I couldn't think – do I go forward, do I back up ..." He didn't finish.

And then Jackson said something awful. "Because I turned the wheel, that's why she fell." And he sobbed a long, breaking "Ohhhhhhhhhhhhh ..." that showed me that Jackson Evans' heart was tearing apart. He should have known it wasn't his fault. I couldn't think what to say to Jackson. Instead I just thought of how bad I had treated Tani when she first came to Ridgeway. And in all the weeks of becoming friends afterwards, I had never once told her I was so sorry for that. I had never even talked about it, like it wasn't important, or that maybe nothing happened, that we hadn't been stupid and mean. Why didn't I tell her? And now I never could. Never say how sorry I was that I didn't try to understand or figure her out or just wonder why. Tani was gone. Moved into the rescue truck. Never to dance. On a stretcher. Never to come home. Covered up. Never to play in the corn. Ever.

But I couldn't see because the corn was hiding me, and I was crying too hard.

CHAPTER 20

I asked Dad the next day how I got home. I didn't remember driving. Or even leaving the corn. That's weird, but I didn't, and it kind of scared me. Dad said our minds can do that sometimes – shut something out that hurts too bad. He said Danny brought me home, that we'd go get the car later.

Mom had stayed with me and Dad went out to Tani's folks' place. I guess he thought they'd need him to be there besides just the emergency people.

Dad said he'd never seen hurt like that, ever, and he hoped he never saw it ever again. He cried as he told Mom. How Tani's dad screamed and her mom folded up on the floor in a heap and just sobbed. How Mr. Paulmann looked at Dad and shook his head, tears streaming down his face.

"Every one of us sat down on the floor with them," Dad said. "You couldn't just stand there at a time like that."

"I learned something, Meg," Dad said to Mom. "I was wrong. So wrong. I longed for something to say that would help them, and there wasn't anything, so I just said, 'God is still in charge.' Tani's dad looked at me and shook his head like I was crazy. He said, 'If God is still in charge, he's sick, downright sick' and then he added fiercely, 'and he's going to have to get down on his blasted knees and beg my forgiveness for letting this happen.' I couldn't blame him for saying that, Meg. I'm sorry, but I just couldn't blame him. There's no rhyme nor reason to this."

I don't think Dad knew I was listening from the hallway.

I'm not sure he would have let me know that. And then he added, "Meg, if this had been Annie, I couldn't bear it." And he started crying and held his head in his hands. I ran into my room and swung the door closed behind me. I really wanted to go grab Dad and hug him and say I'd never die, but I couldn't. I suddenly remembered the log that crashed against the rocks at the beach on my birthday. Just seconds after we jumped from where it hit. I sat on my bed and cried and thought of skunks walking across the cornfield in front of Jackson, so he had to stop the chopper to miss them.

Why does stuff like this happen? Maybe God isn't in charge of anything. Maybe He is sick, like Mr. Paulmann said. I knew then that I never wanted to tell Mom and Dad about the log. And I never wanted to tell God anything. Period.

THERE WAS NO school the next Monday, being Labor Day, and I stayed home Tuesday, even though it was the first day of classes. I just didn't feel like going, and Mom didn't make me. Katelyn called after school. "You should have come, Annie. It helps to be with other people."

"I couldn't."

"Well, come tomorrow."

"Maybe."

"Somebody told Ms. Michaud that they buried Tani beside her sister in a cemetery in Seattle," Katelyn said. "That must have been awful for her mom and dad, don't you think? Ms. Michaud's office was open to anyone who wanted to come in and talk."

"Good," I said. Actually, that was good – both talking, and letting Tani be beside her Jenny-sister. Ms. Michaud is a good counselor, and I wanted to ask her all about Tani's funeral. I wished in a way I could have gone to Seattle to be there. No, not in a way. I wished I could have gone. But nobody thought of it, I guess. And it happened so fast.

What I found out the next day was what didn't happen. There was no funeral. Not even with Tani's friends in Seattle. They just did a gathering with a few relatives at the cemetery where Jenny was and buried Tani. I'm not sure why. That made me sad. The only other person I majorly know who has died is my aunt, my dad's sister, Carla. She was a very strong woman who worked in a bunch of different places around the world as a vet. Places where she could have easily died from some weird disease, but she managed through all of that, and then ended up getting cancer and dying at home. We went to California for Aunt Carla's memorial. It was sad, but I think my cousins, and me too, and my mom and dad, were happy we were there together to remember her and say goodbye. But Tani was just suddenly gone and our remembering was stuffed down inside our hearts.

SCHOOL SEEMED DIFFERENT. For only being there a part of last year, Tani was everywhere. Nobody ate lunch at the table where she and Param sat last year until a few days later when some freshmen, obviously not knowing, scooted into those benches. We postponed the first dance, and planned an all-school bonfire instead, because nobody wanted to think about Tani not being there to teach us line dancing.

Worst of all was Snyder's class, Speech and Communication this year. Even Snyder didn't seem to have any magic words to take away the empty seat in the row by the window. We just left the seat empty. I think that was okay with Snyder. He set a vase of flowers on the desk, and a picture of Tani as the radio station announcer in last year's Scopes trial. Throughout the day other things were added. I don't think Snyder intended that, but it happened. People put out the yearbook, opened to a picture of her dancing, a candy bar, a hair clip, a pine cone, a hat, a bunch of notes and drawings. Nobody said anything, but before or after class you'd see somebody slip into the room and put something on the desk or the windowsill behind it.

I went into Ms. Michaud's office at lunch. After "How was your summer, Annie?" and "Really good, Ms. Michaud," she just looked at me.

"Tani," was all I could say, and I started crying.

"I know," she whispered. She sat beside me on the couch in her office as tears welled up in her eyes too and she just let me cry. When I finally waved my arm in some sign that I hoped meant "later" she managed a smile and said, "Come back soon, Annie." We hadn't said anything. But we had.

I decided to be late for cross country and headed to her office right after school. "I've been thinking, Ms. Michaud. I know what we need, but I wonder if Tani's mom and dad would let us do it."

"What's that, Annie?" she asked.

"To say good-bye."

CHAPTER 21

I asked Dad first. I was surprised that he didn't think a memorial was a good idea.

"I think I've said too much already, Annie," he said. "It feels like they need time. I don't know how we can help. I can't think of anything."

"Remember at Aunt Carla's funeral," I said, "when little Ricky told about her coming in the house covered in mud from catching that sheep, and giving Ricky a big mud hug?"

Dad smiled. "Okay, Annie. You're right. But I don't think it can be the usual – not at church and probably not even with the pastor right now. I'm not sure they would come no matter where it was. Maybe it's just for the rest of us. Even that could be good. I'm realizing how much it hurts us all to have her gone. What do you have in mind?"

"Nothing much yet, Dad, but I want to think about it."

We met at lunch the next day – Danny, Katelyn, Param, and I – and I told them my idea. I wasn't sure of any details, just that we had to do something. "I've never been to a funeral," Danny said. He turned to Param, "So what do Sikhs do when somebody dies?" he asked. Maybe he thought there was some nice ceremony we could change into Christian and use. Or not even to Christian, if that would help Mr. Paulmann. Just something that people would do no matter who they believed in or not.

"We cry a lot," Param said. "Because of how sad everyone is."

"That probably happens whether you try to stop it or not," I said.

"We don't stop it," Param said simply.

"Well, maybe we can have music," Danny said. "That can cover up the sounds of crying if anyone needs it." Katelyn said she'd find some Scott Joplin music, and then something mellow. We decided we'd let people who knew Tani tell about her if they wanted to.

I knew we had to invite Tani's mom and dad. So I got Param to cut cross country with me and do our own running out on Kinsey Lane, to Tani's house.

It was farther than I remembered, and we were both worn out by the time we got there. It wasn't faking it to walk down their driveway to see if we could get some water and rest for a few minutes, though that had been our plan all along.

A car was in the driveway. Tani's mom, Robin, came to the door. Suddenly I realized how dumb this was. I should have come dressed up and with flowers or something. But she was nice. Before I could say anything, she said, "Well, hi, Annie. Thank you for the kind note you sent."

I started to introduce Param, but she turned to him and said, "And yours too, Param." So they already knew each other. Param stepped forward and gave her a hug. "I'm so sorry," he said. She just nodded her head.

"Would you like to come in for a minute?"

"Sure. We could use a little water before we head back to school," I said. As we sat around the kitchen table, I told Robin what we wanted to do and asked if they and any of their family would come. She seemed surprised, but said she'd talk to her husband and call me.

WE STARTED THE run back toward school. "Where are we going to do this memorial?" Param asked.

"Someplace beautiful and quiet and away from everything busy, where Tani would like to be. Like the meadow where I'll get married. Or have my reception," I said.

Param slowed to a walk. "What?"

"Oh, we won't have her funeral there. That would make it weird for a wedding later on. The memories. I just meant that it needs to be a place like our meadow." We walked on without saying anything until I added, "You should come see it, Param. I know you'll think it's a perfect place to get married."

I stopped talking and walking. If my face was slightly red from running, it had to be totally red then. I looked at Param to see if he might have missed what I said and got what I meant, that he'd like the meadow and the creek and the willow trees, not that I wanted him to okay us getting married there.

Param stood in the middle of the road and grinned at me.

"I didn't mean that like it sounded," I stumbled out. "I just meant that you'll like the meadow, for a picnic or something." I was flustered, and Param saw it. He walked up to me and brushed the hair away from my hot face. Then he reached down and took my hand.

"Let's just walk for a while," he said. That was okay with me. We didn't say anything more for maybe a quarter mile, but I held onto his hand. Then he stopped.

"Annie?"

I looked up into his face. Somehow, I knew it was a crazy time for what was happening, but maybe that was all a part of it, the realization that life is crazy, and when something is there that you want, you can't push it away, because it might be suddenly gone. And I wanted it very much. I nodded yes, and Param leaned over and kissed me.

No one came driving by to make me wonder how that happened or if I should be there on the side of the road being held by Paramdeep Singh. He didn't seem to care either. He held me close and said, "I missed you this summer."

"I missed you too." We kissed again. And again.

We walked on toward the school. The thought came to me that we were taking longer than we should and we'd be late getting back to school. If Mom came to pick me up and I wasn't there, she'd ask the coach where I was, and he wouldn't know. Then she'd wait and see me running up with Param and wonder what I'd been doing. I tried to push the thoughts away, but they hovered right beside the nod yes and the kiss.

"Beat you to the crossroads," I said, and I slipped my hand out of his and ran ahead. I smiled to myself, wondering if that was Param's first kiss too. How can a kiss be so easy if you've never done it before? I hoped he hadn't; I wanted it to be his first. He caught up to me and we ran side by side, in total sync. He must have adjusted his stride to pace mine. It was a good pace, steady enough for thinking. I looked sideways at him and wondered what he was thinking, running alongside me. Was it just for the moment? A reaction to the situation, or did Param really mean for it to happen? We had slammed full force into a new school year with everything going crazy, and I hadn't even stopped to hope, let alone think, what it would bring.

As we ran, I did both. I wondered if a Sikh might marry a Christian. Could Param ever be a forever friend, loving me like Danny does but for real? All of me?

It was good no car had come along. I didn't want anyone telling Danny what had just happened. It came to me that nobody had ever challenged Danny's place in my heart, and I guess Danny knew that, but maybe Param didn't. Even though I didn't know what having that place really meant to me or to Danny. Way back in grade school we heard some big high school kids talking about their prom and we promised back then that if we didn't have dates for our prom, we'd go with each other. I think we even promised that we'd marry each other by a certain age. I like to think now it was sixty, or something reasonable, but I've thought since that maybe we said sixteen and we're both forgetting that on purpose. How could we have thought of that in grade school? I wondered if Danny remembered our promises. I wondered why I was wondering about Danny when I had just kissed Param.

CHAPTER 22

School fell into a pattern. We didn't talk about Tani or the memorial for a couple of days, and then Robin called Mom and told her it would be okay, they would come, but Mr. Paulmann asked one thing – no God talk.

"The one time we need God with us more than ever," Dad said, but then he added, "God is. He doesn't need us to plan Him in or out. He'll meet the Paulmanns and all of us where we are."

That's another thing I love about my dad. He was a part of giving me my God-all-wrapped-up-in-a-box, but the reason he did was because he knew what, or who, was in the box for him. And I supposed Dad was right, that God would find a way of being at Tani's memorial, whether or not I wanted to talk to Him.

FIRST, WE HAD to find a place, then invite people who were a part of Tani's life to come – maybe that Jek kid from Seattle who wrote on her skirt or some others from her youth group. Also kids from school who knew what a great Charlie Chaplin she was. Then we'd think about what Tani loved and how we could tell that about her – her dancing, her skirt, her mom's Scott Joplin music, her Jenny-sister, her courage to even breathe after Jenny died, but we might not mention that, and her singing with Myrtle and Lydia. We'd gather pictures of Tani like they did for Aunt Carla.

And we would do it all in the meadow.

I almost cried when I decided that's where it had to be, and I think Mom and Dad were surprised, but for some reason, it felt like it was a gift we all needed to give Mr. Paulmann and Robin. Dad said, "That's a good place, Annie. Thanks." He didn't say anything about my plans to have my wedding there, but I wondered if he was thinking of it too.

Some of last year's seniors who hadn't gone off to college yet heard what we were doing and said they wanted to help. They, and a group of kids in our class, met Thursday evening at our house. We showed them the meadow, and it was settled. A Ridgeway memorial would be held for Tani Ann Bella Paulmann, on Saturday, September 16. We found out what her middle initials, A and B, stood for. Not Miss "Above and Beyond," as we called her when she first came and we didn't like her. Her middle names were Ann Bella, Beautiful Annie. I wished I had been that for her.

We got some Scott Joplin music, and Dad set up a sound system in the meadow. We borrowed chairs from the church. Mom put out a long table with a lace tablecloth and set out pictures of Tani that Robin loaned her. Really cute ones of her as a little girl with her head covered with spaghetti, and dancing in cowboy boots way too big for her. We found out she learned line dancing when she was tiny by watching her mom and dad dance with a western dance club. There were pictures of her and Jenny dressed as pirates and of Tani at a jump rope competition, winning first place. I could have known all this little girl Tani stuff from the very beginning, if only I had been curious instead of instantly judging her. If I had just wondered.

Tani's grandparents from Tacoma came and her grandpa read the thing they put in the paper about her – all the statistics of who she was and where she lived and what she liked to do. It didn't say anything about the cornfield, just that she died in an accident at the age of sixteen. And that she was preceded in death by a sister, Jennifer.

Then people had a chance to talk about Tani. The seniors started and told how they first discovered she could dance. She was stomping her heels down on the floor of the girl's bathroom at school doing dance steps when one of them walked in and slipped into a stall unnoticed by Tani. When Tani started singing "Any Man of Mine" to accompany her solo dance, the girl, Sara, peeked out the door to watch. Sara said she didn't know if Tani was mad or embarrassed, but she was so good at singing and dancing that Sara said, "I don't know you, but if I did, I'd give you a hug for that!" They both laughed, and then hugged, and it ended up with Tani agreeing to help them teach the dance the next Friday night. A lot of people smiled, remembering that, our first big surprise about Tani.

The Jek boy did come. He had been Tani's boyfriend in middle school, and high school, and he could hardly talk. He said she was his hiking buddy first, but then just his everything buddy, and he told that he and Tani promised each other they'd go to the same college so they wouldn't fall in love with anybody else, and they... He couldn't finish, so just started back for his chair. Mr. Paulmann stood up and reached out to grab his hand. I guess he must have liked Jek too. That was hard not to cry through.

Most of our class sat together, and several of us told little things about Tani. Robin cried when Katelyn told how Tani had loved her mom's piano playing. Nobody said much about the first month or so she was at school. It seemed so long ago now. There were kids who had done things with her in the summer that I didn't even know about. She worked in the summer reading program before we started at Maplewood. One little girl got up and said, "Tani loved books as much as I do. She let me read to her. She said I was awesome. I miss her a lot." Her chin shook and she cried and sat back down. That took courage.

Eva and Pam came, and Eva stood to say how much it meant to her that Tani had gone with me to sing with Myrtle and Lydia. She told how Tani taught wheelchair dancing. She didn't admit to the racing, which maybe she didn't know about. I thought if somebody had brought Mr. Taylor and Mr. Davis, they would tell about the wheelchair races.

Param told about Tani biking into town once with cookies she had made for his family to celebrate Baisakhi. I wondered how she even knew what that was.

Tani's grandpa asked if there was anyone else who wanted to say anything. I wish I had stood up right then. I wanted to, but I was overwhelmed with knowing Tani was gone forever and I had wasted part of her life, just being mean. I wondered if she told Robin and Mr. Paulmann how we shunned her, or if she carried that all alone. At least Param was there for her. But I couldn't say all that, and then I didn't have a chance even if I would have thought of what to say.

Suddenly from somewhere Jackson Evans came to the front. I didn't even know he was there. It was okay that he came, because I knew how bad he felt, but I hoped he wouldn't slip back into his dirty mouth at a time like this, maybe swearing at God. I wouldn't have totally blamed him if he did. But Jackson didn't talk at all. He just walked up to the front row of chairs where Mr. Paulmann and Robin were sitting and fell down on his knees and rested his head on Mr. Paulmann's legs. I was on the aisle so I could see what maybe some others couldn't. Jackson's body started to shake and then pretty soon we heard quiet sobs. I don't know if Mr. Paulmann knew Jackson before that minute, but Jackson raised his head and sobbed, "I was driving the cutter, sir. I didn't mean to hurt her. I didn't mean to. Please believe me." And his head went back down and I thought I heard Jackson say, "Please forgive me. I beg you."

On his knees, begging forgiveness.

I DON'T KNOW exactly how it happened then, but I could see Mr. Paulmann gently lift Jackson's head off his knees, and roll out of his chair so that they were both kneeling at that same empty chair together, crying in each other's arms. Sobbing. Can strangers do that for each other? Maybe they weren't strangers. All I know is that Tani's grandpa knelt too and then her grandma and Robin, and then my dad and mom, so that they were all kneeling together in this growing circle. Reaching their arms around each other. It wasn't a church thing. It just happened. Chairs got moved around and lots of people just came and knelt there together, kids from school too, reaching up to the person in the big circle in front of them, crying quietly or silently or not at all, together. I don't think that happens at funerals. But it did.

I don't know who started the song. The really weird thing is that later Katelyn asked how I had the nerve to do that, and I asked what she was talking about and she said I started singing, and how did I do it. I told her I didn't, but she was sure I had. We all, everybody, sang, "This Little Light of Mine, I'm Going to Let It Shine." And then another verse somebody changed to "This Little Light of Tani's, We're Going to Let It Shine."

Let it shine, let it shine, let it shine. I guess Jackson probably sang that too. I hope so, because I knew then that Jackson was carrying part of Tani's light with him. Everybody there was. And right then, all we wanted to do was hold that light and know that it would keep shining. And we would remember her. Always. Ever.

CHAPTER 23

Snyder eventually moved things off Tani's desk and the windowsill, but he put her Monkey Trial WGN radio announcer picture up on the wall of his classroom. He reframed it to make room for the words underneath the picture:

Ponder passion, pursue doubt,
Pursue passion, ponder doubt.
Remembering Tani Ann Bella Paulmann
Who helped us at Ridgeway High School to do both.

I HOPE HE keeps it up so kids will know that everybody has a story, and sometimes it ends before it's done.

CHAPTER 24

S nyder has a way of getting us back to life, even when we don't feel like it. He forced us to begin our speeches that very week. I think we figured it'd be like speech class in junior high or the speeches we had to give when we were running for class or club offices – things you can pull together on the bus on the way to school. Not Snyder. He looked up fifteen different real essay contests from Oregon and around the country and told us we may as well get to work on scholarships now, that our senior year will come rolling around sooner than we think, and then help with college costs will seem very important. He told us we had to choose one competition to enter, research our topic, write an essay, and then give it in speech form to the class. Who knows? Maybe we'd even win.

Danny chose "Why I Am a Christian." It was a scholarship offered by a church in a town near us. Snyder should have refused to let him do that one since Danny is not a Christian and we all knew he'd be making it all up. Maybe Snyder was interested in what he'd make up. Sondra took "Democracy – Catalyst for Development and Achievement in Third World Countries," whatever that means. Param got Snyder's approval for an essay he was already doing through his temple in Salem: "You're a What? Being Sikh, and in the Minority." Katelyn chose "Women Who Overcame" because it didn't say what they overcame, and she wanted to write about a lady who just got out of prison for child abuse, totally changed, she insisted, and ready to fight to get her little boy back.

Mine? I went back and forth between two possibilities. One was the importance of flowers in people's lives, which I have believed in ever since I discovered how to make daisy chains for crowns and necklaces, out in the meadow when I was probably a year old. But the scholarship was to attend Floral Design School which I probably wouldn't do until after college. The other one, which Snyder threw on my desk, was "The Impact of Studying Abroad." That one gave the choice of writing on two places where there were current programs and scholarships available for high school study – Malta and India. I vaguely remembered hearing there is a place called Malta, maybe an island somewhere or maybe a country in Africa, and I knew it would do me good to learn more about it, but then the idea came to me that learning about India might help things with Param's family.

"India!?" Katelyn asked. "Why in the world ...?"

"Ghee!" I whispered. Katelyn winked. Ghee was our new code word for Param. I had told her about Kinsey Lane, and she knew the obstacles I was up against. The thought came to me that ten years from now somebody might do Katelyn's essay on me – A Woman Who Overcame – though I wasn't sure I would overcome in this case.

"No, I mean it," I told Katelyn. "I bet I win this scholarship contest, and then I'll get to go to India and fight monkeys with paper swords and rescue my Ghee from their clutches. Yeah, India, here I come!"

Snyder overhead the last little bit. "Not impossible, Ms. Karten," he said. "Just be sure to tell them why you want to go. Describe your commitment."

I laughed, but I thought about that. Even just to get a good grade on my speech I knew it should be something about world understanding or world peace. Maybe it could even be about understanding a classmate and his family better by knowing more about their homeland. That would be a little more truthful than world peace, since I've never joined our high school Peacebuilders Club or ever gone to a peace march or a vigil. Not that I don't want world peace, or that I like wars and fighting, but just that I was always too busy to get involved. So I knew I couldn't truthfully say that was my priority. The more I worked on my essay, my speech, the more I came to know what it was all about.

Tani.

I thought about her all the time. I thought about how bad it was that she was dead. I thought about Robin and Mr. Paulmann at home and wondered if he was drinking or crying. I especially wondered why I ever started the idea of corn maze parties, because without them, Tani would be here working on a contest speech about heroes of silent movies. And she'd win and get money to go to college with her Jek boy. Most of all I thought about what I didn't do, but wished with all my heart that I had, when there was still the chance.

That's when I realized my essay was about undoing who I had been, by saying in words that I wouldn't let it ever happen again. I would force myself to be different, if only I could start over. People would think it was all about India, and that would be okay for the essay and speech. But there'd be another meaning and commitment there, for Tani and for me.

I'd say that if I had the chance, I'd be curious. I would wonder, rather than be judgmental. When I ran into something I didn't expect or hadn't experienced before, I'd force myself out of my own shoes. When something was jarring, and I felt like writing somebody off because of what they wore or how they looked, or even how they acted, instead of just walking away without another thought, I'd wonder. They'd think I was talking about people in India the whole time, or experiences I might have while I was there. I'd pretend it was about India, but I'd know, and I'd hope that somehow Tani would know that it was really about her.

There was no chance of really going. I knew that, but it didn't matter. It was writing the essay that was important. I could finally say, even in code, how sorry I was for what happened. For the way I treated Tani when she came to Ridgeway. For never having the guts to tell her I was sorry. For whatever role my stupid corn party had in her dying. Most of all I'd say way down deep that I'd do it all differently. Even though I would never have the chance. I cried a lot as I wrote, but I found the words.

I DREW #1, the first person in the whole class to give my speech. I was scared, even though I knew everybody there and could talk to them any other time. But Snyder was great. He said I did splendidly. He told me to make sure I met the mailing deadline for the organization that sponsored the contest. And to start packing my bags for India. I would share much and learn much, he said, and be certain to return to Ridgeway with some more good speech material.

Even though I knew he was teasing about packing my bags, his compliment was almost as good as getting to pet the hedgehog, still in his bottom drawer from last year. And right then the idea seemed a tiny bit interesting. India was scary, actually, way different than Ridgefield, I knew. But it was exciting too. I started to wonder what I'd find to wonder about in India. The next day, I mailed my essay. By then it dawned on me that I was wasting a stamp and an envelope. But I could honestly tell Snyder that it was in the mail. And he might ask.

CHAPTER 25

O n Saturday night, two weeks after Tani's memorial, I went out to the meadow. I took a candle in a glass holder, so the breeze wouldn't blow it out and the light could flicker through. Maybe it reminded me of Tani's light shining. I was missing her. I sat down next to the creek and cried. I wondered if Tani and her Jenny-sister were line dancing in heaven, because regardless of what I thought about God, I felt positively there was some kind of a heaven for them to dance in, and I wasn't giving that up.

I watched the candle flame and then looked around at the creek and the meadow. I knew right then I'd be back here for my wedding. It hadn't been spoiled by a memorial service. I could never find a more beautiful, full of love place, than right here, blessed by tears of people who care. The twilight held the meadow gently, outlines of the trees softening under the sky now dotted with stars. It was lovelier than I had ever known it to be.

I hoped Jackson Evans would come to my wedding. Yes, I did. And he could dance at my wedding too if he wanted. Jackson Evans had a lot more heart than I ever gave him credit for. Of course, the first dance would be for my dad. And the next one would be for ... My mind or my heart just filled in Param's name. I looked back up the path. It was the one I would walk from the house to the meadow, in my wedding gown, and I imagined Param stepping out from the cherry grove, standing beside me. Somehow even Mom would love it, love him.

It's crazy that I would be thinking about a wedding just two weeks after we had a funeral there. Sometimes thoughts just come that I don't count on. I didn't push this one away, like I don't plan on pushing Param away, no matter what. He came into my life from nowhere, suddenly, and he's one of the nicest people I've ever known, besides being smart and beautiful. I always knew I'd take a few years, or at least a lot of months to decide who I was going to marry, but I sat there looking at my candle light flickering and knew right then, logical or not, that I could marry Paramdeep Singh, and I'd love him, and be very happy.

I didn't know how it was all going to happen, because we weren't dating, even if we could. A kiss didn't mean things were decided. I wasn't even sure what it did mean. I had no idea how in the world I would accomplish all my great plans, getting Param to fall in love with me and want to be with me forever, let alone convince four parents that it was a great idea.

JUST THEN SOMEONE called from the path leading down from the house.

"Annie! Are you out here?"

It was Danny, carrying the matching candle to mine.

"Over here," I called.

"Hi," he said, as he approached.

"Hi."

"Your mom said you were down here."

"I am."

He wasn't intruding. It was good to have Danny there. I hadn't talked to him alone since the memorial.

"It was a good day, wasn't it?" he said, and I knew what he meant.

I nodded my head. He sat down beside me.

"Thanks for doing the memorial, Annie. It was a gift for Tani, even though she wasn't here to get it."

Danny and I sat there for several minutes totally silent, just being in that place. Finally we began to talk about her and all that had happened since she came to Ridgeway in March. We even talked about the night she died. I don't know if somebody can come back from heaven to watch you, but when I told Danny about us racing Mr. Taylor and Mr. Davis down the street, I think that happened. It felt like Tani was there, listening over our shoulders, because I could picture her so clearly.

"Tell me how she looked then," he said.

"What?"

"What did she do? What did she look like after you raced?"

I knew Danny hadn't seen either of the things I was going to describe, but I told him it was the exact opposite of when she was crying with her face turned up – that time in Snyder's class and the other time on the track when she told me about Jenny.

"After the wheelchair race," I said, "which she kept insisting she and Mr. Taylor won, she threw her head back and just laughed into the sky, like ..."

"Like?"

"Like she loved being alive, I guess. Like she was glad we were there doing that silly thing together."

He let me finish. "Like maybe she loved me, and knew I loved her, even though I never especially thought about that till right this very minute."

I lay back on the grass and looked up at the stars, now filling the darkening sky. "Star light, star bright," I said. I didn't have to hide my words from Danny. He would know it was reasonable to wish on the first star, even though I wasn't sure which one it was. "I wish that Tani has fun in heaven with Jenny, and that they get to be in each other's weddings." Danny let me cry. It didn't have to make sense. Danny knew that. "I wish it had never happened," I said at last. He reached over and took my hand.

When I sat back up, I noticed a little paper sack between Danny and me.

"What's that?" I asked.

"I made you a present while you were in San Francisco this summer," he said. "There hasn't been any good time to give it to you since you got back. I thought maybe tonight was okay."

"What is it?"

"Look," he said.

I opened the sack and pulled out a beanbag.

Danny and I made beanbags in second grade. It was the first time either of us had ever sewn anything. His mom showed us how, and we were really excited. They didn't work very well. They leaked beans all summer long because our stitches weren't tight enough. We loved them, though, and kept them till all the beans had disappeared and we were throwing around little square pieces of cloth. We changed what they were, from beanbags to doilies, like my grandma puts under all her flower vases.

I recognized the fabric.

"It's material from our third-grade zebra costumes," Danny said. "My mom still has a whole box of scraps from that program. I filled it with flax seeds. They're way better than beans. And I sewed it really tight. Look at the stitches." He moved his candle over close to the beanbag so I could see, then took it in his hands and tugged at the seams. "No way can a flax escape this."

"Nice job," I said.

"Thanks." He smiled. "So you want to play catch?"

I laughed. "Yes, Danny, that's exactly what I want to do."

We set our candles down at the edge of the water. Danny took off his shoes and socks and waded to the other side of the creek. Under the stars, with a moon just rising, we tossed a zebra beanbag back and forth across the water.

"I love you so much, Danny Amado!" I called out.

"I love you too, Annie Karten," Danny called back. "Always have. Always will! Never forget that."

"Okay," I said.

PART III

Cow Crossings
(India)

It wasn't logical. It was too far away. Too fast. But logical wasn't working. Sometimes I couldn't breathe. The water around me would churn up wild because of that crazy storm, and it felt like my boat was sinking. I couldn't hang on.

So I went. And, honestly, I didn't bother to pack my God Box.

Annie

CHAPTER 26

T he Hyderabad crowd plodded through immigration. Annie stayed in line, but set her backpack down on the floor and sat on it, wishing she could fall asleep, afraid that she might. Finally her passport had the needed stamps, and the necessary questions were answered. She looked around, hoping there'd be someone holding a "Welcome, Annie" sign, but all she could see were carts and families and people who had been on the plane waiting for the luggage to start coming in.

Uniformed guards stood at a narrow exit gate, tending the crowd as they stretched and peered around each other into the baggage claim area, straining to get a glimpse of relatives. Just then she saw a small poster bobbing above a wooden half-wall probably seven feet tall. The letters A-N-N-I-E floated along the top of the wall. Annie sighed, guessing she was the only Annie on that flight and knowing there was somebody on the other side of the wall waiting for her. Both bags came through, also a relief since they held everything she had to live in for the next five months. A man in a blue shirt was at her side helping roll her suitcases toward the exit when Annie saw a head peek over the wall beside the sign.

"Annie!" the girl yelled. "I'm Ketsa! Welcome to India!" She waved the sign and her free hand wildly above her head.

Annie couldn't help but grin, as the face framed by tiny braids disappeared behind the wall and popped up again in the crowd at the exit gate.

"We're over there," Ketsa said, pointing back toward a woman Annie guessed to be about her grandma's age. "Well, Ms. Dunlop and me, that is. Lori and Jen are back at the hotel snoozing away. I think I'm still on DC time. Couldn't sleep, so thought I might as well come see your flight arrive. You know it's four in the morning here?"

"*Chaar baje*," Annie said, and then quickly added, "Yes, four. Thank you so much for coming to meet me."

"No problem, girl. We've been doing the Hyderabad scene to kill time till you got here – tombs, mosques, the zoo – white tigers, baby! – and this amazing old gateway called the Charminar. We waited for you for the village visit though, since we all paid through our noses for that cultural add-on. But I must say this, you are in for the shock of your life, unless Oregon is a lot different than I think it is. Never been there, but I've seen pictures. And wait till you step outside. This room here is not the real world. We paid to get the privilege of coming into this inner sanctum to meet you. The rest of the crowd – and the real India – is waiting outside. And it is definitely out of control!"

Ms. Dunlop interrupted Ketsa's chatter. "Hi, Annie. We're so glad you're here. How was your trip?"

"Okay," Annie said as Ketsa and Ms. Dunlop each took a suitcase and led her through the "inner sanctum" toward a glass doorway to the outside.

"Ready, set, go," Ketsa said, as they emerged into the crowd.

"Taxi? Taxi, Madam?" multiple voices called out.

"Would you like a nice hotel, Madam? I can show you."

"No thank you. We're all set," Ms. Dunlop said as she led the girls through the crowd toward their waiting driver.

"And be thankful this city is still 99% asleep," Ketsa said. "You'd go crazy if you got your first taxi ride at noon, guaranteed."

Annie felt the 44-hour journey seep through her body as they rode through the yawning Hyderabad morning. But she pushed away the longing to sleep and stared out the window of the taxi. They passed a line of wooden carts loaded high with grass, pulled by some big cow-looking animals, each with one red horn and one bright blue.

Ketsa followed her glance. "Colorful, aren't they? We just missed a big festival which honors the cow. Only these are actually called bullocks, not cows. Not sure what that means exactly, but Ms. Dunlop knows a lot and can fill us in later. And these giant buzzing things we're passing on your side are called auto rickshaws. They're a blast! We've been going everywhere in them. Cheaper than taxis and way more fun."

The black and yellow, and black and green, rickshaws droned on beside them, keeping up with their taxi, some crowded full even at dawn, others empty, still going somewhere. Ketsa pointed out their features. "You sit in the back on a seat behind this guy riding some kind of a scooter. But it's built right into the whole thing to make you think you're in a tiny little car. I may import one to drive to school next year. The too-cool-for-you dudes would turn green with envy!"

Annie smiled at the thought of this Ketsa girl driving up to Ridgeway High in an auto rickshaw with Annie in the back. Danny would be there to pull her out and give her a big hug, and Katelyn would grab her away from him and start talking non-stop about who was doing what, and she'd look up and see Param standing on the steps by the main door, watching them. Danny would follow her glance and notice Param, and....

Ketsa was quiet and Annie wondered if she had been rude, letting her thoughts drift. She couldn't help it. No matter what she had to work out when she got home, she missed them already. A pang of homesickness shot through her. Annie reached for something inside her to push it away. "I wonder ..." she whispered. "I wonder ... why all those shops have metal garage doors instead of regular doors." Most of the shops lining the road were still closed, but people stirred here and there in front of them.

Annie turned away from the window toward Ketsa. "Is that guy going to the ..." Ketsa finished for her, "Peeing against the wall. Nobody seems to mind. Undoubtedly adds to the aroma of the city, wouldn't you think, all that pee. I mean yesterday we walked right by two guys ..."

"Gross," Annie said.

"Gross is yet to come!" Ketsa laughed. "I saw a little kid go diarrhea right off the sidewalk yesterday. And I stepped over a big blob of poop in the alley coming out the back door from a movie. Might have been dog doo, but it kind of makes you wonder."

Ms. Dunlop turned from the front seat where she had been talking to the driver. "Ketsa, let's let Annie make a few discoveries on her own, once she's settled in," she said.

"Got it, Ms. Dunlop." Ketsa winked at Annie. "I'll tell you more later," she whispered.

CHAPTER 27

Two girls were in the dining room of the hotel when they arrived. "Welcome," one girl said, ushering them to chairs. Pointing at the food on their plates, she said, "We had the same thing yesterday morning. Not bad, actually. The soup stuff is a little spicy, but it's good. Oh, I'm Jen, and this is Lori."

"Hi," Lori said. "They're making us omelets and toast right now, though I'm not sure we can trust it. I don't suppose toast can kill us. Don't eat the papaya though. The coffee should be safe – boiled, half milk and sugar – but good that way, since I never liked coffee before." Annie noticed that Ms. Dunlop had already eaten most of the two slices of papaya on her plate, shaking her head and grinning.

After breakfast, the girls packed their bags to move them into the hotel's storage room for safe-keeping while they were away for their village visit. Annie sat on the corner of one of the beds, and tugged her journal out of her backpack. She turned to the back pages, where her writing wouldn't be noticed, and jotted down:

- Ketsa – sunshine in braids. I love her already.
- Jen – clothes! make-up! I wonder why she chose India.
- Lori – nice, but scared?
- Ms. Dunlop – old, but likes India; what's her story?
- Danny – wish you were here, Bud
- Param – is this really your home? Yikes!
- Tani – why?

Ms. Dunlop apologized for not letting Annie sleep before they headed out to the village but said she had a trade-off. She had scrapped the plan of taking a local bus – there'd be time for that cultural experience later on – and had hired a small van to drive them the 300 kilometers to Gandhinagar. Annie knew the village visit was a purposeful introduction to India before they went on to school, but only now learned that Ms. Dunlop had been a Peace Corps Volunteer in Gandhinagar almost forty years back.

"Wait. How did you do that?" Ketsa asked Ms. Dunlop, pointing to what she was wearing. "Turn around for us!" Ms. Dunlop had been in jeans a few moments before, and here she stood before the girls wearing a beautifully wrapped and pleated light blue sari and matching blouse.

"You are one rockin' lady!" Ketsa laughed. "I mean, look at that revealing skin at the waist. I'd get called into the principal's office for sure if I wore tops that high above my belly button! And toe rings! Ooo-eee!"

"Well, the top is just what you wear with a sari, and the toe rings aren't as wild and exotic as you might think," Ms. Dunlop said. "They were a gift to me from a family in Gandhinagar. For my whole time in the Peace Corps, the village women stewed about the fact that I was twenty-two and still not married. Five years later I came back with my new husband, and they gave these to me, insisting that I wear them as a token of my marriage. It wouldn't do for me to show up now without them."

"So do we get to wear saris?" Annie asked.

"You could. They are the world's most practical and adaptable dress, I'm sure, but they also have a tendency to feel cumbersome to young women used to wearing shorts and t-shirts." She dipped one shoulder, allowing the end of her sari to tumble to the floor. "I usually cheat," she added. She reached into her bag and anchored the sari in place at her shoulder with a safety pin. "But we can definitely learn to wrap a sari before you head up to MMIS," she said. "For now, there's another option for being appropriately modest in the village. Come with me."

They walked next door to a small dress shop with a variety of colorful outfits hanging out front.

"The salwar kameez," Ms. Dunlop explained, holding one up in front of her. "A long dress and a scarf, worn over matching pants. Maybe not what you're used to, but I think we can give up our jeans for a few days."

No one considered it a sacrifice. The outfits were beautiful. Annie chose a swirled lilac and lime green top, with lime green pants to match, and a flowing lilac scarf. Ketsa's was gorgeously red and orange, and both Jen and Lori selected colorful batiked cotton outfits with little round mirrors sewn onto the dresses. They had just finishing changing into them when the van arrived. They grabbed their overnight bags, and Ms. Dunlop loaded a box of bottled water into the van.

IT'S HARD TO suddenly stop a habit after sixteen years, and that's exactly what the van driver was telling Annie to do – just get in and not to worry that there were no seat belts. She knew if they crashed, the newspapers would report that she wasn't buckled up, and everyone back home would think that she died of her own stupidity. She had seen articles like that in the Ridgeway paper, and heard people say that very thing. About people they didn't know.

"Come on, girl," Ketsa said, "I guess they don't make seat belts in India."

"But they do," Annie protested, pointing to half of one belt attached to her side of the van. The driver waved her on inside.

"Seat belts gone, Madam," he said. "No problem. Not worry."

"That's crazy!" Annie protested to Ketsa as they pulled

out, honking, into a swarming mass of traffic – motorized rickshaws, taxis, bicycles, cars, bullock carts, motorcycles, and people trying to maneuver their way through them. "And they don't wear helmets, either!" Just then a motorcycle pulled alongside Annie's open window. The driver glanced her way and smiled, wearing a helmet. "Guess they do sometimes," Annie said, and then she noticed that the woman behind him and the two children between them, were bare-headed.

"Probably thinks his brains are more valuable than theirs," Ketsa said.

"Don't they use yellow lines, Ms. Dunlop?" Jen asked. Annie looked sideways and counted six or maybe seven, rows of traffic, if you could call them rows, proceeding helter-skelter, juggling positions to get somewhere faster. A cycle rickshaw loaded with a huge bundle of plastic water jugs held its ground in front of their van, until their driver blared the horn, leaned his head out the window and shouted at the bundle. It worked its way off to the side, and Annie saw that the man pedaling was a lot older and skinnier than she thought he would be.

"That was a red light we just went through, Ms. Dunlop!" Lori exclaimed.

"I think we'll be okay," Ms. Dunlop said. "The traffic's a little intense, but they seem to manage."

So began Annie's first wakeful nightmare in India, when she wondered if this could be the end of her life. "I hate this," she said to Ketsa. "If I die, they will send me home dead and I will have come here for nothing. No offense, but it's not worth seeing some stupid village if this is how we have to get there." Scholarship promise or not, Annie could not bring herself to wonder why this driver was weaving in and out of traffic like a maniac, going head-on toward other cars, even buses and trucks, only to swerve back in at the last possible minute. Frantic looks passed between the girls in the back of the van, until Annie finally said, "Ms. Dunlop, I've got to go..."

"...pee," Ketsa finished for her. "Me too. Let's hit the next rest stop."

Ms. Dunlop looked back at them. "You need a chai break, girls? We can stop a way farther up the road for tea or soft drinks and bathroom."

When the van stopped, Ms. Dunlop handed them a roll of toilet paper and pointed to a concrete enclosure a short walk away.

"Cool! Let's go squat!" Ketsa laughed.

"And then will you tell that driver to slow down?" Annie pleaded with Ketsa. "You're braver than me."

She did.

He didn't.

"I'm not sure I want India in my bones," Annie said to herself as she leaned her head on Ketsa's shoulder and promptly fell asleep.

THEY ARRIVED IN Gandhinagar safely, and the van was soon surrounded by a group of boys and girls. One of them said, very formally, to Ms. Dunlop, "*Salaam alaikum.*" She answered back, "*Alaikum salaam.*" She looked at him carefully. "Hamed?" she asked. He smiled grandly, nodding yes, and then, pointing to Annie, asked, "Penny?"

"*Illa,*" Ms. Dunlop shook her head, and then added with a smile "Annie." She turned to Annie and explained, "But you do look strikingly like my granddaughter, Penny. I realized that at the airport." Then she introduced the girls one by one to the kids and chattered on in some language that Annie had never heard – Urdu or Kannada, she supposed, because Ms. Dunlop said those were the two main languages in this village. She felt someone's hand take hold of hers, and looked into the eyes of a beautiful little girl at her side.

"Annie," the girl said clearly. Annie nodded, and wished

she had learned something more than *"Chaar baje."* Then she remembered she also knew *"Namaste."* She slipped her hand free, and with palms together, raised as if in prayer, she nodded slightly, saying, *"Namaste."* The girl smiled and responded with, *"Namaste."* Immediately a dozen voices echoed the greeting, then giggled as Annie greeted each of them in turn. Finally, the little girl reached up and grabbed Annie's hand back.

"Ms. Dunlop, how do you say: What's your name?" Annie asked.

"With her, it's: *Tumhara naam kya hai?*"

That's how Annie met Yasmeen, and some others whose unusual names slipped away as soon as she heard them. They all headed up a dusty, rough pathway into the center of the village, where a government traveler's bungalow and people Ms. Dunlop knew awaited them. There were tears in Ms. Dunlop's eyes as she greeted her many friends, and Annie thought of the lady at the Mumbai airport.

CHAPTER 28

"**O**h, come along with me," Annie sang out.

"Oh, come aylong wit mee," echoed back the voices of twenty-some boys and girls circled with Annie, Ketsa, Lori, and Jen under a big mango tree in front of the bungalow.

"To the top of a tree," Annie acted out as she sang. She wondered if they had any idea what they were singing back to her, but she couldn't help but grin at their enthusiasm, and feel glad for her days at Camp Namanu along the Sandy River in Oregon. The song took them into and out of a bear's cave, down white-water rapids, and away from a swarm of bees, each verse being interspersed with, "Iyo, Iyo, Woo-hee, Woo-hee, it's a very fine day, for you and me!" When the English got blurred, motions filled in perfectly, and Annie was happy someone had invented repeat-back songs. After several more, one that Jen led and the rest that Annie called out, Ketsa convinced the kids to sing for them, and then Ms. Dunlop called for them to come.

Pied Piper-like, with ever growing numbers of children joining the parade, they walked along rough dirt roads that wound from the bungalow through the village to the compound of one of Ms. Dunlop's old friends. There the children were shooed away, except for a handful who seemed to belong to the family, Yasmeen among them. Three boys had found a way to get to a neighboring roof and were looking down on them as they entered the yard.

Some of the rooms on the inside of the compound were of brick and some of mud. They were all covered by a sheet metal roof held down here and there by big pots, or maybe that was where these people stored their pots, on the edge of the roof. The outside walls were brightly white-painted and clean. They waited a few moments before going inside, as mats were being spread on the floor.

Ketsa turned to Annie as she ducked to keep from bumping her head on the top of the doorway. "Aren't they amazing, making floors that look like this out of cow pies and water?"

"What?" Annie answered. "It's concrete." She looked to Ms. Dunlop for confirmation, but Ms. Dunlop just smiled as she explained how practical the concrete-looking cow dung finish was. Plates were brought and put before them – plastic red, white, and blue, with stars and stripes splashed across them – as Ms. Dunlop explained they were a gift she'd left behind for this family on a visit to India in the late '80s.

"They kept your American plates for all these years?" Annie asked. But she didn't wait for a reply. Her attention was on a woman in a sari, sitting in the corner of the room beside a variety of brass, clay, and plastic containers stacked next to a trunk on which sat a tiny black and white TV.

"Is she ..." Annie started, but Ketsa interrupted.

"Oh, my gosh! She's talking on a cell phone, here in a mud hut with cow dung floors!"

"Ketsa, they may understand more English than you think," Annie warned quietly. "And their floors are beautiful."

The woman didn't seem concerned about their conversation, but eagerly handed the phone off to Ms. Dunlop, who broke into excited chatter with the person on the other end of the call. When she finished, she translated for the girls, "Two other daughters in this family are headed here by bus right now to see us. They'll be here late tonight. One was a favorite little friend of mine (like Yasmeen? Annie thought) when I was just trying to survive those first months in the Peace Corps, and the other is the one sister in the family I've still never met. Aren't cell phones great! Forty years ago there was one phone in this entire village, but I never saw it. We had to send important messages by telegraph and connected with home by writing aerograms."

Lunch was soon ready. Annie was surprised that Lori and Jen were such good sports about it. By now she expected Ketsa to jump in feet first, but sensed it was more of a challenge for the other two. Annie was reluctant herself. She had never before seen anything they brought out, except the chapatis, which looked like the whole wheat tortillas her mom bought. And the mutton biryani was in the somewhat familiar-looking rice category. Otherwise, it was bowls of green and yellow and brown stuff that was delicious but burned her mouth. Ms. Dunlop said they toned it down from their usual, but it was still spicy hot to Annie. Lori must have liked finger-painting when she was little, because eating with her hands didn't throw her, as Annie would have guessed. It was fun actually, and Annie decided right then that she would learn Indian cooking, and would serve what she cooked to people at home sitting on the floor, without any silverware.

Yasmeen had walked around behind each of them, offering to pour a little jug of warm water over their hand so they could wash up before the dinner began and again now when it was finished. It all seemed quite wonderful, except for the fact that the five of them ate by themselves, with just two of the men of the family, and everyone else waited until they were finished.

What followed lunch was a blur to Annie, with tea and hot milk, biscuits – which were actually cookies – and cashews, raisins, bananas, apples, and bright green tangerines served by two other families, also friends taking their turn at hosting the guests on their arrival day. Annie had just reached down for more apple slices when Lori whispered, "The rule is: 'Cook it, peel it, or forget it,' and let's hope they boiled that milk you're drinking. TB, you know." Annie didn't know, or had forgotten, and felt like crying. Ms. Dunlop should have told her friends not to serve something the girls shouldn't accept, or she could have at least warned Annie to be sly and ignore bad stuff like unpeeled apples. How could Annie be expected to remember that? She had grown up picking apples up off the ground in their orchard, then rubbing them on her pants leg and calling it good.

Finally out of steam, in the last house, Annie scooted back into a corner, leaned her head against the wall, and fell asleep.

She was still on the floor, but lying down with a pillow under her head when she awakened. At first, she couldn't think where she was, but realized she was alone, until she saw the little girl, Yasmeen, sitting across from her. As Annie stirred, Yasmeen moved over beside her, and reached out for Annie's hand. "Iyo, Iyo," Yasmeen sang softly but perfectly in tune. Annie grinned and sat up, echoing back the chorus and adding "Woo-hee, Woo-hee," which Yasmeen sang back to her. Then together they finished, "It's a very fine day," and grandly motioned, "for you and me." Annie reached out and drew Yasmeen to her in a warm hug. "Thank you for sitting with me," she said. "Do you speak English?"

"I speak some little English," Yasmeen answered. "School studying English, 4th standard."

"That's super," Annie said. "I don't know any Urdu or Kannada or whatever it is you speak here. But maybe I'll learn at the school I'm going to. Only they speak English there, and maybe some Tamil, so I'm not sure what language I'll study."

"I school in going, Kannada little learning," Yasmeen explained. "My mother tongue is Urdu. Go garden?"

"What?" Annie asked.

Yasmeen took Annie's hand to help her up. "Come. Peoples all go garden."

Annie didn't think to feel hesitant. It seemed logical that she would walk hand in hand with a little girl named Yasmeen on this sunny January afternoon, in a village she'd never heard of, and that the man they met riding in the wooden cart pulled by bullocks, and the woman leading the donkey loaded with a bundle of grass ten times its size, and the two goats tied together with a rope around their necks would let her pass.

As they walked through the village, people stopped and watched, and both children and adults chatted with Yasmeen. Annie was sure it was about her, yet Yasmeen seemed confident that her short responses were all anyone needed to know. As before, a crowd of children followed along behind them, growing in numbers as they went.

At the edge of the village, the road turned into a path that passed between a small grove of coconut trees on one side, and a patch of very tall green corn-like plants on the other side.

"*Kabu*," Yasmeen said. Annie looked puzzled, so she explained, "Shurgahcane."

Stalks of the sugarcane had been brought from the field and cut into pieces. The children were tearing away the outer purplish peel with their teeth, then biting off and chewing on chunks of the juicy yellow stalk.

"Go for it, girl," Ketsa called to Annie as she arrived, pointing toward the pile of sugarcane chunks. "It's sweet – literally."

Even Lori was chewing on a piece, so Annie supposed it had passed the general safety test.

"What did I miss?" Annie asked.

"You were one tired girl," Ketsa said. "But you didn't actually sleep all that long. We got a tour of this here field – garden, Ms. Dunlop calls it. Those coconut trees over there are the very ones that she helped the parents of this family plant when she was a Peace Corps Volunteer here way back when. Cool, huh?

"The parents both died when their five kids were still pretty little, but the oldest girl was sixteen and she was married, so she and her husband, who lived in Gandhinagar too, took care of the others. Amazing! Ms. Dunlop said she was glad the trees made it, because she hadn't been all that sure she knew what she was doing. She was twenty-two then." Ketsa looked right at Annie and said, "Let's do something in India that changes the place and lasts forty years, Annie, even if we're not in the Peace Corps."

"Okay, Ketsa," Annie laughed. Just then she saw a group of kids emerging from the sugarcane patch. Annie went limp. A feeling of dread washed over her – that they shouldn't be playing there, that she should warn the kids that accidents can happen and they should get away. She sank down on the mat Ketsa was sitting on, and tears welled up in her eyes.

"You okay, girl?" Ketsa asked. "What's happening?"

"Just a memory of home, and a cornfield, and my friend Tani," Annie said.

"Doesn't it just hit you at the weirdest times? I know it does me. Sometimes I suddenly miss my baby brother and think he'll be all grown up before I get back home. Then I relax and know I'll see him in five months, and then he'll be back to bawling his head off, which bugs the heck out of me, and I'll wish I was back in India. You'll see your Tani friend soon enough, girl. She'll manage without you for a while."

Annie knew she should have told Ketsa right that second about Tani, but once Ketsa added, "Come on, girl, you'll be okay," and the moment had passed and Annie hadn't corrected her, it didn't seem like she could just blurt out now that Tani was dead and she wouldn't see her ever again. Annie wiped her eyes, and pushed away thoughts of the accident in the cornfield. The one God could have stopped.

"Yeah," was all Annie said. She realized that she hadn't been near a cornfield since the night Tani died, even though this wasn't quite corn either. "I'm so sorry, Tani," she whispered to herself, and Annie knew that her God Box questions followed her here, regardless of what she meant to leave at home. But the kids emerging from the field were quite the opposite of solemn right then, and they drew Annie away from her thoughts. The boy leading the way, with two or three long stalks of sugar cane over his shoulder, also led the chant: "Iyo, Iyo."

"Iyo, Iyo," the smaller children carrying the other ends of the stalks echoed back.

"Woo-hee, Woo-hee."

"Woo-hee, Woo-hee," they sang.

Annie couldn't help but smile. She wondered if Ketsa noticed that they had changed India, in a crazy little for-one-day way, with only a handful of kids. This place was different today from what it was yesterday. Ketsa did notice and grinned at Annie. Still, Annie doubted that anybody would know that song in forty years, not even kids camping along the Sandy River in Oregon, not even her.

THAT NIGHT THE watchman at the bungalow made chapatis and omelets for their group. Annie tried to stay awake to hear about the hot water that he would carry to them in the morning, and about the mehndi hand painting, and who was going to ride back to Hyderabad with them the next evening, but long ideas were hard to hold onto. Instead, quick thoughts flitted through her mind – *chaar baje*, cell phones, apple skins with TB, no, that was milk, coconut trees, monkeys, bullock carts piled mountain high, Mt. Hood, home. Annie didn't bother undressing, just leaned back on one of the beds in the room and pulled a sheet over her.

The bed cradled her, holding her like her bed at home. She could imagine her mom coming into her room to wish her good-night and kiss her on the forehead. "I love you, Mom." Annie whispered into the Indian night. "I love you, Dad. And you too, Danny." She didn't open her sleepy eyes, but she smiled, "And you, Param. Why didn't you come with me? You'd be home, I guess. If you were here, I'd tell you about a little girl who led me through the village today, hanging onto my hand. Her name is Yasmeen, and we sang, "Iyo, I ..."

CHAPTER 29

The night came and passed, and in the early dawn, as everyone else slept, Annie stirred. Sleep wouldn't come back once her mind cleared and anchored her to this bungalow in Gandhinagar. She let her mind retrace the journey of one long day between home and here. Annie had no idea how long she lay there thinking, but the room began to lighten and as it did, she began to pray. It didn't matter that she didn't believe in prayer anymore. She needed to talk to God, so she did, whispering softly.

"God, please make the driver be safe on our way back to Hyderabad tonight. And take care of Mom and Dad and everybody at home, especially Robin and Mr. Paulmann, and take care of Yasmeen and all these kids in Gandhinagar. Please don't let me get TB or anything awful like worms or malaria ..." She paused and then added, "I'm sorry I'm so mad at you. I want to believe. I wish I could. Especially here where I really need you."

There was a tap on the door. Ms. Dunlop threw back her sheet and crawled out of bed, then slipped into a cotton robe to open the door to the watchman, holding a bucket of hot water. She glanced back over her shoulder and caught Annie's eye, motioning that Annie could have the first bucket bath. "And, God, could you help me figure out how to take a shower with one bucket of water and a cup," Annie prayed as she carried the bucket toward the little latrine and wash room.

Annie took time to journal while the others got ready for

the day. "Questions for Param," she titled a new section of her journal, and made three entries:

- Is English your "mother tongue?"
- Did you ever peel sugarcane with your teeth?
  (Maybe I did something in India you never did.)
- What do you dream?

Annie had dreamed of Param that night. He was in Gandhinagar and could talk with people in other languages. Monkeys came to steal the coconuts from the village, and everybody was worried. Someone called for Param and told him to bring his sword. He had long, floppy paper swords, which he waved at the monkeys, and they bounded away.

And he was in love with Ketsa. That was the other thing that was easy to remember about her dream. He didn't seem to know Annie was there. She kept trying to find him to tell him, but she couldn't. It was a bad dream. For all her not wanting to think about either one of them, they seemed to find their way to Gandhinagar.

"Danny? Param?" she wrote.

She let the question float in her mind as the other girls finished their bucket baths and got dressed. She told herself it didn't matter now. But she couldn't keep from thinking.

Danny had come to the Portland airport to see her off. She pulled back into her mind his smile and the hug, and his whispered words, "Don't fall in love, Annie." She was surprised, expecting him to be funny or at least not serious. But if that's what he really thought, then why didn't he reword it, Annie wondered. Why didn't he just once say, "Fall in love with me, Annie," because she would have told him that she had wanted to. And that maybe she would.

"Sure, Danny! Like who am I going to meet in five months in India?"

Annie went back to the line she had just written in her journal: Param? Danny?

"☺?" she added, shaking her head and smiling.

"SO, ARE YOU getting tattooed today, Annie?" Lori asked, pulling her kameez on over her head. "Or painted with henna or mehndi or whatever it is?"

"You bet! I did that at the State Fair last year, and it's gorgeous. Only I had them do just a tiny little butterfly on the inside of my ankle, and wore socks over it for two weeks till it faded, so Mom and Dad wouldn't freak that it was Hindu or that I hadn't ok'd it with them first."

"How could it be Hindu? These people are doing it for us and they're Muslims," Jen said. "I think it's Indian."

"Things aren't that easy, Jen," Annie said. "My parents think anything even remotely related to other religions is suspect. Acupuncture? Totally out. It's a foreign god kind of thing, with its voodoo needles and all."

"You're kidding?" Ketsa said. "They even got their continents mixed up, girl. Voodoo – Africa, Haiti. Acupuncture – China. But I get you. Unless they've tried it, how would they know it really works? It's like meat-eaters who think vegetarians are weird."

"Welcome to Ridgeway!" Annie said. "That's exactly the reaction at my school. I decided to be a vegetarian for one month last year just to try it, and I got teased to no end. So with that and loving fried chicken, I decided to give it up after four days. I don't actually know anyone who is vegetarian."

"Girl, you are lookin' at me!" Ketsa answered. "Didn't you see me put those chunks of mutton over on your plate yesterday? Nobody I know in DC thinks it's weird. Once we get out of Muslim territory, you're going to find a lot of vegetarians in India. Want to go veg with me? It's your big chance."

"I'll think about it," Annie answered.

Another tap on the door, and with the wooden shutters open Ms. Dunlop must have spotted someone through the window bars.

"Daulat!" she screamed as she ran for the door.

"Not a little excited!" Ketsa laughed. "One unusual Gram, huh? Must be the ladies on the other end of the cell phone." Then she looked around at Lori, Jen, and Annie. "Think we'll be best friends when we're old ladies like her?" she asked. They watched as Daulat and Ms. Dunlop hugged, first to one side, then the other, and cried and laughed, both of them. When Daulat introduced Ms. Dunlop to the other woman, her little sister, the hugging started all over again. The ladies sat on the porch of the bungalow and talked for several minutes, until Ms. Dunlop brought Daulat and Saleema inside to meet the girls.

"Watch me do those fancy two-sided hugs," Ketsa whispered to Annie. "Wise Woman of the World that I am."

As Daulat reached out to greet Annie, she held her at arms' length and looked at her closely. "Penny?" she asked. Ms. Dunlop smiled and explained who Annie was and wasn't, but Daulat seemed not to care and pulled Annie toward her in a hug so gentle and warm that Annie didn't mind taking advantage of this Penny-girl's goodwill from the past.

Greetings over, they all left the bungalow to begin their second and last day in Gandhinagar, starting with newly painted fancy hands.

Annie hoped the mehndi would never wear off, at least not until she got back to Ridgeway High and could hold her hands out like friends did when they had a new ring to show off. She wanted everybody to see how stunning the design was and ask where in the world she got it done. "Oh, some great little shop in India," she'd say first, and then she'd smile and tell them the truth: "Yasmeen's big sister painted my hands, in front of their house, sitting next to me on a straw mat. She held my hand and squeezed dark brown stain from a gold foil funnel with a tiny pointed tip and made these beautiful designs all over both sides of my hands. Without a pattern, even. She just did it free-hand." Annie knew she'd never hide this artwork under a pair of socks.

A cousin and two aunts decorated the other girls' hands. Younger girls passed behind them all, combing their hair and braiding it into one braid down the back, except for Ketsa, whose many tiny braids they passed over with giggles. Annie hadn't even thought of it, but when they started on Lori's hair, she pulled her own comb out of her bag and handed it to them.

"Head lice prevention," she whispered. "Combs are a major way lice spread."

Annie noticed that the little girl combing Lori's hair had looked at the comb and then tried it out in her own hair first, then her friend's, but Annie decided not to say anything to Lori.

Women and children not directly involved sat around the sides of the mats and watched and chatted. From time to time, they'd all break into songs. A few men sat off to the side, seemingly amused yet aware that this was women's and children's work, or play.

"I feel like I have four daughters getting ready for their weddings all at once," Ms. Dunlop said. She sang along on some of their songs, and hummed others. "What a wonderful tradition," she said.

Annie felt Ms. Dunlop's friend, Daulat, behind her, resting her hands gently on Annie's shoulders. Like waking up with Yasmeen watching her yesterday, she felt at peace, as if she had known these people for a long time. Annie sensed, oddly, that she belonged here – even without language, without family, and with food that made her nose and eyes water. Ms. Dunlop told them the mehndi would fade away in a week or two, but Annie knew the design of Gandhinagar would stay.

THE GROUND THEY had come to was sacred, even though there were no crosses, which there wouldn't be, nor even tombstones. There were rocks here and there on the ground, a few large ones, and some smaller ones gathered in piles, marking the graves. So when others slipped off their sandals, Annie reached down and unbuckled hers. She stepped out onto some rough grass and discovered it to be filled with tiny sharp thorns. "Ouch!" she mouthed to warn the other girls, then pulled her lilac scarf up to cover her head, as the women had done with the ends of their saris, and the men had done with handkerchiefs.

They were visiting the place where the parents of this family were buried, along with one of their sons. Annie watched as Ms. Dunlop and the others placed a rose on each grave, roses the family had taken from the single little rosebush back in their compound. Annie wondered how these people had died.

As they turned to leave, Annie saw a patch of ground that appeared to be a new grave. She motioned for Ketsa to look. A woman watching them started to explain to Annie, then turned to Ms. Dunlop who interpreted for her. She told of a young woman, about the age of Annie and the others, who died just a month back when a kerosene stove exploded beside her. Annie thought of the horror of that death, and how awful it is to die when you are sixteen. She wondered if the girl's family was mad at their Allah-god for letting a stupid stove explode and burn her to death, when she could have easily walked away from the stove a minute before it happened, and gone to the bathroom or outside to get some water. But God hadn't let her think of water just then, so she died. And instead of being alive to meet them, here she was in a grave marked with a pile of stones.

Annie wondered if that girl might have found Tani in heaven and asked her if she wanted her hands painted with mehndi, like somehow, they were connected to what was happening on earth. Or was it just that Annie longed for Tani to be part of life again, and mehndi would make that so. Deep down she had the feeling that crappy things happened in India like they did at home.

She thought of Tani's dad at the funeral and how he wouldn't talk to anyone until Jackson Evans came up and kneeled in front of him, and how they cried together, how Jackson needed love, and so did Mr. Paulmann, just like people in India must when somebody they love dies. Tears sprang to her eyes and she quickly wiped them away with her scarf.

ONCE BACK AT the bungalow, they began packing up for their return to Hyderabad. A motorcycle drove into the compound and a young man slid off the seat from behind the driver, anchored a pair of crutches under his arms, and bounded toward the bungalow steps. Ms. Dunlop spotted him through the open doorway and rushed out, calling, "Abid, I'm so glad you came! Girls, come meet a special friend of mine."

"*Salaam alaikum,*" he said.

"*Alaikum salaam,*" Ms. Dunlop replied with a big smile, and they chatted on, until she remembered and paused to introduce the girls. "He's finishing up a book he's been working on for two years," she explained.

"What's your book about?" Ketsa asked. Abid glanced at Ms. Dunlop, but then answered Ketsa. "It's my family story and my story. Also my cousin and my days with polio," he said.

Annie tried to remember what she knew about polio. She thought it had been eradicated for people her age, but evidently not. She was glad this Abid boy was able to run on crutches and write books and win the fight.

THEY FINISHED PACKING up, and as they loaded into the

van and waved goodbye, a little girl with a large red dot on her forehead came to the open window next to Annie, and raising her hands in Namaste said, "*Hoge-burri.*" Several of the little girls picked up the phrase and the van pulled away to the calls of "*Hoge-burri, hoge-burri.*"

"What are they saying, Ms. Dunlop?" Annie asked.

"It's their word for 'good-bye'," she said. "But it really says 'go and come back.'"

"Cool!" Annie said, and she turned and yelled out the window, "*Hoge-burri!*"

"*Hoge-burtini,*" Ms. Dunlop offered. "It means, I'll go and come."

It was dark when they left Gandhinagar, along with the two aunts who crowded into the van with them. It turned out they lived just the other side of Hyderabad in Faraknagar, and although they said they'd catch a bus back, Ms. Dunlop insisted that the driver take them as close to their homes as the road allowed. Annie fell asleep, but woke from time to time, and thought maybe the driver was being more careful than he was the day before, not swerving so much.

She knew they had arrived in Faraknagar when they slowed down, and Daulat was telling the driver to turn here and here until he finally stopped at an outcropping of big boulders where the road seemed to end. Annie sat up and looked out the window to see a trail winding through the rocks to a small white house. She must have slept once more, through the farewell, though she vaguely remembered Daulat reaching out and stroking her head. She wished she had told her goodbye.

When she woke again Annie recognized the shop where they had bought their salwar kameezes, and knew they were back at the hotel.

As they went up the steps, Annie asked Ms. Dunlop, "Did we all get shots against polio when we were babies?"

"Shots or something oral. I don't remember which."

"Why couldn't India afford that for Abid?"

"The health workers came to Gandhinagar to offer inoculations, but Abid's mom was away visiting her sister, and they missed it. Before they came on another round, tiny little Abid had contracted polio..." Then almost to herself Ms. Dunlop continued, "I've thought often about my grandbaby, Penny. She was sick when she was due her first series of inoculations, so my daughter delayed them. It was a few months before she was rescheduled. Nothing happened. That's just it. We have the good fortune of living in a place where often, nothing happens.

"You can sleep in until noon tomorrow if you want," Ms. Dunlop told the girls as they retrieved their luggage from the hotel storage room. "We have just one thing to do, and that's to catch the night train to Coimbatore."

CHAPTER 30

In spite of their late night, they were all awake well before seven a.m. in this day-is-night and night-is-day place, too many time zones away for their American bodies. They decided to get some breakfast, and then find an internet cafe so they could all email home.

"So can we call home too?" Ketsa asked.

"It's getting a little late on the East Coast, but Oregon would be fine."

"My Mama said I can call her any time, day or night," Ketsa declared.

So they did. Everyone talked to somebody at home. When it was her turn, Annie was excited just to hear the ring, imagining the phone on the kitchen wall and her mom or dad jumping up from the table to grab it. But instead of their voices, the answering machine went on. It was her own voice saying, "You've reached the Kartens. Leave us a message."

"Mom—Dad—annnyyy-bodddy hoooome..." Annie said slowly so as to give them time to pick up the phone if they were there screening messages. But they weren't, so she said, rather deflated, "It's me. I'm fine." She was suddenly blank. "India's great... I love you guys!" She hung up before she remembered to add, "Oh, and we've been in this amazing village, and we leave for the school tonight by train." Annie quickly wiped the tears away. She hadn't wanted to leave a message. Where did they go that was so important? When were they going to get cells like the rest of the world? Next time she'd call while they were asleep, as the others had done. Or plan it ahead.

What Ms. Dunlop guessed would be an hour's outing, ended up taking most of the morning, but the girls convinced her that their email was an important kind of journaling, and better than sleeping in till noon, which she had already okayed. Annie had emails from friends at school, several from Danny and Katelyn, and from her mom and dad. Nothing from Param though, and that bothered her until she read one of her mom's messages saying that Param's family was in New Jersey and had called to see if Annie arrived safely. So he's probably busy, she told herself.

Annie sent off answers to each one and, finishing before the others, went outside to join Ms. Dunlop. She pulled out her journal and began writing about Gandhinagar. She titled a section:

Email Omissions – Things that would freak M & D

Under it she wrote:
- No seatbelts
- Mehndi
- TB - Head lice – Polio

Omissions didn't apply to Danny or Katelyn, of course.

THEY HAD TIME for more sight-seeing before their train left that evening. They went back to the Taj Mahal Hotel for a rice meal, Ms. Dunlop's favorite place to eat, then re-visited the Charminar so Annie could see this famous Old City Gateway landmark of Hyderabad. From inside they could look out over one of the world's largest mosques, and Ms. Dunlop pointed out the hospital where Abid had come for treatment. Annie thought it was beautiful, in looks, but also in what it did.

They wandered in and out of the little shops near the

Charminar, and came upon a row of flower sellers seated at their baskets of blossoms. The girls watched as these garland makers picked up the small, delicate white buds and, two at a time, quickly knotted the fiber thread around them so as to anchor the blossoms into a long strand.

"They smell so good!" Ketsa said. "Wait up, Ms. Dunlop. Can you help us buy some?"

Ms. Dunlop turned back. "Jasmine," she said. "Yes, let's all have some. They are definitely a part of India we shouldn't miss." She reached into her bag for some hairpins, and the girls clipped a strand of jasmine blossoms into each other's hair.

They flagged down two auto rickshaws and headed back toward the hotel, though Ms. Dunlop had the drivers stop a couple blocks short of their destination at a small Hindu temple. "Just so you won't think Islam is the only faith in Hyderabad," she explained.

The temple was hidden behind a wall, painted in bold red and white vertical stripes. Inside were pink and blue statues of people with all kinds of fancy layered headdresses, in all kinds of poses. There were carvings of animals here and there, in bright green, yellow, orange, and red, on a deep blue background. People took off their sandals, so Annie did too, but as she approached the central area, she began to feel uneasy. A black stone cow in the middle of the temple was garland with flowers. Sticks of burning incense, flower petals, and coconut halves were at the base, along with tiny oil lamps, and on the center of the animal's forehead was a splotch of colored red powder, like what she'd seen some women wear, and the little hoge-burri girls in Gandhinagar, only this was much bigger.

"Is this an idol?" she whispered to Ketsa. "Because if it is, I don't know if I should be here."

"Beats me. It looks like a fancy black marble cow. But I'm sure it won't bite! Relax, girl."

Annie watched a woman approach the statue, waft her

hand over a lamp flame and then touch her hand to her fore-head. She opened a small newspaper-wrapped packet in her hand and added to the dot on the cow's forehead. The little girl she was holding pinched a bit of powder from the packet and did the same. As the woman finished and turned back toward the exit, her eyes caught Annie's and she smiled. She was younger than Annie had expected, and pretty. Annie wondered how anyone could find that ritual meaningful. I may be mad at God, she thought, but at least He's not a cow.

As the woman passed by, she pointed to Annie's decorated hands.

"They are lovely," she said in perfect English.

"Thank you." Annie waited a few moments as the woman left, then backed away from the temple proper. She turned toward the gate, picked up her sandals, slipped them on her feet, and hurried to the auto rickshaw.

"You are liking the nice temple?" the rickshaw driver asked, as she crawled into the seat behind him.

"Oh, sure, it's fine," Annie said. She paused, then asked, "Do you know anything about the idol in there?"

"No idol, Ma'am," he said. "That is Nandi, the Bull that Shiva rides. Very old. Very good. Do many miracles and heal-ings in this temple."

"Right," Annie answered softly. Why in the world could someone ever believe junk like that, she asked herself, and then remembered her promise not to do this, not to criticize. She said, "I wonder...." But nothing would come. It was all just too crazy.

She took a breath and tried again, "I wonder... I wonder if I would have liked that young woman if I had met her first at a mehndi party instead of at that temple. And I wonder if she knows what the heck she's teaching her daughter."

Maybe a little critical, Annie recognized, but it was the

best she could do. She opened her journal to the back and added under Omissions that would freak –

- Cow gods
- Temple visits

Nobody at home would be ready for those.

CHAPTER 31

"Wow!" Jen exclaimed once they reached the train station and found their assigned rail car. "My name is right here. Imagine! My name in India, on a piece of paper stuck to the side of a train. Yours too, Ketsa, and Lori's and Annie's ... and Lucinda Dunlop."

Ms. Dunlop smiled. "That's me. Named after my very brave great-great-grandma who made it through on the Oregon Trail with her kids in spite of losing her husband along the way. But luckily Indian trains are luxurious compared to wagon trains, and I won't have to be brave, once we get this luggage loaded."

They found their seats, and stowed their bags under them and on an upper bunk.

"We'll reshuffle if we have to," Ms. Dunlop said, "but let's keep our fingers crossed that this section was assigned just to the five of us. I'll do some negotiating if necessary."

It wasn't needed. No one else came to that second-class, three tier compartment, except the two ladies who were assigned to the end bunks across the main aisle from them. The girls ventured out for a quick tour of the "amenities," as Ketsa called them, discovering one squat latrine and one with a toilet. There was no toilet paper and Annie hoped Ms. Dunlop had a supply for them. There was also a little sink and a mirror out in the entry area.

"Don't use the latrine yet," Ms. Dunlop cautioned. "It dumps directly onto the tracks."

"Really?" Ketsa asked. She peeked her head into one of

the tiny rooms and looked down through a hole to the ground below. "Yep," she confirmed.

They settled into their seats as tiffin sellers wandered the aisles calling out, "Chai, Chai," "Caw-pee, Caw-pee," "Bissss-kits."

"What's 'caw-pee'?" Annie asked.

"Coffee," Ms. Dunlop laughed. "Good stuff. Lots of milk and sugar."

Annie glanced at a man carrying a big stainless steel vessel holding tea. He evidently took her glance for a yes. He turned the spigot, filling a tiny plastic cup full of hot chai and handed it to Annie.

"I'll treat," said Ms. Dunlop to the girls, and requested four more cups. The sellers continued on down the car, followed by a woman with a box of barrettes and hair clips, then a man with a basket full of thin paperbacks. He set the basket down on the floor of the compartment in front of Annie and began talking with the women across the aisle. Annie noted the price marked on most of the books was Rs. 50, and quickly realized they would cost her less than a dollar each. She leafed through a book titled *1000 Quotations*, and set it aside, then saw two children's books about Indian gods, or at least people with multiple arms and odd decorations. She wondered if there might be something about Nandi the bull inside, but decided she didn't need that and dropped the books back into the basket. She dug deeper and found one on snakes that looked interesting.

"Can I borrow a hundred rupees, Ms. Dunlop? Mine is all in my money belt," Annie said. She suddenly knew she was too tired to read anything and stuffed the books in her backpack.

A man came through taking orders for supper – rice, vadai and sambar. Annie didn't know what vadai was, but she was hungry, and thought at least the rice would be good. But when the others shook their heads no, and even Ms. Dunlop didn't seem interested, she decided she should pass.

Perhaps the ladies across the aisle read her thoughts or saw the disappointed look on her face. Just minutes after the train pulled out of the station, they began unpacking dinner. One of them looked up at Annie and caught her eye. Annie smiled, then glanced down so as not to seem intrusive.

"Would you like some lemon rice?" the woman asked Annie, holding out a plate of yellow rice and vegetables. "We have plenty."

Annie was confused. Should she accept? How could she ask Ms. Dunlop without hurting their feelings? Lori had crawled up into the empty top bunk and was already asleep, so her reaction provided no safety barometer for Annie. She turned to Ketsa.

"I'm not hungry," Ketsa said, "You go ahead." That was no help. Annie wanted to know if she'd die if she ate this great looking food being offered to her by strangers. Ms. Dunlop was the one to answer.

"I thought my rice meal at lunch would hold me over for the day, but now, well, I'd love some lemon rice. How kind of you," Ms. Dunlop said. "How about you girls?"

Lori slept on, Jen declined, but Annie quickly answered, "Sure," and Ketsa decided she'd have a little after all.

They made up two more plates and lifted three forks from a bag. So they use forks, Annie thought, instead of fingers. Annie wondered who or what decided how things were done in this country.

Hema and Vani, sisters, introduced themselves. They had been to Hyderabad to visit family, just back from travels to the Ganges River. On Ms. Dunlop's invitation, they moved over into the main compartment area, sitting across from Annie and Ketsa, and chatted as they ate dinner together.

"You going to Coimbatore too?" Ketsa asked.

"Yes, our home is not far from there. Our husbands are brothers."

"You live in the same house?"

"Yes. In the family home with their parents and our children." They brought out pictures of the kids and passed them around – Vani's two boys and Hema's little girl. "It's hard to leave them," Hema said, then grinned and added, "but it was nice to travel without them for once. They'll see their grandparents in another month, when they come to Coimbatore."

Talk turned to the present – that the girls were headed for MMIS, a school the women knew of, having worked in a nearby village as a part of their college service project. They had both attended Madurai Women's College, just a few hours away from MMIS, on the plains. They currently ran a quilting cooperative for women who had become newly independent, fleeing abuse.

Hema fetched her bag and scooped another spoonful of lemon rice onto each of their plates.

"The last woman wanting to join us had three little girls," she said. "Her husband beat her for five years, so finally she and the children came to us for help. We didn't have a place for them to stay that first evening, so since she was a Christian, we took them to the pastor of one of our churches for help. He assured us he would find something. She never came back to the Co-op, so we went looking. Two days later the pastor's wife explained that he had taken them back to the husband's house, where they belonged."

"It's not always easy," Vani added. "In fact, it's almost never easy."

"That's shitty," Ketsa said.

The women looked surprised, then Hema looked right at Ketsa and answered, "Yes, it is 'shitty.' And until the abuse stops, it's important that these women at least have a way to escape it. The quilts they make are beautiful. Sometime you must come visit our co-op and see them for yourselves."

"I'd like to do that, Hema," Annie said. Ketsa, Jen, and Ms. Dunlop nodded.

"We just had a quilt show in Chennai in early December and sold thirty-five of the forty quilts we took with us. As we were boxing up the last five, a couple from Australia decided to buy all of them and offered to help us make sales contacts in Australia and the US." Vani reached into another of their bags and lifted out a flier about the show, with pictures of the quilts. Annie had expected bright colors, with gods or elephants in the designs, and was surprised to see daisies and sunflowers and traditional quilt block designs like she had seen at the Oregon State Fair.

"You may keep it, if you wish," Hema said, "to remind you to come see us."

She looked around at them, then lifted a small glass bottle of water from her bag. "We're taking some water back home for blessing of the family."

"Oh my," Ms. Dunlop said. "Water from the Ganges?"

Hema nodded.

"I always thought I'd go in person, but I never have." Her voice held a sense of awe that surprised Annie. It was just river water, after all, though Annie had heard the Ganges River was considered something special.

What happened next happened quickly, before Annie could think what she needed to do or not do. Hema reached forward and took Ms. Dunlop's hand in hers, turning it palm upward. Ms. Dunlop automatically cupped it to receive the gift, and Hema poured a few drops of the water into the center of her palm. Raising her own palm to her lips in illustration, Hema said, "Drink it." But instead Ms. Dunlop asked, "May I?" and tapped her forehead, as the woman had done with the colored powder in the temple in Hyderabad. Hema nodded, and with dampness glistening in her eyes, Ms. Dunlop dipped the tip of her index finger into the water and placed it on her forehead, then leaned over and did the same on the foreheads of Jen, Ketsa, and at last, Annie.

Hema twisted the cap back on the bottle and slipped it back into the bag. For a moment, no one spoke. Annie sensed that something important had just happened, though she didn't know what.

"Thank you for sharing such a precious gift with us," Ms. Dunlop said.

"You're welcome."

Hema and Vani collected the dinner things and packed the remaining food back in their bags. Vani took a few steps across the aisle and threw the used paper plates out the bars of the train window. They went back to their seats and, tucking their feet up underneath their saris, chatted quietly in a language other than the English they had just been using.

Annie watched the lights from villages flicker by as they rolled on, and looked out at the occasional highway crossing where cars or a bullock cart or a bus stopped to let the train through. Eventually they all decided to sleep and took their sheets and travel pillows from their bags. They stood and raised the backs of the long seats they had been leaning against, slipping them into the chains that converted them from seatbacks to bunks. They put their sheets and pillows on the bunks, and covered Lori, still asleep on the top berth.

"Not everyone goes 2nd Class, three-tier," Ms. Dunlop said. "I have friends who only travel 1st Class AC. But I wanted this purposefully for you girls. AC is certainly not needed in January, and you meet the nicest people traveling 2nd class." She nodded toward Hema and Vani.

Annie unclipped the strand of jasmine blossoms from her hair and tied it around one of the bars on the window at the end of her lower berth. She tucked her backpack safely in at her side, stretched out, and settled into the gentle rocking of the train.

Annie didn't know what a 1st Class train ride would be like, but she knew that this was much better than sitting up for two days on the airplane coming over, trying to sleep against the window, or trying not to sleep in the airports en route, afraid she'd miss the announcement of her flight.

"Thank you, God, for Indian trains with seats that make into beds," she whispered, "and for Ms. Dunlop knowing where we're going, and Vani and Hema helping ladies make quilts and stay safe. Thank you for lemon rice and chai, and important water. Thank you for tomorrow coming." Annie sighed and added, "And thank you for not being a cow." She closed her eyes and let herself slip into the rhythm of the night's journey, as the cool, jasmine-scented breeze blew against her face.

Ketsa leaned her head out from the bunk above Annie's. "Are you asleep, Annie?" she whispered.

"Yes," Annie answered.

"Sorry. I just wanted to say it was fun today."

"It was for me too," Annie said. "I'm really glad our group got this village trip and time in Hyderabad before we start school. It's almost like if I had to go home now for some reason, it would still be worth it."

"Ditto here," Ketsa said. Then she added in a whisper, "Hey, did we just get baptized? Because I've never been baptized before that I know of."

Annie looked over at Hema and Vani. They too had turned their seats into beds and appeared to be asleep.

"Shhhh," Annie whispered. "No, we didn't. That's not how baptism is done."

"Did we worship a Hindu river then?"

"Of course not!" Annie said. "We just let Ms. Dunlop tap our foreheads, that's all. Go to sleep, Ketsa."

"Okay, then. But it seemed more special than that." She paused and then sang softly, "Iyo Iyo."

Annie smiled. She thought she sang back a soft, "Iyo Iyo,

woo-hee, woo-hee," but it was just as likely that she only imagined it as she drifted into sleep, awaiting the dawning of the new day that would, if all went as planned, take them high into the cool, green Palani Hills of Tamil Nadu and to their home for the next five months.

Occasional lights flashed through the bars of the windows at her head, stirring her from sleep as they passed through a station, or stopped at one. Sometime in the early morning Hema crawled out of the top bunk across the aisle and slipped down to awaken Vani. Annie heard her whisper to Ms. Dunlop that they were getting off at the next stop as it was closer to their home than the Coimbatore station. Annie knew they'd have to get up soon, but it was still dark and she wanted to sleep. She also realized that she loved Indian trains. "It's a very fine day," she hummed silently in her head, "for you and me," as she drifted back to sleep.

CHAPTER 32

A small bus with a big sign "Megha Malai International School" awaited them at the Coimbatore station. While Ms. Dunlop talked with the driver, the girls loaded their things into the back and then settled into the seats for the ride that took them through Coimbatore, into hillsides dotted with huge white wind turbines, and alongside villages. Annie felt like an eavesdropper, able to watch without being seen, looking into backyards at a woman doing her laundry, slapping cloth on a stone beside a well; a school girl in uniform rushing out of a doorway and grabbing the arm of a little boy, dragging him back to the house; dogs nipping at each other; men gathered around a tea stall here, and out there in the fields, walking along behind bullocks. Then again into the hills with more turbines.

"This looks like the hills on the Washington side of the Columbia River," Annie said, but everyone was sleeping, so she took out her camera and clicked a few shots to email to her uncle who worked in wind energy in Minnesota.

"And this could be on the Old Highway in the Gorge," Annie said as the mini-bus began the ascent into the hills. "Wake up, you guys! Look where we are. This is beautiful!" If it weren't for the monkeys and the hairpin curves, Annie could have imagined she was home in Oregon, on the Scenic Highway that connected a series of waterfalls in the Columbia River Gorge. Then she glanced down at the yellow-green coconut beside her on the seat, a thin orange straw sticking out of the hole holding the cool coconut water inside, and the rice packet, neatly folded and tied in a banana leaf. John, the mini-bus driver had bought them snacks before they started up the steep Ghat Road. Well, maybe it's not exactly like Oregon, she thought to herself.

The bus stopped momentarily at a small temple. John handed some coins out the window to a man who had been sitting in the shade of a nearby tree.

"*Japam. Puja*," Ms. Dunlop explained. "He'll do worship for our safety."

"Oh, great," Annie whispered under her breath, looking closely at the temple, "an elephant this time." As they wound their way up the mountain, the road narrowed to a single lane at times, and the sharp drop-offs made Annie nervous. "Jesus Saves" messages painted onto the rock at blind corners didn't ease her worry. She couldn't tell how far down they would plummet, but it was steep and out of sight. She, in some odd way, felt comforted that this man behind the wheel had been concerned enough about them arriving at MMIS safely that he had asked for help, even if it was from a plaster of paris elephant.

ANNIE NEVER KNEW if the boy Aziz appointed himself to be at the Main Gate when the bus arrived at MMIS or if someone had posted him there officially as part of a welcoming committee. But he was there, full force, and she would never forget it. The bus stopped just inside the gate and within seconds, Aziz was on the bus, handing out bottles of cold *Guav-oh!* juice, telling them their journey of half a world was over at last and welcome to MMIS. He obviously knew John and rattled off something to him in some other language, then introduced himself to Ms. Dunlop, and explained that they could unload their bags in front of Performing Arts and that he'd round up some of his fellow PEERS, student leaders, to help carry their things to the dorms.

Annie hadn't expected that they would have PEERS here like in Ridgeway, and then she realized what Aziz had just said. Dorms. Plural.

It never dawned on her that they wouldn't all four be assigned to the same dorm. Ms. Dunlop introduced Aziz to them – Ketsa, from Washington, D.C., Lori from New Orleans, Jen, from Maine, and Annie, from Oregon.

He nodded to each one in turn. "I'm Aziz, from Jaffna." Then turning to Annie, he said, "I've been as close as Davis, California. My uncle lives there, but I've never made it to Oregon." He smiled and added, "Yet. But I want to go to Smith Rock."

Annie assumed Smith Rock must be somewhere in Oregon. She tried to remember if she'd ever heard of Jaffna. Maybe it was in North India, she thought, where they had a camel fair? Or was it in the Middle East? In any case, she could tell that Aziz was Indian, and Jaffna was evidently a big enough city to sell stone-washed jeans with holes in the knees, Bob Marley t-shirts, bright red running shoes, and a multi-colored knit hat that Danny would try to win off Aziz in some kind of bet. Annie stared at him as he told Ms. Dunlop that the Principal was out of station but the Vice Principal and Dean would meet her at tea in Staff Lounge at four o'clock. *Chaar baje,* Annie thought to herself, and smiled. When Aziz turned back toward Annie and saw her looking his way, he broke into a grin that gave her goosebumps.

"This is the chapel," Aziz pointed out as the bus moved away from the Main Gate. "It's compulsory for the little kids, but not us, though some really good stuff goes on in there besides church. We have a pianist that you won't believe. And a kid from Norway who plays clarinet better than Kenny G plays sax. We did *Godspell* in the chapel last year, clown faces and all.

"And that's called Covered Courts – CC for short," he pointed out, "dodge ball, basketball, and PE classes when it's rainy and we can't use the fields. We have a rock concert and some assemblies there too." The van slowly moved past the buildings up the driveway to the center of the campus. "That old stone building over there is the library. Good place, for several reasons. Do any of you happen to be rock climbers?" he asked.

Annie didn't follow the tie in of libraries to rock climbing, but Aziz went right on.

"My climbing partner just moved to New Zealand and isn't coming back this semester," he said. "None of you climb? I thought that was big in the States."

No one broke the silence, so Annie spoke. "I climbed the National Guard rock tower at the State Fair last summer. Twice. Does that count?"

"We could count it," he laughed. "There aren't many new students coming in this semester, and I'm desperate for a belayer around here, so yes, it definitely counts. Oops, we just passed Tresham, one of the Upper School girls' dorms," he said, motioning its way. "I think one of you is in there. And here is Performing Arts, where we have daily assembly. Compulsory, all grades. The van stops here, but the other three girls' dorms are over there in the trees."

A small group of students came out of the Performing Arts building and gathered around the van. Ketsa turned to Annie in the seat behind her and whispered, "If I make a big stink, do you think they'll put us in the same dorm?"

"It's worth a try," Annie answered.

Ketsa shrugged, grabbed her backpack, and headed for the bus door.

They both ended up in Tresham, without the stink, along with thirty other returning girls – from Korea, Nepal, India, Canada, Tanzania, Bhutan, Jordan, Bangladesh, and England. A huge world map, with photos of the girls mounted on their home countries, was in the entryway hall. Annie would come back and locate Aziz's Jaffna when she wasn't loaded down with suitcases. Among the photos were Annie's and Ketsa's, pinned to both sides of the US, though somebody had reversed their locations. Annie had never heard of Bhutan, and wouldn't have been able to say exactly where Tanzania was, if the girl helping bring one of her suitcases in hadn't pointed herself out on the map as they passed it.

"That's me – Tanaz," she said.

Annie had stayed a week in a college dorm for a leadership camp, and Tresham reminded her of that dorm – old, but majestic, with high ceilings and heavy built-in wooden beds with drawers underneath. Their college host had apologized for the rooms, and said they would be renovated soon, but Annie felt sorry they'd do that. At least nobody here acted as if Tresham needed renovating. The rooms had tables for desks and a standing wardrobe for each resident. The bathrooms down the hall were pretty normal, Annie thought, except for little water heaters hanging on the wall.

Tanaz saw Annie looking up at them. "They finally got new geezers over the break," she said, pointing to the long row of water heaters.

"Geezers?" Annie grinned. "You're kidding!"

"No, really. They're all new. Let's just hope we have enough hot water for everyone's shower this semester. I never could get up early, not even for hot water, so this will be nice."

"Shower?" Annie asked. "You mean we don't have to take bucket baths?"

Tanaz laughed, as if Annie had just made a joke. Ketsa smiled and whispered, "And did you notice – the toilets don't open onto the tracks either." It was good, of course, this bright, tiled, sparkling clean bathroom, and Annie was relieved, but she also wondered if Tanaz even knew that people in a village one night's train ride away did use buckets for baths.

The dorm rooms opened onto a courtyard filled with trees

and plants, surrounded by a tall stone wall. This part isn't much like home, Annie thought, and she wondered if she'd feel trapped inside the wall. Annie looked closely at it, and the thought flitted through her mind that she probably could climb it if she needed out, or in.

STUDENTS NEW FOR second semester, plus a group of PEERS and the student council had gathered for orientation. "Take off one shoe and throw it into the box," the PEER leader called out. "Okay," she continued, dumping the huge box upside down in the middle of the dining hall floor, shoes going every which way. "Now find a shoe! Any shoe but your own." Annie reached down for a flash of color hidden by the white and black and brown pile of shoes and sandals, and picked up a bright red running shoe. "Now, without any talking, go find the person who matches your 'glass slipper.' Go ahead and talk – ask their name, what they like best about MMIS, and what they hope for this semester."

"Aziz, right?" Annie faked uncertainty to the owner of the other red shoe. "What do you like best about…"

"Mr. Chettri's Indian Cooking classes; hiking season; S.S.; cricket – tournament coming in March, by the way; Field Trip Week – we did the Kerala backwaters this year, too bad you missed it; chicken curry on Sundays and banana pudding; our SL village project, Service Learning, if you haven't heard of it; and the Dean's decision to finally provide TP in all the Bs. Student Council had to work on that one for two months. Bs are bathrooms," he concluded.

"Didn't she mean one thing you like best?" Annie laughed.

"Okay." He paused, then answered, "The fact that this place was built a hundred years ago out of stone that has great handholds and so far, I haven't been kicked off them. Those two go together as one. But if we have to report back to the whole group, just say 'TP in the B.'"

"And your hope for the semester?" Annie asked.

He grinned. "That you turn out to be a good belayer."

"Okay, then," Annie said, her face flushing hot. Handing back his shoe, and suddenly shy, Annie turned to a girl she hadn't met yet who was waiting at her side, holding Annie's other sandal.

"Is this yours?" the girl asked.

"Yes. Hi, I'm Annie," she said, reaching out for her sandal.

"I'm Leeza. Welcome to Megha Malai. Have you had time to figure out what you like best about us?"

"I guess I'd say ..." Red running shoes popped into her mind, along with the funny kid who wears them, but of course she couldn't say that to this Leeza girl she didn't know. "Probably the courtyard at my dorm or maybe how friendly everybody is."

"And your hopes?"

"That I survive."

Leeza looked at her intently. "Really? Are you scared it won't be good here?"

Annie knew it was just a warm-up activity, not a time to pour out her heart, but Leeza was asking and somehow made it okay for Annie to acknowledge the fear that had been inside her from the time she arrived in Mumbai, and at the moment was just under her skin. She answered honestly. "I want it to be wonderful, and I hope it will be, but inside I'm scared. I'm afraid I'll miss home way too much, and I'll mess up on grades, and I'll get sick with some weird disease, and it'll all be a big mistake." Tears filled her eyes and Annie wiped them away, embarrassed.

Leeza pulled Annie into a hug. "No one knows what the future holds, but I guarantee you, Annie, it won't be a mistake that you're here."

Her words were calming. "Thank you," Annie said. "I just

worry sometimes." Annie was reminded that there was something too close to the surface that kept coming back, a feeling that she couldn't let go, that something would go wrong here, that God wouldn't care, and that she was too far from home and the people who did.

"You'll like it, Annie. Really. And you have the best roommate – Naveena. She's from Chennai. You'll love her. She'll be up in a couple of days. I know it will be okay."

"Thanks, Leeza," Annie said.

Annie learned more about MMIS in that one activity than in all the reading material the scholarship program had sent her, not to mention everything she'd read on the school's website and in the email attachments they'd sent from the Admissions Office. She didn't get some of the abbreviations or know what Eid and Holi were or where Guiliano's Restaurant was or the Tibetan stalls around the lake, but she had a hunch that there was a lot more to explore and to experience than she had realized, and that the students were glad to be back at school.

When it was her turn to introduce Aziz to the group, she panicked and forgot everything he had said, except "TP in the B," but the group clapped, so she knew it was a legitimate thing to be thankful for. She remembered his hope clearly, but changed it slightly to "Find a good belayer this semester." Several people laughed. Evidently some of these people knew of Aziz's rock-climbing hobby. She looked over at him, but he was shaking his head no, as if to clarify that he hadn't said just any good belayer. He pointed directly at her and nodded.

She had a funny feeling that Danny would tell her to watch out. "I'm not going to be a rock climber, Danny," she could hear herself say, "or if I am, by any chance, I'm not falling in love, so you don't have to worry." She grinned just thinking of Danny's farewell words at the airport, and then she realized that Aziz had seen her grin and was smiling back.

CHAPTER 33

"**W**hat classes did you get?" Ketsa asked as they stood in the lunch line.

"Good ones, I think," Annie said. "And we get so many. My high school at home has five periods a day, all long classes, which I don't mind there, but here I get nine different subjects, plus study hall."

"Which are ...?" Ketsa asked.

"Environmental Science, Maths – they add an s, did you notice? – Modern Religious Thought, which the kids call MRT, PE, SL – which is Service Learning, even Hindi..."

"Me too!" Ketsa said. "I told them I wanted Urdu or Kannada for my language, so I could talk if I go back to Gandhinagar, but my advisor said Hindi would work for Urdu. They're basically the same some way. Isn't that cool? Did you get Indian Cooking?"

"Yeah, and Tabla. How about you?"

Ketsa clapped her hands over her head and whooped. "All right! Girl, we are going to drum up a storm. Promise me you'll come to D.C. and do a tabla concert with me in the White House."

"Of course," Annie replied, "anytime." And then, pushing her tray along in front of the food counter, looking down at the stainless-steel tubs of food, she asked, "What in the world is this stuff?"

"Ladiesfinger here," replied the server behind the counter, "and bitter gourd and chickpeas here."

"Oh, thanks, good," Annie quickly replied.

He followed along across from her, naming each dish. "Sliced beet root, tomato, cucumber, curds, and lime pickle. Papadum." The question had been intended for Ketsa, and once they moved through the line, Ketsa answered, lifting a little of the ladiesfinger on her fork.

"Okra, girl. Can't get too much of this, at least not the way my mama makes it." They headed up the stairs to the upper dining hall and found a table next to an open window.

"My mom would croak if she knew I was eating white rice, and white bread toast and chocolate cereal for breakfast, plus drinking chai and coffee. Those are banned items at home," Annie said. "Mom started us on this whole grain, low sugar thing last year. But I like the taste of white rice, so what can I say? They force it on us, right?"

Lori and Jen waved from across the dining hall and came to join them at their table by the window. "We'll probably get in trouble if we hang out with only us," Jen said, "but let's risk it. I'm dying to know how you guys are doing and what your dorm is like, who your roomies are, and your classes."

"And how you got that *Guav-oh!* juice guy to fall in love with you so fast," Lori added.

"What!?"Annie protested.

"What!?" Ketsa mimicked. "This girl is one innocent babe who swears nobody is in love with nobody, but seeings as how you two noticed it as well, then I think we have something on our hands here."

"There is no one in love with me," Annie insisted. "Besides, I promised."

All eyes were on Annie. "Promised who, what?" Ketsa asked. "You holdin' back on me, girl? You got some boyfriend back in Oregon I haven't even heard about?"

"I haven't even dated, Ketsa, so how could I have a boyfriend?"

"Really?" Jen asked. "You've never dated?"

Annie was irritated by Jen's reaction, but she knew it was

curiosity, not a criticism, so she answered honestly. "My folks had this rule. Group outings only until I was sixteen, which was last May. I guess I got used to it, and since I didn't like anybody anyway, it was fine. Except then along came Param last year, who is from India actually, at least when he was little. He is very awesome..." Annie paused.

"And..." Lori asked.

"And not much. His parents want him to marry an Indian girl who understands 'how things are with families,' and my parents would freak if I married a non-Christian, which he is, being a Sikh, so they don't want me to even date him. I have never gone against my parents in my whole life. Well, my mom on a few little things, but never my dad. I think he'd be hurt. But I'm thinking it's crazy to have rules like that. So there I am."

"What are you going to do?" Ketsa asked.

"Well, nothing for five whole months. After that I'm not sure. But I'm not letting him go. He's way too wonderful. That's about as far as I got trying to figure it out. Actually, I'm hoping I learn something in Modern Religious Thought that would prove to Mom and Dad that Christians and Sikhs are closer to the same than anyone at home realizes, or that we're the same enough to not worry about it, or something. Or that I just get the courage to do what I want to do."

"Which is?"

Annie grinned. "I have no idea." She shrugged. "And then of course there's Danny."

"Whoa!" Ketsa cried. "I have so misjudged you, girl. How many other men do you have on the line?"

"Ketsa, I don't have anyone on the line! Danny's my best bud, from pre-kindergarten days, that's all. And always will be, I hope. I don't want to mess that up. And I don't even know this Aziz guy."

"I'm taking bets," Ketsa said. "Ten to one you definitely know him before this semester is up. I accept dollars or rupees."

Annie laughed. "You'd love Danny. He bets on everything. Never pays up, though, or collects, for that matter."

"How would he bet on this one?" Jen asked.

Annie fiddled with her fork. "He'd … he'd tell me to … Hey, I ate that whole pile of chickpeas without even thinking how they tasted," she concluded.

"Spicy," Ketsa said.

A NEW WAVE of middle school students came up the stairs, filling the tables around them. The girls had chatted the lunch period away.

"Let's meet again on the Green before tea time," Ketsa said, "and if your roommates are around, I want to meet them. Hey, I better get a move on it. I have PE next… Crap! I left my PE clothes back at the dorm. And they lock the dorm gate until after school!" Ketsa threw her hands into the air. "So I start out with a zero for the day? And I love hockey, which we're supposed to play today."

A girl from the next table walked over to Ketsa. "I'm Daychen, and this is Hannah," she said, introducing another classmate. "I have an extra set of PE clothes in my locker if you'd like to borrow them. I don't have PE until tomorrow."

"Sweet," Ketsa answered. "You're from Bhutan, right? In our dorm. I'm Ketsa. Thanks for saving my skin."

"The exact thing happened to me last semester. That's why I always keep the extra set of clothes in my locker now."

Ketsa headed off with Daychen, and Annie left for another of her classes, Service Learning, curious to find out what Aziz meant about their SL village being one of his favorite things about MMIS.

The class was small, a dozen students, and they sat on cushions on the floor or on benches along the walls.

"I've been back out to Chinnakadu during the break," the

Service Learning teacher, Mr. Hausden, said. "The biosand filters are working fine, and the village *panchayat* wants us to work with them on another fifteen, if we can, this semester. Oh, would some of you catch up our new students, Annie and Sandesh, on our SL village? First, where it is, a little about their potable water project, what the *panchayat* is, and what we've been able to do with them. Bijeen, you'll probably want to tell about where we stay when we go out there."

The class laughed, so Annie knew there was a story to hear, which Bijeen offered. The students had worked with the people of this village and stayed overnight in their school building, all except for him. He had insisted on sleeping outside and was surrounded by a troop of monkeys which robbed his open backpack of its food stash, and sent him dashing out of his sleeping bag, screaming, to the safety of the school building. He learned his lesson though, he said, which is not to scream, hard to avoid if a monkey has just jumped on your sleeping bag, you in it. So second best would be to set up motion sensor cameras at night so you could have some good action photos for your final SL paper.

"That would have earned me an A for sure, right, Mr. Hausden?" Bijeen concluded.

"You got an A," Mr. Hausden said, grinning. "Now, could someone relate how we chose the project?"

It was probably all review for the students, but it was exciting for Annie to listen to them. Community service hours were required at Ridgeway in order to stay in National Honor Society, but there was no special project that they all worked on together, except the one time the school granted a group of them eight hours for repainting the bleachers in the football stadium. Annie loved helping build a house in Mexico and volunteering with Tani at Maplewood Care Center last summer, but those didn't have anything to do with school.

Here the students had SL class and had been working together with the people of this village.

"We worked with the village council, called the *panchayat*," someone explained, "to learn their top priority need. They said it was water – safe drinking water. They said long term they want a tube well drilled, and a reservoir with a piped water system, but that's too far away, so for now they have to find some way of making the stream water safer to drink."

"We got on the internet," another student picked up, "and found out that this organization from Canada is already here in Tamil Nadu doing a water project. So we got them to come up to MMIS and put on a workshop for our SL program and for representatives from several villages in the Nilgiri Hills, including people from Chinnakadu. They showed how to make and set up these biosand filters."

"After four weeks in use, they eliminate 99% plus of the bad stuff in the water," another student explained to the newcomers, "and that's huge when so many people here suffer from waterborne diseases. Huge. Kids die from diarrhea sometimes. But once the filter's built, they figure it will last for thirty years. The lady from Canada said she's personally been back to Nicaragua where they helped put these in homes, and she found them still there in use after ten years. Very same filter, working fine."

Mr. Hausden asked a student to play the DVD he had made of one of their workdays in the village last semester. Annie saw the filters being made, as well as MMIS students playing tag with kids from the village, and then a girl leading a call and response camp song.

"That's really impressive," Annie said, and then added, "and who's the girl leading the songs?"

There was a giggle behind her. A girl held out her hand. "It's me, Vidhya. Glad to meet you, Annie. Kids love singing, even if they don't exactly know what the words mean. Camp songs are a great way of breaking the ice."

"I know," Annie said. "I went to camp all through grade school and junior high, and we sang that very same song." She discreetly wrote the name Vid-ee-uh on the palm of her hand so she wouldn't forget. Annie wondered what camp she might have gone to. In India or some other country? She had guessed wrong about Leeza, thinking she was from India, only to find out later that she was American and grew up in Chicago. She met a girl who looked Indian, but was from Brussels and had come to MMIS because her family wanted her to know something of their Indian roots. Looks didn't tell her much here.

"We're expanding our village program," Mr. Hausden said. "Beyond water. Do you remember the speaker who came last November from Madurai Women's College, Ms. Jayashree? She works in tribal and village health and is doing research on women's issues in the villages. She asked me if we'd help by interviewing women in Chinnakadu. It would be a project for girls only, at least the interviews," Mr. Hausden continued, "and though it isn't a requirement for everyone, some of you would need to be Tamil speakers."

The room was quiet. Then Vidhya spoke. "I'm in," she said.

Annie slipped her hand up. "I'd like to do that too," she said, "but I'm sorry, I don't know Tamil."

"No problem. *Nan irukiran.* I'm there for you," Vidhya answered.

CHAPTER 34

"**I**'d like to know why you signed up for Modern Religious Thought," Mr. Das said to the class, "...what you hope to accomplish in here this semester." Annie knew she shouldn't have sat in the second row, the first row with anybody in it. She needed more time than that to figure out what she could say – that she wondered what Modern Religious Thought would even mean to a bunch of kids of different religions, that she wanted to learn about Sikhs in order to justify dating Param when she got back home, or maybe that she wasn't sure about God anymore and wondered if there was anything modern about that. She decided to say that her advisor told her to take the class, but luckily, Mr. Das started in the back of the room.

"I liked your Ethics class," a kid in the last row said. "I decided to come back for more."

"Thank you, Hajime," Mr. Das responded. "Others?"

"Religion is a big part of life, at least for some people." It was a girl, maybe from Korea or Japan. "Sometimes I think it's important and other times I'm not so sure. I want to know what other people think, especially people my age." She didn't say what her religion was.

"Frankly, I think things are a little too Christian-y around here," a girl said. Annie looked back and saw it was Vidhya from her SL class. "I want a chance to defend Hinduism," she said. Annie felt a twinge of disappointment. She supposed that somebody who knew camp songs and wanted to help village women would be a Christian or at least would like Christianity and avoid cow and elephant gods. Evidently not.

"How many faiths or paths do we have represented in this class?" Mr. Das asked. For the first time, it dawned on Annie that she should scan the room for turbans. One. In the back row.

"Call them out," he said.

"Islam," two boys said simultaneously.

"Buddhism." It was a girl from Annie's dorm.

"Me too," the girl from maybe Korea or Japan added.

"Come on, you Hindus," Vidhya said. "Speak up." Several kids waved or raised their hands.

"Sikhs?" Mr. Das questioned.

Annie raised her hand, then realized the awful mistake she had made and quickly retracted it.

"The new girl is a Sikh?" she heard someone say. "Mr. Das, we have a Sikh up there." It was said seriously, like Annie really could be a Sikh in that kid's mind.

Flabbergasted, Annie intended to explain that she wanted to learn about Sikhs but that she was a Christian. Someone said, "Let her speak for herself, Sam," and a response came, "But she put her hand up."

Mr. Das turned to Annie and asked, "What do you hope to learn? Annie, is it?"

She nodded, then answered, "I guess I'm in this class to learn about other religions and maybe why God lets people die." It was the truth, but she felt embarrassed by what she just said. There was silence.

A voice in the row behind her said, "I'm Sikh." Like he was irritated with Annie for drawing attention to Sikhs or something. Annie turned around to look, supposing she had missed the turban in her earlier count, but he was not wearing one. He did have long hair, but it was pulled back in a ponytail. Watered down version of a Sikh, she thought. Not much to learn there. She didn't like him, whoever he was. Then talking directly to her rather than the class, the boy said, "Death is a crap shoot. That's all."

"We will have some natural groupings over questions," Mr. Das explained, "and of course, I can assign you randomly if you prefer. Since Ajit and Annie have expressed interest in a similar question, let's have this section take 'The role of God in life and death.' Other questions for discussion will be...." And here he turned and wrote on the whiteboard:

> The role of God in life and death
> Talking with God – the efficacy of prayer
> Images and imaginings of the Holy
> Religious practice as a formulator of moral codes
> When religions clash
> Positives and negatives of various faith practices

Mr. Das posted signs on the walls of the classroom – Prayer, Images, Life and Death, Morals, Clash, Pro's and Con's – and the class divided up into groups around each one. Annie noticed no one chose Prayer, and the biggest group was with "Clash." Feeling obligated by the teacher's directions, Annie joined the boy Ajit and a girl for "Life and Death."

"Today I want you to introduce yourselves in your group and give a short personal example of the topic from your life or others you know. For tomorrow you will need to bring to class a one-page summary of your group's comments and a library resource that in some way applies to your discussion. I am available for questions."

"Can the whole group submit the same one-page summary?" the boy Sam called out.

"Nice try, Sam," Mr. Das replied.

The girl, Irfana, opened Annie's group's discussion. She told about a neighbor who was killed when a coconut sitting on a window ledge in a second story flat rolled off the ledge and fell to the ground, striking the woman on the head on its way down, killing her instantly. She didn't know the lady, so it wasn't as sad as it could have been, but she had thought how many times she and her family walked in front of the building and could have been killed if something that random happened. The only good thing that came of it, Irfana said, was that the woman's mother-in-law announced that they weren't going to cry for the rest of their lives and they would start doing something positive. So she put all three of the kids in voice lessons. Classical Indian voice. They're really good singers now. They've traveled to Mumbai and Delhi and other places to perform for big crowds.

It seemed bizarre, this person whom Annie had never met, telling her something like this. She wondered if the story was really true, or if the girl made it all up, right there on the spot. But when Irfana said it had happened two years back and the children's father was her dad's good friend who was still so sad that her dad cried because he didn't know how to help, she decided it was real.

It reminded Annie of what she hoped to forget about in India, and though she hadn't planned to tell anyone, she found herself saying, "I had a friend who was in my class at home. Some of my friends, including her, went to check out a corn-field to see if we could use it for a maze for this party that we do every year before school, in a corn maze ...." Annie paused. She didn't know if they even knew what a corn maze was.

"And?" Irfana pressed.

"And she was hit by the corn harvester. The medics came, and they were going to call Life Flight. That's this helicopter that gets them to a bigger hospital fast, but she was already dead. Somehow this boy, Jackson Evans, thought it was his fault, but it wasn't." Annie was remembering out loud, more than talking to the others. "I was the one who was planning the party. The thing is, God could have easily prevented it.

We could have played volleyball like my mom suggested. It makes me feel that God doesn't have anything to do with life or death, or if He does, He's wa ..." She was going to say "warped," but thought better of her words, and wanted to give God the benefit of the doubt in front of these people who might already have the wrong idea of Him. "It's confusing," she finished. Annie sat quietly and waited for Ajit, thinking about skunk naps.

"I think everybody at MMIS but you knows why Das would put me in this group," he said to Annie.

"Why?" she asked.

He didn't answer. Maybe Irfana didn't know either, because she didn't explain anything. Instead she said, "It's hard to figure out why such awful things happen, when looking back you could see that a little thing would have prevented it."

"I know," Annie said.

Mr. Das gave further instructions on their assigned paper, and the bell rang. Ajit gathered up his books and rushed to the door. As Annie and Irfana walked out of the classroom together Annie said, "I know of a girl about my age who burned to death when a kerosene stove exploded next to her."

"Wow, that happens in the States too?" Irfana said.

"What do you mean?"

"Well, just that I didn't know you have those problems in the U.S. too, and... "

"And?" Annie didn't get where this was going.

"And... Well, I thought with love marriages, maybe you wouldn't have dowry deaths or bride burnings."

Annie stopped in her tracks. Shocked, she turned to face Irfana. "What are you talking about?"

"You know. Like a bride who hasn't paid enough dowry, burned to death, to get rid of her," Irfana said. She looked into Annie's eyes. "Or maybe you don't know."

"On purpose? Are you crazy? The girl I was talking about wasn't even married. People would never do that!" Annie cried.

"Sure. No, of course not. I didn't mean anything." Irfana's voice trailed off as she hurried up the steps in front of Annie and turned toward the Performing Arts building. Others drifted out of the classroom, and Vidhya caught up with Annie.

"Assembly's next," Vidhya said. "Going that way?"

"Uh-huh," Annie mumbled. Then she added, "Vidhya, I was in the Life and Death group. Somebody mentioned a kerosene fire. Have you ever heard of that in India?"

"It's so messed up, isn't it?" Vidhya answered. "Ghastly. I don't get the mentality. You'd think somebody in Delhi could just pronounce it insane as well as criminal and that would be the end of it. People are trying, and who knows, maybe in a few years it will be considered so shameful that it will end on its own. Tamil Nadu isn't bad compared to some places."

"What?" Annie asked.

"You're right. If it still happens at all, it's bad. I remember a dowry death in Chennai that happened last year. Not long afterwards, there was another one. The girl didn't die, but she has awful scars from it."

Annie was stunned. Did the whole world except her know about this? Or were Irfana and Vidhya just a coincidental minority? She decided she'd talk to Naveena about it at tea or maybe in the dorm at night. Annie had study hall after assembly. She signed out to go to the library to find her MRT resource on life and death, and came up with a book called *Questions That Hurt to Ask.* Then out of curiosity she went to an empty computer and Googled "bride deaths india burning" to see what she'd get. The search took 0.07 seconds to give her 1,190,000 entries.

"Holy crap!" Annie said. "Is this place hell or what?"

CHAPTER 35

"**A**nnie, wait up!" Aziz ran toward her and Naveena as they walked from the dining hall toward Tresham. "Hey, Naveena. How was break?"

"Good. I mostly did nothing. I loved it. Did you go home or to the States?"

"Both. I brought you something from California."

"Really?" The way Naveena said it brought a new thought to Annie. Maybe Naveena liked Aziz. Bummer. Annie knew she shouldn't care, but disappointment flitted through her mind. She wondered what kind of a souvenir Aziz would buy in the U.S. and bring back to Naveena, and why. Maybe he was just friendly and smiled at everybody, like he did her.

"You'll see. I'll bring it to class tomorrow. It's at dorm," he answered. Then to Annie: "Hey, I've been watching for you, but I didn't see you at dinner. Where do you hide out?"

"We ate upstairs tonight, but we weren't hiding out. I just wanted a quieter place."

"Didn't work, did it?" he asked. "Whoever designed the dining hall didn't think about sound. But it's great for singing. Have you tried it yet?"

Annie laughed. "Well, this is my first week, but no, I haven't tried singing in the dining hall. What? You rock climb and sing, both?"

"Not at the same time. Well, not always. But speaking of rock climbing...."

Two girls from Tresham came by just then and started

talking with Naveena. Aziz nodded toward the Covered Court. "Come on, I need to talk to you." Annie slipped away from the other girls, saying, "See you back at the dorm."

"Want to climb the rock wall with me?" Aziz asked.

"What rock wall? There really is one?"

"Yes. Out behind Performing Arts. Actually, it's the back of the building. Somebody had a good idea – use the stone that's already right here. It works for climbing. They added anchors to create a couple different routes up. But they let it all go when the staff who were into rock climbing left," he said. "So, it's all mine now. But I need a belayer. Like I said, the guy who climbed with me last semester didn't come back, and I haven't been able to recruit anybody else. So I have to find somebody who likes rock climbing."

"Me? I don't really know how to rock climb, Aziz, and I sure don't know how to belay anybody. I just did what the guys running the tower told me to do."

"I'll teach you. Most kids around here just aren't into it. I thought, maybe, since you climbed that tower... I need a partner. What do you think?"

"Now?" she asked.

"No. We have to be in dorm in fifteen minutes. We'd get busted if we tried skipping out at night. I learned that the hard way. But the back of Performing Arts is better than your National Guard towers, guaranteed."

"When?" Annie asked.

"Tomorrow morning. Early. There's this thing with adults. If we're out late or up late, we're bad. If we get up late in the morning, we're lazy, regardless of how many hours sleep we need or got. But if we get up early in the morning, then we're self-disciplined, role model kids. I don't get it, but that's their theory. Besides, they never suspect you of doing bad stuff at six a.m. So that's when I climb. Maybe 6:15, just as it's getting light."

"Bad stuff? They don't allow climbing then?"

"I wouldn't put it that way. I heard it was a big thing around here a couple years before I came. I asked some guys when I first got here, and they didn't think it was allowed, because nobody wanted to chaperone or knew how to climb, they said. Which is lame, because that's one of the reasons I was interested in this school. So I decided not to ask, officially. I just keep quiet and do my own thing. I figure if you don't make a big announcement or anything, nobody will stress. I just got bold when your bus came in because I still hadn't found a belayer. Even if I don't talk about it, some people know. But the only ones out checking on things early in the morning are the watchmen, and they all know me and can see I'm not hurting anything. I buy them chai from the stalls across from Main Gate. It has nothing to do with keeping quiet, of course. They're just cool guys who like chai as much as I do."

"But if we're not supposed to ..."

"Dean Carr knows I climb. I'm positive he does. But he hasn't asked me a thing about it this whole year, and he talks about everything else, so he would if he really wanted to know. It's not like our fingertips are going to wear down these old stone buildings."

"But I'm just here for one semester, Aziz. If I get kicked out it would be a total disgrace."

"You won't get kicked out, Annie. I guarantee it. Nobody will care what you do before breakfast. Kids go running around the lake in the mornings. There's even an early morning yoga class you can leave dorm early to go to. So come on, okay? I'll teach you how to belay."

She shook her head. "I really don't know how to climb, Aziz. I just tried it, that's all."

"That's what it takes," he said. "Annie, it'll look good on your college applications. Rock climbing is big these days. Just what admissions officers want to see. Better than good TOEFL or SAT scores."

Annie grinned. She had no idea what TOEFL was, but Aziz was so enthusiastic he sounded almost convincing.

"I assure you, at the top of this building is a view of the lake worth getting out of bed for, and I'll even bring *Guav-oh!*." He was beaming, and Annie couldn't resist.

"Okay, if you're sure we won't get in trouble."

"All right! Meet me at the side of Performing Arts at 6:15. If Tresham gates are still locked, then come at 6:30. We'll climb till breakfast." He turned and ran, then called back over his shoulder, "Wear shoes."

She wondered if he thought she'd go barefoot, then looked down at her sandals and guessed that they weren't what he wanted.

ANNIE SET HER alarm for six, and when it went off, she threw on her clothes, and to Naveena's sleepy inquiry if everything was okay, Annie answered that she was getting up early to study. Rocks, she whispered under her breath. Or maybe Aziz.

It was darker than Annie thought it would be, but the Tresham gates were unlocked. She decided that if Aziz wasn't there, she'd pretend she was running the loop through campus for exercise, then head back to Tresham and hop back in bed. But he was there, waiting, wearing his multi-colored knit hat as usual.

"Hi, Oregon," he said.

"Hi."

Annie slipped into the extra harness he brought, glad she had climbed the National Guard tower and knew a little about what to expect. "Are you good at this?" she asked. "I mean – safe?"

He looked her right in the eyes. "I've been climbing since I was ten. Any place in Sri Lanka that there's rock, my dad and I have done it. I've climbed in California, and Nepal and India.

If you want me to brag a little I will, but bottom line is – yes. I never free solo. I climb safe. I know how to belay – meaning the rope will hold you if you fall, and you won't fall more than the rope stretches. I joined a climbing club back home so I'd learn how to do it right, and was taught by some great people. On top of that, I've read lakhs of climbing books from their library."

"Lax of books?" Annie questioned.

"Okay, not lakhs, but way more than a lot of climbers ever read, I'm sure. A lot of books."

Annie didn't say anything, so Aziz continued with his credentials. "I've checked the anchor bolts they put in. They're solid. I've also done several routes outside campus with Mikhail, my friend from New Zealand, and a guy who ran an Eco-Tourist place in Megha Malai, who unfortunately moved to Madurai at the end of last year ..."

Annie interrupted. "Which we aren't doing. Ever! I'm not climbing real cliffs, Aziz."

"No pressure, Annie," he promised. "But you might start loving it." He pulled a coil of rope, and then two helmets, from his backpack. "And we wear these, just in case."

"In case what?" she asked.

"In case there's an earthquake and the top of the building breaks off and falls on our heads. Or just because we always do."

He showed her how he would be holding the rope to belay her, what he'd do in case she slipped, and how the knots would hold. Aziz moved behind a bougainvillea bush, then scrambled up a couple footholds to where he could reach behind a protruding stone, and flicked a looped cord loose. It fell to the ground in front of Annie.

"What's that?" she asked.

"That's how we get our rope up through the anchor at the top."

"How'd it get up there?" she asked, looking up at the cord running alongside the building.

"There are ways," he said.

As he tied their rope to the cord and hauled it up and through the top anchor, Aziz asked her what she knew about being lowered, and then about how the climb starts.

"They had us do that at the State Fair," she said. "I say, 'On belay?'"

"Yeah," he nodded. "Good."

"Then 'Climbing,'" she said.

"Right."

He hooked a chalk bag into the side of her harness and had her try a few holds from a standing position.

"And what do you holler if you're almost to the top and you lose your grip?" he asked.

"Save me! I'm dying!" Annie said.

"'Falling' will do, but 'Save me, I'm dying' might help make sure I'm not digging around in my backpack for a *Guav-oh!*"

"You better not! My life depends on you."

"Vice versa, you know," he said. "You'll be fine. For now just get a feel for the climb, and in a week or so we'll work on you belaying me. Only I just read an article in a climbing magazine that said you shouldn't team up with somebody you...." He stopped too suddenly.

"You what?"

"Somebody who forgets her shoes and wears sandals."

"Oops," Annie said. "I got ready in such a hurry. I didn't even think about it."

"It'll be okay," he said. "But sandals are about the worst thing to climb in. Barefoot works, but kills you after a while." He looked at her feet. "I'll bring one of my old pair of climbing shoes for you next time. They're way too tight for me, but I couldn't throw them out." Aziz rechecked her harness and the knots.

Annie stood up to the wall, dipped her fingertips in the chalk bag, and placed them on holds above her head. "On belay?" she said softly.

"What?"

"On belay!"

"Belay on."

"Climbing."

"Climb on."

Annie thought someone could make a camp song out of that routine, but it made her feel good to know that Aziz went by the rules and used clear communication to make sure everyone was ready. It made rock climbing seem more of a sport than something wild and crazy. Her fingers dipped in and out of the chalk bag, onto holds she found among the stones. She felt an ease she hadn't expected, as the strength in her arms and legs moved her up the side of the wall. Aziz took up the slack in the rope each time she reached and lifted herself to a new level.

"You're doing great!" he called. "There's a good set of holds just over to the left a little."

Annie shifted direction and continued up, until she finally paused and looked down at Aziz below her. "Oh, my gosh!" she said.

"Now about a meter more and you'll be above the eucy trees blocking your view. There's a rock that makes a kind of ledge to stand on too." She climbed on as he directed and turned slightly to glance over her shoulder.

"Keep the rope tight, Aziz!" she called, and then, "Oh, it's gorgeous!" In the distance she could see the mist rising on the lake, and the silvery rays of the sun hitting its surface. Around the perimeter was a red stone path, with runners and walkers already out. Tiffin sellers were rolling carts into place, and a small herd of cows had moved into the water to drink. "I'm going running there, starting today. It's so close, and so beautiful," Annie said. Looking out over the treetops gave her an exhilaration that crowded out the hesitation she had felt earlier. She leaned back away from the wall and checked the tension on the rope with her hand, letting her harness hold her. "You got me?" she asked.

"I do," Aziz answered.

"You sure?" she called.

"I've got you," he said.

Feet anchored firmly against the wall, Annie released her hands from the rope and shook out her fingers. She re-tested her balance, and then slowly raised her arms in the air. She held the stance, hovering there on the side of Performing Arts, above the treetops, breathing in the crisp cool of the morning. A feeling came over her that she was part of something big and wonderful.

Annie slowly lowered her hands to the rope. She looked down on Aziz. "Okay, I'm ready."

"Lean out a little. Keep your legs straight and just walk your feet down the wall," he instructed. "Just the way you said you did before. You can do it."

"But this is higher than the National Guard Tower."

"You'll be fine, Annie."

Pushing off from her position at the top of the wall, Annie walked herself down as Aziz fed the rope she needed. As her feet touched the ground she cried, "I'm a rock climber!" then looked around to make sure she hadn't made too much noise. No one was in sight. "Or maybe a stone building climber." She slipped out of the harness, still grinning, as Aziz handed her a bottle of *Guav-oh!*.

"Congrats, Annie. You did great. Let's celebrate."

"Thank you, Aziz. So did you. I'm still alive. Hey, where do you get this stuff?" Annie asked, lifting the guava juice to her lips.

"The shops outside Main Gate, but I keep a stash in my room. In my backpack too, for emergencies."

"I wonder if we have fizzy guava juice at home. It's really good!"

"You're welcome."

"So you've been doing this climbing since you were ten?" Annie asked. "Your parents must be a whole lot different than mine. I didn't even tell them about the National Guard tower until a couple months ago, and then just because it slipped out. I'm their only kid, and they're overly scared something will happen to me."

"So you think because I have two sisters, my mom and dad take me to rocks and say, 'Go for it,' like they'll still have two kids left if I fall?"

Annie laughed. "No! I just mean, I can't imagine my parents letting me rock climb for real when I was ten. Or even now, for that matter."

"Mine didn't, at first. Then my uncle, the one who lives in California now, came home from college and talked my dad into it. They went all over Sri Lanka. Finally my mom put her foot down and said they were at least taking me along if she had to stay home with the babies. So I went, and learned to climb."

"Why'd they go all the way to Sri Lanka," Annie asked. "Is it better climbing than India?"

"That's home, remember. I live in Jaffna."

"Oh, yeah," Annie said, like she knew all along that Jaffna was in Sri Lanka, not North India or the Middle East or wherever else she had never heard of before.

CHAPTER 36

"**I** hate to get up early on Saturdays," Annie told Naveena on their way to breakfast. It was the third Saturday since arrival at school, but the first village workday for the Service Learning classes.

"You'll get used to it. We had hiking season last semester to break us in, and this semester we have to finish up all our SL hours for the year. So, we just get up. Besides, you'll get into the projects, and then it feels worth it. You get to sleep in on Sundays, unless you go to church."

Annie didn't comment. Of course she went to church – every Sunday in her whole life except when they were on backpacking trips or ski trips. Even then they had devotions before they left camp or the cabin. It's what you do. Maybe, Annie thought. Maybe I go to church and maybe I don't. For the first time in her life, Annie realized she could decide for herself, and nobody would know. Nobody who would freak, that is.

She chose pancakes and syrup over the indistinguishable cream-of-wheaty looking stuff with vegetables in it, which Naveena took. The syrup tasted weird, so Annie smeared peanut butter and jam on her second pancake. Someone hollered that the SL buses were loading. Annie rolled her pancake for eating later and gulped down her coffee. It was too hot, and she burned her tongue.

Four different Service Learning projects were scheduled for the morning – Annie's own class's project at Chinna-kadu; Grace Home, to visit and play games with the elderly;

Santosha, an orphanage within walking distance of MMIS, where Naveena was going; and another smaller group, gathered around a jeep loaded with computer monitors, going to the polio home in Megha Malai. Annie wanted to go to all four places, but headed for the Chinnakadu bus. Mr. Hausden was there, checking their names off a list and handing out a green MMIS t-shirt for each, with the words, "Earth's Child" on the back, overlaid on a photo of the Earth from space. The students pulled them on over their shirts or jackets and loaded on to the buses. Annie wondered if any of them objected to being called Child. They didn't seem to.

"Sit here, Annie." It was Vidhya. "We can talk about the interviews. Mr. Hausden said we can start with a few women today and see how it goes. Ms. Jayashree gave him a list of questions."

"Remember, I don't know Tamil at all," Annie said.

"That's okay, as long as you at least learn '*Namaskaram*' or '*Vannakam*'."

"Which means?"

"More or less, it means 'hi.' And then we'll figure out what else you need to know, or I'll translate. But mostly, you just record."

"*Namaskaram*," Annie repeated. "How'd I do?"

Vidhya smiled. "Good. And then be ready with that Iyo camp song you told me about the other day, just in case the kids want to sing. Okay?"

"Sure," Annie said, as they pulled out of Main Gate. They wound through a part of town Annie hadn't seen. Thoughts of both Hyderabad and Gandhinagar flooded her mind. In just three weeks the passing scenery had become an odd mix of familiar and puzzling. It seemed normal now, that the bus would stop for cows wandering across the road. Annie was occasionally startled by a cow on the sidewalk or one coming up alongside her as she crossed the road outside the school gate, but she'd never seen them bother anyone, and she realized that cows cross roads too. But what about the old man digging through a concrete garbage bin, fending off dogs, asserting his right to the garbage over theirs? Was that normal?

She saw a chai seller's stall, with shabby paint and a rusted metal roof, and mentally compared it to the new drive-through latte shop that just went in across from the high school at home. She knew that kids at Ridgeway would laugh at this chai stall if it were there, which it wouldn't be, because it wouldn't pass some kind of inspection. But she had already been to one like it with Naveena and the girls from her dorm and bought chocolate bars and chai. Even Lori had agreed that it was safe since they boiled the milk. This morning there were three men gathered around the stall, waiting in turn as the owner poured their tea from one cup high in the air, to a second cup a good two feet below it. Again and again, cooling it down before handing it to the next person in line. Annie sucked in cool air over the burned spot on her tongue.

The bus passed a group of women walking, almost running, single file. Each carried a long bundle of wood on her head, young saplings that they somehow balanced, though their load was twice as long as any woman was tall. They came in groups of ten or so, and Annie wondered if it made it bearable to carry that kind of load because others did it too. Did they get paid a lot? She hated filling the wood box at home, carrying wood from the garage into the living room, but she did it because she loved the fireplace, and because it was her chore. Was it easier to carry something on your head than in the crook of your arm? Annie wondered if she could even walk from the garage to the house with a pile of wood on her head.

Annie and Sandesh were the only new students in this SL group, so once the bus parked in Chinnakadu, Sandesh went off with Bijeen, and Vidhya took time to show Annie around the village. She felt an even stronger admiration for Vidhya as she stopped and visited easily with people along the way. She introduced Annie often, and Annie smiled, but didn't venture to try out *"Namaskaram,"* hoping her smile would be enough.

They circled back to the school, which Annie recognized from the DVD she'd seen in SL class. They found the work already underway on the new biosand water filters. Annie watched from the side until Mr. Hausden came by and said, "You can figure it out better by getting in there to help, Annie. Ask Bijeen what needs done."

Annie spotted Bijeen with a man wearing the same narrow skirt she had seen on the airplane coming into Hyderabad, only it was plaid instead of white. She offered to help.

Bijeen handed her a tape measure and a pencil and pointed to a square of sheet metal on a worktable. "Mark off an edge five centimetres wide on each side and then fill the center with a grid, lines spaced 2.5 centimetres apart. You can use that straight edge to draw in the lines so holes can be punched where they intersect."

Annie liked Bijeen. She smiled thinking about his story in class, about the monkeys. He deserved an A, for more than stories. For caring so much. She started measuring and marking.

"What's this for, anyway?" Annie asked.

"The diffusers. Remember Won Tae's DVD? They break up the water being poured in so it doesn't just dump straight onto the sand and wreck the biolayer growing there."

They talked as they worked, and Annie began to understand how the filters did their job, how a layer of micro-organisms built up in the first few inches of sand, boosting the effectiveness of the filters from just pretty good to 99%.

"It's all because of the *schmutzdecke*," Bijeen said with a grin.

"The what?"

"The *schmutzdecke*. Nice word, huh? We learned it from the Canadians. It's the bio part that eats up more bad stuff in the water."

"I want to finish one whole diffuser myself, Bijeen," Annie said after she had marked out the grid for two of them. She could imagine one of the ladies she had just met, pouring water into her new filter, over the diffuser Annie had made with her own hands. She wouldn't be here forever, she knew, and even though the concrete was still being mixed and shoveled into molds and would have to dry before the sand could be added, Annie knew her diffuser would become a part of a filter eventually. She wanted to be able to think of someone in this place taking a drink of good water long after she'd gone home, because of something she helped do. Because at home, all she did was turn on the faucet. Or grab her stainless-steel water bottle from the frig. It didn't seem fair.

Earth's Child, Annie read off the back of Bijeen's shirt. It was true. They were. All of them. She looked around the school courtyard at the project – students from both MMIS and Chinnakadu; volunteers from the village, mostly men, all ages, but a few women too; Mr. Hausden; three little boys playing, making pretend sunglasses from straw; an old lady sitting, watching it all from under the tree, holding a baby on her lap. No music blasted in the background, no chips and salsa, chocolate chip cookies, or gummy bears for snacks, no movies planned for afterward, but in Annie's eyes, this was one of the best parties she'd ever been to. For Earth's Children.

THEY GATHERED AROUND the bus to get their sack lunches. "Veg in this box; non-veg in that one," someone directed. They make it so easy to be a vegetarian here, Annie thought, then wondered how kids at Ridgeway would respond to that announcement. "Gross," someone would say. Or "Sure, like we're supposed to survive on lettuce! All vegetarian dorks, please step forward and get your bag of carrots." It came to Annie that it made no more sense to make fun of vegetarians than of football players or people who like to go to scary movies, but she doubted that she'd be any different than everybody else once she was back home. I'm basically a chicken, Annie thought.

Or at least a chickpea. She grinned at herself for the way the words followed each other. She had never heard of "chickpeas" at home. They were garbanzo beans. English was funny here. Not just the yards to meters, or metres, stuff. Or Bijeen giving her directions in centimetres. Annie had expected that. But garbanzo beans were chickpeas. Okra was ladiesfinger. Flashlights were torches, and trucks were lorries. And there was the actual pronunciation. Annie had grown up hearing words the way they were supposed to be said. But here, very smart teachers said in-**TEG**-ral for integral and **CON**-tri-bute for contribute They even spelled words wrong: *organise, apologise, colour, diarrhoea.* So much for rules.

Annie realized she was hungry and that the box of lunches was emptying out. She decided to try a veg lunch, then seeing it contained a potato patty sandwich and the non-veg kids got fried chicken, she faked that she had made a mistake, and traded her sack for the other kind. They all held a bag of Lay's potato chips, which Annie had never guessed would be in India, and a small Cadbury chocolate bar, plus a fruit drink. Annie's was labeled Green Mango. "What the heck?" she said when she saw it.

Bijeen looked her way. "Want to trade for Fruity Berry?" he asked.

"Sure."

The students split up for the afternoon. One group continued their work on mixing concrete for the filters. Another did an English conversation class on the theme of traveling: "Going to Chennai," complete with props. Another group led a hike from the village to a nearby waterfall, or rather, let village children lead them.

Annie and Vidhya went to three homes to interview women. They asked to talk with each person separately, as Ms. Jayashree had directed, thinking that the young women in the family might not be comfortable talking while others listened in. Vidhya asked the questions, while Annie recorded the translated answers:

Is Chinnakadu your native place, or which village did you come from to this place? That's English, Annie wondered? Native place? But she wrote the question down as Vidhya called it out.

Did your parents want you to go to school? How long?

How many children do you have? Do you want more?

Are you satisfied in life?

Annie learned that of the five women they talked with, three had stopped going to school after 3rd or 4th standard; one had never gone. One was a recent bride, expecting her first baby in a few months. One looked very young, but had been married for three years. No children yet, she said. She seemed reluctant to admit that. An older woman had five children and twenty-one grandchildren. The other two had three children each.

However Vidhya had worded things, the last question seemed to be the one they wanted to stop and think about. Had she said satisfied, or happy? The answers had come in – yes; yes, I have a good life; there is much work, but that is a woman's duty. At the last home, where one young woman was alone, they got an unexpected answer. Wiping back the tears that sprang to her eyes when Vidhya asked the question, she said, "*Illay.*"

Vidhya talked with her some more, then turned to Annie and said, "Things haven't been easy for her. She said it would be better if she had never been born or had died as a little girl. Vidhya slipped over to Radha, the young woman, and held her in her arms. "No, it would not have been better," she said. Then, at first so softly Annie thought maybe it was just her breathing, Vidhya began to sing. A gentle song. A rocking song.

Radha swayed to the rhythm and now and then sang a word with Vidhya.

Annie didn't know what to do, but she sensed this young woman's heart was breaking, and it hurt hers to watch it happening. She could hum, and so she did. She scooted nearer to Radha herself and stroked her hair away from her damp face, then reached for one of her hands and held it in hers. "*Namaskaram*," Annie whispered, because somehow she wanted to speak a word of caring to this woman, not so different in age from herself, and that was the only Tamil word she knew to say. Then she leaned her head against Radha's and said, in English, "That means I love you," which it didn't, except in the heart of the girl who said it.

ANNIE AND VIDHYA were the last two students on the bus.

"Highlights?" Mr. Hausden asked when they were loaded.

"It's a tradition with SL trips," Vidhya explained to Annie. "We have to come up with at least ten. The drivers all know not to start the buses until they get Hausden's okay."

Responses came in: the waterfall hike; four new filters poured; fried chicken; the English class made it to Chennai and back; the *kabaddi* game against the village boys.... Annie let it all drift around her and held onto her own thoughts. The bus pulled away from the village, and a troop of waving children ran after it through the dust until they were lost from sight. The SL class would be back in Chinnakadu in two weeks. Would Radha be okay until then? Annie would ask Vidhya what happened when they talked, but it was too noisy on the bus for that now. She felt tired, and wished she could sleep. She pulled off her green MMIS t-shirt, folded it in a square against the window, and leaned her head against the world.

So what does Green Mango fruit juice taste like, Annie wondered.

CHAPTER 37

"It may seem early," Dean Carr announced at the end of assembly, "but you need to start thinking about Long Weekend. Many of you from here in India will plan to go home. And, hopefully, as you've done in the past, many of you will invite a classmate or two along. For those who find that choice not open to you, we are offering four trips, chaperoned by staff: Kerala backwaters; Hampi temples; Bangalore, where we'll be visiting some high-tech businesses, Lalbagh Gardens, and yes, Pizza Hut; and for those who want some time just to kick back and yet get out some too, we'll be taking an overnight trip down to Madurai – the Meenakshi Temple plus the water park. Information sheets on these options will be available in your next period class. March will be here sooner than you think."

Annie was not quite out the door of the Performing Arts when she felt a tug on the back of her sweatshirt.

"Hampi, Annie," Aziz said. "Sign up for Hampi. I've been waiting two years for this. They only have twenty slots, and I hear one of the art classes is going, so sign up in the Activities Office today."

"What?

"Long Weekend. You heard Carr's announcement. Sign up for Hampi."

"I never heard of Hampi until assembly. And I'm not especially interested in temples, to tell you the truth."

"Trust me. Hampi is not just temples."

Annie was confused.

"Want me to sign your name?" Aziz asked. "What's your account number?"

"Aziz! What? Why do I want to go to Hampi? Maybe I'll go to Naveena's in Chennai."

"Because across the river from the temples you will find some of the world's best bouldering. You've got to, Annie."

"What about the Kerala backwaters?"

"It's good. But you can do that anytime. Next time. Another time. Really. You can always cancel later if you don't want to go, but you can't always ..." He paused, and Annie sensed that was the end of his sales pitch. Then he added, looking her straight in the eyes, "You can't always go climbing in Hampi with me. I want you to come, Annie."

This was different some way from the other arguments, and from the belaying she'd been doing. He needed her for that because his old climbing partner hadn't come back to school. Other kids would be going to Hampi, but here he was, asking her. It made her stomach feel funny, and she knew right then that she wanted to go. She was at the door to her 5th period class. "I have Study Hall right now. Can I think about it?" she said. "Ask me at lunch."

Annie checked in and got a pass for the computer room. She Googled "hampi india." Beside the list of sites, there were pictures of temples. History, religion, and architecture seemed to be the theme. Annie clicked on a couple of the linked sites, and noticed that behind each temple pictured was a pile of rocks. She went back to the main page and changed her search entry to "rock climbing hampi india." In an instant she knew what Aziz was talking about. This time the temples were in the background, and the pictures were of climbers hanging on huge boulders of all shapes, rising up from the hills above the rice fields in the most amazing combinations – mounds or pillars here, jumbled piles there, one lonely, huge boulder filling an entire picture.

So Hampi obviously had a side that Dean Carr hadn't stressed, and though she didn't feel excited about temples, Annie decided to sign up. She had climbed the back of Performing Arts a dozen times, and had begun belaying Aziz, and she liked it. Aziz never said anything about it for a long time, but finally told Annie that he and Mikhail had discovered the back of the library was bolted, and confessed that they had climbed it multiple times last semester. It wasn't long until Annie had learned firsthand how the library tied in to rock climbing. Now she felt she was ready for this, for more. Climbing in one of the world's best bouldering sites sounded good. And being there with Aziz sounded great. If she changed her mind, she could always cancel, like Aziz said. That would give her time to email home and make sure the trip idea was okay with her mom and dad. To the architecture-and-history-Hampi, that is.

She didn't see Aziz at lunch, so ate by herself quickly and headed back to the Computer Lab for a few minutes of emailing before afternoon classes started. As incoming messages downloaded, she typed a note home to tell them to look up Hampi and let her know if they were okay with paying Rs. 12000 extra for the trip. Otherwise she could stay at school or do the Madurai overnight trip for almost nothing, though she hoped they'd be okay with Hampi.

She didn't mention going to Naveena's as an option. Naveena had gone on the Hampi trip her freshman year and said it would be great for Annie and that she could come visit her family in Chennai on her way back to the States in May. Nor did Annie mention anything about bouldering. It wasn't being deceptive. She would see the temples. They had to, because that was the real purpose of the trip. But Aziz had assured her they would also have plenty of free time for the rocks, and that he'd make sure they got assigned to Boulder

Haven, the bungalows across the river that bordered some of the best bouldering grounds in the world. A fact that wouldn't especially impress either her mom or dad.

Annie looked at the clock on the wall. She was still okay. She clicked open her inbox.

Param Singh.

"Oh, my gosh. Finally!" Annie said.

"Hey, Annie. It's me. Sorry I've been so slow writing." Slow was hardly the word Annie would have used. Non-existent was more like it. She read on eagerly.

"Things have been really busy. Major overload. We stayed in New Jersey two weeks after school started in January and it took me over a month to catch up. I'm not sure it was worth it, but it was fun at the time. Track just started. Guess what? We have this new exchange student who is going to run long distance. You probably heard about her from other people. She's taller than you, so maybe she'll be pretty fast. She's from Germany. How's it going? I miss you! Param."

"Oh, great!" Annie said out loud. "Param! That's all you can write?!" He didn't seem to know the kind of news Annie was waiting for. As if she cared about a tall girl from Germany who ran her events! After all these weeks, that's all he had to say? And what did he mean by "I miss you"? It sounded like "I haven't written but now that I type your name I remember I used to know you."

"Gosh," Annie said, "what the heck?" She moved the cursor disgustedly to "Sign Out" but saw she had a message from Danny and clicked it open:

"gotta tell you something. i'm married. that's first and biggest. second is that i got a new mountain bike. Will you ride bikes with me oh yah and my wife too, when you get home that is? Fourth is about param and rob the new blind kid I told you about. guess what they're doing in track? long distance – 1500 and 3000. rob can't see a thing and here param went up to him and said he could do track anyway and rob said he would and they practiced running around the track holding hands. and get this. nobody not one person in the whole school made fun of them. that's a first for ridgeway huh! now they go out and run on the nature trail too but they hold a ribbon between them that the coach gave param. can you believe being blind and running on ridgeway's nature trail? Not exactly the smoothest freeway to run on. i wasn't going to tell you this because you'll like param for doing it but actually i like him for doing it and i sure admire rob so just thought you'd want to know that ridgeway is a pretty cool place. wantta come home early. i'll meet you at the airport. won't tell anybody ☺. by the way i'm not married i just wanted to see what you'd say, so tell me. your first reaction. your bud, dantheman p.s. in case you think param is too cool - rob said he ran him into a tree, but they both laughed so I don't think he got hurt. love you, but you know that already."

Annie hadn't cried or even felt homesick the last couple weeks, but after she read Danny's email she did both. She just wanted to see him. She wanted to hear him laugh. She wanted a hug. She wanted to be home. Back walking Ridgeway's halls where she knew everybody and everybody knew her. She wanted to meet this new Rob kid and see him run, and cheer for him. And she'd tell Danny that she loved him all the more for thinking she'd want to know that, even if it was about Param, because it was just as much about Danny too.

The thought did come to her that Param could have just as easily talked about Rob in his email. Why was the only news he sent about a new girl from Germany? Maybe that was another reason to get back home. Or maybe she didn't care. Danny could give Param a few pointers on how to write an email that somebody would want to read.

She sat at the computer thinking about home, realizing that everyone would be asleep right then. A loneliness washed over her, to be in her own bed in her house asleep too, waiting for the morning to dawn on a Ridgeway day. She'd wake up and eat wheat puffs and applesauce and whole wheat toast, and talk to her mom and dad about nothing or everything and then drive to school. Drive. On roads without cows. People would call out to her as she walked down the halls and she'd go to classes where she knew her teachers and their kids who she babysat for, and all her classmates. Everybody would have normal names that she could say without even thinking. Not things like Jyotsna, Gowrishankar, Bharati, Hyunju, Lhundup, Yashonandan, Vrusti, Minm-Hiep, Amrithavalli. The names at home would make sense because they were regular names, not random sounds put together and called names, that you had to figure out word tricks to memorize.

She would stay after school for the Spirit Committee meeting, and then go running for track practice. She'd suggest the long-legged German girl try hurdles instead of distance, and she'd ask Param if he had an extra ribbon she could hold onto, and they'd run together. And they'd stop, like they had on Kinsey Lane last fall .... Of course she cared. She couldn't pretend she didn't or that his stupid email didn't bother her. That girl would go back to Germany and Annie would come home.

Annie couldn't think of any reason she had wanted to come to India.

She wiped her eyes dry, put her fingers to the keyboard, and hit Reply to Danny's email:

"You better not get married, you dork! Besides, who would you marry? (Tell me!!!) And tell Rob hi for me and that I'm glad he's going out for track. That's a cool story, especially because it's happening at Ridgeway. If Rob can run the nature trail maybe he'll go out for X-C next fall. You should get a positive referral for spreading good news. Tell Thompson you deserve one. Or ask Snyder if you can pet the hedgehog for being my hero. Almost time for class so I gotta go. I miss you!

"P.S. I hear we have "Track Week" here next month. I'm not sure how it works, one week for a whole track season, but they say everybody does something in it. Even you if you were here! Maybe it makes up for in numbers what it loses in speed. Not that you'd be slow. If you ever decided to run, that is.

P.S. What's third? You skipped it.

P.S. Love you, Dantheman!"

She asked him to tell Param "hi," then went back and deleted it. She didn't want to push things with Danny, so she pulled up her note from Param and hit Reply.

"Thanks for the email! I know what you mean by busy. It's like that here too. We have nine classes – ten with study hall. And homework's a lot heavier than at Ridgeway. In fact, I'm almost late to class, so I better go. I'll write again soon. Annie"

She had written "Love, Annie," then went back and changed it to "Annie." At the moment, she didn't feel Param deserved anything more. She would ask Katelyn what was happening, and if this new girl was anything important. Katelyn would have told her if Param really started liking somebody else. Even Danny would do that, happily.

Knowing that Danny would check his email in the morning before he left for school, somehow made her feel closer to home. She'd be in his house, on his computer screen, through her words, and he'd be reading them about the time she finished dinner and headed for dorm that night. How nice it was to have somebody always love you, and remember to tell you so.

CHAPTER 38

A s the weeks passed, Annie found that things fell into a comfortable pattern, a school routine of sorts, yet she wasn't taking life for granted. There were odd things that happened too often for that to be the case. Things that jarred or hurt or made her question, things that made her marvel and feel grateful, or, when she remembered to do it, made her wonder.

The server in the dining hall who had described ladiesfinger and beet root to Annie that very first day, brought a picture of his family to show her. Sarmila, his wife, worked at the women's craft cooperative in Megha Malai and he invited Annie to go there and visit. She went the next Saturday afternoon.

Annie found Sarmila working in a small room above the sales floor at one of two dozen sewing machines lined up in rows behind two large cutting tables. Bolts of fabric stood in shelves along the front wall. Women came here to order their tailoring done. Sarmila smiled when Annie asked to speak with her.

Annie had just bought an apron in the showroom downstairs to give to her grandma, and, taking it out of the bag, asked Sarmila if she could make another like it for her mom.

"This is my apron," Sarmila said pointing out the ID number on the tag. "I will make a nice apron for your mother." They selected fabric, and Annie tripled the order on the spot – one for her dad and Mr. Snyder, and then she decided to get one more for herself and one for Param's mom, too.

Annie asked if Sarmila could make shirts, pointing to the one of Naveena's that she was wearing. Sarmila smiled again and pulled several bolts of fabric down for Annie to choose from. "Because of the embroidery work, and tomorrow shop is closed, it will be ready Wednesday next. Is this good?"

"This is very good," Annie replied. Sarmila took a tape measure and in an instant jotted down Annie's measurements. This kind of shopping was an example of something you didn't take for granted. As were the rows of sewing machines and the little room, or Sarmila's happiness to be there doing that work. I could do this for maybe half an hour, or forty-five minutes max, Annie thought to herself, before I'd have to get out of here and go running. Yet both she and Sarmila were excited about what was happening and the work Sarmila knew how to do.

But other things in Megha Malai and at MMIS jarred Annie. They did a current events day once a week in Modern Religious Thought, and Annie's group read about and discussed an article that told of Hindu fundamentalists pouring kerosene on the jeep and the house occupied by American Christians. The family escaped from the house in time, but their son was badly injured when metal from the exploding jeep hit him. He remained in critical condition. The article in the paper said they were looking for those involved and that it was believed to have been done in retaliation for the people coming to India under false visas, pretending to help with a medical project and then blatantly trying to convert the people in that area to Christianity.

"What is the deal with kerosene here?" Annie asked. "And what is so bad about becoming a Christian that you'd try to burn somebody up?"

"It's pure stupidity," Ajit answered, and then added, "and there's no way it's okay. But why do Christians get in the habit of thinking they are God's messengers to the whole world? I never could understand that."

"It's because of something their Bible says that tells them

to convert people," another student added. "Isn't that right, Annie? Wouldn't these people be doing what they thought they should, working in medicine, but all the time they're really missionaries trying to save the heathen? At least that's what I've heard."

Annie surprised herself. Six months ago she would have had the answer, and she would have told them immediately, but today she turned and looked over her shoulder, saying, "What Annie are you talking to?" They laughed, and Annie continued, "I don't know anymore. I'm trying to figure it out myself. I don't know why, because I used to think everybody needed to become a Christian, or..." She was going to say, "... or they'd go to hell," but instead she said, "Things changed for me when this kid named Param moved to my hometown. He's a Sikh, and he's okay. I can't see God being mad at him.

"I only have one other major close friend at home who says he is not a Christian, and sometimes I don't think he really means it. But, you're right. I think I've always believed that it was my job to at least hope people will want to become Christians."

"So we're not okay being who we are?" Ajit asked.

"That's not really the point, Ajit," Annie said. "Isn't it a whole different thing to ask somebody if they want to become a Christian than to try to burn them up for doing it? That's sick. Are these Hindus crazy or what?"

"Maybe." Vidhya shifted chairs to join them. "I agree it's horrible, but maybe they're sick and tired of know-it-alls putting down everything they've ever been or known or learned, and saying their past has to go and their lives have to totally change. I can't imagine life without Pongal and Holi and celebrating with special food, and not being able to offer *puja* at the temple. Could you imagine not having Deepavali and the stories, and rows of flickering lights on the window sills? My mom refuses to go to candles or electric lights. We still fill the lamps with oil like we've always done. They are so beautiful. I'd never give that up for anybody! Or any sales pitch from Christians."

"Who's asking you to give up stories and food and lamps on the window sills?" Annie asked.

"Christians, Annie! They say the stories are of the devil. There's a teacher here at this very school who wouldn't let her kids buy clay Deepavali lamps at the bazaar last semester. I was right there when they asked her to get them. 'These are used to represent the path people lit for Hindu gods, Rama and Sita, to find their way back home,' she told her kids. 'We Christians don't believe in that.' End of story. I felt like asking her if she believed in the triumph of light over darkness, or understanding over plain stinkin' narrow-mindedness, but I didn't.

"She had no idea I was in the bazaar for that very reason. We got permission from the Activities Office to buy three hundred clay lamps for the dining hall. We got oil from the cooks to fill the cups and had the lamps burning when people came in for dinner. It was a very different atmosphere in the dining hall that night. Quiet. A beautiful glow, and we were so happy. Everybody was, including the Christians who didn't know they shouldn't love it! But that teacher freaked when she found out. In spite of her protest, the administration had approved it all. Thank God!

"'We're supposed to be a Christian school!' she said, 'and this is compromising our witness.' Exact words!"

"Who's the teacher?" Annie asked.

"That's not what's important, Annie! So many Christians have that attitude. It was her, last semester. Next year, it'll be somebody else. But for me, the dining hall made it a tiny bit bearable not to be home for Deepavali. The cooks made a great dinner, and at the end of the serving line there were trays and pans of gulab jamun, kaju kalinga, ladoo, jalebi, and barfi. It was awesome. I bet she would have stopped them from doing that too if she had known. Or maybe she didn't figure out that the sweets are a part of the holiday too."

"Barf?" Annie asked. "Did you actually say the cooks made barf-y?"

"Annie! Just shut up! That's what I'm talking about. People who don't know a dang thing, and still make fun of everything that's important."

"Sheesh, Vidhya, I was just joking," Annie said.

Mr. Das wandered over to their group and stood behind the chairs, listening. Vidhya lowered her voice and said, glaring at Annie, "Well, don't. It's not funny. I know criticizing Deepavali is way different than kerosene, and I'd never ever say they're right in doing that – ever – but neither should people try to destroy the beauty of our traditions."

ANNIE THOUGHT OF that discussion in chapel the next Sunday morning when she noticed the candles burning beside the altar. She supposed the light flickering from a candle looks pretty much like that from an oil lamp, and she wondered when candles first got used in churches. At least they weren't tied to some make-believe Hindu gods. Maybe there was something weird and dangerous about the story that Vidhya failed to mention. Who were these Rama and Sita people? And what did they do? Maybe the teacher was right. It could have been compromising her faith, and she had to stand up for what was true.

Had Vidhya called the holiday Deepavali? Deep as in Paramdeep? Annie suddenly remembered the day on the track last year when Param and she had talked about God and he said he liked the idea of being God's lamp. She had never thought about his name meaning something. Any more than "Annie" did. It was just who she was. But maybe Param was a lamp. She liked that idea too. She had always loved the song,

"This Little Light of Mine." Candle light and Sikh lamps could mix, couldn't they? If he wanted them to, that is.

The chaplain was well into his sermon, though Annie couldn't have said what it was about. Her thoughts were back in Ridgeway High, with Param. Maybe she didn't need to be so mad at him for his email. Some people weren't especially great writers. He had said he was on overload. And he missed her. She wanted to believe him.

As the service closed, they sang "Somebody Prayed for Me." It was a song they sang often at her church at home and it reminded her that her mom and dad and grandparents, and Pam from the fruit stand, and kids from school and youth group at home were praying for her. She was glad for caring and prayers. She couldn't be mad at God. She was God's girl in God's world, and at least this day, He loved her.

Tears flowed down her cheeks as the song filled her heart. A hand reached her shoulder from the pew behind, gently, and Annie turned. It was Leeza.

"Is everything okay, Annie?" she asked.

"It is, Leeza. I was overwhelmed, in the good sense of the word, to remember how many people are praying for me while I'm here. The song reminded me."

"You can add one more to the list, Annie. I pray for you every day, since that day we first met and I knew you were scared about coming to Megha Malai."

"Really? Thank you, Leeza. Thank you."

CHAPTER 39

The man who sat just across the street from Main Gate and begged as people approached the small shops was hardest of all for Annie, because he was always there. His legs folded under him like little sticks, and ended in something that Annie knew should be feet, but had probably never been used as feet. She stood inside the campus gate and watched as he moved down the row of shops. He rolled up over onto his knees and swung himself along on hands and knees on the filthy pavement, then in one smooth motion, rolled back onto his bottom, lifting his hand to beg just as a woman in a sari passed. The woman stopped, then reached into a small cloth bag for some coins which she dropped into his outstretched hand.

"Why can't somebody do something?" Annie said. The watchman standing nearby evidently followed Annie's line of vision and thought she was talking to him.

"They tried. He was taken up to Grace Home and told he could live there. They gave him a bed in the men's dormitory. He didn't last a week. He said he couldn't live up in the woods away from town and people, and he came right back here to beg."

"Where does he go at night? Where does he go when it pours down rain? Where does he wash his hands?" Annie asked, but the watchman had turned to talk with someone inquiring about an extra set of keys.

"This is crap!" Annie said to herself, and then remembered her pledge. "I wonder," she started. "I wonder why there isn't a cure for polio. Or why it doesn't work in India? And why there aren't wheelchairs and sidewalks with ramps? And why there aren't jobs for people with stick legs. He could work in a cell phone shop. Like Abid."

Annie remembered the computers at the Megha Malai polio home, one of the SL projects her class was working on. Maybe there were jobs, and no one told this man. On an impulse, she walked right out the Main Gate, crossed the roadway, and approached the man she had been watching. Not having planned exactly what she would say, Annie began. "I'm sorry about your legs," she said. "Did you know..."

She never finished. He held out his hand to her, his shoulders and his face pleading. He moved his hand back and forth toward her – outstretched, and then cupped, touching his forehead, and back to her. He seemed suddenly pitiful, yet what startled Annie most were his eyes. It was as if he were looking through her, not really seeing. She knew he wasn't blind. He saw everyone who approached. What was this look then? He didn't seem to know English. She should have thought of that. She turned to walk away.

"Mah, Mah," he called loudly, stretching his hand toward her. Then softer, as if convincing her she must act, "Mah ... please, Mah."

Annie stopped and twirled around. She swung off her backpack and unzipped the side pouch. She reached into the pocket, pulled out a twenty rupee note, and put it in the man's hand. His fingers quickly closed around it, then slipped the bill under a little towel that was sitting beside him. He hadn't even looked at Annie.

She turned quickly and started back across the road, forgetting to look over her shoulder, and nearly walked right into a cow. "Yeow," Annie cried. "Can't you watch where you're going?"

"You shouldn't do that!" the watchman said sternly as Annie re-entered the Main Gate. It surprised her. It was obviously the cow's fault, which should be out in a field and did not belong on streets in town, yet here the watchman was criticizing her. Then she realized he must mean she shouldn't have given the money to the man with the shriveled legs. She remembered Ms. Dunlop suggesting that they not give to the beggars outside the hotel in Hyderabad. "We'll be swarmed by others once word is out we're here," she had said. But this was different. This was Annie's place now, her community. Even though Annie had planned just to ask the beggar if he knew about the polio home and the computer training there, she wasn't sorry she had given him the twenty rupees. She could do without part of a candy bar.

"Why?" Annie decided to ask the watchman. "Why shouldn't I?" She truly wanted to know.

"You must know the rules by now. No leaving the Main Gate during school hours without a gate pass from your dorm parent." He hadn't meant cows or beggars. Just rules.

"I'm sorry," Annie said. She was. Not about gates, but about polio and hands and knees on the dirty road, and malaria and typhoid fever; tiny workrooms with rows of sewing machines; kerosene fires, and protests against clay lamps.

Yet on the other hand, there were hospitals and scooter-riding survivors; aprons and embroidered shirts and smiles; watchmen who cared about rules; inoculations; water filters that keep typhoid away; hockey games played with Buddhists, Hindus, Muslims, and Christians on the same team playing against Buddhists, Hindus, Muslims, Christians, Parsis, and Ketsa on the other team, and nobody caring. Or even thinking about it until Annie and Ketsa decided to figure out who was what one afternoon. And this was just one moment's thoughts. Yes, Annie had forgotten the gate pass rule. Yes, she would try to remember next time. But in a way, there was no gate pass now. Annie had already passed through the gate, without even realizing it, and there was no turning back, no matter who tried to give or take away permission.

CHAPTER 40

The bus loaded for Chinnakadu, and Annie was ready, two rolled pancakes, no syrup, in her sweatshirt pocket. She and Vidhya had tallied their survey sheets from their prior visits, having covered much of the village and trusting that word would get out to the women whom they hadn't talked with. Radha agreed to help, and had managed to invite ten or twelve other young women to join Annie and Vidhya in the courtyard of the Hindu temple at the opposite end of the village from the school.

Annie wasn't excited about the location, but was excited about the meeting. They had finished their interviews in one other Saturday. The next time they checked in with the women, they shared, with permission, the kinds of responses other women had given. This was a turning point, Annie felt, and the women began to speak more freely. They had learned so much about each other that they thought applied only to themselves. Annie felt the project had already been worthwhile, regardless of where it went from there.

They learned that few women had had more than three or four years of school. There was more they would like to study now, and some of them had not yet learned to read. Most of them felt isolated. Though a part of their husband's family, they felt lonely and cut off from their own families and from other young women in the village. They recognized their total dependence on their husbands and extended family, and several expressed a longing to be stronger and more able to help make decisions or do something that they chose. Today they were going to meet together for the first time, talk, and perhaps even make a proposal to Annie and Vidhya about one or two things that could improve their situations.

The women sat in a corner of the temple grounds under a shade tree. Vidhya spoke to them briefly. They talked around their circle, and Annie guessed it was introductions, but she couldn't pick out names from any of the other words, so just studied their faces as they talked and decided to ask about names later. Once they began, Vidhya slipped out of the circle and sat down beside Annie, translating quietly what was being said:

"They'd like some kind of school just for them, or some classes, but they don't think that will happen. They would like to earn money of their own so they'd feel they had a right to spend it for what they needed. That lady just suggested they start a small library for the village. This girl has heard about women's cooperatives and is suggesting they start something here in Chinnakadu that could include earning money and taking classes. She just suggested getting an older woman in the village to teach them, but that idea seems to be going down."

More talk. More translation for Annie. How would they justify meeting together when Annie and Vidhya weren't coming anymore? Would they still come after the water project was finished?

Vidhya reminded them that their school year ended in May and that Annie would be going back to the US, but that she, Vidhya, would come back again in July, even if the water filters were finished. There was a pause, and Vidhya suggested they take a break. She called to a small boy hovering right outside the temple gate and told him to go to a tea stall and ask that chai be brought to them. "Milk Bikis too," Vidhya added.

As they sipped tea and ate cookies, the atmosphere lightened, and someone started singing. It was a song everyone except Annie knew, and they moved from that into two or three others, or maybe it was just one very long song with breaks. There was lively conversation, and Vidhya explained to Annie as they finished, "The singing gave them another idea. It won't be easy for them to leave their houses to get together with each other on a regular basis, because there's too much work to do, but..." Vidhya smiled at their ingenuity. "But if they come here to the temple to worship and sing, they will be doing something worthwhile and good, and no one at home will say they shouldn't go to temple. Even if they just happen to show up here at exactly the same time! They've all agreed to it."

Annie could see the relief and joy they were feeling to have this plan. The young women giggled and continued their discussion. Vidhya again translated: "They're talking about beginning, even in a little way, some kind of craft project that they can market as a group and earn a little money. They'll use part of the money for books for a village library and the rest will be divided among them personally."

"That's cool!" Annie replied. "I bet they could get the women's co-op in Megha Malai to sell what they decide to make. They have that little store under the sewing shop."

Vidhya knew the place too, and relayed the idea to the women. "They want us to talk to the director of the co-op. We can do that."

"And tell them," Annie added, "if they get some things ready before I leave, I will fill one of my suitcases with their work and take it back home with me. Our church has a humongous craft sale every June to raise money for the Children's Health Clinic in Ridgeway. Doctors and dentists volunteer time there, but that doesn't cover all of the costs, so we do a bazaar."

"Hold on, not so fast," Vidhya laughed. She relayed Annie's message back in Tamil, and Annie could tell Vidhya felt her excitement. The women nodded and spoke their approval.

"People at the bazaar pay big bucks to have a table," Annie continued, "but they get sponsors to help, and that's how the

Clinic gets its money. The people who make the crafts actually get to keep their sales, so I could send the money back here." Annie felt a surge of joy. People at her church would like to do something tangible to help these eager young women in Chinnakadu. Everybody would go for money for a library. And they'd understand why the women would want to earn some money for themselves. The church ladies doing the bazaar would love the idea.

They talked a bit more, then the women stood and Annie assumed they were ready to leave. But they all walked toward the inner temple instead of the outer gateway. Annie was puzzled.

"*Puja*," Vidhya said. "Worship. That's part of their plan, remember. Come on; they want you to come too."

"I can't."

"What?"

"I don't want to – go in there..."

"Why? Annie! It's important to them. Just walk through the temple. You don't have to do anything. Close your eyes if you want, but just come."

"Vidhya, you don't understand."

"Oh, come on, Annie! You're the one who doesn't understand! Here you sit with them for two hours while they make all these wonderful plans. You drink tea with them. You offer to help them sell their crafts and let them think you're their friend, and you won't go into their temple! I mean, they invited you. They don't do that for everyone who comes along. You are trashing them. What is with you?!"

Vidhya's tone of confusion turned to anger, and she finished with, "Fine. Be that way! I have been in the chapel at school a million times. But if this pinches your little Christian heart to walk alongside these women here in their temple, then go on back to the bus. Go! We don't need you."

"Vidhya, you don't get it. I went to the temple in

Hyderabad, and I didn't like it. I don't want to go to a temple that has a stone cow that they pretend is God."

"Just leave!" Vidhya yelled. "Get out of here!" Annie glanced at the women and saw they were upset. Vidhya told them something, then took one lady's arm, and walked with the group toward the inner part of the temple. Annie wished she knew Tamil. She'd make them understand. Or she'd tell them she was sorry. But she didn't know Tamil, so she turned to leave. As she rushed through the gate, she stumbled, bumping into a young woman sitting on the edge of the step, partially blocking the doorway, looking into the temple grounds. She hadn't been there before or Annie would have noticed her and remembered the awful scars on her arm and the side of her face.

"Excuse me," Annie said as she rushed past.

She heard Vidhya calling out behind her, "And for your information, there's no cow here! It's an elephant, to your little brain!"

Annie left, crying. She had messed up. But she knew she shouldn't have to do something that made her feel awful, just to help somebody else feel better. Especially when they were wrong. So she ran back through the village past the school building and headed for the bus.

"If you've finished up early," Hausden said as she passed him, "you can help this group carry the leftover lumber to the luggage compartment under the bus."

"Okay," she said. Hausden was busy and didn't seem to notice that she was barely hanging on.

"How did your interviewing with the women go?" Bijeen asked as he gathered up some of the tools they had been using.

"Mostly good," Annie said, trying to fake that she wasn't choking back tears.

"And?" he asked. For being so funny, Bijeen was pretty perceptive.

"And Vidhya and I just had a huge fight, in front of the women we're working with. It was terrible."

"Well, Vidhya can be intense sometimes, but she's pretty cool. Speaking of, here she comes now. I will leave you two to your misery." Bijeen lifted some boards onto his shoulder and started toward the bus.

"Bijeen, don't leave me. I don't want to talk to her now. She's irate."

"Then take that pile of boards over there," he said, pointing to some scrap lumber. Annie took her time, stacking and restacking the boards, all the while watching the bus so she could see when Vidhya got on. At last Annie took her load to the luggage compartment, then stepped up into the bus and took the seat right behind the driver.

"Sit with me, Bijeen," she said as he got onto the bus.

"What about Vidhya?"

Annie pointed to the back of the bus, making a face. She mouthed the word, "Mad."

"So what happened?" Bijeen whispered as Hausden called out for Highlights. They sat quietly until the bus pulled away from Chinnakadu.

"Are you a Hindu?" Annie asked him.

"Why?"

"No. Are you? Just tell me. Because if you worship stone cows and elephant gods, I will croak."

"So what happened?" he asked again. "Something to do with Ganesh?" Bijeen asked.

"What?" Annie questioned.

"Ganesh. 'The elephant god,' as you'd call him. The remover-of-obstacles and giver-of-good-fortune."

"That is so archaic, Bijeen. So you are a Hindu!"

"More or less," he answered.

"You can't be more or less. Either you are or you aren't. And worshiping a stone elephant to give you good fortune is like worshiping fortune cookies. Nobody worships fortune cookies! They eat them and throw the paper fortune away once they've read it. It's a joke. I watched them get made in a little factory in San Francisco once. There's nothing holy about it at all. Somebody makes up those sayings on little pieces of paper. They get randomly put into the cookies before they're folded up. And the waiter puts them on a plate for you. There's no 'good fortune' about it. No more than there is in a rock, chipped out in the shape of an elephant!"

"Ohhh-kaay," he said slowly. "Tell you what ... let's talk about what movies you saw in the US that I might not have seen here."

"No, Bijeen, I'm serious. Okay? I need to ask this one thing. Are you a real Hindu?"

"Well, if I can't be 'more or less,' then, yes. I am."

She groaned. "Do you really believe that a stone elephant will bless anybody or this new project the women have?"

"Why not?" he answered. "Now how about the movies?"

Annie hit her forehead with her palm and said, "Yes, let's change the subject. This makes no sense at all!"

THAT NIGHT IN the dorm, Annie found Ketsa. "We gotta talk," she said.

"What's up, girl?" Ketsa asked. "You look stressed."

"Something happened in our SL village today."

"Which was?"

"I didn't go to a temple with some women, and Vidhya got mad at me," Annie said.

"I thought your SL project was water filters and the interviews. What's that got to do with temples?"

"Nothing. But this was at the end of the interviews, and I didn't feel like going inside the temple."

"So don't go. Why would she get mad at you?" Ketsa asked.

"That's exactly what I'm saying! Ketsa, just tell me. Do you think it's right to be in a place where people are using idols, like all the stone or metal gods around here, animals and dancing people with a bunch of arms and legs? I mean, they worship them, like in that temple in Hyderabad. Aren't we compromising our witness to let them think we believe one ounce of that's okay?"

"And you're asking me, girl?" Ketsa grinned. "I guess I don't worry about compromising witnesses much. I've grown up with a lot of variation in my life. You get it in D.C. Or at least in my family. We did a unit on holidays around the world in sixth grade, and what I found out is that those holidays live in D.C. And then there's my mom. She looks for things that expose us to other faiths.

"We actually host Hanukkah at our house every other year, and we're not Jewish. Mom got us on this whole veg thing a month after she started going to the Hare Krishnas on Sunday nights. But I know what you mean about the statues. They seem kind of gaudy to me."

"God-y?"

"You know, an overdose of bright colors and all those garlands and powder and incense all over the place, and arms and legs going every which way and people with animal heads or animals with people bodies. But, I mean, if it floats their boat, does it matter to us, really? If it helps them?"

"Ketsa, how could it help them?"

"There you go. You answered your own question."

"No, I didn't."

"You told me you made an agreement to wonder, right? So, wonder how it could help them. The idols. How they could make life better for people, for real. How could it make God more real? It might be like Hanukkah is for me."

"What are you talking about?"

"Well, at first I figured it was just a nice way to remember their tradition of oil lasting a long time by lighting candles each day. But what I found out is that it's good for people today too."

"Like how?" Annie asked.

"Like, during Hanukkah you can't get up and do the dishes or your homework while the candles are burning. We just have to be there or pray or play. And so it's great! Our life is so hectic we would never take time as a family to gamble over chocolate money, spinning tops to see who gets all or half or none. But we do it. We play with these dreidels with two other families, and we all love it, and we love each other, and when I grow up, I'm going to light Hanukkah candles every year and not do a blessed thing while they burn.

"My mom didn't know the tradition, about hanging out while the candles burn down, and she drilled eight holes in this log she decorated and got some big dinner candles for it. When we got ready to light it, our guests were nice, but they laughed and said they were going to have to sleep over since those candles would burn for a long time. They didn't, sleep over that is, but the next year Mom found a regular menorah at a second-hand store, and we got some real Hanukkah candles for it.

"So, I don't know. Maybe there's something you could learn from Hindus that would make you a better Christian."

"Ketsa! I'm leaving! This conversation is insane!"

"Okay. *Hoge-burri.*"

Annie couldn't help but smile. "Okay. *Hoge-burtini*. But let's go run around the lake before dinner. Please."

CHAPTER 41

Annie got the go-ahead from her folks for the Long Weekend trip to Hampi. It turned out her dad had done a research paper on Hampi back in his college archaeology class, and he was excited for Annie to go.

"So did you tell them we'd be bouldering?" Aziz asked.

"I didn't *not* tell them. It just didn't come up," she answered. "My dad wanted to know if they're still excavating things, and told me to be sure to see the Pampa-something temple for him. It had been too long since college, he said, and he forgot its name. He never asked about rocks."

"It doesn't matter," Aziz said. Then he added, "Do they even know about me?"

Annie laughed. "Of course. They've known about you since *Guav-oh!* on the bus the day we got here. Mr. Red Shoes."

"And rock climbing?"

"A little."

"What does that mean?"

"Aziz, they're a long way from here. I can tell them you are a rock climber and that you climb rocks in Sri Lanka. But I can't tell them about Performing Arts and the library. They're not here to see what it's like. If I told them what we do, I know exactly what my mom would say: 'Annie, I can't imagine that it's okay for you to climb buildings!' or 'Is the PE teacher in charge of this climbing? Are adults there supervising?' She's strong on supervising.

"The thing is, I was freaked of it myself at first, so how

236   *Encounter: When Religions Become Classmates*

could I expect them to be okay with it? And I think it would just confuse things to tell them Hampi is both temples and bouldering. Especially if we don't even know if we'll go bouldering."

"I can assure you we will go bouldering," he grinned.

IT FELT AS if half of the campus was gone by dinner that Wednesday night when Long Weekend started. Both school buses and three minibuses rented from town had been parked outside Performing Arts when 10th period class finished. Bags had been piled in front of the building earlier that morning, so after a quick run to the dining hall for tea, students loaded onto the buses and left to make their train or plane connections. The atmosphere was charged with energy, and Annie momentarily longed to be going home too. "Soon," she said to herself. "Half-way done."

After dinner, the Hampi group loaded onto another bus for their trip to the railway station at the bottom of the Ghat Road. They caught the overnight train to Bangalore, 2nd Class Sleeper again, but much easier than when she had come to MMIS because they were traveling with just one small bag each. Their group had all of the seats in three sections to themselves, so the chatter and laughter ran high until the train lights around them began to go off and they realized the rest of the car was quiet. They would have liked to stay up all night, but the art teacher, Mrs. Kaur, came through the compartments reminding them the train would reach Bangalore shortly after 5:00 a.m.

Annie climbed onto a top bunk, and as she lay there, rocked gently by the motion of the train, she thought back on that other train journey from Hyderabad to Coimbatore two and a half months back. Before Megha Malai. Before Aziz and Vidhya. Before Chinnakadu. Before Sarmila's aprons and the man with polio. Before MRT and "Climb on!" Just hours ago she had been longing for home, but at that moment, Annie asked God to slow things down.

ANNIE MUST HAVE slept, for her thoughts moved into dreams, yet she was tired, not ready to wake up when Mrs. Kaur first came to their compartment. It was still dark outside. But when Mrs. Kaur returned, calling out that they'd be in Bangalore in fifteen minutes and they should start packing their bed rolls, Annie slid out the end of the bunk, making record time from wake up to feet on the floor so she could use the train's latrine before they got to the station.

Once off the train they moved with the crowd toward the station exit. Porters in red shirts ignored them, since the students carried their own small bags. Some of them stopped to get chai, but the teacher rushed them on, saying that they'd have a two hour wait if they didn't make the first bus out of Bangalore for Hampi.

They walked a short distance through an underground passageway from the train station to the Karnataka State Bus Depot and boarded a bus that would leave for Hospet, the town nearest Hampi, in thirty minutes. Better they sit on the bus and wait, Mrs. Kaur told them, than try to get on at the last minute and have to stand the whole way. They took seats in the back, and a couple of boys took orders, then went back out for soft drinks, bananas, oranges, and biscuits for the group. Others bought chai and little packets of something hot, wrapped in banana leaves, from sellers holding them up to the bus windows. Annie wouldn't risk it, but succumbed to a small plastic bag of banana chips. After she had eaten half of them, she wondered where they came from, but let the thought pass, as their saltiness and crunch tasted good.

The bus departed right on time. Once out of Bangalore, it

moved onto a smooth, wide, double-lane divided freeway. It seemed out of place. Annie wasn't sure why. Had she seen a highway like that when she first got to India, it would have been normal, but after Hyderabad and the drive to Gandhinagar, and then the journey to Megha Malai, it just didn't fit. It eventually trailed off into a narrow, paved road, passing through small towns where music blared into the streets from loudspeakers mounted on poles, and alongside villages where groups of women worked in fields with their saris pulled up around their legs like shorts. The bus stopped three times for groups of school children, then let them off farther down the road.

While MMIS students sat three to a seat, other seats often had four, plus children, and people were standing, crowded in the aisle, when the bus arrived in Hospet. As they stepped down from the bus, they were shuffled directly into auto rickshaws. It was a short distance on into Hampi, and the road was beautiful, trees lining both sides, reminding Annie of the country roads between Ridgeway High School and home.

Aziz was out of his rickshaw, waiting for Annie's as it pulled up.

"I signed you up to stay at Boulder Haven," he said. "It's across the river, so after lunch we'll go down to catch the boat."

They ate banana pancakes with the chocolate hazelnut spread Annie loved at home but only got at Christmas. They sat on reclining chairs made of rock slabs with a rock table in front of them, flanked by banana and coconut trees blowing in the breeze, overlooking the river. It was like the freeway – something that didn't seem to fit. It made Annie wonder what else she'd learn about India. Maybe she should have expected pancakes with chocolate spread.

After lunch ten of them loaded into the rowboat for the other side of the river. They walked up the riverbank, past a garbage dump where three cows and some dogs searched for edibles, through narrow dirt streets, and back out into open fields of rice paddies. Then in the distance she saw the reason Aziz brought her here.

The whole horizon opened before them with its landscape of boulders of all shapes and colors, scattered across the earth in piles, as if giants had played here and left their stacks, their marbles, for another day. God must have loved this place, Annie thought. She knew why people would build temples here. As far as she could see, the outcroppings of rock continued in one huge, beautiful jumble.

She looked up at Aziz. He grinned, giving her a thumbs up. They followed the road to its end.

"Boulder Haven," he announced grandly. In the front yard, a rope stretched tight between two coconut trees, just a meter off the ground. Aziz dropped his bag and jumped up onto it, thrusting his arms out to his side as he wobbled a bit at first, then regained perfect balance. In a few seconds he had impressively tight-rope walked his way across the line. The owner of the lodging came out just as he was bounding off. "I see we have a climber here," she said to Aziz. Annie wasn't sure what this had to do with climbing, but Aziz looked pleased.

He introduced himself, and they exchanged climbing information while the others got their room assignments from an assistant.

"We have crash pads for our guests," the owner said, "but you might already know that."

"I read online that you did," Aziz answered. "I hoped it was still true. It might have looked questionable if I brought my own, since we're on a temple art tour. Uh, during the mornings," he added quickly. "But in the afternoons, a couple of us plan to do a lot of bouldering." He pointed over to Annie, and she nodded hello.

Annie was assigned to room number 503, in a cluster of orange buildings with thatched roofs, along with two other girls from the Art II class. She liked the room number. It was her Area Code at home in Oregon, a coincidental sign of good luck sure to come. She also liked the room. It held a chest of drawers and three beds with mats, sheets, and mosquito nets held up by a frame. Annie had never slept under a mosquito net. The hotel in Hyderabad hadn't had mosquito nets, nor had the bungalow in Gandhinagar. Ms. Dunlop had the girls wear long sleeved shirts over their kameez tops in Gandhinagar to protect against mosquitoes at twilight, and they were never outside by dawn, when the mosquitoes were out most.

"So are we really going to use these?" Annie asked her roommates, SangMo and Chechong, motioning to the net above her bed.

"Sure," SangMo answered. "We'll sleep better without mosquitoes buzzing in our ears all night long, and their bites are no fun. Besides, there's no sense inviting malaria into our lives."

"Malaria?" Annie asked.

"Don't worry. Ms. Kaur brought spray repellent for all of us to use when we're out. I don't think they'll bother you."

"But what if I get one bite and that one happens to carry malaria?"

"That's why you take your malaria tabs."

Annie froze. Malaria pills! She had stopped taking them the required thirty days after they arrived in Megha Malai. The altitude was high enough that mosquitoes weren't a problem.

"Did you guys take malaria medicine?" she asked. They nodded. Annie ran out of the room, back to the veranda of the main building. Mrs. Kaur was still there.

"I don't have any malaria medicine," Annie said. "I forgot to take it before we left. I forgot to bring it with me. What can I do?"

"Slow down, Annie," Mrs. Kaur said. "You don't have it with you? It was on the handout for the trip." Annie shook her head and Ms. Kaur continued, "You were to arrange with your dorm parent to have any needed medication sent to the Activities Office before we left."

"I forgot all about it. What should I do?" Annie fought back tears. Something told her she had made a bad mistake. She had pushed away the feeling that something would go wrong on this trip to India. Annie had been sensible and positive and had not given in to the fear. But this time, it wasn't just fear of something out of her control that might happen; it was something she had done to herself, something that could have dangerous consequences.

"We might be able to get some chloroquine in town," Mrs. Kaur said, "though I'm not sure if this is an area where the mosquitoes are chloroquine resistant. Is that what you were using?"

"No, that wasn't the name. It was some antibiotic. But I'll switch if something else works. I'll take anything."

"You'll be okay, Annie. We live with the possibility of malaria all the time, but since we know we're not going to take medication our whole lives' long, we carry coils and use repellent and stay inside at certain times. But I know the worry. I had malaria as a teenager, and it was hard. So let's see what we can do."

That didn't make Annie feel better. She waited while Mrs. Kaur called the school dispensary, the whole time feeling angry at Aziz for not mentioning mosquitoes or reminding her about her medication. I'm not going to die of malaria just to climb around on some dumb rocks, she said to herself, and the tears came unbidden to her eyes.

What could she do? This kind of wondering was not what Annie had intended with her commitment to wonder. But that afternoon, once back from the medical shop in town and having downed a chloroquine pill, she couldn't help but wonder. Her roommates were gone, so she crawled onto her bed and sat under her mosquito net and thought, then prayed her heart's desire that God would watch over her and keep her well. She examined her ankles and feet carefully, then her arms and hands. She ran her fingertips over her neck and face for any little bumps that might be mosquito bites. She was sure there were none.

This thing was bigger than Annie, and she told God she needed Him. She prayed that He would take away the panic she felt and that she would be okay in Hampi. The thought of Leeza came to her, and though she knew Leeza had gone to visit relatives in Pondicherry and would be too busy to think of school, she wondered if she might also have found one moment to whisper a prayer for her. She knew her mom and dad would.

"I need you, God," Annie said simply. She lay back on her pillow and closed her eyes. A peacefulness came.

"Thanks," Annie whispered.

SangMo and Chechong came back into the room just then. "Aziz is looking for you, Annie," Chechong said.

CHAPTER 42

"**R**eady? We have two hours free time before we tour." He was carrying a big black suit-case-shaped mat on his shoulders like a backpack, and carried his backpack in his hand.

"What's that?" she asked.

"Climbing shoes. Chalk bags. Wantta carry it?"

"No, I mean that," she said, pointing to the mat.

"A crash pad."

"What for?"

"For when we fall."

"Aziz!"

"Annie, what? 99% of the time you land on your feet anyway, but it's just good to have it in case you don't, and it's easier on the ankles. I thought you wanted to climb safe."

"I do, but I don't want to crash."

"Okay, it's a landing pad. Better?"

"Okay."

They walked down a footpath through the rice paddies and then caught a dirt road and continued on it a short way before turning again onto a pathway that led directly toward the boulders. Annie grinned. Never had she expected, back in Ridgeway, that she'd be bouldering in Hampi, India, with this guy from Sri Lanka. A guy who was funny and fun and passionate about life and rocks and maybe a little about Annie coming along. She decided not to rail on him about the malaria pills. It wasn't his fault, she knew, and besides, what were the chances that something would happen?

"Aziz," she called out to get him to slow down.

"Yeah?"

"Wait up."

He smiled, then stopped walking and threw his arm out over the horizon. "Look at this place, Annie! It's paradise!" Annie caught up with him and looked out over more rock than anyone could climb in a life-time.

"It is beautiful," she conceded.

There, anchored to a large boulder, was a rusty metal sign-board: "BEWARE OF ROBBERS IN LONELY PLACES."

"Beautiful, and deserted. So should we expect to get mugged?" Annie asked.

"Come on, Annie!" Aziz said, running back to her. He whirled around her, grabbing the backpack she held in one hand, and caught her up in his momentum. "I've waited my whole life to climb in Hampi. Whatever a lonely place is, it's not here, and there'll be other climbers, and if there were robbers, what would they rob?" He ran in circles around her up the pathway.

She caught his spirit and took off jogging, down through boulders more than twice Annie's height, and up again, to emerge on an overlook of the river and fields beyond, and in the distance, more temples and a village. "Here we climb!" he said, "and nobody can rob this moment from us."

Annie was glad the climbing they'd done at MMIS had become a part of her. She slipped on Aziz's extra pair of climbing shoes, snapped the chalk bag around her waist, and dipped her fingers into it, trying some holds. Aziz did the same thing a few meters away. He stopped and spread the crash pad out under the spot Annie had chosen. "Not that you'll need it," he said, "but try sitting on it and starting from the ground position up."

"Why not start from the highest handhold you can reach?" But she didn't really pursue the question. She sensed that challenge somehow overrode height here. Aziz had gone to check out another side of the rock. She sat down on the crash pad and found grips for both her hands and feet and began working her way up to where her fingertips had rested when she stood. It worked!

Annie realized she was scaling the rock at two meters, then three. She found a wide crack open above her and let the fingers of her left hand move up along it as her right hand dipped back into the chalk and searched out handholds. Her climbing shoes pressed against the curvature of the boulder and found small footholds to balance her weight. Slowly she worked her way toward the top. She couldn't see the form of rock above her, but she could tell she was nearly there. Annie held her weight on her feet and left hand, and threw her right hand up, searching out something to pull against. In one fluid movement, her hand slipped over a rough but solid hold, her body momentarily touched the rock, then with all she had she lunged upward, feet and hands simultaneously digging in, then springing loose, heaving her up over the top. Annie lay for a second and caught her breath, then shimmied onward, wiggling her legs up underneath her until she was on hands and knees. From there she stood, and stepped out, easily scrambling over uneven rock a few easy meters to the center of the boulder. She let out a whoop!

"Aziz! Did you see that? Look what I did!" Suddenly sensing the height and not seeing Aziz, she sat down and carefully scooted along the downward slope opposite where she had climbed and looked over. Aziz was standing, looking up at her.

"Annie! What are you doing up there? Are you crazy?"

She had expected congratulations, a smile.

"I'm bouldering in Hampi," she said. "I thought that's why we came."

"Yeah, sure," he answered with a weak smile. "I thought we'd practice spotting for each other first. Get used to falling, I mean, landing. I thought you were just warming up."

"The holds worked, so I kept going," she said. And then sliding on to the edge above where Aziz stood, she looked down and added, "Yikes! How do I get down?"

CHAPTER 43

T wo hours of bouldering went by quickly. They reached Boulder Haven just in time to put their things away and join the rest of the group leaving for their guided tour of Hampi's temples, just an introduction to what they'd explore in more detail with Mrs. Kaur the next day.

Annie would tell her dad that she'd seen the Pampa-something and its real name was Virupaksha Temple. It was magnificent, its gray-white stone tiers rising pyramid-like against the deep blue sky. It didn't bother her like the temples in Hyderabad or Chinnakadu had. She was a tourist, at a palace.

She had trouble understanding the guide's English, but decided to just look instead of listen, and then read the details later in one of Mrs. Kaur's books. She also decided that the people who destroyed Hampi seven hundred years ago were stupid and mean.

Nightfall came as early there as it had in Megha Malai, and by 7:00 the students at Boulder Haven were back across the river, seated on cushions at low tables, awaiting their rice meals. There were other tables outside beneath the trees, under strings of lights. Annie and Aziz chose one of these.

Chapatis with two vegetable dishes were served first, then rice and sambar, curds, and crispy papadum. Better than at the dining hall, Annie thought, or maybe I'm just hungrier. She realized they hadn't eaten much that day, just the pancakes for lunch, unless she should count the banana chips at the bus station. But the server continued to come around with steaming hot pans of white rice, and even though she had planned to stop with a second serving, she had been talked into one more.

As they sat and talked, Annie wondered if they might have walked through something that had irritated her ankles, like nettles in the woods at home. Her feet itched and she caught herself scratching one foot with the other. She finally swung her feet out from under the table and looked at them. Every place her sandals weren't, her skin was covered with welts.

"What's this?" she said, running her hand over the bumps.

But Aziz had struck up a conversation with the server, making his rounds again with the rice, finding out about a group of climbers arriving tomorrow from Germany. Mrs. Kaur called for attention, going over the program for the next day, and suggested the students move into their rooms. Lights out at 10 p.m., if they were still awake by then. The day had started early, with the train's arrival in Bangalore, and Annie doubted that anyone would fight Mrs. Kaur on the early bedtime.

"G'night, Annie," Aziz said as they walked from the tables toward their bungalows. "Save the afternoon break for me," he said, and then added, "and the rocks. You were pretty awesome today, once I knew where to look for you."

"It was fun," she said. "I really like it."

"I'm glad you came."

"Me too." Their eyes met, and Annie didn't pull away. Neither did Aziz. She just looked at him, this boy she hadn't tried to find and never expected would come into her life. Annie knew the feeling. "I'm in enough trouble with my heart already," she told herself. "I can't let this happen." But neither of them turned away, and in that moment, something much stronger than words was said. She knew that he knew that too.

"See you in the morning," Aziz said at last, reaching for her hand.

"Okay then," Annie said, returning a gentle squeeze.

ANNIE WALKED TOWARD her room, falling in step alongside Mrs. Kaur. "Long sleeves," she said to Annie. "Or get under your mosquito net right away. They're out tonight in big numbers!" She swatted at her cheek and wiped away a flattened mosquito.

"I will," Annie said.

Chechong and SangMo were under one mosquito net, with a pile of cards spread out in front of them on the bed when Annie got to the room. "Want to play Teen Pathi, Annie?"

"What's that?"

"Cards. But we play with chickpeas instead of rupees."

"Sure. But I don't have any chickpeas."

"No problem. We have plenty."

So on one single bed under one mosquito net, Annie and a girl from Nepal and a girl from Bhutan played Three Card Bluff for chickpeas and talked about far away homes and parents, little brothers and sisters, jeans and sweatshirts and prom dresses and saris, clear skin and pimples, test scores and colleges, dancing and boys, old temples and new churches, wars and kingdoms with royal families. With two chickpeas left, Annie told the girls goodnight and slipped under her own mosquito net. Ketsa would have loved this, she thought. She wished Ketsa had chosen the Hampi field trip too, instead of Kerala. Annie missed her. Though she saw Lori and Jen occasionally, she didn't have any classes with them, and being in separate dorms, they had been content to develop their own circle of friends. But Ketsa was Annie's for keeps, she knew, in India and back at home. If Ketsa had been here Annie would have told her that she might be right about Aziz, after all.

CHAPTER 44

"**A**nnie... Annie, wake up." The voice was a whisper at first, then just a bit louder, but her bed was right under the window, and she stirred as she realized it was Aziz. She rolled over on her knees, and still under the mosquito net, pulled herself up to the window ledge, brushed a curtain to one side, and looked through the bars right into his face.

"Annie, you've got to get up. The guys from Germany came in last night, and they asked if we wanted to go out to the boulders for sunrise. I said yes."

"You said yes? Why didn't you tell me last night?" she whispered.

"It was too late. I'd get busted if I was caught on your porch at midnight."

"What time is it?"

"A little after five."

"Aziz!"

"Come on, Annie. You can sleep tonight. Or on the train going back to school. We're only here once, and these guys are cool. Besides, we'll be back before breakfast."

SangMo and Chechong hadn't awakened.

"Okay, I'm coming," she whispered.

Annie crawled out from under the net, pulled the curtains closed, and slipped into her clothes. She grabbed a bottle of insect repellent and gave her clothes, neck, wrists, and ankles a good spray, going over her ankles twice. The welts were still there, itchy, but not as swollen. They didn't really look like mosquito bites, at least she hoped not. Annie tiptoed into the bathroom, then picked up her backpack and water bottle and quietly slipped out of Room 503. Aziz and three other guys were waiting for her around the corner at the main building.

"This is Annie," Aziz said. "And this is Lars, Georg, and Tab. She's from Oregon, USA," he said motioning back to Annie, "and they're from Hamburg, Germany, all three of them." Introductions finished, Aziz offered them each an orange. They flicked on their torches and started out across the rice paddies toward the boulders. The boys spoke easily in English to her and Aziz, and from time to time slipped into and out of what she supposed was German, as they talked with each other.

They walked past the Beware of Robbers sign, farther into the boulders than they had the day before. The Germans seemed to be looking for a specific place, as they pulled out a guidebook from time to time and compared where they were to what was pictured. When they stopped and set down their crash pads and backpacks, Lars said, "This is it. Liam's Landing. I have a teacher at home, an Englishman called Liam, who told me about this place. He claims he did a first ascent on it, so he said he had the right to name it. Not sure how he confirmed that bit of history. Liam's Landing, he calls it, because he landed twenty-six times before he made it on the twenty-seventh try. I told him I'd do it in twenty-five."

"Why is it so hard?" Aziz asked. But at that moment a family of monkeys came bounding up the trail behind them. They stopped and sat on their haunches a few meters away from the group. A baby hopped into its mother's lap. Another picked up an orange peel and began turning it around in its hands, inspecting it carefully. Annie was fascinated. She hadn't seen monkeys this close before, not even in a zoo, and they had kept their distance in Chinnakadu. But she was also wary when Aziz waved his arms to frighten them away and they didn't budge. "They probably suspect that our backpacks have more goodies," he said. "Whose orange peel is that?"

"Sorry," Tab said. "I'll get them away." He picked up his backpack and flung it toward the monkeys.

"Mistake!" Aziz yelled. In an instant Aziz dashed forward and snatched the backpack up just as a large monkey lunged for it. The monkey backed off. Aziz stepped back toward Tab and tossed his backpack at his feet. "That could have been the end of your climbing shoes. Those guys are fast, and they figure any bag left unclaimed is theirs, even if it's for ten seconds."

"Oh, sorry again," Tab said, "and thanks."

As if at some inaudible signal, the monkeys all rose and in a few short bounds were on Liam's Landing, springing up its mound, suddenly at the top, even the babies. The climbers stood in awe, then laughed.

"Twenty-five tries, huh?" Annie said. "Too bad we're not monkeys! I hear we have 98% the same DNA. So climbing must be the missing 2%. This is a picture for home," she added and reached into her backpack for her camera. It wasn't there. She left it back in the room. Annie watched as the others snapped shots of the monkeys on top of their boulder. In a few moments they were gone, bounding off the rock and down the trail as quickly as they had appeared.

Annie secretly hoped her luck on the rocks would repeat itself and she would hold her own with these four climbers. Maybe she'd even make the top before any of them. She just watched for a while, and saw that she had a lot more to learn about spotting for another climber. Lars fell a dozen times, mostly at an overhang that he couldn't manage to hold onto, and Tab and Georg took turns directing his fall toward the crash pad. It looked trickier than the couple of times she'd done it with Aziz yesterday. She eventually chose another side of the boulder and began working her way up and, losing her hold, found herself repeatedly landing feet first back on their pad.

"Annie, come spot for me." It was Aziz calling from the back of the boulder. "Bring the crash pad. This is tough, but I want to try it." They repositioned, and Aziz made several attempts. Annie nudged him back toward the mat on a couple of the falls. Finally his dyno worked and he made the hold.

"Great leap, Aziz! Keep on!" Annie yelled. "You'll make it! Keep going!"

Two more holds, and then it all happened. His fingers slipped, his foot popped off the rock, and down he came, his back leading the fall. Annie knew she had to direct him toward the pad, and she was ready, but the angle of the fall and his weight were too much, and her knees gave way as his body hit her outstretched arms. She collapsed along with him, all but their legs hitting the crash pad. They were in one big heap, with Annie underneath Aziz, pinned tight against the mat, when the Germans appeared.

"You are all right?" Lars asked.

"You okay, Annie?" Aziz said, not moving.

"So this is what Americans and Indians do behind the rocks," Georg joked, looking down at their bodies intertwined at the base of the boulder.

"I'm okay. You?" Annie answered.

"I'm okay." Aziz rolled to one side, and accepted Georg's hand up, then reached down for Annie and helped her up. He brushed himself off, stood straight and leaned from side to side, testing his movement. "Sure you're okay," he asked Annie again. She nodded. Aziz turned to Georg and the others. "Yeah, this is what Annie and I do all the time," he said with a grin, "only I'm Sri Lankan."

They all returned to the other side of the boulder. More attempts were followed by more sudden landings, until they lost count, and decided to move to another outcropping, leaving Liam's landing for Liam's return.

As the sun rose over the Hampi horizon that morning, five young climbers sat together on the top of another beautiful boulder and let its rays welcome them into the new day. Annie felt Aziz's shoulder comfortably leaning against hers. The guys chatted in German, and she let the language carve a gentle seclusion around her and Aziz. As much as they all five were doing this together, it was Aziz who brought Annie to this place, and it was with him she chose to be as the day began. She leaned into Aziz, and said softly, "We do this all the time." It didn't make sense. It didn't need to. It was just what she wanted to say, and the shift of his shoulder toward hers said it was so.

CHAPTER 45

"**W**elcome back from Long Weekend," Mr. Das told his MRT class. "What Modern Religious Thoughts did you have over the break? Or experiences?"

Annie knew something had happened to Ajit. He was wearing a turban, and she wanted to know why. She liked Mr. Das's question. Maybe it would make it easy for Ajit to tell what happened. They had talked several times on their own after that first class in which he seemed so sullen and disappointingly un-Sikh. Annie had judged him too quickly.

She had learned more about his mom's death, and the fierce betrayal Ajit felt over his dad's quick acceptance of it and the flippant announcement he made when Ajit left for boarding school that he'd just have to remarry so they'd be a family again. As if both Ajit and his mom were dead to him now. Ajit had threatened to cut his hair in defiance and stormed out of the room, and when his dad turned on him in anger, Ajit threw off his turban, then pulled the bracelet off his arm and threw it at his father with a promise never to wear either again.

"Of course I regret it," he had told Annie. "But there's no going back on something like that. I did it to hurt him, but he deserved it. How could he forget Mom just like that, as if she didn't mean anything to us, and then treat me like dirt? So for now, I'm stuck in my own stupid pledge never to wear a turban. I'll cut my hair when I go off to college. And he'll get married again and never talk of Mom, so we'll be even." But here Ajit sat in a turban, wearing a bracelet.

"We'll divide into fours," Mr. Das directed. "Within each group, I'd like you each to describe something you experienced during the last week that touches on the practice of religion or spirituality. Then I'd like each group to select one of the four experiences and role play or describe it for the class."

Chairs shifted and groups formed. Annie turned her chair directly facing Ajit's.

"Looks like we're in the same group," he smiled.

"Heck yes," she said. "Why are you wearing a turban and a bracelet?"

"I'm in here too," Vidhya said.

Annie hadn't expected Vidhya to join her group. She had come into the room and sat on the other side by the wall, obviously still avoiding Annie. They hadn't talked since before Long Weekend, since the yelling at the temple in Chinnakadu, to be exact. Twice when Annie knew Vidhya had seen her in the dining hall and another time on the way to class, Vidhya walked away and began talking to others. Annie felt bad, but there wasn't anything she could do about it. It seemed to be Vidhya's choice to retreat into her own little Hindu world. But when Mr. Das announced they'd be working in groups, Irfana scooted her chair over, and Vidhya joined their circle.

"You start first, Ajit," Vidhya announced. Annie realized she wasn't the only curious one.

"It's nothing as dramatic as it seems," he said. They waited, so he went on. "I flew home to Lahore for Long Weekend. My aunt and uncle came from Australia with cousins I hadn't seen since elementary, and my dad's cousin and his wife and little girl came from Toronto, and we spent two days together with my grandparents and other family from Lahore. It was good. When Saturday came around we were supposed to go to the temple, and Dad asked me if I'd be one of the servers at lunch for a group of people who were visiting Lahore from northern Karnataka. I didn't expect that.

"'I can't,' I told him. He asked me why. I didn't answer, but my dad left the room and came back with my turban and bracelet. I guess he had kept them. He just looked at me and said he was so sorry and could I ever forgive him. My dad had never talked about my mom dying. He just said things like, 'You'll be okay. We'll be okay. You're strong, Ajit.' That day I finally told Dad that I had never been strong, and all I wanted was for him to miss Mom with me. I had never seen my dad cry, ever, until then." Ajit stopped talking. Tears filled his eyes, and he wiped them away, as he looked down at the floor.

"It's been a pretty awful year, hasn't it, Ajit?" Vidhya said tenderly. Annie was glad she found those words to say.

Ajit looked up and nodded. "For the first time," he continued, "I told my dad that I had wanted to die too. It hurt too much, yet he didn't care at all. About Mom or about me. Instead he sent me away to boarding school so he could start a new life. He held me then, and told me I would never know how much he hurt from missing her. And me."

Here Ajit paused, but they knew he wasn't finished.

"And ..." Irfana said.

"I realized that after almost a year, I wasn't the only one who still missed Mom or didn't understand why she had to die."

The classroom was silent. They realized the groups had all turned toward Ajit to hear his story. Letting out a big sigh, he shook his head.

"Go ahead with your group discussions," Mr. Das directed the class. When the noise level resumed to normal, Ajit continued quietly, "We went on to the temple and I worked alongside my dad and the other men. I was proud that we have this tradition of welcoming visitors by sharing our meals.

"That evening we talked a lot about my mom. Everybody. My aunts told me stories about her that I never even knew, and I laughed. Before I fell asleep that night, I said goodbye to Mom.

"That's all." He paused, then added, "Except for coming back here and wondering how people would treat me when I came back wearing a turban."

"We'll treat you like Ajit, who you are," Vidhya said gently. "At least I hope people aren't stupid." She looked right at Annie when she said that. Unfair. Annie would never make fun of Ajit. Even though Vidhya was so adamant about some things, Annie realized how easy it was for Vidhya, a Hindu, to accept Ajit, a Sikh, and his turban. Annie couldn't help but think of all the mess at Ridgeway when Param had first come to school wearing a turban. Maybe it's good for people to grow up with gods that have green and blue faces and elephant noses and ten arms and legs, she thought, because then something like a turban doesn't throw you. Doesn't throw you at all.

"So, Irfana, you next?" Vidhya said.

"Nothing really happened that I noticed," Irfana said. "I don't think I thought of anything spiritual. I just veg'd for five days – movies, out to eat, shopping. Except ..."

"That 'except' is probably the answer to the question," Vidhya said. "What's the except?"

"Except there was this family that had moved in next door, and they have two little kids who made this creative lookout tower out of boxes and boards so they could see from the corner of their compound into ours. We were having tea on the veranda and there they were, their little heads peering over the top of the fence, looking at us, a boy and a girl, maybe kindergarten age. Mom and I started giggling, and so did they, and we told them to get their parents and come over for tea. Which they did, and the adults were horrified that their kids were little spies. But we all laughed. And I guess I just felt that the world is an awesome place with little kids like that around." She paused, then added, "Is that a Modern Religious Thought, by any chance?"

"I think so," Vidhya said. "A good one. My 'happening' was just about the opposite of that."

"What was it?" Annie thought maybe Vidhya had decided to put their argument at Chinnakadu behind them, and hoped she'd answer civilly.

She answered, but didn't even acknowledge Annie's presence. She kept right on talking, looking at Ajit and Irfana. "Our cook got sick when I was home, and she didn't come the whole time. What I saw was that my dad and mom are great cooks, and they even sent some of the dinners they made to Kamala's house; that's her name, our cook. But what happened was, I had a friend from my old girls' school come over, and she was shocked that my folks would do that – fix our meals themselves instead of getting a temporary cook or having one of the other ayahs fill in. 'And I suppose your parents empty the dustbins too, and clean the bathrooms!' she teased. I just looked at her. Because they do.

"And I do too. My dad said way back before I was born, that two things our ayahs would not do would be to empty our rubbish and clean our bathrooms. So I grew up doing my own. I hadn't really thought about it very much, until I heard her make fun of the idea, because it had never seemed especially unusual to me. Now I'm afraid that I ..." Here Vidhya let out a big puff of air. "I'm afraid I'm headed for another Cause."

"What?" Ajit asked.

"You know. A Cause. Something that bugs me till I do something about it. Maybe I'll just get the library to buy the book *India Stinking*, and call it good. I noticed the cover in a bookstore display while I was home and bought it. Maybe I'll write a letter to *The Hindu* about Dalits still cleaning dry latrines and challenge people to get over the idea that somebody else has to clean up their dirty work. 'Shit,' if you will," she added. "Maybe I'll tell Maintenance that we need to have the students take a turn cleaning the Bs here at school."

"Not me," Irfana said flatly. "That's exactly why we pay lakhs of rupees... not just for classes and teachers, but for the cooks and for the ayahs who clean the Bs. I will never do that!"

"See!" Vidhya said.

"See what?" Irfana asked. "Oh, Vidhya, go take your revolution somewhere else! Certain things are meant to be, and me cleaning Bs, even my own, is not one of them. Besides, you said yourself you have a cook."

"So?"

"So!"

Annie looked at Ajit, and her eyes said as clearly as she could, Do something! It was bad enough that Vidhya was mad at her, but now she was tearing into Irfana. He rolled his eyes, in a look of helplessness, then smiled. "So!" he said in a perky voice. "So, we have to hear from Annie still. We can always get back to the shit later, no pun intended." Vidhya did not laugh. Irfana grinned.

"Yeah, I do have something," Annie said. Vidhya looked at her. An improvement. But she didn't smile.

IN THE END it was Annie's experience they decided their group would role play for the class.

Ajit made a dash for the kitchen, and was back with a small packet of white flour before Mr. Das realized he was gone. Their group presented second. They arranged their four tables, plus two extras, in a pyramid, and asked another group to donate their tables for a second pyramid. Irfana and Vidhya made a doll-like being with Ajit's jacket. They set it in the middle of the second tier of table legs in the first pyramid. It was quite a stretch of the imagination to see the deity they were trying to create, but when they put a hastily written sign on the top table, reading "Virupaksha Temple, Hampi," the class got the idea. On the second pyramid, they placed a second sign "Hampi boulders."

Ajit, Vidhya, and Irfana dipped their fingers in the flour, made three horizontal lines across their foreheads with their whitened fingertips, and proceeded one by one to approach the temple tables and bless the image inside with another dot of flour on its forehead.

Having finished their worship reenactment, they stepped to the side. Annie approached the boulder-pyramid and sat down on the floor. Students leaned forward or stood to see what she was doing. She dipped her hands into the paper sack of flour which she had tucked into the waistband of her jeans, and reached for the edge of the table. Matching patches of flour that had been placed strategically on the pyramid earlier, Annie rose from seated position to knees, then crouched, then stretched upward and mimed the motions of reaching for each of the chalk-marked handholds above her as she went. She stepped up on a chair they had placed next to the "boulder" and onto the first level of the pyramid, re-chalked her hands, and placed them both on the top table. Then she turned, bounded down from the table, and when the class was quiet, she spoke.

"I went to Hampi over Long Weekend, and I saw both the colored powder used for worship in the temples and the white powdered chalk used to give us a better grip on the boulders we climbed. Three guys from Germany were with me and Aziz, and we climbed one day just as the sun was coming up. When I jumped back down off the boulder that morning, and looked at the bright white chalk patterns up the side of the rock, I had this funny feeling that it wasn't all so different from the ash we put on our foreheads at home on Ash Wednesday, or the powder they used to bless the Shiva in a temple in Hampi, except for the color.

"I guess not many people would think this, and maybe you'll think I'm crazy, but that day, I was thinking about what a great world God made and how lucky we were to be in it. And how much I hoped it stayed beautiful forever. All of us there loved the rocks and the sun, and the green of the rice paddies beyond us. We were all part of something amazing that God made in that spot. I was part of it.

"I didn't think about it right then, but on the train back I started wondering if that's the feeling people had when they first built the temples in Hampi, that this place with these amazing boulders was so beautiful, that they wanted to build something that would make people notice what God created. Then I got to wondering if maybe some people think about the real God when they go into the temple, if that whole process of doing that helps them remember God and feel like they're near Him. Because I know people who would think I was crazy for saying I felt close to God climbing boulders. But I did. That was my thought."

The class applauded when she finished. Annie turned to join her group and caught Vidhya's eye. Something had softened in her look. She wanted to tell Vidhya that she hadn't totally changed her mind about temples and she hadn't changed her mind about idols at all, so she could stay mad if she wanted to. But instead she reached out for Vidhya's hand. If this Hindu girl knew camp songs and cared so much about ladies in Chinnakadu, and made Ajit feel okay when he cried, then maybe they shouldn't stay mad for months. After all, there wasn't that much time left. Vidhya didn't pull away. She just looked at Annie, and tears filled her eyes.

Annie continued to get questions from the students around campus, students in MRT and others too. Nobody asked much about the temples; they asked about bouldering. Did you do that in the US? Are there places around Megha Malai where you go? Why didn't they tell us we could go rock climbing in

Hampi? Are you the one who climbs Performing Arts with Aziz? Annie down-played the whole thing, thinking it wasn't news to be spread around campus. It was just something that came to mind in MRT, not something she wanted other people to know. But word traveled fast.

Ketsa found Annie in the dining hall. "The new camping director is looking for you, girl. Aziz too."

"Yikes."

"No, the director talked to me, and he's not mad. In fact he's excited. He heard you're a rock climber, and he wants to know what you know about rock walls."

"Nothing, except the National Guard tower that they had at the State Fair." And the walls of a few buildings, she thought, but didn't say.

"So stop in at his office, he said. They're thinking of putting up a rock wall where the school goes for its camping trips. He didn't even know there was an old rock wall right here on campus."

Just then Aziz came up to Annie's table. "Have you heard?" he asked. "We may be able to tell the world about what we do!"

"Starting with me, right now!" Ketsa said. "So what do you do, Aziz? With Annie..." She grinned.

"Climb," he answered, grinning back.

CHAPTER 46

M r. Hausden announced on the bus out to Chinnakadu that they would be finishing up this batch of water filters today and next week. The women's project needed to wrap up too, or at least be under the women's own direction completely until school started again in July.

"Can we finish this project together without getting mad at each other," Vidhya asked Annie on the ride out to the village. "Because the women deserve it, don't you think? They could use our help."

Annie nodded. "But I'm not sure how … how I'll react in the temple. I'll just warn you about that right now."

"Would it do any good for us to talk about it?" Vidhya asked.

"Probably not," Annie said. "I just can't make sense out of it, no matter how hard I try."

"But you said that at Hampi…" She didn't finish.

"I know. And I do wonder. But maybe I was going too far."

They rode along in silence until Annie said, "How does a stone elephant mean anything to you, Vidhya, really? How can it possibly be God? I really, truly want to know."

"It's not like I have everything figured out, Annie, even though I might act like I do. But it is real. Ganesh makes a lot more sense to me than what Christians do. They talk to some man up in the clouds who everybody knows can't possibly be there. And they call him Father God sometimes and Jesus God sometimes, and then say they're the same thing anyway – the one and only true God. Like that makes sense?"

Annie shrugged.

"What is God, anyway?" Vidhya asked. "Something way big. Brahman. And how does 'something way big' care about me and a little group of women from Chinnakadu who are lonely and scared and want to start something new to make things better. How does 'way big' bless us? It's hard to feel something in the clouds, except the mist or the rain, or something everywhere, so we go into the temple, and there is Ganesh, right there in front of us, reminding us that God is solid and real and as close as right where we are. God may be big, but God is also in Chinnakadu and cares about us and wants to give us blessings. So we honor him."

"God or the elephant?" Annie asked.

"Does it matter? If one is a reminder of the other, a reminder that it's true?"

"It matters to me."

"That's the thing about Christianity," Vidhya said.

"What's that supposed to mean?" Annie asked.

"Nothing."

THE BUS BUMPED along and Annie looked out the window at the green terraced fields held in place by the red soil walls built up to encircle the contour of the hillsides like a giant topographic map. "It's amazing here," she said. "I almost wish I were coming back next year."

"Do."

"I can't. But will you email me and tell me how they're doing?" Annie asked.

"You know I will," Vidhya said. "I'll find a way to get back here next year and see how it's all going, even if we're done with the water."

"I wonder if they've figured out how they're going to earn money," Annie said.

"We'll soon find out."

The bus rolled into Chinnakadu and stopped in front of the school. Annie and Vidhya left the group immediately and headed for the other end of the village, along with Leeza, who had joined the Chinnakadu group this time, as a rep from National Honor Society. Annie had told her about the women's project and Leeza decided to see if National Honor Society and the Scholastic Book Fair people would donate some books to jump-start the village library. The girls stopped at Radha's house and found six young women already there, waiting for them. They had tea and then moved to the temple grounds. A group of women were also waiting there.

There was excitement in their voices. Annie could feel it in the air. Vidhya talked with the women, and then with Annie and Leeza to bring them up to date on the plan.

"They've decided on a craft," Vidhya explained. One of the young women, Chandra, told Vidhya that it was something her mother taught her years back, but she had done it only as a hobby, for fun. "And they've already figured out how to get started," Vidhya added.

"What are they making?" Annie asked. Vidhya relayed the question to the women. Three or four of them opened the cloth bags they were carrying and gently lifted out small packets. Untying the thread that held them, and unfolding the newspaper that protected their treasures, they showed the girls that each of them had made three sample greeting cards, along with handmade envelopes. The inside of the card was blank, but the cover was a picture of something or someone from village life made from little scraps of paper and fabric glued in place on the card stock. They handed the first set of three to Annie, and the bright colors and clever artwork clearly showed what they were portraying: a *dhobi* carrying a bundle of wash on his head; a woman holding a Deepavali lamp in her hands; two girls doing a dance with sticks raised above their heads, hands crossed. The arms and faces were of brown paper. The rest was cloth.

"These are awesome!" Annie said. "They made these?" Her reaction brought smiles.

Vidhya chatted with the women and then with Annie and Leeza. "Chandra and Anandhi have already been to Megha Malai and managed to get a small loan from the Women's Cooperative to cover the cost of scissors and cardstock. Others gathered fabric scraps. They plan to sell the cards through the Co-op, as well as from a little shop here in Chinnakadu. They want you to take some home to sell too, Annie. And Leeza, they're excited to hear about the picture books for the library."

The next set of cards the women unwrapped included a temple, like the one just a few meters from where they sat; Ganesh, with flowers sprinkled at his feet and a garland around his neck; and a tree with two women sitting in its shade. Because of the wall behind it, Annie was sure it was the tree under which they were sitting.

Vidhya looked over her shoulder. "Oh, my gosh, that's you!" she said. "And me!" The women burst out in laughter, and Annie held the card to her heart. Radha had just handed the last set of cards to Leeza.

"This is mine!" Leeza said seeing the design on the top card. "Look!" She held up the card showing two brightly dressed bunny rabbits, each carrying a pan full of fabric Easter eggs, on their heads, like the women who carried gravel to repair the road in front of the school. "Who knew to do this?" she asked. "Can I buy it right now?"

Radha, obviously pleased by Leeza's enthusiasm, chatted with Vidhya.

"How much should it bring?" Vidhya asked Leeza. "Forty rupees?"

"More."

"Fifty?"

"More."

"Seventy?" Vidhya asked a bit cautiously. "Would they bring seventy rupees?"

"In the States, for sure. That's just less than a buck. I'm not sure about Megha Malai, but I think so, with the tourists and all. Let's try it."

"They are awesome cards!" Annie said.

"I would buy them over any you find at home." Leeza agreed.

The young women explained that they had already chosen a treasurer to keep track of payments on the loan and take the extra funds to the bank in Megha Malai to put into an account for their group under the name Kurinji Women's Cooperative. They would also keep sub-accounts for each woman. Annie wondered what the word *kurinji* meant, but Vidhya was already talking about the first batch of cards they'd have done by next Saturday, forty of them, and their plans to get them to Megha Malai. Leeza said she'd see that they had a bag of books to bring back to their new library when they returned.

By this time, a group of older women had gathered at the temple, perhaps just to see what was happening, but they were welcomed, and the sample cards were brought out again and passed around. Tiny scissors were taken from a bag and added to little packets of fabric and paper which would be each woman's personal supply. The three women who had brought the samples began showing the others how the patterns they had made could be copied onto their cardstock. Annie noticed that the girl with the scars had come back again, the one she almost tripped over the day Vidhya yelled at her for not going into the temple. The girl had quietly slipped inside the gate this time, and sat off to the side by herself until one of the older women motioned for her to join them. They handed her a pair of scissors and fabric scraps and paper. Annie noticed that her scars didn't show quite so much when she smiled.

The women decided they would meet at the temple

grounds, under this tree, and cut and paste their pictures as they sang together, twice a week for an hour. And so they began by singing about the *kurinji*, their namesake, though it was only later, on the bus ride home, that Annie learned from Vidhya that this was a flower of delicate purple hue which blossomed there in the Western Ghats once every twelve years. Chinnakadu had fields of *kurinji*, sure to bloom within the next month, in this very time of their group's beginning, and that would bring the good fortune they knew was sure to come.

Once every twelve years, Annie thought. How could a flower know that twelve years had passed and it was time to bloom? And how could these women of Chinnakadu have known that there was something within them waiting to bloom into just what they wanted it to be. Annie had never seen a *kurinji* flower. Nor had she ever seen a village women's card-making cooperative. But she had a feeling that these cards would be popular in Oregon and wherever they went in the world. These women would surely find all kinds of village life scenes to show on their cards, and their pictures would tell stories as wonderful as the books in their new library. Tiny miracles, Annie thought. And I'm here to see it happen.

Chandra, took Annie's hand as they closed their meeting. She spoke in Tamil, "*Vannakam.*" Then, as if testing her voice, she began again softly in English. Annie stood quietly so as not to miss what she said. "Thank you. You are a good Animator." Had Annie heard right? An animator? Someone who draws cartoons? She didn't understand, but she felt the warmth of the compliment. Annie reached out and folded Chandra into a hug.

Annie slipped away from the group as they walked toward the center of the temple. She stepped out of the temple compound gate into the bright sunshine. She tipped back her face, feeling the sun's warmth seep into and blend with her smile. "Thank you, God," she whispered, "for Chinnakadu and for the miracles of this day. *Vannakam.*"

She turned and saw Vidhya and Leeza, together with the women, emerging from the inner temple. Vidhya didn't look mad. Maybe she hadn't noticed that Annie left.

AS THE BUS pulled through the Main Gate into the school, Annie turned to Leeza. "Thanks for coming with us, when you didn't have to."

"Thank you for telling me about the project," Leeza said, "and inviting me. I wouldn't miss it for anything. I love what they're doing. I'm excited to see it happen. And I love books, Annie. I hope to be a real writer someday. And to think that I could help people in Chinnakadu have books is just, well, worth way more than sleeping in on Saturday morning."

Mr. Hausden collected the green t-shirts and asked for volunteers willing to work with him and Won Tae on the year-end report on the water filter project. It would be presented in an all-school assembly the first week of May. Vidhya hollered up to Annie from the back of the bus, "Let's do it, Annie. We can get something in on the Kurinjis." Annie raised her hand. As they filed out of the bus, she waited for Vidhya.

"It was a good day," Annie said. "Thanks for understanding."

Vidhya laughed. "Understanding what? That a Hindu and a Christian who aren't fighting have a little more fun together. That our women are very cool. That we have multiple reasons for re-assimilation of our friendship."

"Yeah," Annie said, smiling at Vidhya's terminology. "All of those things." Then she asked, "Is 'animator' a Tamil word?"

"No. It's English. Maybe British English if you don't say it in the States."

"We say it," Annie replied, "but it means somebody who draws cartoons or makes animated movies."

"I suppose it means that here too, but mostly it's the name we give to the government *sevaks*, or development workers. Why?"

"Nothing. All this time I thought it only meant somebody who draws cartoons."

"Around here, it's somebody like Ms. Jayashree who takes on a village and is their resource person, or encourager."

Annie slipped into the library before going back to Tresham. She pulled a dictionary off the reference shelf. There was no listing for "animator," so she settled for "animate": to fill with breath, to give life or spirit, to infuse with vivacity. Annie felt honored by the title. Why don't we ever use the word that way at home? she wondered. All those questions about what she wanted to do when she grew up, what she planned to major in at college … "I plan to be an Animator," Annie could say, and that would cover it.

CHAPTER 47

"Thirty-nine," the nurse read out, taking the thermometer from Annie. "Another sick girl."

"How are you feeling, Annie?" Doctor Mary asked.

"Awful," she said, "... headachy, and hot, and my stomach." Annie didn't feel like talking, and pulled the sheet up around her ears.

"It looks like this bug doesn't care where we're from or what resistance we might ..." The doctor's words trailed off as another nurse came to report that two more students just came in with fever, nausea and cramping. "Let's get word out to the dorms to watch for gastrointestinal flu," Doctor Mary said, "and to send their students over to us. We want to contain it as much as possible."

"Word is already out," the nurse replied. Three girls stood in the doorway in pj bottoms and sweatshirts, wrapped in blankets. "We're sick, Miss," one of them said to the nurse. "Our dorm parent said we should come to the dispensary."

"Where's the bathroom?" one of the girls asked, and dashed away in the direction the nurse indicated.

Annie rolled over on her side and slept, vaguely aware that others too had come, though she was unable or unwanting to stir herself to see who it was or if she knew any of them. She just wanted to sleep.

Annie awakened, shaking, not sure if it was day or night, and someone nearby called the nurse. Annie was crying.

Maybe that's why the nurse ran, she thought. Doctor Mary was there too. Or was it Vidhya? Annie was scared, but she was too hot to do anything, so she let them take care of her and went back to sleep again. She had to sleep.

Was this all happening today, or was it last night or yesterday? She thought she remembered someone saying Ketsa was sick too, but the hours blurred as she slept and woke and slept again, knowing that she was hot, always hot, except when she was cold, and that someone threw up in the bed next to her, or maybe it was her, and they forgot to tell her she had puked in her bed. Or was that a dream?

The dream came again, that the welts from Hampi had come back around her ankles and were swelling bigger and bigger. She knew she was supposed to spray them to make them melt, only when she did, the spray melted the mosquito net instead and Annie was left in her bed, hot, always hot, except for the mosquitoes singing to her. People were talking about Hampi, and the singing mosquitoes.

The mosquitoes sang on, pulling her back from the hospital. But she wasn't at the hospital; she was at school. And Danny was there asking if she wanted to pet Snyder's hedgehog. And Tani was there. She told Annie she could borrow her black velvet hat because she didn't need it in heaven, unless Annie wanted to come to heaven with her.

Ketsa was holding her hand, Annie thought. But not at the dispensary. She was in a hospital. Where? Had she gone home? Were Mom and Dad in the other room? She cried out to them.

"We called them, Annie," someone said, "They know."

Hurry. Hurry, Annie thought. And sing.

"I'll sing." Annie recognized the voice, but she couldn't think who it was. "It's me," the voice said.

It's Leeza and Mom, Annie supposed. They came to pray for me. Annie was sure she nodded yes, for Leeza to sing, and Mom to pray, and so they did:

"Right where you are, you couldn't be more precious.

Right where you are, the wonder of you ..."

The song went on, but Annie couldn't hear the words, only the birds singing.

Another night, or was it the hot sun on her head?

Aziz? The sun's coming up over the boulders. It's time for us to go. I'll just sleep here on the rock. And Param will hold me.

For one long night and one day Annie slept and dreamed, and woke and slept again, and fought against the sickness that was attacking her body, the same virus, they assumed, that hit others less intensely throughout the campus. The dispensary was full, and two or three rooms in each dorm were designated as sick rooms, taking the doctor and nurses on continuous rounds throughout the campus. But Annie's fever did not subside as quickly as the others' had.

"I'm doing *puja* for you, Annie, right here. Regardless," a voice said. "You don't have to open your eyes. Just feel the light. You'll be okay. Ganesh will bless you, I know." The girl was crying, in Tamil, or was it German? Annie couldn't feel the light. It was too dark. And she was falling. She wanted chalk for her fingertips, so she could hold on, but she was too tired to reach for the chalk, so she let go and fell into the darkness.

WHEN THE SEIZURE hit, everything became more than clear. It wasn't a bad case of the gastrointestinal flu that Annie was fighting. It was malaria. She was moved from the dispensary to the hospital in Megha Malai for immediate treatment. Her parents were called, and they left for Seattle to get emergency visas for a flight to India. Twelve hours passed, and everyone but Annie felt it as an eternity.

A hand touched her forehead. "God, you're still hot!"

"Vidhya?" Annie stirred. "Vidhya?" Annie opened her eyes and raised her head from her pillow, then struggled to push herself up on her elbows. Vidhya was there, crying. "Vidhya, what's wrong? Where's the doctor? I think I'm sick."

"Miss Shanthi!" Vidhya called. "She's awake!"

The nurse came quickly and stood at Annie's side. "How are you, Annie?" she asked.

"Okay. Tired. And I have a headache." She looked at the nurse, then at Vidhya. "Where in the world am I? Where's Doctor Mary?" she asked.

The nurse put her hand over her mouth as if to hold back a sudden cry. "Rani, call Doctor Mary and tell her that Miss Annie is awake and is asking for her. You're in the hospital, here in Megha Malai," the nurse said. "You've had the onset of malaria, but you're going to be okay."

"Malaria?" Annie said. "I don't want malaria. Please ..." She began to cry. Vidhya sat down next to her on the bed and pulled Annie into a hug, rocking her gently back and forth. "Don't worry, Annie, you're going to be okay. The nurse said so."

Her parents had not yet left Seattle when the call reached them that Annie had come out of the coma.

"She'll be fine," Dr. Mary told them, "but we'll keep her in the hospital or in our dispensary for the present."

"They want to talk to you," Dr. Mary said, handing the phone to Annie.

"Hi, Mom." Annie started crying again. "Dad, are you there?"

"We're right here, Annie. Do you want us to come? We will. We can be there in twenty-four hours."

"I don't know. I think I'm okay. But I got sick. They said I have malaria. I'm scared."

"We'll come, Sweetie," her mom said. "I'll be right there."

It was just what she always said when Annie called home to be picked up after track practice. It made Annie smile through her tears.

"What?" Vidhya whispered.

"My mom ..." Annie said. "Mom, I think Dr. Mary wants to talk to you again." Dr. Mary stepped out into the hall, but Annie could hear her voice and knew it was a long conversation. In the end, Dr. Mary told Annie that her folks decided they would call again in a few hours and see how she was doing.

"You don't need to come," Annie said when they called back, "but thank you for saying you would."

"We still can if you need us or want us to."

"Thanks, Mom," Annie said.

"So many people were praying for you, Sweetie. We're just praising the Lord that you're okay!"

IN THE HOURS that followed, Annie learned that friends from MMIS, those who weren't sick themselves, had kept vigil at her bedside in the hospital during that twelve-hour coma when she slept so deeply.

"Aziz came?" Annie asked. "And Ketsa?"

"Aziz, yes," the nurse answered. "But Ketsa has been down with the bug that got so many sick, so we kept her away. And you, little girl, gave us a real scare."

"I'm sorry," Annie said. "I didn't mean to. I don't think I knew what was happening. It all got mixed up, like a dream. I even thought Vidhya came ..."

"She did, many times," the nurse answered.

"No, I mean I thought she came and prayed to her elephant god for me. Gosh, that shows I was in lah-lah land for sure!"

Annie was glad that medicine had been discovered that could fight malaria. She was glad her body was strong and that there were doctors and nurses who knew what to do. She was grateful for friends who would sit with her even though she slept and dreamed. And parents and grandparents and friends at home who would pray for her. Most of all Annie was thankful that God stayed by her through all this and had kept her safe.

Then in a sudden moment of clarity, Annie realized something else. Vidhya had come. She remembered a tiny light burning somewhere nearby, and Vidhya praying for her, praying when she desperately needed it. And Vidhya had cried ... and cried ... to Ganesh. The Remover of Obstacles.

CHAPTER 48

T here was a tapping in the girls' ward of the dispensary. Annie looked up to see Aziz through the window, outside, rapping his knuckles against the glass. "Come open this," he mouthed. Annie crawled out of bed and walked to the window. She fiddled with the handle, then managed to push it open.

"What are you doing here, Aziz? You'll get in trouble."

"Okay."

She smiled. "Wow, it's good to see you!"

"You too. So when are you getting out?" he asked.

"Dr. Mary said I should be back in school next Monday, at least part time."

"Annie, you were sick. Bad."

"I know that now. Thanks for coming to the hospital to see me. They said you did."

Aziz nodded. "I realized that climbing isn't as important as I thought it was," he said.

"Of course it is, you dork! I love it!" Annie said. "But to tell you the truth, I don't exactly feel like climbing rocks, or buildings for that matter, right now."

"That's what I mean. All I wanted to do was have you wake up and talk to me, or eat rice with me, or walk, not even run, the lake – with or without me. I realized we had so much more to do and things to talk about and not much time left."

"What things?" she asked.

"You know, like how you're going to survive without

Guav-oh! in the States." He looked away. "Wait a minute. I'm going around to the front and coming in. Ask the nurse if you can come out to the lounge, okay?"

He was gone before she could answer, and in a few moments he reappeared in the hall just outside the girls ward. "The nurse said okay, or she would have if I could have found her. Come on, Annie."

She picked up a blanket and wrapped it around her, then followed Aziz to a bench at the end of the hallway.

"I thought about you a lot while you were sick, Annie. Did you realize that not once since I met your bus coming up from Coimbatore back in January, have I ever told you, till right now, that I think about you? But I do. A lot. I've talked about climbing and classes and home and Oregon and music, but I've been scared to say what I really want to tell you. I like you. And I don't know what that means, except that you're fun, and you smile, and you try things, and you're nice, and you like to learn, and... and you like my red shoes." He paused. "And you've sat with me and watched the sun rise in Hampi. I want to keep you, but I don't know how. And I was scared."

Annie slipped her hands out from under the blanket shawl and into Aziz's. He gathered both his hands around hers and lifted them to his heart, looking deep into her eyes.

"I want to keep you too, Aziz," she whispered, lifting the edge of the blanket to her face to wipe away the tears in her eyes.

ANNIE WAS STILL in the dispensary on Saturday when her SL class went back out to Chinnakadu for the last time that year, but word had somehow reached the village that Annie had been seriously ill. In addition to news that the women had almost doubled their goal in card making and that the women's co-op in Megha Malai had invited the Kurinji Co-op in as partner-members, Leeza had played photographer and brought back a good hundred digital photos for Annie, including a short video clip of the ladies at the temple singing. For Annie.

"And they sent you this," Leeza said, handing her a flat little packet, wrapped in newspaper, tied with thread. Annie opened it carefully. It was a card. The outside of the envelope had something written in Tamil, and underneath it, in English, the words: Animator Annie. She slipped the card out of the envelope and saw a delicate fabric bouquet of lavender blossoms, bordered by a narrow satiny purple strip of cloth. Annie's name was in one corner in tiny letters, and across the bottom, the words *Kurinji Women's Co-op.* Annie opened the card. It was written in Tamil, by several different authors, she guessed. She handed it to Leeza. "Can you read?"

Leeza smiled. "A little Hindi. But no Tamil, sorry to say. But I can fake it. Let me see. It says: 'Dear Annie, We're glad you are getting well. We hope you can go to the store in Megha Malai to see all the cards we made. Please tell Leeza we love the books she sent." Leeza stopped and took a little bow, then continued her charade. "Tell Annie..." She paused for the idea to come. "Tell Annie to come back and ... and dance with us."

"Okay, I will," Annie said.

CHAPTER 49

I t wasn't the only thing she wanted to do before the semester ended – return to Chinnakadu. But it was first on her list, and Mr. Hausden said he'd arrange with the Travel Office to get a jeep to take her out, even though the bus wouldn't be going again that year. But finals were approaching and Annie had a lot of school work to catch up on once she was okayed to return to classes.

"I've kept good notes in all the classes we have together," Ketsa said. "You can use any of them you want. But don't stress about grades. Ask yourself one of those Wonder Questions, like: I wonder who ever came up with the idea of grades anyway?"

"But these grades transfer home," Annie said, "and they'll wreck my GPA if I mess up now."

"The real question you need to be asking, girl, is have you been here, really been in this place, with your whole heart. And I, Ketsa Darlene Ostrander, affirm that you have. So whatever grade you get for not having your work caught up in time, and deciding not to take Incompletes, is not yours to worry about, period, exclamation mark!"

Annie knew Ketsa was right. It wasn't that she overdosed on report cards and getting A's, but MMIS was different than Ridgeway, and Annie realized she could easily end up with several C's or maybe even a D if things didn't go right in the next two weeks. So far in high school, she had managed to earn grades in the A/B range with only one C her freshman year and she hoped to keep it that way. Ketsa was still talking.

"So when in your little high school in Oregon did you ever learn to drum the tabla like we do, girl, or have fights with Vidhya look-alikes about idol worship, or make idlis and coconut chutney in cooking class? Or find some gorgeous Sri Lankan in red running shoes to climb buildings with? If it comes to that, this experience is worth getting a C in Maths or Environmental Science, I assure you. Maybe even a D, because you'll have another chance at math and science some other time and place, and you won't have another chance at living and loving your last two weeks in Megha Malai."

It wasn't a lecture. It was just Ketsa talking her talk. And it was what Annie needed. She thought about what Ketsa said, and for the first time in her life, she purposefully went too fast and did a mediocre job on two papers. She handed them in knowing she could do better and get a better grade if she'd take more time. It felt awful and wonderful.

She couldn't do that for Modern Religious Thought, though, simply because their final paper was something she really had to do for herself: *Three Questions for Our Times, A Personal Reflection.* She didn't have to have the answers, Mr. Das said, which would have been impossible anyway, but just ask the questions and provide some "leanings." Annie decided her three questions would be:

1. Is there or was there ever an American equivalent of kerosene?

2. How does our "picture" of God affect what God is for us?

3. In what ways are Sikhism and Christianity alike?

She included #3 because it was a major reason for taking MRT and she still needed to know. Or hoped she did. Param's last email had been there when she got back from Hampi – a forwarded collection of jokes. They weren't even funny, and she decided not to answer it. That would be a test to see if he noticed. He evidently didn't, because he hadn't emailed again. Not even when she was so sick.

Annie worked on the MRT paper throughout the next week and had it ready to turn in at the end of the day on Friday, leaving her last Saturday morning free for one final visit to Chinnakadu. Mr. Hausden arranged for the jeep, as he said he would, and Annie, Ketsa, Vidhya, and three other girls from Tresham loaded in as soon as they'd had breakfast.

They were expected, and when they arrived at the school, a large group of girls greeted them, along with the women from the Kurinji group – Nirmala, Jayanthi, Leelakumari, Chandra, Radha, Asha, and Anandhi. Annie realized that somewhere along the way she had learned their names. The fancy long skirts and blouses and saris told Annie this was a time of special celebration. Tea and biscuits were brought, and afterwards Radha asked Vidhya if they would make a speech.

"*Kattayam!*" she replied. "Sure!" She turned to Annie. "They said they want you to make a speech."

"Me?" Annie asked.

"Well, not specifically you, but the rest of us will be back next year. You're the one going home. It's your time in the sunshine."

"So what am I supposed to say?"

"Thanks for the chai, and then whatever else you want," Vidhya replied. "I'll translate."

So Annie began: "When I first came to Chinnakadu, I didn't know what to expect. I knew we were working on water filters, and I knew I wanted to help because everybody needs good water to drink. Oh, and thank you for the chai and biscuits." She paused for Vidhya to catch up.

"And I did help build one filter and I hope it works forever, but what I really want to tell you is that when Chandra took my hand a couple of weeks ago, when you first showed us the cards you'd made ... she called me a name in English that I didn't know. She said I was an Animator. And I found out later what it meant, and what I want to tell Chandra and all of you ..." Again she paused for Vidhya.

"I want to say that you are my Animators." Annie's throat tightened and she tried not to cry as she looked for the words to finish. "The dictionary at our school says it means giving breath or life or spirit. You have given me so much that I didn't know about life. You let me know you and what you hope for and what you work so hard to make happen. Your cards are awesome."

She remembered something, and once Vidhya had finished, she added, "Thank you for my *kurinji* flower get-well card. I'll keep it for always, and remember you and pray for you."

Some of them came up to Annie and touched her hair or her cheek, and the rest gathered around, holding the moment, until Radha pointed out that the light bulb had just come on above their heads. "The power's back on," Vidhya said. "They can use music for their dance now."

The girls from MMIS moved their chairs around to be nearer the dancers lined in two columns in front of them. The music peeled out a lively rhythm, and Annie began using her knee as a tabla top, sliding, then tapping, her fingers to the beat of the song.

Ribbons unfurled between the columns of girls – ribbons tied to the ends of two sticks. Each girl held onto one of the sticks and let the ribbon flow between her and the dancer across the way. Then pairs of girls stepped forward, in and out of their places in a way that left the ribbons twisted firmly together in the center, forming the hub of a fluttering ribbon wheel. Once the wheel was set in motion, they began a horizontal pole-less May Day dance that Annie loved because it was so much like winding the May pole at home. She watched closely, trying to memorize the motions, and stared in amazement as the girls wove a design in the ribbon wheel, then tipped it toward them to show the pattern, all the while keeping time with the music. When the song ended, Annie hopped up from her chair, clapped her hands, and cheered. The girls bowed, then stepped backward, smiling.

They dropped the ribbons in a corner of the courtyard, and lifted a bundle of colorfully painted dowels from a cardboard box that sat nearby. Each girl took two of the sticks and quickly formed a circle. A new song began and they stepped into the dance, clicking sticks together over their heads, then with the girl ahead, the girl behind, turn, turn, step forward, and all the while the clash of the sticks kept the rhythm perfectly.

"Oh, my gosh!" Annie said. "I want to do this!" Spotting a few sticks beside the box, she grabbed Ketsa's hand and pulled her up. "We're dancing! Come on!" She picked up four sticks, handed Ketsa two, and alongside, but out of the circle, Annie and Ketsa did a fair job of guessing each other's next move, joining the stick dance with passion.

"*Kol atum*, it's called," Vidhya said when they came back to their chairs. "When I was in elementary, the high school girls always did it on Republic Day, but when I got to high school somebody forgot the tradition, I guess. I haven't seen it at school for several years. In fact, the PE department has a whole box of sticks in the storeroom. I saw them when I was looking for racquetball racquets."

"Let's do it!" Annie said. "Before school's out, so I can learn it for real. And the ribbon dance too. Then I can show people at home." She rolled her eyes and laughed. "Sure! Like kids at Ridgeway would do this! Who am I kidding? Unless we could get the seniors to introduce it at dances like they did with country line dance. Well, actually, I'll be one of the seniors next year, so maybe we could do it."

"You do country line dance at school in Oregon?" Ketsa asked.

"We do. I know it sounds crazy, but it's a tradition at Ridgeway, and a lot of us are getting pretty good."

"Okay. I'm coming to Oregon," Ketsa said.

"Deal," Annie said.

The power went out again in the middle of the next dance, but the girls in the circle and the women on the side picked up the tune and sang the dance to its end.

Nobody at home would do that, Annie thought, then realized what she was doing and stopped. "I wonder," she said softly, "I wonder if we could do that at home – learn to sing if the power goes out?"

CHAPTER 50

Mr. Das was in charge of worship on the last Sunday of the school year. He asked students from his MRT class to take part – lighting candles, reading Scripture, telling anecdotes, and singing. He asked Annie if she would share one of the questions from her MRT final paper, as the message for the service. "Seriously?" she asked. "I don't think I can. Talk in front of all those people? Besides, you know I didn't come up with any answers, Mr. Das. Preachers in church are supposed to have the answers, right?"

The funny look on his face made her laugh. Yes, that was Mr. Das. Yes, she would agree to read her question and tell about her leanings. It was her second question he asked her to talk about:

How does our "picture" of God affect what God is for us?

"My friend, Aziz, is a Muslim," Annie began that Sunday morning. "He reminded me that he doesn't have a picture of God and tries not to have one, even in his mind. For him, Allah is beyond what our minds could grasp anyway, and it's better if we don't try to capture him in the hot, sticky road tar of our ideas, he said. But personally, I think he finds God in the rocks he climbs, or at least when he's climbing. Because I've seen him run in a circle down a trail because he was so amazed by the beauty of a place. And I've watched him hold his arms up to the sky when he's standing on top of a rock, like I do when nobody's looking and I reach up to show God how wonderful something is. So not having a "picture" of God at all seems to help one friend keep God big.

"My friend Ajit is a Sikh, and he says God is with us in the holy writings, in the words of the Gurus, but I've seen him find a new piece of God, or a new peace from God, in his aunts' stories and in serving food at his temple. So I think his picture of God includes his family in Lahore and in Australia and Toronto. I think that makes him feel like God is somebody he belongs to, like he does to his family. Somebody everybody belongs to.

"My friend Daychen is a Buddhist, and I didn't know that for a long time, because I didn't think to ask her and she didn't say anything about it. She comes to church with some girls from our dorm, so I assumed she was a Christian." Annie could see Daychen in a pew near the back of the chapel, her head lowered, but she had said it was okay for Annie to include her in the talk, so Annie continued.

"She asked me once if I wanted to go to the rose garden with her to meditate. I didn't tell her I might not know how. At first I kept wondering what would happen if I fell asleep, and then I wondered what would happen if I suddenly sneezed or yelled or just started looking around at all the roses. I wanted to be quiet, but sometimes I'm hyper inside.

"I learned from some kids in MRT that there isn't 'God' for Buddhists, like for Christians and Jews and Muslims, so although that was a little hard to hear, or actually, really hard to hear, I guess I have to admit that Daychen might not have a picture of God at all. I notice that she has stillness, though. Something I want to learn."

Annie took a deep breath. "And then there's Vidhya, my friend who knows God is found in the form of an elephant-headed creature. That bugged the heck out of me for four whole months here at MMIS, but I couldn't find my pearl-handled hairbrush recently, and I knew I had it, because I took it to the dispensary when I got sick, so I went back and asked the nurse, and she said it had been at the hospital but she hadn't seen it since. So I walked up to the hospital and I asked if I could just look in the nightstand of the room I was in. It was still there, in the very back of the drawer. And along with it there were some dried flower petals and a little brass oil lamp, and this..."

Annie held up a tiny statue of Ganesh. "I think the nurse must have put them there, because she told me right away that 'Lord Ganesh' was Vidhya's and that Vidhya had prayed over and over that Ganesh would make me well and bless me and take away my malaria fever.

"I was really sick when all that happened, but I had this feeling that Vidhya prayed for me. And that she lit a candle, or I guess an oil lamp. Nobody ever mentioned it, though, and I started thinking it was one of the dreams I had.

"When I got back from the hospital I went straight to Vidhya and asked her if I could possibly have her Ganesh. She asked where I got it and why I wanted it. I think she was afraid I wanted to make fun of it with my friends at home. She didn't realize that's not what I was thinking at all. Most people at home wouldn't even know what it was, but those who did, the ones I know, would probably call it an idol, and they'd freak. So I thought hard before I asked her if I could have it.

"I won't say that it's to remind me of God in any way, but it does remind me of Vidhya's prayers to God for my healing. And I like to look at it and remember that. That's why I want it.

"So I think Vidhya's picture of God is different than mine, but in the end, it seems like God is something she can talk to or cry to when she cares." Annie nodded her head. "I can understand that." She took in and sighed out another big breath.

"One of my favorite verses from the Bible is John 10:10: *I am come that they might have life, and that they might have it more abundantly.* That's Jesus talking, but I know some women in a village not far from here who call themselves the Kurinji Ladies, or that's what I call them, who seem to have the same motto, probably without knowing it's in the Bible. They are Hindus, and they are making life "more abundant" by what they're doing for each other and their village. They're doing the very reason that Jesus came, helping him meet his goal, which is pretty cool if you stop and think about it. Which they probably don't, but I do, now.

"One of the Kurinji Ladies called me an Animator. I didn't know it was an English word for *gram sevak*. Besides being a helper, it means to breathe spirit or life into things, into what you do. They made me want to be an Animator for the rest of my life.

"But still, I had to ask myself: How does Annie's 'picture' of God affect who God is for her? I need to mention something. I was mad at God when I first came to India, because I couldn't understand why He let my friend die in an accident. I guess my picture of God was somebody who was supposed to be in charge of things, but instead decided to hibernate for the winter. And the winter just kept going. That hibernating God picture made God cold, in some cave far away where He didn't care. So I didn't care back.

"I planned to forget about God, but I couldn't, and I can't, because I've realized here, maybe more than ever, that I reach out. I expect something to be there. And it is. Usually, it just is. So even though I don't have any answers, I do have 'a leaning,' as Mr. Das calls it.

"My leaning is that Aziz and Ajit and Vidhya and the Kurinji Ladies in Chinnakadu, and Daychen too, are reaching out and finding what they are reaching for, and I wonder … I wonder if that is God. And because I've found them, I think I'm finding more of God, in new and unexpected ways. I want to know God better, because the little box that used to hold Him for me, doesn't have a lid on it anymore. Maybe it doesn't even have sides. But I'm not scared.

"I made a promise when I came to India, to be curious and to wonder about things instead of being afraid or comparing everything to home. I haven't always remembered to do that, or been able to do that, but sometimes I have. It never dawned on me that I was doing the exact thing to God that I was trying to avoid doing to people. I was judging and criticizing Him. I knew exactly who He should be and what He should do, and when He didn't do things the way I thought He should, I was ready to junk Him.

"But because of these people, I started wondering about God. And then when I was working on my final paper for MRT, that's my Modern Religious Thought class, it dawned on me that maybe it makes more sense to wonder about God than to judge.

"When you start loving people, and then you encounter something that you didn't expect, love makes you wonder about all kinds of things, whether you planned to or not. I'm still learning what that means.

"I'm still learning what God means. And I'm glad I got to come to India."

Annie finished, stepped down from the lectern, and slipped back into her pew. Now that it was over, she took one more big breath. She felt glad that Mr. Das had asked her. Otherwise, she might never have heard herself say those words.

CHAPTER 51

Aziz met Annie in the dining hall after church. Now that it was over, she wished he had come. But she was the one who told him not to, so she let it go. They walked through the food line, filled their trays, and found a table upstairs by the windows overlooking the Green. "I'm going to miss the dining hall's Sunday chicken curry," he said.

"And?" Annie replied.

"And curds and rice."

"Oh, good," she laughed. "Anything else you'll miss?"

"And the plastic cups we drink out of, and the warm water in the plastic cups we drink out of," he said, holding one of the cups in a toast. "And, oh yeah, I'll miss Annie! To Annie," he concluded, "the Oregon climber in my life."

"And to Aziz," she replied, "the sparkling *Guav-oh!* in mine!"

"I have a surprise for you!" he said, once they had eaten. He grabbed her by the hand and pulled her up from the table. "Off campus, but no passes needed. The camping director got a school car and wants me to go along with him and his assistant to see a rock face out on the new property they have for camps. They discovered that it's already been bolted. Can you believe that? And we never knew it existed. I told him you'd come too."

"Really?" Annie asked, disappointed.

"Is that not good?" Aziz asked. "We don't have to pay for a taxi or figure out if we can make it by bus. And it's rock we've never seen. Right outside of Megha Malai!"

"No, it'll be fine," she said. She had hoped to spend one

last Sunday afternoon alone with Aziz, but he seemed excited about the plan, so she decided to make it work.

And it was fun. The rock face was great – solid and clean with good holds, not as high as they would have liked, but it had easy trail access to the top and two large trees that could be used for top-roping. They agreed that it had scope for the outdoor camping program. Both Aziz and Annie got to climb, and she realized how much she had learned, and how much she loved the rock. "Especially on a day like this," she said, "with the sun and the mist mixing as it rolls in off the hills."

"Today is a true Megha Malai day," the camp director said. "Misty Hills."

"That's what it means?" Annie asked. She laughed at herself. "All this time I never realized Megha Malai meant anything." She liked the name. From where she stood, she could look far below to the plains and imagine the heat rising – from everything. For four and a half months she had lived in these high misty hills, and she loved their coolness and their lush, green beauty.

IT WAS LATE in the afternoon when they got back to school.

"In a hurry?" she asked Aziz once they were dropped off near their dorms.

"No."

"Then wait right here. I'm going to dorm, and I'll be right back." She left her backpack in her dorm room and grabbed up a shopping bag she had ready. Once again with Aziz, she led him to the back of Performing Arts, where they first climbed together. "It's our spot," she said, "for now. It sounds like they're going to reopen it as an official rock wall next semester. All because I talked too much."

"Well, it's time they did. Other kids will finally see how

great climbing is. And it was ours for a while. Maybe they'll call it the Annie-Aziz Rock Wall. We'll be famous, probably."

"Probably," she echoed. She opened her bag, and took out a bright red table cloth with batiked yellow and gold designs throughout. Next came two bottles of – "Tadah" Annie called out – "*Guav-oh!*... and chocolate spread... and Milk Bikis. My favorite tea for our last Sunday together."

"Until Yosemite," he corrected. "I'm serious, Annie. You've got to meet me there. It's awesome. Even to hike in if we don't want to climb, which we will."

She opened the packet of biscuits and spread a thick layer of chocolate on each one.

"Will you?" he asked. Annie kept spreading, setting out their snacks on plates made of pressed, dried leaves.

"Aren't these paper plates, I mean leaf plates, the coolest things?" she said.

"You didn't answer me, Annie. Will you?"

"Will I what?"

"Marry me?"

"Aziz!"

He laughed. "It was just a test to see if you were even listening. I thought you were paying more attention to those biscuits than to me. I meant to say, 'Will you meet me in Yosemite a year from this June?'"

"Yes."

"Okay then," he said, obviously surprised. "That was easy."

Annie had no idea how she would meet Aziz in Yosemite in thirteen months. But she'd find a way. She meant it when she said yes.

They ate the cookies and drank the *Guav-oh!* and then both of them lay down on the grass in the last rays of sunshine filtering through the eucy trees.

"Remember Liam's Landing in Hampi?" Aziz asked.

"Always."

"I want to do it again," he said.

"We never made it once. What do you mean, do it again?" Annie asked.

"I want to fall and have you catch me. But without the Germans watching."

"Okay," Annie laughed. "But you're already down."

"That's no excuse not to do it," he said.

Annie knew what he meant. They were leaving India and each other and, even with Yosemite, it would be at least another year before they'd see each other. Life had given them the gift of crazy, precious time together, and she longed to hold him close, to let him fall into her arms if he wanted to, and not hurry to move.

"Well, we can fall up, I guess," she said.

"And you'd catch me?"

"Definitely."

He stood and held out his hand to Annie, pulling her up, and to him, closely, gently. She didn't resist, just buried her face in his shoulder. He stroked her hair as he held her, then spoke softly, though she heard clearly. "I love you, Annie."

She looked up at him. There was so much of life she was unsure of, yet this one thing she knew certainly: "And I love you, Aziz."

She made no move to pull herself away from his arms.

CHAPTER 52

A nnie didn't even know the word "invigilate," nor had she ever taken exams like they had at MMIS. Lines of ayahs, the women who normally swept the classrooms and walkways, now carried desks and chairs on their heads, moving from the classrooms to the gymnasium and back again, and again, until hundreds of exam tables were set up ready for the first test at 8 o'clock Tuesday morning. For the next three days, in two-hour blocks, teachers invigilated the exams, wandering back and forth among the rows of desks, making certain that all was in order. A hush fell over the campus, and except for mealtimes there was little activity other than studying, until a group of boys said things were getting ridiculous, and set up a dodge ball tournament on Covered Courts both nights after dinner.

So it was that at three o'clock Thursday afternoon when the last exam finished, the chapel bell peeled long and loud, and students cheered from wherever they stood. The work of another year at MMIS had come to a close. Tea was served early, on the lawn outside Performing Arts, and students were transformed with the relief of it all being done once more.

Seniors talked about graduation and their families soon to arrive. The others talked about vacation and where they'd be and what they planned to do.

Buses were parked, ready to load for the trip down to the train station or to the Madurai airport. Some students would leave late that afternoon, including Ketsa, Lori, and Jen. Aziz was to leave that night by taxi. Annie, and most of the others, except for the seniors, were booked to travel on Friday. By graduation time on Saturday, only the seniors would remain.

Annie and Naveena would catch the Friday night train from the bottom of the Ghat Road to Chennai where Naveena's family would meet them. She'd visit there for four days, celebrate her birthday with them by going to a sketching symposium Naveena's mom was in charge of, and then fly out of Chennai for home.

"They shouldn't do it this way," Annie said to Ketsa, "have exams right up till the end and then, bam, it's all done and people are gone. I haven't even started to pack, let alone say goodbye."

"Speaking of which, I have a present for you," Ketsa said. "An early birthday present, or a going away present, or just a me-to-you present." Annie took the cloth bag Ketsa handed her.

"You can keep the bag too," Ketsa said. "Isn't it pretty?"

"Yeah, I like it," Annie answered. She reached into the bag and pulled out a plaque, painted in rich blues, reds, and greens on a light green background. "Is it Tamil for something?" Annie asked.

"No, it's Kannada. I had the librarian help me. He's from Karnataka. I told him about us going to Gandhinagar when we first came and he said he'd help with my plan to make this for you."

"You made it?" Annie asked.

"Actually, I made two. One for you and one for me. Down in the art studio. All by myself, girl! After the librarian outlined the script on the wood, I filled it in. Love those colors, huh! It says, '*Hoge-burri*' in Kannada."

"Go-and-come," Annie said.

"That's it, girl," Ketsa said. "That's what we gotta do for each other. No 'Good-bye,' just 'Go and come' till we're old ladies, remember. So keep this, and remember Gandhinagar and remember Megha Malai, and most of all, remember me."

"I will, Ketsa. I love you, and I love this present. Thank you so much," Annie said. "We'll do it. And call me at home in a week, okay?"

ANNIE WATCHED AS the bus pulled out of the parking lot, taking Ketsa and the others away, and then it suddenly stopped. Ketsa came tumbling out the doorway. "Annie..." she called back up the parking lot. "I forgot to tell you. You're in today's *Hindustan Times*. In the library. On the bulletin board in the entry. Grace has a copy for you." Ketsa waved madly, threw Annie a kiss, and rushed back onto the bus.

Since Annie wasn't the only one seeing the bus off, several students heard Ketsa's departing cry, including Vidhya. Once the bus was out of Main Gate and beyond waving range, Vidhya said, "Okay, the library's still open. Let's go see Hindustan Annie on the library bulletin board."

It was the Thursday, May 24th edition, and the guest editorial headline above Annie's picture read: "India Gifts American Teen with *Kairos*." The picture was taken outside church last Sunday after Annie's talk. The reporter was a guest writer from Mumbai who was visiting Megha Malai. She compared Annie's questioning attitude and empathy with the dogmatism of a group of fundamentalist Hindus and Christians deep in violent conflict in the Northeast. She mentioned Annie's experiences of friendship and faith, then said:

"Like the Greek word *kairos* suggests, time seems to have paused and extended a special opportunity of insight that this American high school teen eagerly stepped into. Completing a five month stay in India this month as a student at Megha Malai International School in Tamil Nadu, Annie Karten, USA, addressed the Megha Malai community on Sunday. Without using the word 'pilgrimage,' she described a journey of thought and experience that India can be proud to have afforded her. This young woman lights a path to inquiry and wonderment that would do her elders of all nations a world of good."

"So I missed your talk, Annie," Vidhya said. "What did you say, exactly?"

"I said that I loved my friend Vidhya, who's way cool," Annie said.

"Why didn't they write that in the paper?" Vidhya laughed. She reached her arms out toward Annie and pulled her into a warm hug. "You're the one who's way cool, and I love you too, Annie."

"Thank you, Vidhya. Don't forget, you have to email me the news of the Kurinji Ladies. For sure!" Annie said. "And news of Vidhya."

"I will. For sure," Vidhya said. She turned and walked away, but Annie saw the tears in her eyes as she turned. India should be closer to home.

Annie reread the article, then sat down at one of the library computers to check her email. A message had come in from her dad:

"Annie, a friend at work called me and told me to Google HindustanTimes.com. You're in the news! It's odd to see an article tonight dated tomorrow, especially about YOU in India! What did you say in your talk? Bring us a copy.

"Have a wonderful time in Chennai with Naveena's family. Email when you're ready to leave there. Then come home! We'll be waiting at PDX! Email from Singapore if there are any flight changes, and call the minute you touch down in LA so we know you're back in the country. Call my cell. (I do like having it.) We'll be on our way to the airport by then. Love you!!!!! Dad"

What a world, Annie thought, when questions can bounce

from one side of it to the other and back before you even know they've been heard.

"I'm sorry, Annie," Grace, the librarian, said. "We're closing now."

Annie looked up at Grace. "What?"

"The library is closing early. I'm ready to lock up. We'll open again at 7:30 in the morning if you need to use the computer. Oh, and I made a copy of the *Hindustan Times* article for you. It's very nice."

"Thank you, Grace," Annie said.

Annie didn't go to the dorm just then. She headed for Main Gate, folding the article and slipping it into her pocket. When the watchman looked the other way, Annie broke into a run and turned toward the lake path. One last run around the lake, she told herself. And if I push, I can still meet Aziz at dinner.

THE DINING HALL was nearly empty by the time she got back to campus. She picked up a tray, went through the line, and realized the cooks were putting things away right behind her. She was late. She looked around for Aziz, and, not seeing him, took her tray to the nearest table, sat down, and gobbled some rice. "No, I can't do this," she told herself. "This is my last dinner and probably the last white rice I'll get for a long time." She left her tray where it was, went to the corner sinks, and washed her hands. Like running the lake path, Annie had to take time to do it all once more. She sat down and ate her dinner with her fingers, like she had in Gandhinagar. Rice, ladiesfinger, brinjal, curds, sambar. And banana pudding. All with her fingers, even though she was sure that wasn't allowed with banana pudding.

The lights flashed, signaling that the dining hall was

closing. Annie took her tray up, washed her hands, and walked slowly back toward the dorm.

THERE WAS STILL packing to do. Everything she could think of leaving behind that could be used in Chinnakadu, she put in a big cardboard box marked "Mr. Hausden, SL." The set of tabla she had special-ordered to take home filled most of the space in one suitcase, so she packed some of her clothes around the drums. In the other suitcase she put a few books, the school papers she wanted to keep, and the gifts she was taking for people at home.

She sat with her backpack, arranging and rearranging the things she couldn't take any chance on losing – the thumb drives full of digital photos, her camera, a tiny bottle containing filtered Chinnakadu water, her Kurinji flower card and the packets of cards to sell at the Children's Clinic bazaar, her favorite salwar kameez, and two CDs of Indian music for dancing to at home.

Remembering one more thing she had intended to do, Annie ran to her dorm parent's apartment, got a gate pass, and left for the shops just outside Main Gate.

"Hi, Abbas," she said. "I need banana chips for the trip home, Cadbury chocolate bars for my dad, and Milk Bikis so Mom and I can splurge on chocolate spread. Oh, and two bottles of *Guav-oh!*, please."

"You are taking *Guav-oh!* back to USA?" he asked.

Annie smiled. "I don't think they have it in Yosemite, where I'll be going," she said. "I'm meeting a friend there who really likes it." She didn't mention when or who.

Annie started back across the street, but stopped and let three cows pass in front of her, wandering somewhere, late though it was, then a car, and a tourist bus. She was in no hurry now. The packing would get done. She knew that at this time tomorrow, she'd be gone from Megha Malai.

Kairos? The word from the *Hindustan Times* suddenly came back to Annie. *Chronos* and *kairos* were the two Greek "time" words her pastor had talked about the Sunday before she left for India last January: *chronos* – clock-ticking, calendar-turning time, the time it takes a cow to cross the road; *kairos* –an "ah hah" critical moment of insight, the time you wake up to a new idea or first realize something. The news article was right; India had gifted her with *kairos*, and was doing it again. Annie understood right then, deep down, this was not the last time she would see cows crossing the road in front of Main Gate. She would come back.

"*Hoge-burtini,*" Annie whispered.

INSTEAD OF GOING directly to Tresham, Annie turned and went down the steps toward Wiebe Hall where Aziz lived. She had to make sure when his taxi was leaving, and she had something to ask. She checked in with the dorm parent who opened up the back door of her apartment and hollered into the hallway. "Aziz, you have a visitor!"

He grinned when he saw it was Annie. "Hi," he said. "I missed you at dinner. I was afraid maybe…."

"I know. I got there late. I'm really sorry. You're still leaving tonight?" she asked.

"In about two hours. Taxi to Madurai, night flight from there to Chennai, and then on to Jaffna."

"I'll be at Main Gate to see you off," Annie promised. "Ten o'clock, right?"

"Yeah, but come early. I'm almost done packing. I'll treat you to one more *Guav-oh!*."

"Okay. I'll go put this stuff in dorm and then be back," she said. "Hey, Aziz, I put both pairs of my running shoes in a box to go to Chinnakadu, and my good shoes and my sandals."

"That'll make somebody happy."

"So I need yours."

"Mine? My extra climbing shoes?" Aziz asked.

"No, your red shoes," she said with a smile.

Aziz's smile matched hers. He turned and ran back into the dorm, and in an instant was back with his red running shoes. He held one out to Annie and put the other behind his back.

"Only one," he said. "I keep the other. And we take turns deciding when we both wear them, at the very same time."

Annie laughed. "No fair. Your feet are bigger than mine. It'll fall off."

"Then why do you want it?"

"You," she said, touching her fingertips gently to his chest right where he had held her hands over his heart.

"I know." Then he added, "Wear a big sock."

"Okay," Annie said, "but I get to go first. We wear them tonight when you leave Megha Malai. For three hours. All the way down the Ghat Road to Madurai. Think of me."

Aziz smiled. "I would have, even without the shoe." He paused. "Hey, Annie. Thanks for coming here." He just stood and looked at her. She met his gaze. "It's really hard to say good-bye to you. I don't want it to be over. Even if there's Yosemite."

"Which there is," Annie said.

"Just don't forget."

"I won't," Annie promised, knowing that they both meant more than Yosemite.

Aziz reached down and took both of her hands in his. "So, how do I put this?" he asked. "I want to kiss you."

"Then do," she said.

ANNIE HEADED BACK to Tresham, twirling the bag of goodies from Abbas's shop in one hand and holding Aziz's red running shoe in the other. "Help me find room in my luggage for all this stuff, God," she said out loud.

Annie walked on in the silence of one last wonder: How am I going to take India home?

Her heart answered: You are.

PART IV

Coyote Calls
(Back Home)

*Home has advantages. One of them is **not** that you automatically know who you are. Or what you should do. But I do know one thing.*

Annie

CHAPTER 53

My flight got into Portland a little before noon. Our plan was to eat at a Thai restaurant we love and then my parents would drive me to school. I was that excited to see everyone. Mom and Dad and my grandparents were at PDX to meet me. I cried when I saw them.

We headed for baggage claim, and as I stepped off the escalator, Danny jumped out from behind a concrete pillar! He skipped class to be there. I was so happy to see him! I didn't expect anyone from school to come. Ridgeway was hosting the district track finals and most of my friends had to be there, Katelyn and Param for sure. This was the one time in my life I was glad Danny didn't go out for track. It was perfect to have him and my parents and my grandparents together for my first lunch at home. I felt so surrounded by love.

I talked non-stop half the way home and then leaned my head over on Danny's shoulder and closed my eyes, just letting the feel of him fill the empty place of five months apart. He reached down and picked up my hand, and after a while I must have fallen asleep. When I woke up, we were pulling into our driveway, not the school parking lot.

Danny's car was there and he said he'd take me over to school if I still wanted to see the track meet. I didn't want to go anywhere. Home seemed more important. I just wanted to go inside and sit at our kitchen table and run upstairs to my room. I wanted to wander in the meadow and see the creek. Everything was so green. I could smell the wild roses along our driveway. School could wait a day. Danny hugged me and told me he'd come over later that night.

I fell asleep right after dinner and didn't wake up until 3 a.m. I couldn't go back to sleep so I reached for my phone and checked email. There was a message from Aziz. I was wide awake by then, so I got up and started unpacking. A couple hours later, when the sky lightened my room, I crawled back into bed and didn't wake up again until almost noon. Mom said Danny came by and several kids called, but she let me sleep through it all.

It was a day later than planned, but that afternoon, I walked into Ridgeway High School. Wearing a red running shoe. Well, I thought about doing that, because it was what Aziz had emailed, that it was his turn to choose when we wore them again and he picked my first day back to school. I might have been able to explain it away as some Indian holiday tradition. Ridgeway kids would have no clue about Indian traditions. But the shoe was big, and I'd feel really stupid wearing it. That was not the feeling I wanted for my first day at Ridgeway after being gone forever. I was already feeling weird about going back when the school year was almost over. Besides, Aziz would never know if I wore it or not. I smiled at that thought. Of course he would know. Aziz would just ask me outright if I did, and I couldn't lie to him. So Mom had dropped me off at school wearing a backpack that had a note-book and one red running shoe inside. I was also wearing the salwar kameez I bought in Hyderabad before that crazy ride out to Gandhinagar.

I should have worn jeans and a shirt. And I should have timed it not to arrive during the break between classes. That hit me when a group of freshmen, or at least some kids I didn't know, stared at me on my way to the office. I was to spend the last two weeks of Ridgeway's school year finishing up the independent study World Geography class I started before I left for India. I didn't mind. It would be weird to come back to my own school as just a visitor. This way, I was there with a purpose and still got to see everybody. And I actually liked the idea of learning world geography now that I have friends who live in those real locations. I realized at Megha Malai I know almost nothing about where any place is.

But my worries about timing or what I wore that day didn't matter. I knew I was back the minute I spotted Katelyn. She screamed from the other end of the hall and came running through the crowd straight toward me. "Annie! Annie! Annie!" We cried and laughed, and as I wiped my eyes, I saw someone step out of the library doorway, watching us.

Param.

He smiled and nodded his head. I smiled back.

Then at his shoulder I noticed a tall blond girl. She said something to him, but he seemed not to hear and walked slowly toward me. "Hi, Annie. Welcome home."

"Hi, Param. How's it going?"

"Good."

His smile and his voice erased everything I was mad about. He was who I remembered he was – awesome. Then just that fast, she was at his side again, saying, "Param? This must be the girl from India." Accent. I got it. This was the exchange student from Germany. The one in his email.

"Annie, this is Trina," he said, and turning to her, "and this is Annie."

"Nice to meet you, Annie," she said, putting out her hand.

"I'm glad to meet you too," I said. I acted like I didn't see her hand. Bad idea. Param reached up and took her outstretched hand, right as the bell rang for the next class. She pulled him close to her side. "Math," he said, as if that explained something. They turned and slipped into the math room. I stared at Katelyn.

"I would have told you, but you were really sick, and

Danny told me not to. Then you were coming home and I figured it would be easier just to tell you when you got here. They've been together since track started, or earlier." Katelyn motioned me into the stairwell leading to the side exit and told me to sit down on the steps. "I mean, they're not official. She talked to some of us girls a month or so ago and said she was dating someone at home, and if she weren't, it still wouldn't make sense to start going out with someone here when she's headed back to Germany as soon as school's out, but the truth is, they do everything together. And I think his parents have even given up the not dating thing."

"Really?" I said. "That stinks. I go all the way to India to learn what they'd expect of me and here they just let him date Germany, like she somehow automatically qualifies."

Katelyn continued, "Besides hanging out at school all the time, they go to movies. I've seen them there. And they sit together on the bus for every away track meet. I'm so sorry, Annie. This is not the way you were supposed to find out."

"How was I supposed to find out, Katelyn? I was on the other side of the world. Someone could have emailed me at least."

"I'm sorry. I'm really sorry. I didn't know what to do. Annie, if he likes her, he isn't worth it. That's what I decided when I realized what they were doing. I mean, couldn't he wait five little months for you to get back? How would he feel if you did something like that to him?"

She put her arms around me. I wondered if she'd feel the red running shoe in my backpack.

"Thanks, Katelyn," I said. "You should be in class right now, and I'm supposed to check in at the office before I go to Independent Study. We'll talk later."

Katelyn gave me another hug, said she loved me, and headed for class. I waited for her to leave, then I turned and walked out of the building.

CHAPTER 54

I couldn't figure out how something so important could change so fast. I didn't want to be around Param right then. I have to admit, I had some bad feelings about it all in India and maybe I was just denying what I really knew inside and didn't want to be true. It still seemed crazy that what Param and I had shared was ripped away and replaced by a total stranger. It was not the right afternoon to start school again. I wanted to go home.

I could have called for a ride. I had my cell phone back, and Mom would have been there in an instant. But I needed to think, so I started running. Part way home I stopped and opened my backpack. I sat down on the grass at the side of the road and pulled out Aziz's shoe. I held it for a while, then slipped it on. Then I had to walk, so it wouldn't fall off.

It dawned on me that time didn't stand still while I was gone. Param and Germany were proof of that, but so was I. People seeing me back at school, and at home, would think I am Ridgeway Annie. Except for the salwar kameez, which I probably won't wear to school again, I look like that Annie, so what could I expect? What nobody knew was that I wasn't me. At all.

When I got as far as Fulgham Bridge, I stopped again and sat down on the river bank. Even though it was sunny, it was obvious we'd just had a big rain. The water level was really high. The river flowed silently over the boulders that lay deep beneath its surface. In the middle of the summer, when the water level was down, that section of river was a minor rapids. The water crashed its way from boulder to boulder as it rushed down-stream. Those who believed their eyes today were deceived. They didn't know this quiet river at all.

I was the river. Nobody could see beneath my surface. They didn't know I was the Annie who came home and realized at three o'clock in the morning that she didn't need any of the clothes she brought back in her suitcase. My closet and dresser drawers were full. I should have left everything in the box for Chinnakadu. I didn't need most of the stuff in my closets and dressers either. You can live fine out of two suitcases.

I was also the Annie who now missed a whole other world of people who no one here even knew existed. I was a rock climber with chalk on my fingertips after the mehndi designs from Gandhinagar wore off. I was a water filter maker and a *Child of the Earth* t-shirt wearer who was scared of temples. But I was also Annie who couldn't go back to church and pretend that God hadn't changed. How was I going to manage that?

There was now a pile of cards on the desk in my room, made by the Kurinji Ladies, and I wondered if anyone would understand why they were so important – the cards, the ladies, their hopes, and their "life abundantly" work. I wouldn't be okay with people talking about converting the Kurinji Ladies to the Lord. Or if somebody pulled their cards of Ganesh and the temple off the church bazaar table. They could do that. Easily. "What is this? An idol! Who in the world ...?" they'd say. And the cards would be gone. Because their questions weren't questions at all. They already had the answers they needed. The same answers I had a year ago, that didn't work for me now.

Underneath this Ridgeway Annie, I was the memory of polio and cows at Main Gate, and chapatis and chickpeas in the dining hall. I was clay lamps and flickering lights that I wasn't sure I should celebrate. I was a kerosene-protester, even though I didn't know what to do about it. I was malaria and

Vidhya's Ganesh and Leeza's songs and prayers. I was Tabla and Indian Cooking, and eating ladiesfinger and rice and sambar with my fingers. I was bucket baths and geezers and 2nd Class 3-tier sleeper trains that rock you to sleep with the smell of jasmine blossoms swirling around you with the night breeze. I was a dancer with sticks and ribbons with Ketsa and with girls from Chinnakadu who sing when the power goes off.

I was Annie, the Animator.

And I was scared she'd just disappear in Ridgeway.

CHAPTER 55

I don't know how long I would have sat there, thinking, but the fire siren went off back in town. It's this thing about Ridgeway. I know fire departments have switched to using pagers, but we still have the siren too. We've grown up with it forever. Dad said they used to blow it at noon in the old days, so people would know when to quit for lunch, because most people didn't have watches. It's that old. Somebody told us when we hear it, we should say a prayer for whoever is needing help, because it's one of us. I especially thought of that after Tani, even if I'm not sure any more how prayer works, or if it works. But the siren reminds us that everybody in and around Ridgeway who goes running for their cars and pickups when it goes off is a volunteer firefighter, ready to help us. Without the siren we'd forget that. We wouldn't remember how we care for each other.

The other thing about the siren that I hadn't thought about for a long time, is that almost always, in the evenings or at night, the coyotes begin to howl when they hear it. You don't notice that in town, but out at our place, or Danny's, or down on the bottom ground, you do. When they howl with the siren, their calls carry over the fields like there are dozens of them. Dad says they throw their voices and there may only be three or four, but they sound like a whole huge pack. They're part of the unseen Ridgeway.

As the siren faded, the coyotes started calling. In the middle of the afternoon, which they don't always do. I stood up to look beyond the river, towards the woods, though I knew I wouldn't see them. And right then I knew something else.

Kairos.

I was home.

I was the old Ridgeway Annie too, who had grown up with fire sirens and coyotes. I belonged to these fields, even the new corn fields I had run past on the way home, with the memories that made me cry. I belonged to this river that I know the highs and lows and seasons of, and the unseen boulders beneath the water. I belonged to the kids at Ridgeway, who all have way more clothes than anyone needs but we don't know it.

I probably don't belong to Param, but who knows what will happen when Germany goes back home, though I don't even know what I want to happen now. "Germany?" Didn't I learn anything in the last five months? Param said she had a name.

I belong to Mom and Dad, and our house and the meadow.

And I definitely belong to Danny. In some way that I don't quite know, but it will be an adventure to figure out. However it goes, I've got to make it good, so that Danny and I stay friends forever. Even if I end up marrying Aziz and climbing the Empire State Building for our honeymoon. Or if I marry some guy I meet in Malta, when I finish World Geography and learn where Malta is. Or if I marry Danny.

Wow, I never heard myself say those words before, but it may be as likely as marrying Aziz or Malta.

It felt good to be back home. I remembered Danny jumping out from behind the pillar in baggage claim. I stood there by the river bank thinking about things I wanted to tell him and ask him. I slipped off the red shoe, held it to my heart, and put it back in my backpack. I needed to walk the rest of the way home in my own shoes.

The coyotes were still howling. I raised my face to the sky and called back to them. Yes, I was home. All sides of me.

I don't actually know what triggered the next thought, but

it came. "I wonder ..." I said out loud, "I wonder how I keep Animator and Coyote together."

I WALKED BACK up to the roadway just as a small blue Honda Civic approached, then screeched to a stop on the side of the road. Danny jumped out.

"Hey!" he said.

"Hey," I answered back.

"You left school before I even found you. But it turns out I'm headed out to the Karten's. Want a ride?"

"Sure." I said.

Danny looked right into my eyes. "I'm really glad you're home," he said.

"Me too."

Danny stayed for dinner, and we all sat up late, talking about what happened while we were apart. Then Mom and Dad finally went to bed. Danny and I were going to watch a movie, but we never put it in. We talked on about changes at the high school and about the food bank where Danny had started volunteering. We talked about Gandhinagar, Megha Malai, water filters, and temples. We talked about being sick. Everything. Well, not exactly everything. I hadn't figured out if I should tell Danny about Aziz, so I just skipped that one detail of the last five months. Then Danny told me something that totally blew me away.

He was leaving me.

Well, not me, exactly. At least not just me. He was leaving Ridgeway and Oregon, and the whole United States. Danny was going to Greece.

My heart sank. I couldn't say anything. I just looked at him.

"Did Snyder do that?" I finally asked, mad. I knew at that moment how my mom felt when I had announced I'd won the scholarship to India.

"What?"

"Did Snyder help you win some Computer Greek Club speech about going to Greece? Why? When? I just got back, Danny."

"Hold on, Annie. I'll tell you. I don't leave until September. No, Snyder didn't tell me about it. An announcement for student interns at a business-university project in Athens was put out for all the Computer Greeks. But Snyder did let me pet the hedgehog when he found out I got accepted. I didn't tell you about it, because I figured it was a too much of a long-shot, and I might not get to go. But I got in. It's four months, and I'll be back home for the last half of the year and graduation. You can video call me every day."

He paused and grinned at me. "I thought you'd be excited, Annie. It's the first big thing I ever got to do."

Tears sprang to my eyes. Bad timing. I didn't want to make Danny feel bad. Of course, I was excited for him. I know he loves everything computer, and he's good at computers, and this was probably a huge opportunity. But it dawned on me then that one of the things I was most excited to get home for was Danny. And the stuff I was scared to come home to, well, Danny would be there while I figured it out. Things like what I'd do about church, and what if Mom and Dad got mad at me, and what about the way people treat others who are different from them. Danny seemed to have some things figured out a lot more than I did. Either that or he didn't worry about it.

Besides, when people go away, things change. They meet people. They go climbing. They make promises. They give away some of their heart. I had lost Param. I was back home, and I couldn't stand the thought of losing Danny.

"What, Annie?" he asked.

"I love you, Danny. That's all." We had said that to each other since we were little. Not around people from school, but just sometimes when we were alone and having fun. It didn't mean anything romantic. But this time it felt different. Yet I couldn't look at him when I said it. For all my thinking that Danny should just say something if he really cared about us being more than friends, I realized it wasn't so easy to do when it was up to me. Because the other person might not mean it back, like you do, and then you'd be left alone.

"Let's make a fire," I said. It wasn't really cold, but I love our fireplace and we hadn't had a fire since I got home. Somebody had done my chore while I was gone. The wood box was full and the kindling was cut. Danny built the fire while I went in the kitchen and made some popcorn and cut up some apples, which I could eat, skins and all, without worrying that I'd die of diarrhea or some weird disease.

We sat on pillows on the carpet in front of the fire eating popcorn and talking. About Greece and how Danny was going to an international youth web innovation project. He was so psyched about it. My tears should have been happy ones for Danny, not sad ones for me. This was his 3000-meter run, or maybe his marathon. He was doing something he believed in. If Danny had asked who'd bet that he'd change the world through this trip, I would have put money on it. But Danny didn't think to take bets on this one. I had been so wrapped up in India, that I forgot to notice his world changing. Thankfully, I had to stop for a breath, or he might not have found the pause to tell me about Greece.

When we finally began to run down, we lay back on the pillows and just listened to the fire crackle. Danny fell asleep. I think I was still on India time, and I was glad, because I loved lying there, looking at the firelight flicker on his face. I got up and retrieved my sketch journal from the table, my birthday present from Naveena from the International Sketch Symposium in Chennai. I glanced through the sketches I'd made there and at Naveena's house, then started a new one of Danny.

Sitting there looking at him, I realized how true it was what they said – that you become more present and aware of what you're seeing when you sketch. The firelight on his face glowed gentle and warm, and it matched exactly who he was – with bursts of flame every now and then. I noticed his eyelashes and the way his dark hair curled right in front of his ear. When I was finished, I wrote "Always" underneath the sketch, and whispered, "Danny... Danny, wake up."

CHAPTER 56

O ne thing about Ridgeway is that you can't go into town without seeing somebody you know. We were out of ice cream, so I volunteered to drive in and get some. Partly just to drive for the first time since I got back, and partly because we were going to make brownies, which I hadn't had since Christmas, and you can't have brownies without ice cream. The who-you-know at the grocery store was Jackson Evans, in the freezer section. I didn't especially mean to, but I reached out to give Jackson a hug. He didn't mind.

"Welcome home, Annie. How was India?"

"It was great, Jackson. How have you been?" The normal way of talking when somebody's been away. But then Jackson surprised me.

"They have a new little coffee shop up by check out," he said. "Can I buy you a cup of chai? In honor of India?"

"I haven't had chai since I left Chennai. Sounds great." I set my ice cream in Jackson's cart and threw my jacket over it so it wouldn't melt. Jackson pushed it along as we talked, then parked the cart next to a booth against the wall, and ordered two cups of chai and two apple caramel muffins.

I told Jackson how tea sellers cooled down hot chai, pouring it back and forth, high up and low down, between two cups. He agreed that was smart. And then, out of the blue, he up and asked me, "Annie, do you ever feel guilty about Tani dying?"

I started to get a bad feeling about Jackson again, like he was back to being mean. Nobody had ever mentioned that it was my

Encounter: When Religions Become Classmates

fault, her dying, because the corn maze party was my idea. Even if they thought about it. I wanted that to mean that nobody figured I had anything to do with it, or if they did, they'd forgotten about it. Then here was Jackson just asking outright.

Before I could get mad, he said, "Because I do. Every day. And I've been wanting you to get home so I could talk to you about it."

"Why me, Jackson?" I said it seriously. I needed to know. "Do you think I was the cause of her death?"

"No, Annie, no. I'm asking you because you really liked her, and you did the memorial. You and your mom and dad. It made a difference. But I know you didn't like her at first, and I wondered sometimes if that was a way to make up to Tani for how so many people treated her – not you necessarily – when she first came to Ridgeway. Maybe I'm all wrong. But, Annie, if there's any way anybody knows for me to make up for something horrible that I did, I need to know it."

"Jackson, did you ever talk to Ms. Michaud about this? She's cool, you know."

"No. I'm not a counselor kind of person."

"What does that mean?" I asked.

"Well. My dad always said, 'We don't air our dirty laundry in public. If you have a problem, deal with it.' He didn't let me join Group at the counseling office in grade school. And you know I could have used it." He grinned.

"Yeah." I didn't say more.

"But while we're talking, Annie, I want to get one thing cleared up. I never in my life stuck anybody's head in a toilet, like you accused me of at the Monkey Trial. If that's why you've hated me, you've got to come up with a better reason."

"I don't hate you, Jackson." It was true. I might have resented him for what he did, but ever since the cornfield, I have not hated Jackson Evans. I had begun to believe Danny's idea that everybody has a story, and I mostly felt bad that

Jackson's story tied in with what happened that night in the cornfield. "But that's what people said you did, Jackson."

"You're smarter than that, Annie. People say a lot of things that have nothing to do with reality. I used to threaten kids with that, just like a whole bunch of people I knew threatened me: 'Do that, and I'll push your head in a toilet.' Nobody did. It was just talk. But I'm getting off track. What I wanted to say is, I'm glad you got to go to India." He took a breath and paused. "And if you ever have any idea about what I can do to make up for hitting Tani with the wagon, tell me, because I don't know what to do."

Jackson bit his lip, and his eyes filled with tears. He buried his face in his hands. I reached over and took one of his hands and pulled it away from his face. "Jackson, look at me." I waited. "I do feel responsible for Tani's death. If I hadn't planned to have a party in the corn maze, they wouldn't have been in that field you were cutting. It would never have happened. I want to forget that, but it's the truth. And there are other truths, Jackson. I was in the field that night. I heard you tell the medics you warned her away from the cutter. Danny said the other night that Tani had told him she couldn't go look at the field with them, and he talked her into it. He had never told anybody that till right then. If only he had let her be, he said."

"So how do you ignore the feelings?" he asked.

"I don't know. I haven't got it figured out. I mostly just left and went to India. The second day I was home, I ran home from school, past some cornfields with a new crop of corn coming up, and it started coming back. Sometimes I just tell God that I'm sorry and I didn't mean for Tani to be hurt, and that I wish it never happened."

"Does that help?"

"Yeah," I said.

"Well, I don't know much about God or who he is or what

he's like. I wouldn't know how to tell him something even if I wanted to."

"God comes in all shapes and sizes, Jackson," I said, "and I'm sure one of them will be ready to listen to you when you're ready to talk." That was a pretty weird thing to say, but I guess it's what I thought right then. "And I will too, especially if you treat me to chai again."

Jackson smiled. "Deal, Annie. Thanks."

I wondered if it had been a long five months for Jackson.

CHAPTER 57

W e had only been out of school three weeks when I got an email from Vidhya saying she was back in Megha Malai, starting their senior year, and did I miss them dreadfully. She was going out to Chinnakadu that Saturday and wondered how the bazaar had gone and if I sold any of the Kurinji Ladies' cards. I wasn't sure I should tell her. It would probably spin her into another cause – reforming my mom. As much as Mom irritates me sometimes, I didn't want Vidhya to think Mom was ridiculous. In the end, I told Vidhya everything – almost: The bazaar was last weekend. We sold all but fifteen of the cards for $3 each. The money was already on the way to Mr. Hausden at MMIS. Tell the Kurinji Ladies that I love them and miss them so much. And if they can get more cards to the U.S. with somebody coming back at the end of November, or if it won't cost too much to mail them, then I'll sell more at the Christmas Bazaar too.

What I didn't tell her was that the fifteen rejects were not left-overs at all, but had been taken out by Mom as "not appropriate" for the church bazaar. Only Mom didn't bother to tell me what she had done until the bazaar was closing and I realized the count was off.

"Oh, there are a dozen or so back at the house," Mom said.

"Why? We could have sold them all."

"I don't think you noticed, Annie, but someone gave you pictures of idols – elephants and cows – obviously objects of worship by how they were covered with flowers and the marks

Encounter: When Religions Become Classmates

on their foreheads. I knew you wouldn't want them included on your table."

I stared at her. "You knew I wouldn't want them included? How did you know that?"

"Annie, they were idols."

"Mom, they were my friends' cards."

"Of idols. Of a stone elephant, Annie."

"That's Ganesh, Mom."

"What?"

"Ganesh, the Remover of Obstacles. The one the ladies ask to bless their new co-op project."

"What are you saying, Annie? Surely not that you believe a stone elephant idol is going to bless them?"

"What I'm saying is that you had no right to take those cards out and leave them home. I arranged with Ms. Kushner personally to have this table and sell the cards from Chinna-kadu. She was excited about the idea of helping the women. We are fifteen cards short. That's $45 worth of sales. That's over 3,000 rupees, Mom, a huge amount of money to those ladies."

"Well, if it's that important to them, I'll write out a check for $45 to cover the cards. And then I'll destroy them. Next time you volunteer to sell for their group, you can ask them to be more thoughtful about what they depict in their cards."

"I don't want your money, Mom. They don't want your money. They wanted to sell their cards to someone who appreciates them."

I couldn't believe it was my own mom who had carried out my imaginary scenario of sabotage. But I do have to say I felt a little guilty for being so mad at Mom over that incident. The thing is, I think she said to me the exact things I said to Bijeen on the bus that day when I told him it was as crazy to believe a stone elephant would bless somebody, as it was to believe in fortune cookies. At least Mom hadn't thrown the fortune cookie argument at me.

So I took a deep breath and said, "Mom, sometimes I don't

even know what I think. It wasn't very long ago that I would have said they were idols too, and I wouldn't have wanted them around. But now I know the people who made the cards and why. And I believe in them."

"You believe in idols, Annie?"

"No, Mom. Not idols. Not Ganesh. Not idols on cards."

"Then what? What are you saying?"

"Mom, I believe in Radha and Chandra and the other girls and women. I know they want good for each other and their kids and their village. And they're trying, Mom. Things are hard for them, but they're trying. Besides, Vidhya says Ganesh makes God feel closer to them, makes Him feel solid and real, so they can expect His blessings. Yes, Mom. At least I believe that selling their cards is a good thing to do."

She looked at me and shook her head. "I don't understand what's happening, Annie." She just stood there. Then she reached out her arms, like she was asking if she could have a hug. "Just keep talking to me," she said. "I don't understand, but keep talking, okay?"

"Okay, Mom," I said, accepting her hug.

I took the reject cards to work with me at Abbey Road Produce Stand, where I was back on staff for the summer. I showed them to Pam and Eva. Pam said, "What a beautiful depiction of Ganesh. Of course, we'd love to sell them for your women's co-op, Annie." Just like that. Like it was normal to see a stone elephant-man and know its name. They took all fifteen and put them in the blessings corner with the other cards. Eva had me make a little sign about the village women's project. Within a week, the cards were gone, including the two Eva bought for her mom and Lydia, who were still at Maplewood. I could hardly wait to see them and tell them in person about the women who had made their cards. I was sure Myrtle and Lydia would love the idea.

That night I told Dad what had happened at the church bazaar and with Pam and Eva. He's so loyal to Mom I knew he wouldn't criticize her, but I finally outright asked him, "Dad, do you ever wonder if someone who isn't a Christian could be saved and could be loving God, even if they don't do it our way?" I didn't say "your way," because I didn't want Dad to think I was Lost. Not "lost" as in "can't find your way home," but "Lost" as in "out of God's will, heading for hell," though Dad wouldn't have said the hell part about me. I needed Dad to love me and accept me, and I hoped he could, even when he knew what I was thinking. We wandered around the meadow as we talked.

"Your mom and I have grown up in the church all our lives, Annie."

"I know, Dad, but that's not what I asked. You went to college. They must have had classes on world religions there. And what about the people you work with? Don't you know anybody who's not a Christian?"

"Yes. Many."

"Or someone who's a completely different religion?"

"A few."

"And? Are they all Lost? Do you think they're all going to hell unless you witness to them and get them to accept the Lord?"

"Some of them are looking for more, Annie. They want meaning in their lives... What do you think?"

"Don't do that, Dad! I can't figure out what I think. Sometimes I know what I feel, and it doesn't make sense to even me, so I don't want to believe it or don't think I should. And sometimes I don't believe what I know I'm supposed to. And I won't, because I can't. I'm afraid it's going to mess up things for our family."

Dad didn't say anything, so I just kept going. "Because I don't feel good being where people rail on Muslims and Hindus as the 'poor unsaved' that we need to reach for the Lord. And that's our church, where we've gone together ever since I was born. Dad, if you knew Aziz and Vidhya, you would love them, and you would know that God loves them, and they don't have to dump their mosques and temples and come to church."

"And it seems that we're saying they do have to?"

"Not just seems, Dad. That is exactly what people say at church. And I don't like it any more. Surely you've noticed all the '2/3' posters up around the church."

"I have. They're for our summer international missions' promotion."

"I know, Dad. But I didn't know that when I first saw them, so I asked this girl who was standing in the hall looking at a '2/3' sign. She was a little kid – grade school age – and even she knew what it meant. Right off she said, 'Oh, that's to remind us of missions, because 2/3 of the people in the world don't have Jesus in their hearts. Missionaries go win them to the Lord. Our church sponsors missionaries.' Like she had it all memorized even.

"Dad, does anyone ever stop to wonder if 2/3 of the people in the world might be okay without missionaries coming? Do they even wonder what 'Jesus in your heart' actually means? I picked up one of the fliers under the poster. It said we need to reach the 2/3 who haven't yet heard God's Good News. Dad, I keep thinking that God's Good News is that everybody matters and our earth matters and we need to be good to each other. Anybody could spread that news, not just Christians."

Dad was more of a listener than a talker right then. We sat down beside the creek, and I told him about the Kurinji Ladies and life abundantly. I told him about making the diffuser plate for one water filter. I told him about Hausden saying that turning water into water was a pretty awesome miracle, and we were Earth's Children at work with each other – MMIS students and the people of Chinnakadu, together.

"That's what makes sense, Dad. That's what I can believe in. I think it would be good if everybody would be open to looking at what's messed up about their own religion, because I'm not saying I buy into everything. I heard some pretty crazy things about some people in India while I was there. But that could also apply to Christians here, as well as everybody else. Instead, we just plaster the walls with '2/3' and brainwash little kids."

"Do you feel that you were brainwashed, Annie?"

"Yes. No. I don't know. It all seemed important and good at the time. It was how we did it, but we never talked about how some people do it another way."

Being in the meadow stirred memories. "Dad, I remember what you said when we were planning Tani's memorial last year, when Mr. Paulmann said he didn't want any God-talk. You said, 'God is. He doesn't need us to plan him in or out. He'll meet us where we are.' I remember that. Can't we just leave it there? And let the 2/3 be?"

Dad surprised me. No lectures about having faith through hard times, or praying more, asking the Lord to give me strength, or inviting the Spirit to walk with me and show the way. He just said, "You're asking some tough questions." He picked a blade of grass and chewed on the end. Then he turned and looked at me and said, "Annie, I know if I had been born into a Muslim family, I would have been a good Muslim. That would have been my world."

I didn't expect my dad to say that.

WE WALKED BACK to the house, with questions and thoughts all mixing together.

But the next Sunday, I knew I had to unmix things and start figuring it out. I was back at Ridgeway Community Bible Church, where I had gone my whole life, with Mom and Dad and Gram and Gramps and friends from school. I could run church myself if I had to. Things might fall apart, but probably not, because I know it all by heart. But I didn't know what to do when our pastor, who's awesome, asked if I'd do the sermon on Youth Sunday coming up at the end of August. Dad had shared with him the article in the *Hindustan Times* and he thought it would be wonderful if I'd give the talk in our church that I'd given in the chapel at Megha Malai. He obviously had no idea what I had said!

I knew I had to get out of it, but I wasn't sure how. I told him I didn't think I'd have the courage to do that, but I'd let him know. He teased me a little, saying people in Ridgeway don't bite, and that it would be a great learning opportunity for so many of us who never had much chance to learn about India.

I got an idea.

You know how it is when you first notice things you've never seen before, and then suddenly you start seeing them everywhere. Or like somebody asking if you can see the arrow on the FED EX truck and you follow it for ten miles, staring at it. But there's no arrow anywhere, and then when you finally see it, not a single truck can come within sight without that arrow being the first thing you see. So I decided to see if I could notice any "variations" at Ridgeway Community Bible Church that I had never noticed before. If I found some, maybe I'd have a chance of fitting in. If Danny had come, I could have counted him as a variation, but he never came. When I was little, I would have peeked to see who didn't close their eyes during prayer, but I was looking for something more substantial now, some evidence that they didn't buy the whole exclusive truth bit.

I asked Eva and Pam if they had any friends who went to our church. They didn't know of any, but said they might be overlooking someone, and why? I decided to tell them. They said the whole wide world was full of variation and they were sure there would be some of that at our church too, even if it seemed hidden. And then Eva said, "Just don't throw the baby out with the bath water, Annie. Sometimes people try to get away from what seems empty to them and they head straight for more emptiness. We need to nurture the spirit in ourselves and others, Annie. Remember the monks: Balance. And fresh bread."

I took a loaf of fresh bread home to Mom, and kale, green onions, and a crookneck squash to make soup.

CHAPTER 58

Another email came from Vidhya. "We're expanding our SL class in a huge way, Annie. We need you here! Actually, you are here. You gave us the idea, even though you might not think so. Remember when you asked me what Animator meant? I loved what you found out, and people who heard you speak in chapel that Sunday remembered it too. Animator stuck. When we got back from break and Hausden asked what we wanted out of our SL classes this year, there was a feeling that we wanted to go wider. Keep the biosand water filter project, but involve more people.

"Annie, we have registered a brand new organization with headquarters in Megha Malai – Teen Animators Networking India. We've already invited other schools to set up groups too. We're starting in Tamil Nadu and Karnataka, but we know it will catch on. We're going to use Field Trip Week to do a training in Bangalore, and then the groups will ask for villages who want to host a training in exchange for a filter for their school and their *panchayat* office. We figure that will plant the seeds. And we'll get to work alongside teens from the villages too.

"I think I've found my cause for the year, Annie. The good thing is, even after I graduate this year, I'm a teen for two more years, so I can keep on with this, and then I'll just change the name of our group to Twenties Animators Networking India.

"If that wasn't good enough, Hausden is letting Wan Tae direct a video project to record it all. We see these groups forming all around the world. Yours in America could be Teen

Animators Networking America. Do you know any computer people who could work long distance with Wan Tae to put together a multi-country video report?

"But first things first. I was asked to write to you and see if you'd be a charter member of our group, since it was your idea in the first place, to be an Animator. Will you join our TANI, Annie? Another cool thing about TANI is that we wrote a problem-solving procedure into our charter. Now, people like me, who tend to get a little vocal and can't let things go, won't have to go crazy or stay mad at people. We voted, and Hausden is getting some teens from Ooty to come train us on how to mediate disputes for each other. It may even spill over into the rest of the school, which couldn't hurt. Figure out how to come back soon, Annie, and in the meantime, keep emailing. Yeah! Love you!"

I sat there and cried when I read that. TANI.

I reached for my cell.

"Jackson?"

"Yeah? Annie?"

"Don't think I'm crazy. I just have to tell you something. There's this new group in India, kids our age, that you and I need to be a part of. And Danny, and anybody who knows Tani and wants to keep her memory alive. They need our help, Jackson."

"I'm not following you, Annie. What could we do in India? And how would that have anything to do with Tani?"

"I don't know. Yet. Maybe we can sell chai here to raise money for water filters there. Maybe we can just tell them we believe in what they're doing and cheer them on. Maybe we can figure out what Ridgeway needs and do that and say we're a local spin-off of their group. They call themselves Teen Animators because they "give breath or life or spirit" to things. That's what Animator means. They're Teen Animators Networking India, and they call their group T-A-N-I,

Tani, for short, but we would be Teen Animators Networking Ridgeway."

"Tani?"

"Yeah. But they don't know her. They just came up with the name sort of accidentally."

"Really? That's cool," he said.

We talked a little more, and he said he'd help me, just keep him posted. Then I called Danny. He came over and we got on MMIS's website and watched three of Wan Tae's videos about SL and the water project. I told Danny about TANI and that they were looking for Computer Greeks to help with their website and in networking with other groups. We talked for an hour, and Danny said he'd see what he could do from Athens. That it sounded exactly like the kind of project they would be looking for there. Maybe he could tap into some other talent too. Teen Animators Networking Greece. He liked the sound of it.

I emailed Vidhya and told her I would be honored to be a charter member. That I loved what they were doing, and I was talking about it here. And that I knew a computer guy who would get in touch with them once he got to Greece and figured out what he was doing. Danny assured me they could get a video conference set up to talk over their projects. I also told her to hurry up and learn mediation so she could come mediate for me in case I needed her for multiple reasons of re-assimilation at home.

It was a crazy busy summer. But I did remember Daychen too, and I found time for stillness, which I probably wouldn't have before India. I purposefully went and sat by Fulgham Bridge and watched the water tumble over the boulders. It was noisy, but it made me quiet. Yet mostly, I was excited. I felt the Animator inside me. I decided not to worry about what I believed or didn't believe or what people wanted or expected of me as a Christian. At least not for a while. I would just live one summer and see where living landed me. Maybe Mom would meet Vidhya through Won Tae and the Greeks, including Danny, when they put Vidhya on film, and they'd love each other. Vidhya might even take Mom on a virtual journey to Chinnakadu to see the water project and meet the Kurinji Ladies. Then Mom and I could decide together if we wanted to go into the temple.

CHAPTER 59

There was somebody else I wanted to tell all this. Trina had gone back to Germany, but I hadn't felt like finding Param until now. I heard he was traveling again, but then somebody said they saw his family back in Ridgeway, so I finally decided to call.

"Want to go for a run, Param?" I asked.

"Sure," he said.

I was scared, but I wanted to know what he had to say, about a lot of things. We met at the track at school, but instead of running laps, we took off down a country road heading off from the school. I pretended not to notice it was the one that ran into Kinsey Lane. Part way out Param asked, "Are we headed out to Paulmann's?"

"Not unless you want to go that far. I thought we'd run for a while and then cut over to the nature trail."

"Sounds good," he said.

We didn't say anything at all for a mile. Then Param slowed to a walk, and I met his pace.

"I disappointed you, didn't I, Annie?"

I should have been honest and said, "Big time," but instead I asked, "What do you mean?"

"We haven't talked since you got back from India. There's so much I've wondered about, but I felt a silence around you, like there wasn't anything you wanted to say to me, so I pushed my feelings away and let it go. But I'm glad you called. I've missed you, and I don't like it this way."

"You've missed me? That sounds pretty unlikely, Param.

You found someone to take my place. You were busy with Trina."

"That's what you thought? She took your place?"

"Didn't she?"

"You were gone, Annie. Her host family lives right across the street from our house. It was natural that we'd see each other and hang out some. And she runs, as you know, so we saw each other at track events."

"And at movies, and on every bus ride to track meets. Katelyn told me."

"Did Katelyn also tell you how things were for Trina when she first got here?"

"Not especially."

"Well, Winter Formal happened shortly after you left for India. A bunch of guys in our class decided it was way too expensive, so they banned together and wore jeans and t-shirts to the formal, didn't get dates, and got people to vote for Trina for Formal Queen. As a joke, since nobody even knew her yet, and to show the girls in the class that they thought the whole thing was a little crazy. Trina didn't know what to expect, and she took it seriously. She thanked everyone for their vote of welcome, and said it was a wonderful dance. But the girls got mad. Because the guys made fun of something important, because Trina took an honor that was "rightfully one of theirs," and because "she ruined things." They started talking. It was bad. I could see a repeat of last March. You know what our class did to Tani. Well, I wasn't going to let that happen again, if I could help it.

"She was being used, and that's not cool. I decided to hang out with her and show people she was okay. More than okay. She's nice, Annie. And she throws herself into what she does. You would have liked her if you would have given her a chance. But you wouldn't even shake hands with her when she offered."

He stopped walking and looked right at me. "I didn't get it.

I thought you had made up your mind to do things differently, and I saw how things changed after your birthday. How kind you were. How hurt you were to lose Tani. But here you came back home, acting just like you had before, and it scared me, Annie. You scared me. And I didn't want to be swept up in it if that's what it was going to be. You're right. I don't think I especially wanted to be around you then. But I felt your silence, and it hurt. So I kept telling myself that it was for the best."

"There was more going on, Param, than just being nice to somebody new at school. Why didn't you write? I was gone five months, and you emailed, what? Three times? And when you did, it was to tell me about Trina."

He nodded. "I told you the truth, Annie. I got behind. Maybe I just got used to not writing. I don't do email that much. But I'm sorry, if you were expecting it."

"That's why you're sorry? Because I expected it? Not because you wanted to talk to me? Did I ever mean anything to you, Param? Why did you kiss me? Was that all just a joke to you?"

"Annie, just stop. What are you doing? You know how much I cared for you. Care for you. I kept telling myself that you cared for me in the same way. That you and Danny weren't together. That maybe I had a chance. But I was just pretending. I finally figured it out, about the time you left for India. And when I accepted it, everything fit. It's obvious to anyone who watches you, or listens to you, or knows you, that Danny's the big thing in your life. I can't compete with that. But I thought we were still friends.

"While you were gone, Danny let me read some of the email you sent him, so full of ... I don't know – energy, fun. 'Love you, Dantheman.' To be honest, it was good to have Trina here. Not just to be nice to someone new, but because she liked being with me. She made me forget the hurt. And

I'll admit it. I started liking her back. She turned from being a neighbor, someone I wanted to stand up for, to being special."

"I thought so."

"Annie!"

"What?"

"You have no idea what it was like for me to see you in the hall that day you first came back to school. You were wearing a salwar kameez. You were beautiful, and I could see that India had made a difference for you. It made me want to know what you had done and seen and thought. It made me want to hope. In that moment, I wanted to think I might have been wrong about you and Danny being a done deal. Then I heard he'd gone to the airport with your parents and grandparents."

"That wasn't my doing. You could have come."

"No, I couldn't have. I don't hold the place he does, Annie. I know that now. Trina guessed you were special to me, and we talked about how we'd all be friends when you got home. She wasn't my girlfriend, Annie. She has a guy in Germany and wasn't interested in dating. It didn't make sense to her, and it didn't make sense to me, so we were friends. Good friends. But I didn't expect that to turn you and me into some kind of enemies."

I didn't know what to say. I pulled my hair up away from my face and just shook my head. "So, you saw things with Trina turning into what had happened with Tani, and you didn't want a repeat. You decided to be her friend. And you found out that she's fun to be around, and you started liking each other, even if you weren't officially dating. And then you were disappointed when I came back and acted mean that day in the hall."

"I didn't say you acted mean."

"But I did. Because I still wanted to be special to you and I felt left out and maybe discarded when I saw her close to you. But I know that's no excuse for not trying to understand. Which I didn't. I wrote her off. I called her 'Germany.'"

"And that started others calling her that too. She might not have minded, but it wasn't said in a good spirit, and I think it hurt her."

"I don't want to be like that, Param. I don't. Really."

"I believe you, Annie."

We turned off onto the nature trail and walked along under the trees without talking. I kept thinking about what Param had said, about Danny and me. How could it be so obvious to him when it didn't seem at all clear to me? It was Param I had kissed, not Danny. It was Param I had imagined marrying in the meadow. It was Param I had gone to India for, to see if India could "get in my bones" and please his parents. Well, Param and Tani. And it was Param I had waited and waited to hear from.

Or was it? I remembered getting Danny's email and laughing and crying and loving to know my reply would be waiting for him when he woke up the next morning. Over and over again. If Danny hadn't written, I would have made Katelyn personally go see if he was okay.

I had just been accusing Param of deserting me for Trina, and not writing to me because he was with her. All that was probably true, but as we walked, I realized things had changed for him before I even left for India, before Trina came. I could have known that if I had talked to him. But I had closed my eyes to what I didn't want to know.

Param had a right to do what he did, and like who he liked, and it hadn't brought the end of the world, for either of us. I also knew he was right about Danny. Danny had been a big thing in my life – since forever.

"Danny's a cool guy, Annie. And he loves you probably more than you can imagine. We've become good friends, and he talks about you, a lot. Somewhere along the way, I got to thinking that if you were home, you and Danny and Trina and I could do things together and have a lot of fun. I had no intentions of replacing you. I didn't think I had, but I knew things had changed, and I accepted it. I guess you weren't here to realize it with me."

"I guess not."

We emerged from the nature trail two blocks away from the school. "Param, I can't bring Trina back from Germany to shake hands with her and be nice, though rewind would be good, and..."

"And...?"

"And if I could, I don't know how I'd feel about her and you being together again. But if it were to happen now, I hope I'd be glad to have another strong runner on our track team, and if I got to know her like you do, I would probably think it was cool that she was Formal Queen for real. I might try to talk her and some of the girls into wearing jeans and t-shirts to the dance too. When I was in India, I estimated how many water filters could have been made with the money Ridgeway spent on the Junior-Senior Prom. The boys were right. Those dances are way too expensive. But that's beside the point.

"I don't know, Param. I might even think that it's cool that you and Trina liked each other and wanted to do things with Danny and me."

I had planned to tell Param about TANI, but decided it could wait. I just wanted him to understand my heart. "Param, you came to Ridgeway and you were like nobody I knew. I admired you – your positiveness, your openness, the things you said sitting in the Royal Chair, the warmth you showed me, the way you were nice to everybody. Then when we kissed that day, it was big. But you're right. I felt something shifting before I left for India, and I didn't want to believe it, so I didn't. I held on, and I was mad that you didn't write. Because I liked you a lot. Actually, I still like you."

"Thank you, Annie."

We didn't say anything more until we got back to the school.

"Param, I don't want to be selfish or unkind. Especially not to you. Not to anybody. I've been thinking about this word they use in India. It's a name they give to their *gram sevaks*, people like our extension agents, who work in the villages. They call them ..."

"... Animators," he finished.

"You know that word?"

"Yes. It's a good name."

"That's what I want to be, Param, an Animator."

"That's what you are, Annie."

It was silly, but because we'd just been talking about being nice and shaking hands with Trina, I held out my hand to shake with Param. He took it and held it gently, then leaned over and kissed me on the cheek.

"Annie, let's be friends."

"For sure, Param. For sure."

CHAPTER 60

A s we said good-bye and I started for home, I realized there was something else I wanted, and I decided right then it was worth risking for.

I turned around and headed for Danny's.

Danny was working on the fence line in the field in front of their house. I pulled over and parked on the side of their driveway. He waved and walked up to the fence, just across from me.

"Hi," I said.

"Hi. What's up? You came to help me fix fence?"

"Not exactly."

"More news from India?"

"Nope. Just news from me."

"And what is that?" he asked. "You're coming to Greece with me?"

"I wish!"

"Then what?"

"That I'm going to be waiting for you to come home. And that you better not fall in love with anyone while you're gone."

He grinned. "Really? Why?"

"Because."

"Not an answer."

I looked him straight in the eyes. "Because, Danny, I came out here to tell you I love you."

"That's an answer," he said. "An answer I've waited a long time to hear, Annie Karten."

He reached out for my hand, through the fence. And then lifted his other hand to the side of my face and gently pulled me to him. With the fence between us, Danny and I kissed.

"Well," he said, "I have to repair this section next anyway." He put his hands on top of the woven wire, crushed it downward, and bounded over it to my side.

"Wow! You could have been running hurdles all along," I said. "Or doing high jump."

"Just didn't have the motivation until now," Danny replied. He picked me up, twirled me around, then set my feet back down and drew me into a hug. I felt home in his arms.

"One more kiss?" he asked.

"Yes, please," I said.

AS I DROVE toward home, I realized I would sooner or later need to tell Aziz I was bringing a guy with me to Yosemite next June. I wondered how I was going to get Danny to fall in love with rock climbing. I've heard that Yosemite is great for hiking too, and if Danny can jump fences, he can surely hike Yosemite. I pulled into our driveway, grinning, just as Dad was pulling up in the pickup. Dad smiled back at me.

"Hi, Annie," he said. "How's my girl?"

"I'm good, Dad."

WE WALKED TOWARD the house together.

"Hey, now that you're back to your chores, want to grab an armload of wood for the fireplace?" He set a pile of kindling into the crook of my arm, then loaded his own arm with five or six big chunks of wood. I started to tell Dad about the women outside of Megha Malai who carried long, heavy bundles of wood on their heads, running toward town, but I stopped. India could wait. It would be a good night for a fire.

Maybe not for talking, but just for being by the fire with Mom and Dad.

I thought of Dad's "what if" – he had been born into a Muslim family.

"Dad, I was wondering. Would you be okay with me giving my Megha Malai chapel talk at church in August, even if people hate it, and everyone at church wonders how you and Mom could have possibly raised a kid to turn out like me?"

"Absolutely," he said. "Now, let's get this wood inside and see if we can help Mom rustle up some dinner."

"Okay then," I said. And I had a feeling that somehow it would be okay.

Everything.

Eventually.

Book Club Discussion Questions

1. As Chapter 1 (Oregon) opens, Annie says the new girl is going to have trouble at Ridgeway. Why might Annie say that? What do you think eventually caused her to see Tani differently?

2. When Annie "learned" that Param carried a knife to school, she had a bad feeling that she was wrong about him. Why do you think she so easily believed this could be true?

3. Have you ever been invited to "pet a hedgehog" because of something special you've accomplished? What unique things have you seen teachers do to affirm or encourage their students?

4. All Tani said was, "Dad, don't hit that skunk!" and their lives were changed forever. She sobbed to Annie, "Why didn't God have that skunk take a nap?" How did Annie react? Would you have done or said something different?

5. Mr. Snyder's class studied the 1925 Scopes Trial. The students found it opened current day discussion for them, as well as taking them back in time. What do you think are the pros and cons of exploring ideas and questions about religion in a classroom setting today?

6. Annie's impression of Jackson Evans changed from the time of the Scopes Trial to the memorial in the Karten's meadow. What made the difference?

7. Why do you think it was so important for Annie, Danny, Param, Katelyn and others to plan the memorial?

8. Would you have gone to India? Why, or why not?

9. There were a lot of things that jarred Annie as she arrived in India. Can you guess how those things would have hit you? Why? What changed to make her feel comfortable in Gandhinagar?

10. How would you describe the difference in Annie's and Ketsa's reactions to things? To religious traditions?

11. Aziz obviously loves the rock. Is it likely that he could have convinced you that it would be fun – and safe – to climb with him? Why or why not?

12. Annie found the MMIS Service Learning class very different from what she had experienced in Ridgeway. How would you describe your experiences as a volunteer? What has been most meaningful to you in helping others?

13. If you had the opportunity to help build biosand water filters in another country, do you think you'd do it? Why do you think it was important to Annie to make one diffuser plate by herself?

14. What does the title ENCOUNTER mean to you? What do you think are some of the significant encounters in this story? Is there one encounter that was especially unexpected for you? What would you say was the most powerful encounter for Annie – the happening that changed her life the most?

15. Annie left for India with a commitment to wonder. How did she do fulfilling it? What made that promise easier to keep, and what made it harder for her? What helps you hold a sense of curiosity and openness rather than criticism and exclusion?

16. Annie didn't report to us about her first essay question: Is there or was there ever an American equivalent of kerosene? What would be your comment on that?

17. How was Annie changed by her semester at MMIS?

18. Annie was upset with her mom over the card sales at the church bazaar. Why do you think she reacted that way, when just a few months earlier she had some of the same thoughts?

19. Why do you think Annie tried to get out of giving her MMIS chapel speech in Ridgeway?

20. Annie had some strong feelings about the "2/3" campaign. Why do you think she felt the way she did?

21. In what ways have you seen teen Animators at work? Adults?

22. Annie worried that changes in her would wreck things for their family. Do you think that was likely to happen? Why or why not?

23. Diversity of religions can give rise to conflict or to new learning and understanding, or both. How would you describe the experience of religious diversity in your community? At your school? In our world?

24. What do you think Annie will do now to keep Animator and Coyote together?

25. What else would you like to say about this story?

26. [Trick question; an answer follows] Who is the author of this book?

About the Author

AUTHOR KATHY BECKWITH grew up on an Oregon farm. After college, she and her husband Wayne went to India with the Peace Corps to work in village horticulture. Later, a boarding school in South India became home to their family. Back in the U.S., Kathy became a community mediator and a mediation trainer and coach, a work she has done both in India and in Oregon. Their "family sabbatical" tradition has taken them back to "their school" and always back to their Peace Corps village in Karnataka. Like Annie in ENCOUNTER, after discovering another meaning for "Animator," Kathy says, "That's what I hope to be when I really grow up." Stop in for a visit at Kathy's website: www.kathybeckwith.com.